FROST

ANTONIA WHITE was born in London in 1899, and educated at the Convent of the Sacred Heart, Roehampton and St Paul's Girls' School, London. She trained as an actress at the Royal Academy of Dramatic Art, working for her living as a freelance copywriter and contributing short stories to a variety of magazines. In 1924 she joined the staff of W. S. Crawford as a copywriter, became Assistant Editor of *Life and Letters* in 1928, theatre critic of *Time and Tide* in 1934, and was the Fashion Editor of the *Daily Mirror* and then the *Sunday Pictorial* until the outbreak of the Second World War. During the war Antonia White worked first in the BBC and then in the French Section of the Political Intelligence Department of the Foreign Office.

Antonia White published four novels: *Frost in May* (1933), *The Lost Traveller* (1950), *The Sugar House* (1952) and *Beyond the Glass* (1954).

Her other published work includes a volume of short stories, *Strangers*, and the autobiographical *The Hound and the Falcon*. She also translated over thirty novels from the French, and was awarded the Clairouin prize for her first one, Maupassant's *Une Vie*, in 1950. She translated many of the works of Colette. Like Colette, Antonia White was devoted to cats and wrote two books about her own – *Minka and Curdy* and *Living with Minka and Curdy*. Formerly married to H. T. Hopkinson, editor of *Picture Post*, Antonia White lived in London until her death in 1980.

Also available

The first two novels in
Antonia White's sequence of four

FROST IN MAY
and
THE LOST TRAVELLER

are separately available from Fontana
in one volume.

ANTONIA WHITE

FROST IN MAY
(2)

THE SUGAR HOUSE
BEYOND THE GLASS

FONTANA PAPERBACKS
in association with Virago

The Sugar House

First published by Eyre & Spottiswoode 1952
First published in paperback by Virago Press Ltd 1979
First published in this edition by Fontana Paperbacks
in association with Virago Press Ltd 1982

Beyond the Glass

First published by Eyre & Spottiswoode 1954
First published in paperback by Virago Press Ltd 1979
First published in this edition by Fontana Paperbacks
in association with Virago Press Ltd 1982

Made and printed in Great Britain by
William Collins Sons & Co. Ltd, Glasgow

The Sugar House

To
SUSAN

Introduction

It is unusual for the publisher of a book to provide its preface. Antonia White wanted to write a new introduction to the three books – *The Lost Traveller*, *The Sugar House* and *Beyond the Glass* – which complete the story she began in her famous novel *Frost in May*. Now eighty years of age, and a novelist whose small output reflects the virulent writer's block which has constantly interrupted her writing life, she preferred to talk to me. For though separated by age, country of birth and nationality, we share a Catholic upbringing which has been a dominant influence on both our lives. What follows is based on a long conversation I had with Antonia White in December 1978, and on the many times we've talked since Virago first re-published *Frost in May* earlier that year.

'Personal novels,' wrote Elizabeth Bowen in a review of Antonia White's work, 'those which are obviously based on life, have their own advantages and hazards. But we have one "personal" novelist who has brought it off infallibly.' Antonia White turned fact into fiction in a quartet of novels based on her life from the ages of nine to twenty-three. 'My life is the raw material for the novels, but writing an autobiography and writing fiction are very different things.' This transformation of real life into an imagined work of art is perhaps her greatest skill as a novelist.

Antonia White was the only child of Cecil Botting, Senior Classics Master at St Paul's School, who became a Catholic at the age of thirty-five taking with him into the Church his wife and seven-year-old daughter, fictionalized as 'Nanda' in *Frost in May*. This novel is a brilliant portrait of Nanda's experiences in the enclosed world of a Catholic convent. First published in 1933, it was immediately recognized as a classic. Antonia White wrote what was to become the first two chapters of *Frost in May* when she was only sixteen, completing it sixteen years later, in

9

1931. At the time she was married to Tom Hopkinson, writer, journalist and later editor of *Picture Post*.

'I'd written one or two short stories, but really I wrote nothing until my father's death in 1929. I'd worked in advertising all those years, as a copywriter, and I'd done articles for women's pages and all sorts of women's magazines, but I couldn't bring myself to write anything serious until after my father died. At the time I was doing a penitential stint in Harrods' Advertising Department . . . I'd been sacked from Crawfords in 1930 for not taking a passionate enough interest in advertising. One day I was looking through my desk and I came across this bundle of manuscript. Out of curiosity I began to read it and some of the things in it made me laugh. Tom asked me to read it to him, which I did, and then he said "You must finish it." Anyway Tom had appendicitis and we were very hard up, so I was working full time. But Tom insisted I finish a chapter every Saturday night. Somehow or other I managed to do it, and then Tom thought I should send it to the publisher – Cobden Sanderson – who'd liked my short stories. They wrote back saying it was too slight to be of interest to anyone. Several other people turned it down and then a woman I knew told me that Desmond Harmsworth had won some money in the Irish sweep and didn't know what to do with it . . . se he started a publishing business and in fact I think *Frost in May* was the only thing he ever published . . . it got wonderful reviews.'

Between 1933 and 1950 Antonia White wrote no more novels. She was divorced from Tom Hopkins in 1938, worked in advertising, for newspapers, as a freelance journalist and then came the war. Throughout this period she suffered further attacks of the mental illness she first experienced in 1922. This madness Antonia White refers to as 'The Beast' – Henry James's 'Beast in the Jungle'. Its recurrence and a long period of psychoanalysis interrupted these years.

'I'd always wanted to write another novel, having done one, but then you see the 1930s were a very difficult time for me because I started going off my head again. After the war and the political work I did I was terribly hard up. Then Enid Starkey, whom I'd met during the war, suggested to Hamish Hamilton that I should have a shot at translating and they liked what I did. After that I got all these commissions and I was doing two or three a year but I was completely jammed up on anything of my own, though I kept on trying to write in spite of it. I always wanted to write another novel, and I wanted this time to do something more ambitious, what I thought would be a "proper" novel, not seen only through the eyes of one person as it is in *Frost in May*, but through the eyes of the father, the mother and even those old great aunts in the country. Then suddenly I could write again. The first one [*The Lost Traveller*] took the longest to write. I don't know how many years it took me, but I was amazed how I then managed to write the other two [*The Sugar House* and *Beyond the Glass*]. They came incredibly quickly.'

In 1950, seventeen years after the publication of *Frost in May*, *The Lost Traveller* was published. In it Antonia White changed the name of her heroine Nanda to Clara Batchelor. 'Of course Clara is a continuation of Nanda. Nanda became Clara because my father had a great passion for Meredith and a particular passion for Clara Middleton (heroine of *The Egoist*). Everything that happened to Clara in *The Lost Traveller* is the sort of thing that happened to me, though many things are changed, many invented. I wanted *The Lost Traveller* to be a *real* novel – *Frost in May* was so much of my own life. So I changed her name . . .' In every other respect this novel begins where *Frost in May* ends. It is a vivid account of adolescence, of the mutual relationships of father, mother and daughter as Clara grows to maturity and comes to grips with the adult world.

'When I finished *The Lost Traveller* I thought of it as just being one book, and then suddenly I felt I wanted to write another one about my first marriage. That was *The Sugar House*, which I think is much the best of the three. In it I see Clara's relationship with Archie (her husband) entirely through the eyes of one person, as in *Frost in May* – I think that suited me much better.'

The Sugar House was published in 1952 and takes Clara through her first love affair, work as an actress and a doomed first marriage. Unsentimental, often amazing, it is unusual for its moving description of a love between a man and a woman which is not sexual but which is nevertheless immensely strong.

Beyond the Glass, which completed the quartet in 1954, is technically the most ambitious of the four novels, dramatically using images of glass and mirrors to reflect Clara's growing mental instability. For Antonia White describes her first encounter with 'The Beast' in this novel, interweaving the story of Clara's new love affair with a vivid description of her descent into and recovery from madness. Antonia White remembers every moment of the ten months she spent in Bethlem Asylum (now the Imperial War Museum) in 1922–3. It is the extraordinary clarity of her recollection of that madness which makes this novel so convincing.

Antonia White's portrait of the life of a young Catholic girl in the first decades of this century is dominated by two themes – the heroine's intense relationship with her father, and the all-pervading influence of the Catholic faith. Antonia White's father centred everything on his only child, and Antonia was absolutely devoted to him. But to the end of his life he refused to discuss one of her earliest traumas – the expulsion from the convent she recorded so faithfully in *Frost in May* – and she has obviously felt that she disappointed him bitterly by going her own way in life. As a Catholic, her relationship with Catholic belief and practice has always been intense, a wrestling to live within its spiritual imperatives in a way which accorded with her own nature, clinging to her faith, as she says, 'by the skin of my teeth'. The struggle is brilliantly felt in this quartet, permeating everything that happens to Clara, affecting her adolescence, sexuality, her relationships with men.

To a modern reader these could be seen as experiences intimately connected with Clara's slow progress towards madness, but to Antonia White they were influences which were also profoundly enriching, in no way negative, part of an extraordinary life which she recalls with a mixture of astonishment and laughter, and which she recreates with consummate skill in these four novels.

*   *   *

When Antonia White completed *Beyond the Glass* her career as a novelist was over, but she always hoped to finish the story of

Clara's life. 'I tried and tried because everybody wrote to me and said you can't leave Clara like this, and for years I tried, but only managed one chapter. Clara by this time is married again – to Clive – and has given up her religion and is living the sort of life her father doesn't approve of . . . going out to work and having a wonderful time. Her father is very upset because Clara has given up her religion and he feels she ought to have a child, because he wants a grandchild, but her mother doesn't disapprove at all, she thinks Clara has had such an awful time that it's time she had some fun. Clara gets on much better with her mother now. I finally finished what I still think is a very good chapter: Clara's father has retired and they're living in the Sussex cottage. Apart from his trouble with his daughter, he is having the most lovely time of his life . . . they've extended the garden and he's at last got his great desire – a full-size croquet lawn where he spends all his time, playing out there in the blazing sun . . .'

Carmen Callil, Virago, London, 1979

PART ONE

Chapter One

The train for the Number One Company of *A Clerical Error* was for nine o'clock. At half-past eight Clara Batchelor had already been sitting for a considerable time in the Refreshment Room at King's Cross spinning out cups of tea and trying not to turn her head hopefully every time the door swung open. Stephen Tye had promised, if he could possibly manage it, to come and see her off. He would be off on his own first tour next week, and, having failed to get into the same company, it might be months before she saw him again.

'I shall make inconceivable efforts to break away,' he had said at lunchtime as, perched on stools in a crowded bar, they gulped beer and sandwiches in the brief space between his two rehearsals. 'I'd cut the whole thing if this chap who wants me to have a drink hadn't some sort of pull with the management. You *do* understand, dear girl?'

Naturally, Clara had understood. For several months the main object of her life had been to understand, comfort and amuse Stephen Tye. This excuse was, at any rate, reasonable. For three weeks the two of them had been no longer acting students but professionals. And, of all the new batch who that summer of 1920 had begun to haunt agents' offices, Stephen could least afford to miss any chance. He was thirty, far older than the other ex-officers who had used their gratuities to train at the Garrick School of Drama. Though his age gave him great prestige in Clara's eyes, he himself was sensitive and occasionally morose about it. He was fond of exaggerating Clara's youth and treating her as if she were a schoolgirl instead of just turned twenty-one. Whenever she tried to claim any experience of life he would say inaccurately: 'You were in the nursery when I was mouldering in a Flanders dug-out.'

Since Clara was in love with Stephen Tye, she found it wiser not to argue with him. Above all, she tried never to make a fuss however much he teased her, patronized her, missed appointments, or turned up late in various stages of drink; wildly gay, pugnacious or suicidal. It was the war that had made Stephen drink, and, though she hated to see him drunk, she took it as a sign that he was more sensitive than other people and felt a respectful pity. She knew that Celia, the wife some years older than himself, who had died in the 'flu epidemic of 1918 had been in the habit of making fusses. Clara was sure that the faint hope of Stephen's asking her to marry him depended on her being as unlike Celia as possible.

As she sat forlornly, trying not to watch the buffet clock and see how few minutes she would be able to snatch with him, she almost hoped he would not come. Try as she would, she could not help feeling hurt. How terrible if, from sheer tension, she were to make a fuss at the last moment. Better to lose her farewell kiss (he had, after all, kissed her very sweetly in the bar at lunchtime) than spend the long night journey to York tormenting herself for having said the wrong word or used the wrong voice or look.

Already, at distant tables, she could see some of the members of the *Clerical Error* company. There were the two elderly ones, Merton Mordish who played the heavy comic and Millicent Cooke who played the spinster aunt, deep in conversation. No one could have mistaken Merton Mordish, with his mane of grey hair, his wide hat and his caped ulster, for anything but an old actor. Even the way he slammed down his tankard and threw back his head as he drank suggested 'business'. Millicent Cooke, whom the whole company instinctively addressed as Miss Cooke, looked more than ever like a real spinster aunt as, wearing a raffia-trimmed hat and a suit obviously knitted by herself, she sipped her tea with her prim unpainted mouth. At another table, alone, sat Maidie Spencer who played the bigger of the two girls' parts and who was to be Clara's room-mate. Under a black velvet hat with a stiffened lace brim, Maidie's wide blue eyes were scanning the room as if in search of someone. Terrified that she should see her and come over, Clara bent down and pulled out of the suitcase the Herrick that had been Stephen's parting gift and propping it open against the teapot, she kept her face well hidden and hoped that her new hat and coat would act as a disguise.

Her anxiety now became acute. She dared not raise her head to look towards the door for fear of catching Maidie's eye. Yet, if Stephen were to come in, he would not know her new clothes either. He might waste some of those ebbing minutes searching for her. He might even give up and go away.

Without raising her head she managed to glance sideways into the steamy mirror behind the counter. Each time the swing-door was pushed open she could see the face of the newcomer dimly reflected. But it was never the narrow high-nosed face of Stephen; that face so easy to pick out at a distance because of its bleached pallor and hair so fair that it looked almost white. Her own reflection, at that odd angle, looked like a stranger's. She could see little but her anxious eyes and two tufts of fair curls pulled forward on either cheek under the small unfamiliar hat. Her cheeks were still pink enough to need no rouge and her hair, though darker than in her teens, still bright enough for enemies to accuse her of peroxide. Stephen was fond of studying their two reflections in bar mirrors. 'The sun and moon,' he had said once: another time, when he was feeling morose, 'the milkmaid and the ageing Pierrot'.

She stared into the mirror, as if by sheer force of will she could conjure the beloved face into it like a girl on All Hallow E'en. Her first sight of Stephen had in fact been almost like an apparition. She had gone one evening into the rehearsal-room at the Garrick, believing it to be empty as it was almost dark. Just as she was about to switch on the light she saw a man's face reflected in one end of the long ballet practice mirror which took up the whole of one wall. She stood, frightened yet fascinated, half convinced she was seeing a ghost, for she could not make out anyone in the room itself. The narrow white face under the thin crest of hair almost as pale in the dimness, appeared to be suspended in air. Then two long hands appeared gesticulating, and she realized that the man in the mirror was wearing a black doublet and hose which, in the dusk, made his body almost invisible. She watched for a minute or two while the face and hands performed over and over again the same series of movements with very slight variations. By now she had realized that the reflection must have an original but that the real person was screened from her by a curtain. But already she had felt so strangely drawn to the face in the mirror that when a few days later, she recognized it in the students' canteen, she was already half in love with Stephen Tye.

It was not till some time after they had become an acknowledged and almost inseparable pair that she had asked him what he had been doing at that moment.

'Rehearsing Biron. "Love's Labour's Lost." I'm not worried about my voice. I can get most of the effects I want with that. But I need a lot of practice for gesture and facial expression. I must have looked slightly insane, mopping and mowing at my own reflection. I keep it up for an hour sometimes till I get what I want.'

'But you get what you want in the end?' she had asked earnestly.

He had laughed the musical, slightly ironic laugh she was to come to know so well.

'As a stage character, yes, on the whole. In private life, by no means invariably.'

Much later she had ventured to ask him when he had first noticed her. He considered, with his head on one side and one pale eyebrow cocked.

'Let me see now. Such a momentous occasion should not call for a great effort of memory. But 'pon my soul it does. I think you must just gradually have impinged upon my consciousness till I was aware of a certain hiatus when you weren't about.'

Looking at the buffet clock and seeing how little hope she had left, she sighed. Already, absent from him only a few hours, she was conscious, not of a 'certain hiatus' but an enormous void. She wondered how she could possible endure weeks, possibly months of separation.

Suddenly a large lace-brimmed hat blocked her view of the mirror and two large, angry blue eyes flashed accusingly at her.

'There you are, you silly Wurzit,' exclaimed Maidie Spencer.

14

'What the hell are you doing, sitting there as pop-eyed as a ventriloquist's dummy?'

'I . . . I was waiting for someone,' Clara stammered.

'Well, he's left you in the lurch, old dear. And you'll get left in the lurch if you don't stir your stumps. Our train's been in five minutes. Everyone but you is aboard and Lister's fuming. I signed on in this show as leading ingénue not as a bloody nursemaid.'

Chapter Two

Clara sat crushed between two other members of the company in the middle of the seat of their reserved compartment. The lights were dimmed and she was the only one left awake. A heavy head lolled on each of her shoulders so that she could hardly move her own. Occasionally she dozed for a few moments only to be woken up by a crick in her neck or cramp in her legs. Though it was an August night and the carriage was stuffy, her feet were so cold that she wished that, like the others, she had brought a rug or a shawl or even a newspaper to wrap them in. They had chattered and played nap till midnight; then one by one, heads had sagged, eyes shut and mouths opened till the smoky air was filled with uneasy sighs and snores.

Maidie had cursed her soundly for making them too late to snatch corner seats. She had taken the cursing meekly, realizing that it would be rash to quarrel on the first night with someone with whom she would have to share a room for months.

Clara, who had never shared a room with anyone, was by no means sure that she wanted to to share one with Maidie Spencer. At one moment Maidie would be so refined that Clara felt she could never live up to such respectability; the next she would swear like a coster. Sometimes she behaved like a convent girl carefully guarding her modesty at a wild party; at others her great blue eyes would glitter knowingly as she egged on the men to outdo each other in dirty stories and found a double meaning in the most innocent remarks.

In three weeks of rehearsing that aged farce *A Clerical Error*, Clara had seen the theatre from an angle very different from that of the Garrick School of Drama, Never at student rehearsals had a producer addressed Clara as 'You bloody little cow' or shouted '*Walk* to that chair, damn you. Don't teeter as if you thought your drawers were coming down.' There had been moments when she had felt like walking out and never coming back. It was not as if she had always set her heart on being an actress. She had gone to the Garrick just as she had gone, at seventeen, to be governess to the Cressetts simply because someone else had suggested it and she had been anxious for a change. Her father had been strongly against it as, at the time, he had been against the other plan. Both times her mother had backed her up. In the end he had become reluctantly reconciled to the idea. As she had paid her own fees by writing slick short stories and advertisements, an aptitude she had discovered during a penitential year of war-work in a Government office, he could make no practical objection. Later, when he had come to some of the Garrick student shows and discovered that two of the actors on the staff had been at Cambridge with him, he had gone so far as to admit that the profession appeared to be becoming almost respectable.

As she studied the unconscious faces of the people who were to be her only companions for months, she realized that his worst fears would have been confirmed. The grey-haired Miss Cooke, sleeping composedly in her corner with a rosary twisted round one hand and a book on landscape gardening on her lap, was the only one to whom she would have dared introduce him. James Munroe, the elderly-looking young man with the frightened expression who never swore and never gave her beery kisses in the wings might have passed muster till he opened his mouth and piped 'Pleased to make your acquaintance, I'm shore.' But what would Claude Batchelor think of Brett Wilding, the rather more than middle-aged lead with his dyed hair so ingeniously pasted over the top of his head to hide the bald patch, his stock, his pointed shoes and his absent way of squeezing Maidie and herself every time he caught one of them alone? Lister, the stage manager, looked like a racing tout and swore like a sergeant; Sam Brilliant, the A.S.M., was pure Commercial Road. She glanced down at the heads, one sleek and dark, the other fair and wavy, of Peter Belsize and Trevor Eton, leaning so heavily against her shoulders. She rather liked this preposterous pair, partly because they never tried to make love to her, partly because they had been kind and covered her mistakes in the first alarming days of rehearsal. Nevertheless their behaviour puzzled her as much as their strange, synthetic accents; a compound of cockney and stage public school spoken in a high-pitched lilt. They called each other: 'Peter dear' and 'Trevor dear' and criticized each other's clothes in minute detail. During the first part of their journey, they had sat side by side manicuring each other's nails. Then, as they grew sleepy they had asked Clara to sit between them. 'We'll protect your virtue, dear. You don't mind if we use you as a pillow?'

Peter had said, rather unexpectedly: 'Like Alice with a queen on each shoulder,' and Trevor had giggled. 'Naughty, naughty.' Maidie had giggled too and then had asked: 'Who's Alice when she's at home? A fairy?' Whereupon they had all three giggled again and Clara had thought it diplomatic to giggle too. There were many occasions in the *Clerical Error* company when Clara was extremely vague as to what the joke, if any, might be. She found it safest to take her cues for laughter from Maidie so as not to risk being thought stand-offish.

As the train wheels turned in her weary head and the sparks flew past the window crowded with dim, sprawling reflections, she seemed to be embarking on a dream rather than a new life. The sense of isolation she always felt on railway journeys was emphasized by her being the only person awake. Already Stephen seemed remote, almost unreal. Her mind slipped back to other journeys; to a particular journey with her parents to Paget's Fold, the cottage where they always spent the summer holidays. She had been fifteen then . . . a child as it seemed to her from the huge distance of six years. War had been declared while they were down there, but that was not her most vivid memory of the August. She remembered a hot day alone on the downs and a sudden, intense desire to find a companion, a lover with whom she could share her most absurd and secret thoughts. No one had appeared but a horrible, red-faced man as old as her own father who had leered at her and called her 'Missie'. Her thoughts grew scrappier and scrappier till, cold and cramped as she was, she fell into a doze. Only a second later, it seemed, she was awakened by a smart kick on her ankle.

'Rise and shine, old dear,' said Maidie's voice. 'We're nearly there.'

Clara blinked at her with aching eyes. 'It's on – only about two, isn't it?' she yawned miserably.

'It's four a.m. and raining like hell,' said Maidie briskly. She looked incredibly fresh as, with a hatpin between her white teeth, she powdered her nose and tidied her hair. Having tied a scarf over it before she went to sleep, the smooth plaited shells needed only a pat before she skewered on the lace-brimmed hat at a smart angle. In a few seconds she was gloved, shod, buttoned and preened till she was as neat as a doll just unwrapped from tissue paper. Struggling to her feet, Clara caught sight of herself in the mirror. Her face was pale and sticky; there was a smear of soot on her nose; her hair hung in limp tangles under the crushed hat that had slipped over one ear. For the first time she was glad that Stephen was not in the same company. There was nothing of the milkmaid or the pink-tipped daisy about that reflection. Before she could attempt any repairs, she was pushed from the mirror by Peter Belsize.

'My dear, I look like the morning after the night before. Trev, you don't know how lucky you are not having to shave twice a day.' He felt his blue chin anxiously. 'I'm *positive* I've got a spot coming.'

Clara, who had never seen men wake from uncomfortable sleep at dawn, was relieved to see that they looked worse than she did. The older ones, with their faces sagging in pouches, seemed to have aged overnight; even Peter and Trevor had jaundiced eyes and a leaden tinge. The train drew into the station; the yawning actors huddled into their coats and began to pull down their suitcases. Clara half expected one of the men to help her with hers but none of them offered a hand. It was

Maidie who helped Miss Cooke with her heavy old-fashioned bags.

At last the whole company stood yawning and shivering on York platform. In the murk under the sooty roof on which the rain drummed steadily, it was hard to realize that it was half-past four on a summer morning. Everyone was longing for a cup of tea, but no buffet was open at that hour.

Dismissed with a call for half-past two on the stage, the actors scattered in twos and threes. Clara, lugging two leather suitcases, found it hard to keep up with Maidie who carried only an oilcloth hold-all and an umbrella. The rain poured steadily on Clara's unprotected hat and hair and sent cold trickles down her neck. After what seemed to her miles of wet grey streets, she panted:

'Is it much further? Perhaps we could get a taxi.'

'Taxi,' snorted Maidie. 'If my screw won't run to taxis yours certainly won't. Unless you've got private means, Lady Clara Vere de Vere.'

Clara was silent. She had four pounds in her bag; all that was left of her last cheque for a set of face-cream advertisements. Apart from that she had only her salary of three pounds a week. Out of that she would have to pay ten per cent to her agent and all her expenses except railway fares. Expenses included not only food and lodgings but the shoes and stockings she wore on the stage, make-up and tips to the theatre staff.

'Five bob every bloody week to the dresser,' Maidie had warned her. 'A bob to the callboy. And if you're wise, you'll slip the baggage man half a crown now and then. Otherwise you may find your heavy stuff getting left behind.'

Clara became so absorbed in alarming mental calculations that she almost forgot the rain and the ache in her arms. Blind to the beauties of York she staggered along with her heavy cases till at last Maidie stopped in front of a shabby house in a back street.

The bell was answered at last by a woman who seemed surprised to see them and kept repeating:

'Ah tell you, ah never got postcard. Ah'm full up back and froont.'

To Clara's surprise, Maidie merely said, in her most refined voice: 'Sorry to have troubled you, Mrs Canning. There must be some mistake.'

Not till they were halfway down the street did Maidie begin to curse volubly.

'Old bitch bloody well had got it an' all. But you daren't get on the wrong side of landladies. Never know when you might play their town again. The girl who gave me this ad said Canning's place was clean. More than you can say for some of them.'

She stood in the rain, consulting a map, while Clara, thankful to drop her luggage for a moment, admired her competence.

'The boys gave me a couple of ads. We'll try those. Where the hell are we? Micklegate . . . Blossom Street . . . at least we don't have to cross that bloody river again.'

Even Maidie's spirit began to flag when Park Street and South Parade turned out also to be full up. A *Chu Chin Chow* company which was playing at the other theatre had arrived the night before and snapped up all the good lodgings. Her pink mouth was drooping and her doll's face looked washed out under the black lace brim which was losing its crispness in the damp.

'Nothing for it, Vere. We'll just have to ask wherever we see a card.'

They tramped on in silence. Maidie's patent shoes were splashed with mud. Occasionally she stumbled from tiredness and swore, but without conviction, as her ankles twisted on her high heels. The first house that displayed an 'Apartments' card between its lace curtains was also full up. The landlady of the second, though they begged and pleaded, was resolved that never again would she take in actresses.

'I'm fed oop with you professionals,' she said, crossing her arms and eyeing them with implacable disapproval. 'Smoking in bed an' all and wanting hot water all hours of the night for what purpose I don't know.'

As they started off again, Clara began to get a kind of moral second wind. The fact that Maidie, who was always extremely tart about people who did not use their handkerchiefs, was sniffing, could only mean that she was on the verge of tears. This unexpected weakness made Clara feel protective.

'Look here, Maidie,' she said. 'I've got four pounds in my bag. Let's go to a hotel . . . just for today. I mean . . . on me of course.'

Maidie said quite meekly, 'Decent of you, Vere. But never say die, as the monkey said.'

Suddenly she stopped. 'Nothing for it, old dear. We'd better pray to St Joseph.'

Clara was startled.

'Why . . . are *you* a Catholic then?'

'I should bloody well think I am,' said Maidie indignantly.

'I'm sorry . . . I didn't know.'

'All the women in the company are R.C. thank God.'

'How did you know I was?'

'Don't ask silly questions. Get busy with St Joseph,' ordered Maidie. She stood still, shut her eyes tight, and Clara saw her pink lips move. She was so fascinated by the sight that her own prayer was so vague as to be negligible.

'Come on,' said Maidie, snapping her eyes open again. 'He'll find us something. Never failed me yet. I warn you it won't be the Ritz. Hasn't got modern ideas, the dear old Wurzit. But it'll be something.'

Sure enough, the very next landlady, who looked a good-natured slattern, could take them in. By now Clara was so exhausted that she would have been grateful for a heap of straw. She could have slept on the landlady's slack bosom as she heard Maidie say they would like to go to bed at once please as they had to rehearse in the afternoon.

'You'll 'ave to wait a bit, dears,' said the landlady. 'The beds isn't made yet. The two other young ladies only went off by the early train. Sit down and make yourselves at 'ome and Florrie'll make you a nice cup of tea.'

The strong leaf-speckled tea sweetened with condensed milk tasted better than anything Clara had ever drunk. Her aching head cleared; she began to take in her surroundings and even to feel a thrill of adventure. For the first time in her life, her parents would not even know her address and this gave her a delicious sense of freedom. The dingy surroundings were to become so familiar that, after a few weeks on tour, Clara had the impression that, though towns changed, landladies' sitting-rooms remained the same. There were always round tables with red or green serge cloths, aspidistras, photographs of seaside towns in plush frames and, in lucky weeks, a tinny, yellow-keyed piano.

Maidie was in bloom again after her tea. Even her lace hat seemed to have revived like a watered flower. She wandered about the room making unflattering comments on the photos of landlady's relatives and running a critical finger over the tops of furniture.

'You could write your name in the dust, and her lace curtains are filthy,' she said. 'Pity she's not a Yorkshire woman; they're ever so clean and they give you butter, not marge. Not used to this kind of thing, are you, Vere?'

'Oh well – it's rather what I expected.'

'I don't know what *my* mother would say if she saw some of the places we have to live in.'

Maidie sat down again after having dusted the chair with her handkerchief.

'We have some really beautiful furniture at home,' she went on in her most genteel voice. 'Antique. My mother always dusts it herself. She says you simply can't trust maids nowadays. She's ever so particular. And I take after her, that's why I wanted to room with someone refined. My mother would have kittens if she knew what common girls there *are* in the profession.'

'Did she mind your going on the stage?' Clara ventured.

'She'd ever so much rather I'd been a music teacher. But Mr Finkleman . . . he's a great friend of the family persuaded her that I ought to train for ballet. I sing too – Mezzo-soprana. I was on the road for two years in *The Maid of the Mountains* playing the *soubrette*.'

'Is musical comedy what you like doing most?'

'I'd prefer Opera. Think, dear . . . I might have been billed as the only Mimi with genuine T.B. Had to put in six months in a San. Only a spot. I'm all right now. But I'm not allowed to dance for a year.'

'You're awfully young. You'll soon get back.'

'Twenty-three,' said Maidie. 'No chicken for a dancer.

Specially when you're out of practice. I've been on the stage since I was fifteen.'

Clara sighed.

'I envy you. I wish I could do one thing and do it really well.'

'You're ever so brainy though, aren't you? The boys told me you have things printed in the papers. True? Or s'only a rumour?'

'Only advertisements and rather silly short stories.'

'They pay you for them?'

'Why, of course.'

'Then they must be quite snappy. Honestly, Vere, I can't make you out.'

'What's so puzzling?'

'If you can make good money just sitting on your fanny writing whatever comes into your head, why on earth did you go on the stage?'

Clara mumbled something about the experience. Maidie took her up sharply.

'Some people might call it taking the bread out of other girls' mouths.'

'Hang it all. I took a training course. *And* paid for it.'

'You'd have learnt more playing the hind legs of a donkey.'

'No doubt,' said Clara, yawning.

Maidie snapped: '*If* you're going to yawn in my face, you might at least say "Pardon". Not to mention putting your hand in front of your mouth. I *thought* you'd been decently brought up.'

Luckily the landlady arrived before they both lost their tempers. The prospect of a few hours' sleep was so delicious to their edgy nerves, that Maidie even squeezed Clara's arm as they went upstairs.

They were shown into a dismal bedroom. Clara was relieved to find that, at least, there were two beds. She was careful to offer Maidie first choice. The sheets looked suspiciously grey and the mattress sagged like a hammock but at least it was something on which to lie down and sleep. Clara hastily pulled off her clothes, instinctively remembering the convent technique of 'undressing with Christian modesty' and plunged into bed. Through her half-closed eyes she could see Maidie's pink mouth pursed in disapproval as she surveyed the clothes flung in an untidy heap on a chair. Maidie shook out her skirt, brushed her coat and carefully folded each of her garments before she put on a virginal nightdress of white lawn threaded with blue ribbons.

'I didn't think *you'd* be so untidy, Clara,' she said reproachfully. 'Still, I'll forgive you this once. You look bloody tired, poor kid. Got that fed-up, blank and far from home feeling?'

'Mmmm,' murmured Clara, conscious of nothing but overwhelming drowsiness.

'Nighty night and sweet dreams.'

Maidie was half in bed when suddenly she leapt out again and fell on her knees.

'Oh damn,' she exclaimed. 'Forgot to say my night prayers. S'pose they count when you go to bed in the morning?'

Clara opened her eyes guiltily, trying to pull herself out of the exquisite gulf of sleep, to do the same. She kept them open just long enough to see Maidie with her long gold plait and her long white nightgown, her eyes closed in an expression of such spotless piety that she looked exactly like little Eva before her lids dropped like plummets and she remembered nothing more.

Not long afterwards she awoke with the certainty that someone was sticking pins into her. She sat up, ungluing her eyes with difficulty, to feel new and sharper jabs.

'Maidie!'

'What the hell's the matter with *you*?'

'I think I'm being *bitten*.'

In a moment Maidie was out of bed and pulling back Clara's sheets.

'If it's bugs,' she said authoritatively, 'we move. If it's only fleas, wet soap will fix them.'

Luckily it was fleas. Maidie handsomely stood by, directing Clara's unskilled manoeuvres with a damp cake of soap.

'Live and learn, as the monkey said,' she observed as she returned to her own bed. 'You said you wanted a spot of experience, didn't you?'

Chapter Three

The first night of playing in a real theatre to a real audience had an almost miraculous effect on Clara's spirits. From the moment she found a telegram from Stephen stuck in the cracked mirror of the dressing-room, the blight that had settled on her since she had left London, lifted. Even the most seasoned actor is excited on an opening night, even if it is only the opening night of a tour. Clara felt a passion of gratitude to Stephen for his telegram, not only because it contained the magic word 'love' and a hope that their companies might coincide some week, but because it made her feel like a real actress. Everyone in the company had telegrams; Maidie, half a dozen, and the lead so many that Merton Mordish swore that he must have sent them himself.

'Pathetic,' he said, as he came into the girls' dressing-room and presented them with a bottle of Guinness with a gesture which converted it into champagne. 'He's signed them Matheson Lang, and Godfrey Tearle and Gladys Cooper, and the Lord knows who. Poor old Brett.' When the callboy banged on the door, shouting 'Overture and Beginners, please,' letting in the faint sound of an orchestra playing 'Take a pair of Sparkling Eyes', Clara began to shiver with delicious apprehension. She shivered so much that she dropped blobs of eyeblack on her newly made-up face and had to begin all over again. When, after what seemed only a few seconds, the callboy knocked again and yelled 'Curtain Up' excitement gave place to panic. She would never be made-up in time for her entrance.

As she fumbled frantically with hare's foot and wet white she made an appalling discovery.

'Maidie,' she cried. 'I can't go on.'

Maidie clapped her hand over Clara's mouth.

'Don't shout. Curtain's up. They'll hear you in front.'

Clara muttered: 'Maidie . . . I've forgotten all my lines.'

Maidie removed her hand from Clara's mouth and deftly rearranged her hair.

'Then make 'em up as you go along.'

'But . . .'

'You'll be O.K. once you're on. It's only stage-fright. Everyone gets it.'

'I've never felt like this before,' said Clara in a hoarse whisper. She was now convinced that her voice had gone as well as her memory.

'Well, you've never played to a real house, have you? Cheer up, kid. We're on together most of the show. I'll pull you through. You look a picture and that's all *they* care about.'

Somehow she found herself standing in the wings at the right moment, though with an agonized conviction that the words she could hear being spoken on the stage bore no relation to the play they had been rehearsing. Her knees were trembling so much that when her cue came Lister had to push her on. However, the moment she found herself on the stage, her legs carried her to the right place and she heard herself say her entrance line in a clear, composed voice.

For the rest of the evening she thoroughly enjoyed herself. The stale, creaking old farce suddenly came to life. Even its dreary jokes seemed witty when they were greeted with a roar of laughter from the tiers of pale masks in the darkness behind the glare of the floats. The first time one of her own lines was interrupted by one of those roars she was panic-stricken. Soon she began to sense when the laugh would come and pause for it.

Her scenes with Maidie went better than she had ever imagined possible. She knew she was not doing too badly from the fact that Maidie risked one or two unrehearsed pieces of 'business' and she found herself playing up to them. At the end, Lister thrust the two of them on for a curtain call of their own and the claps and appreciative whistles, though Clara knew she had only a small share in them, were the most intoxicating sounds she had ever heard. Almost more intoxicating were Lister's slap on the back in the wings and Maidie's, 'Not half bad for a beginner, Vere. You might make an actress yet.'

During the next few weeks, Clara became accustomed to a

diet of sausages, strong tea and grilled herrings, to having a perpetual smear of blue on her eyelids and to never feeling properly washed or groomed. She could not acquire Maidie's technique of 'living in a suitcase' yet always appearing perfectly neat and fresh. Her own were overloaded with second-hand books she could not resist buying and which crushed her clothes and seduced her from ironing them. She became used to sitting up all night in trains and playing nap at dawn in station waiting-rooms. She even became used to seeing her own name in print coupled with such phrases as 'sprightly performance', 'promising newcomer' and 'vivacious freshness' in the Tuesday editions of provincial papers. At first she was interested in each new town and would explore its streets and even take a bus into the country outside. But soon, like the others, she no longer bothered to find out more than the shortest way from that week's digs to that week's theatre. Except for the long letters she wrote to Stephen and which he quite frequently answered and the postcards she occasionally scribbled to her parents in return for their faithful weekly budgets she was quite cut off from the outer world. Maidie curbed her natural extravagance so successfully that she just managed to make both ends meet on her salary. Only once or twice did she reluctantly force herself to dash off a few pieces of copy to mollify the advertising agents with whom she dared not break completely in case she suddenly found herself out of work.

A company on tour is not unlike a boarding-school. There were times when its changing feuds and friendships reminded Clara absurdly of Mount Hilary. She thought ironically how horrified the nuns would be that she should find any connection between this slipshod existence and the ordered, spotless life of the convent. Yet here, as there, she found herself both accepted and a little apart. She was beginning to wonder if there were any place where she did perfectly fit in; any life to which she could wholly commit herself. Ever since her childhood, she had believed that, just round the corner, her real life was waiting for her. Perhaps, after all, there was nothing. Nothing . . . or possibly something so frightening that she would dash blindly up any path to avoid it.

Friendships struck up in Huddersfield would dissolve acrimoniously in Nottingham: people who had cut each other dead in Leeds would be found rooming together in Liverpool. Apart from herself and Maidie, who, though they quarrelled, never quite split up, only one pair remained inseparable. Occasionally Trevor would complain that Peter had been 'really rather beastly, dear', or Peter would sulk because Trevor had snatched a corner seat twice running on night journeys, but they were usually a most peaceable couple. They made a kind of protective alliance with Clara and Maidie. Though they would not, of course, give up a corner to either girl, they would hold seats for them against other claimants and sometimes offer them the dregs of their Thermos flask. Clara had found them puzzling at first but she came to accept them as she accepted Maidie's extraordinary switches from primness to bawdiness and her own nickname of 'Vere'.

She soon discovered that Trevor looked up to Peter with almost worshipping awe. Peter knew just enough French to decipher *Le Jardin des Supplices* with great labour and translate it in whispers to Trevor on train journeys. He was also an expert at embroidering. Sometimes, on Sunday mornings, the four would meet at each other's digs. If it was a piano week, Maidie would sing, while Trevor admiringly watched Peter stitching sprays of almond blossom on a cushion cover. 'Why not pansies, dear?' Maidie had asked once and Peter had giggled, 'Too obvious, darling.' Maidie had an unexpectedly pure small soprano. When she was not in the mood for indecent songs, she would sing 'my classical pieces', 'Caro mio' or excerpts from *Aïda* and *Butterfly*. When she sang these she would sit bolt upright, like a schoolgirl practising before her mistress, breathing very conscientiously, and wearing her most refined expression, occasionally breaking off to snap: 'For God's sake, turn over, Vere' or 'Damn that bloody wurzit of a chord.'

Those Sunday mornings in dingy furnished parlours had a character of their own. Sunday, if they were not travelling, was the only day they had to themselves; there was a sense of peace, even of luxury, in being for once out of harness. They reminded Clara again oddly of the Sundays at her convent school though they had little in common beyond the fact that she and Maidie and Miss Cooke went to early Mass. She was not surprised to find that Miss Cooke went to Mass nearly every day but she was amazed at the devoutness of Maidie. Often when Clara herself could not face the thought of getting up before breakfast after a late journey, Maidie would walk a mile or more fasting to go to Communion. Clara felt that Maidie had a right to reproach her, as she often did, for slackness. During the last few years, and particularly since she had known Stephen Tye, her religion had become a habit rather than a preoccupation. Stephen was fond of saying: 'How lucky you are to be able to believe in something. I have no refuge of that kind,' or 'Poor Celia should have been a Catholic. Women need religion.' Such remarks made her feel that there was an unfair advantage, almost a kind of mental cheating in being a Catholic.

Though she and Maidie frequently exasperated each other, they never quite came to the point of splitting up. Clara, bookish, untidy and accustomed to privacy, would have found it a severe strain to share a bedroom even with someone of her own type. Maidie was as horrified by Clara's disorderliness as Clara was alternately shamed and irritated by Maidie's almost pathological neatness. She could keep up neither with Maidie's heights of refinement nor her moods of rollicking relaxation. Maidie, whose prim rosebud mouth could produce the most startling language Clara had yet heard, was deeply shocked when Clara once exclaimed '*Mon Dieu*'. 'God, Vere,' she had said. 'You shouldn't say that. It's not just unladylike, it's blasphemous.' She was almost as shocked because Clara sent her underclothes to the laundry instead of, like herself, washing them in a basin at their digs. 'I'm surprised at you, Vere. Why, you went to a convent, didn't you? For all you know, there may be *men* working in laundries.' Sometimes the two quarrelled bitterly and continued to share bed, board, and theatre dressing-room in silence broken only by: 'May I trouble you for the sugar, Miss Batchelor,' or 'I *believe* that's my number five, Miss Spencer.'

If it had not been for their both being Catholics, their feuds might have been permanent. But, inconsistent though they both were, it was impossible for them to kneel side by side at Communion and return to their lodgings to glare in icy silence at each other across the breakfast table. Sundays, for this reason, were usually an oasis of peace before the next quarrel began to brew.

Chapter Four

One particular Sunday morning – it was in Nuneaton – Clara and Maidie went round to Peter and Trevor's digs. It was a warm morning in late October; a strong smell of tanneries came in through the open window. Maidie was sitting at the yellow-keyed pinao playing and singing; Trevor was manicuring his nails and Peter, as usual, stitching his cushion cover. The photographs on the piano jangled every time Maidie struck a powerful chord; at intervals a cracked bell sounded from the neighbouring chapel. Clara listened idly to the old musical comedy songs, watching Peter's needle moving expertly in and out.

Maidie broke off in the middle of 'Florrie was a Flapper' which she sang with great verve and said primly:

'I don't think I ought to sing that on Sunday. Let's have something classical.'

Sitting very upright, with the sun glinting on her coiled golden plaits, she began in her unexpectedly pure, violin-like voice:

'One fine day you'll notice
A ship . . . a ship arriving . . .'

Inevitably, Clara's thoughts flew to Stephen. Her situation was becoming very like Butterfly's. Week by week she went on hoping that his company would catch up with hers; sometimes they missed each other only by a day. In Liverpool there had been a chance that he would get over from Chester for the

Sunday but a telegram had cancelled their meeting. Lately she had begun to wonder whether he would come at all.

Maidie sang without passion, like a conscientious schoolgirl, yet the very impersonality of her choirboy voice made the song more poignant. All the yearning of all women waiting for their lovers to return seemed to rise and fall like a fountain jet in the ugly parlour crowded with plush and bamboo, among the smells of cabbage water and tanning, the scratching of Trevor's nail file and the tinny clang of the chapel bell. All at once, Clara forgot Stephen and was carried into that other realm where everything had a significance beyond itself. She thought 'This moment is like no other. Only *now* will all these things come together in this particular way . . . this music, these smells, these sounds, these people.' At the same time she felt not that violent yet vague urge to write which usually turned to impotence after a few pages, but something calmer and more concrete. Certain loose threads which had been floating in her mind for weeks spun themselves together; she saw the rough shape of a story quite unlike the slick mechanical ones she constructed for *London Mail*.

Maidie banged down the piano lid; the pink glass lustres on the mantelpiece shuddered and tinkled. Peter pricked his finger and swore.

'Nothing like a spot of classical music,' she said. 'My soul feels better already. Think I'll even go to twelve o'clock Mass and hear a sermon. Coming, Vere? We've just time.'

'N–no,' stammered Clara. 'I'll go back to our digs. Something important I've remembered I must do.'

'Can't be more important than going to Mass.'

'I *have* been once.'

'I should bloody well hope so.'

'Tst. Tst. Girls, girls,' said Trevor.

'Shall *we* go with Maidie?' asked Peter. 'Anything for a new sensation. I adore incense and candles.'

'There won't be any. It's Low Mass.'

'Oh, we can't abide anything low,' he giggled. 'I'll stay here and let Trev do my nails.'

For the rest of the day, Maidie had one of her fits of exceptional piety while Clara stayed in their stuffy bedroom writing hour after hour with a sustained concentration that amazed her. Her attempts to write anything serious usually petered out in impotent misery after a few paragraphs. Today she was too absorbed to tell herself as usual that she could never hope to be anything but a hack with a certain trite facility. By seven when Maidie returned, announcing that she had been to the Rosary, Benediction and Holy Hour, she was busy on the third draft of her story.

Maidie burst into the bedroom in the best of tempers.

'I've brought us some Guinness – I need it after all that praying. What have *you* been up to?'

Clara hastily retrieved the pages which littered the floor.

'Inspiration flowing, eh?' she snatched up a page Clara had overlooked. 'Come on, let's have a peep.'

'Please, Maidie,' implored Clara, trying to rescue the page.

'Why . . . what is it? A hot love story?'

'No,' said Clara almost in tears. 'It's something you'd find awfully boring.'

'How d'you know?' Maidie's face turned suddenly suspicious. 'I'm not educated enough. Is that it?'

'No . . . no . . .' said Clara in agony. 'Of course not. Only I can't bear people to look at things till they're finished.'

Maidie stared. Then to Clara's relief, the suspicious look relaxed into a patronizing smile.

'Diddums then. You are a rum kid. Like a rabbit about to eat its young. Come on, have a Guinness. I'm dying for a spot of fun. Shall we ask that stuck pig Jimmy Munroe to have a drink?'

Clara nodded. The elderly young man with the frightened expression was rooming in the same house that week.

'Do him good,' said Maidie. 'He nearly jumps out of his skin when I ask him to pass the mustard. He's terrified of girls. Too pure to be true, my dear. If he were a Catholic there'd be some excuse. But when you don't *have* to be pure . . . well, it's unnatural. I'd like to give him a *real* scare.'

The young man with the frightened look drank his Guinness readily enough and became almost talkative though his expression did not change. Maidie drank several. With each one her spirits rose and her language became less and less inhibited.

After supper she suddenly rushed upstairs. Ten minutes or so went by and she did not reappear.

The elderly young man asked Clara:

'Does your friend often drink quite so much Guinness?'

'I've never seen her have more than one at a time.'

'You don't think she might be feeling poorly?'

'I shouldn't think so. She's in tearing spirits.'

'Oh, yes. Ever so cheery,' he said nervously. 'Pardon the suggestion. But don't you think you ought to go up and see if she's all right? She might have come over queer.'

Clara agreed. Before she could reach the door, Maidie bounded through it, dressed only in a pair of black silk stockings and a pink chemise. She had let down her hair which now hung in long golden strands almost to her waist.

James Munroe looked more terrified than ever, but he was not going to be driven out of his comfortable sitting-room.

'I feel like dancing,' announced Maidie gaily. 'Haven't practised for months. Wonder if I can still get up on my points.'

After one or two unsuccessful attempts, she balanced on the tips of her toes, a slender, charming figure. In spite of the pink chemise, her face was a study in angelic innocence.

'Wonder if I can remember a routine.' She skipped a few steps, then stopped.

'Damn,' she said sweetly. 'I'm as stiff as a poker. Can't get my leg up. Come here, Jimmy – hold my foot.'

Very gingerly, as if it had been a live shell, Munroe took hold of the small black-stockinged foot.

'That's right. Now lift it up. No . . . higher. Hell, man, don't look so frightened. Haven't you ever seen a girl's leg before? Well, you're bloody well going to now.' She whipped her foot out of his hand and sent it flying up in a head-high kick. 'And again – *and* again,' she panted. 'Now you've got something to write home about.'

The sight of Munroe's panic-stricken face sent her into peals of delighted giggles. Then she relented.

'Poor lamb,' she pouted. 'Was he shocked then? Did naughty Maidie commit a spot of *faux pas*? Well, it's all come out in the wash as the monkey said.'

Averting his eyes, the unhappy Jimmy collapsed into a wicker chair. Maidie sat down at the piano and regaining her most virginal expression, began to sing:

'Hark, hark, my soul,
Angelic songs are swelling.'

'You sing beautifully,' said the frightened man. 'But aren't you a little cold, Miss Spencer?'

'Maidie to you, and I'm not as cold as I look.' She leapt up from the piano stool and bounded lightly on to Munroe's knee.

'I bet you don't know the difference between a man and a woman, Jimmy,' she said, winding her slim arms round his eck. 'Sweet thirty-five and never been kissed.' She pressed her lips to his recoiling mouth.

After he had, with some difficulty, unwound her, Maidie rushed up once more to the bedroom and returned with an empty Guinness bottle and a rosary. Flinging herself on the floor and waving the bottle in one hand and the rosary in the other, she proceeded to pour out alternate strings of 'Hail Mary's' and unpublished limericks. Munroe, now pale and sweating with fear, dashed out of the room and Clara heard the key turn in his bedroom door. After much persuasion, she induced Maidie to come to bed. Once upstairs, Maidie disappeared into the bathroom, and returned, rather pale but quite sober. She plaited her hair with her usual deftness, exchanging the pink chemise for her white schoolgirlish nightdress and knelt down to say her prayers. When she had finished, she opened her limpid blue eyes and looked at Clara reproachfully.

'You're a good sort, Vere,' she said. 'But I wish you'd take your religion more seriously. I get quite worried sometimes thinking what might happen if I weren't there to keep you straight.'

Chapter Five

The next day, when they moved on to Gainsborough, Clara found two letters waiting for her in the stage doorkeeper's pigeonhole. One was from Stephen; the other from her father. Stephen's pencil scrawl contained such wonderful news that she entirely forgot her other letter.

'I'll be outside the theatre at Gainsborough on Sunday morning at eleven. We're playing Lincoln this week and I've wheedled Miss Lane into letting me hire a car and drive over. Official reason; get local colour for possible stage version of *The Mill on the Floss*. Real reason; see you. My love – for what it is worth. S.'

It was not till she returned to their digs after the show that she remembered her father's letter, thrust unopened into her coat pocket. She saw that it was a long one and thought remorsefully how faithfully he wrote to her every Sunday, busy as he was, and how carelessly she skimmed through his news. But this time she read the letter attentively and with disquiet. Archie Hughes-Follett was in England and her father had told him the theatres where she would be playing in the next few weeks. She had not seen Archie since she had jilted him nearly four years ago on the verge of their wedding and she had no desire to see him now.

'I hesitated,' Claude Batchelor wrote, 'but it seemed churlish to refuse. I could not help feeling sorry for Archie. He seems rather lost since his mother's death. His job in South America does not seem to have been a success. At any rate he is back in England with no home of his own to go to and, as far as I can see, no definite plans. He has changed a great deal since I last saw him in 1917. In case he should come and see you, I should warn you that, superficially anyhow, you may find him changed for the worse. The war seems to have affected some of the very best in that way. But I am sure that, fundamentally, he is as sound as ever. I was always fond of Archie, as you know, and I was touched by the way he spoke of you: not a trace of resentment or bitterness. Now that he is down on his luck – financially as well as in other ways – I think it would be nice if you could make some little gesture of friendship towards him. I am sure he would not misinterpret it and I feel you owe it to him. Don't imagine that I am blaming you in any way for Archie's present state. The fact remains that, magnificently as he took it, you gave him a great blow when you broke your engagement. I am *sure* he has got over it . . . but equally sure that he needs any friends he can find.'

Weeks of the tour when there had been nothing definite to look forward to had flown. This one dragged interminably towards the distant brightness of Sunday. Though Clara dreaded the thought of seeing Archie again, she would have welcomed almost any distraction to make the slow days go more quickly. Each night she expected to find a letter in his cramped, childish writing but the only other letter that came that week was from her mother. Isabel, too, wrote about Archie.

'Daddy will have told you that your ex-fiancé turned up here last week from South America. He looked untidier than ever; almost dirty, to tell the truth. I am afraid he was also rather tipsy – *so* sad to see a young man from such a background going downhill like that. Poor Philippa Hughes-Follett! It is almost a mercy that she is dead; she would have been heartbroken to see her son in such a state. I *always*, you know, had an intuition that there was some fatal weakness in Archie. More than ever now I realize how *disastrous* it would have been for you to marry him. Daddy still has a very soft spot for that young man, however! I didn't want him to put Archie on your track but you know how obstinate Daddy can be! I implore you not to do anything rash. *I* know you have a very tender heart, however hard and "modern" you like us to think you are. Women are so dreadfully liable to be moved by pity and though Daddy is sure he has got over everything, *I* believe he's still in love with you. And now, less than ever, would he be a fit husband for my darling, pretty clever daughter. Even *you* admitted I was right in 1917 and realized your frivolous mother was not such a fool after all. You may have forgotten that day I found you crying your heart out in the Oratory but I never have and never shall.'

Clara had forgotten neither the day nor the conversation with Isabel that had led to her breaking her engagement but she intensely disliked being reminded of it. It was the one occasion in her life on which she had turned to her mother, whom she normally despised, and had found her displaying a most unexpected wisdom and firmness. Clara had long since slid back into her old superior attitude and Isabel into the vain, inconsistent, peevish self which so comfortably justified it. This letter, unlike her father's, had the effect of making her feel a faint, remorseful renewal of interest in Archie.

However, as Sunday came within measurable distance, she forgot all about Archie in preparing to meet Stephen. Examining herself anxiously in the glass, she saw that she had lost some of her freshness in the last three months. Her skin was duller and her eyes looked tired. She began a hasty beauty campaign and made herself take long walks among the warehouses and gabled buildings along the banks of the river where Tom and Maggie Tulliver had drowned in each other's arms.

When Sunday arrived at last, she could only deal with her distractions at Mass by turning her thoughts of Stephen into prayers for him. She kept imploring, 'Please let it come right for us,' without daring to formulate what 'coming right' might mean. Before eleven struck she had passed the theatre a dozen times, forcing herself to walk a hundred yards beyond it either way without looking round or hiding up a side street which gave her a clear view. She laughed at herself for behaving so exactly like Madam Butterfly and even sang softly, 'I without answering, hold myself quietly concealed' ironically imitating Maidie's careful vowels. At last she saw a car drive up and stop in front of the theatre. She sauntered towards it as slowly as possible, not daring to raise her eyes in case the man at the wheel should not be Stephen. She did not look up till she heard the door slam and saw his tall figure in the familiar old trench coat hurrying towards her. She stopped dead with a sudden wild impulse to run away. The next minute she felt his hands on her shoulders and found herself looking up into his face.

'My *dear* Clara!'

'Stephen!'

He looked different, she thought. His pallor was faintly tanned, making his fair hair and moustache seem almost white by contrast.

'How incredibly well you look.'

'Almost indecently fit.' He smiled down at her, tucking her arm under his. 'By Gad, it's good to see you. This calls for a celebration. Damn, they won't be open yet. What shall we do . . . drive out somewhere?'

'Absolutely anything you like,' Clara said happily.

'Perhaps I'd better not use too much petrol. Eliza might get suspicious. After all I'm supposed to be getting local colour in St Ogg's, not roaming the countryside.'

'Eliza?'

'Miss Lane. My boss.'

'Of course.'

'You've no idea of the wangling I've had to do. Naturally she wanted to come along. I invented an eccentric old gentleman who was a great authority on George Eliot and couldn't abide women. Recognize yourself?'

She laughed.

'Character part. Give me time to get into the skin of it, as old Merton Mordish says.'

It was a grey morning yet the prim red streets where she had taken her dull duty walks seemed suddenly flooded with sunlight. Every gable, even every shuttered shop window became beautiful and significant; every passer seemed to look at them with affectionate envy. She could hear Stephen telling her about his parts and the people in his company; she could hear herself laughing and answering but all the time she was saying to herself, 'This isn't a dream. I really am here in Gainsborough on a Sunday morning, walking with my arm in Stephen's.'

At last she became aware in one of the streets leading down to the river that neither of them had spoken for some time. Stephen detached his arm.

'I must have a cigarette. Isn't there anywhere in this place where one can sit down?'

She guided him to a bench by the river. Between puffs at his cigarette he looked down at her with narrowed eyes.

'Well,' he said. 'Here we are. Still the same little Clara. Or *are* you quite the same?'

'Do I look awful?' she asked nervously.

'Good lord, no. Perfectly recognizable. A little *distraite*, possibly.'

'I still can't believe you're actually here.'

'You would if you realized the prodigious efforts I've made to get here. I've not merely perjured myself but I was out of bed by eight on a Sunday morning. I doubt if many men in your life will do as much for you as that.'

'All right. You *are* here. If I can believe you got up at eight, I can believe anything.' She spoke lightly but her heart was unaccountably heavy. It was more of an effort than usual, having been away from him for so long, to keep up the careless note he liked and expected. She wondered if he had the least idea how it hurt her when he suggested there might be other men in her life some day. It was inconceivable to her that she could ever love anyone else. The mere possibility of 'other men' implied something too painful to imagine; the loss of Stephen himself.

She began to ask him questions about his life in the last three months. Once or twice he said impatiently:

'I've told you that already. I don't believe you've listened to a word I've said.'

She knew that she had been too excited by his mere presence to notice what either of them had said as they walked down to the river. This made her self-conscious and for some moments she was afraid to speak at all.

'Absent-minded or sulking?' he asked, pinching her arm rather sharply. 'I can't stand these pregnant silences. I get too much of them with Eliza.'

'What's she like – Miss Lane?'

'My dear, I've told you that too. Very matriarchal but a damn good actress. No doubt you were too *distraite* to hear me say I was going to play Richard II in Oxford.'

'No. That's something I did grasp. I'm terribly excited. It's *absolutely* your part.'

Stephen stared at the river.

'By God, it is. I've longed to play it ever since I was in the O.U.D.S. What a part . . . and what poetry.'

Clara said softly: 'Oh, that I were a mockery king of snow.'

He took it up and went through the whole speech, muting the resonance of his beautiful voice, but making every pause, every inflection perfect.

Clara felt a chill of sheer pleasure run down her spine.

'Stephen . . . if you can do it all as well as that . . . this is going to be *something*. Oh, if only I could come and see you.'

He turned to her with his face alight.

'Aha . . . I've woken you up at last, have I? There's my old crony of the taverns. I was beginning to think I might as well have stayed in my comfortable bed. Listen – I've got an entirely new idea how to work the mirror scene.'

She listened intently for several minutes while he explained and illustrated his idea. She was rewarded by his suddenly flinging his arm along the back of the seat and looking at her affectionately.

'My God, talking to you makes me realize how much I've missed you. No one listens as intelligently as you do. *When* you listen, that is. Have you missed *me*, Clara?'

'What do you think?' she said happily.

'You didn't mention it in your letters.'

'I thought it was too obvious to mention.'

'Hmmm. I wondered if some dashing contemporary might have cut out your middle-aged admirer.'

'I wish you'd stop once and for all harping on those ten years.'

'My dear, it's only with you I feel so confoundedly old. With the Lane I feel a positive Peter Pan.'

'How old is *she*?'

'Forty if a day. She doesn't look it on the stage. Remarkable woman. A slight strain, sometimes. Goes in for plain living and high thinking.'

'You sound as if she were trying to reform you.'

'She makes attempts in that direction. Do you know Clara, I

have had precisely two pints of beer since last Thursday? And not a drop of whisky.'

'It sounds like Swinburne and Watts-Dunton.'

'It is rather. However, I intend to relax today. What time do they open in this appallingly smug little town?'

'I've no idea.'

'Very proper. I see life on tour hasn't corrupted you. When I first saw you . . . I thought for a moment the milkmaid had ever so slightly lost her bloom.'

'More than slightly. And probably past recovery,' sighed Clara. 'Touring seems to suit you all right. I've never seen you looking so well.'

'My face hasn't got fat or anything awful?' he asked anxiously.

'Good heavens, no.'

'I shall need all my haggard charm for Richard. And for Wakem if we do the "Mill". Eliza wants me to play Stephen Guest but I'm sticking out for Philip.'

'I think it's absurd to try and turn the "Mill" into a play. When a thing's conceived as a novel – when all the drama is internal and the whole thing's an accumulation of tiny incidents – it's just sheer mutilation.'

'My dear Clara . . . what eloquence! It must be your father coming out in you. I've always believed you would have made an admirable schoolmistress.'

'Beast. You know I hate people to say that.'

'Have I lost my ancient privilege of teasing you? Actually I agree. But Elizabeth has a fancy to play Maggie Tulliver.'

'At *her* age?'

'I tell you she doesn't look it on the stage. Besides she's got all the technique in the world. Also she's rather the type: intense, humourless, high ideals, touch of fanatical mysticism, et cetera.'

Maggie Tulliver was one of Clara's favourite characters in fiction. She was beginning a spirited defence of her when Stephen interrupted.

'Spare me another literature lesson, dear girl. In my opinion the book's a bore and Maggie's a bore. Maggie's a bore because she's George Eliot and George Eliot was the supreme bore of the nineteenth century.'

'You've *never* appreciated George Eliot,' said Clara, too angry to care whether or not she was boring Stephen. 'I don't believe you've even read her properly.'

'No female novelist is worth reading,' said Stephen. 'Women can't write novels any more than they can write poems. There's only one book approaching a work of art even *signed* by a woman . . .'

'Emily *did* write it,' insisted Clara. This was an old ritual quarrel of theirs.

'Branwell wrote it,' said Stephen, with his most exasperating smile. 'Branwell, who was a drunk of genius. And like Branwell, I propose to make for the nearest pub. Are you coming or do you wish to remain glaring at the Trent and waiting for the eagre to overwhelm you?'

Clara laughed, but not as convincingly as she could have wished. It was nothing new that Stephen should tease her but she was out of practice in hiding the fact that she was hurt. Today, his old joke about women writers went deeper than usual. She had too often rashly imagined this first talk with him after their long separation and hoped that, when they got back to her digs, she might be able to mention, even to show him the story she had written in Nuneaton.

She walked in silence beside him as they hunted for a pub. This time he did not take her arm but strode along, with his hands in his pockets, so fast that she could hardly keep up with him. An east wind was blowing, whipping the ends of her curls into her eyes and raising Stephen's hair in a crest above his high-boned profile. He sang as he walked, in the thin, not quite true tenor that matched so oddly with his resonant speaking voice.

> 'Then one he singles from the rest
> And cheers the happy hen.
> With a "how d'you do?" and a "how d'you do?"
> And a "how d'you do?" again.'

When they were settled at last in a pub and Stephen had ordered some food and a double whisky, he said:

'You're looking gloomy again. What's the matter?'

'The hen's quite happy, thanks.'

'Hen? Hen?' he frowned. 'Stop being cryptic and have a drink. What do you want?'

'Anything. A Guinness.'

'Quite the old pro, eh? But you'll put on weight if you drink too many.'

'All right. A small gin then. It's Maidie who has such a passion for Guinness.'

'Maidie? Ah yes, of course. Your fantastic room-mate. You wrote me some rather amusing letters about her.'

'Too kind.'

'Women *can* write letters. They should stick to that.'

'I'll remember.'

'Still making masses of money out of those deliciously absurd advertisements? I wish *I'd* got the knack of writing profitable nonsense.'

'Precisely three guineas since the tour started.'

'Pity. I find theatrical life appallingly expensive, don't you?'

'I muddle along somehow. Maidie keeps me in order.'

'Eliza tries to keep me solvent. But I've usually subbed most of my beggarly salary by Friday. You couldn't possibly lend me a quid, Clara dear?'

'I've only got about fifteen shillings.' She emptied her bag on the table. 'You can have that.'

'Forget it. I don't rob children's moneyboxes. I daresay I can manage.'

'Let me pay my share, anyway.'

'I hate it but I suppose I'll have to let you. I forgot this absurd situation when I started ordering doubles. God, it's humiliating at my age. You should have known me when I was a gay captain. But I forgot. You were still in pinafores.'

'How often have I told you I left them off about 1907?'

'Don't be so maddeningly literal. You're still in mental pinafores. I don't suppose you were even aware of the war.'

'Aware enough to have lots of my friends killed in it. Boys who were only two of three years older than I was.'

'Killed,' he said with the sudden moroseness Clara remembered so well. 'They were the lucky ones.' He stared at her almost accusingly; his blue eyes hard and glazed.

She said unhappily: 'I couldn't help it. Being too young and not being a man. I did *try* to imagine it.'

'Imagine!' he said bitterly. 'I've seen things you *couldn't* imagine.' He swallowed a great gulp of whisky. Ashamed of her inadequacy, burning with sympathy for all Stephen must have gone through, Clara could not quite stop herself from noticing that his voice and gesture would have registered well on the stage.

She said humbly: 'Of course you're right. I can't imagine it. It's silly even to try.'

With another of his abrupt changes of mood he said:

'Don't look so sad. It doesn't suit you. Come, let the canikin clink. Can we afford another?'

After his third double, he became extremely lighthearted.

'My God, it's good to be with you again, you absurd creature. Trying to look like an actress and sipping your gin like a schoolgirl drinking a particularly filthy cough-mixture. I'm sure you haven't changed since you left that celebrated convent.'

'The nuns would think I'd changed. Considerably for the worse.'

'Rubbish. I doubt if you've got it in you to change. I believe you're immune from experience.'

'Am I as stupid as all that?'

'Very refreshing when it isn't exasperating. There are times when I adore this convent aura of yours.'

'You don't know anything about convents.'

'If you entered one, I should come and rattle at the grille.'

Clara said angrily: 'I'm not in the least likely to enter one.'

'Of course not. They're your church's admirable solution for unattractive females.'

'They're nothing of the kind. Oh, it's hopeless to try and make you understand.'

'Don't try, my sweet. The only time I find you slightly tiresome is when you attempt to explain your religion. Mark you, I approve of religion for women. It's a safety valve. Poor Celia should have been an R.C. Then she could have complained about me to the saints or gone to confession about me or whatever comforting thing it is you do. At any rate it might have stopped her from making such a fuss. Waiter . . . another double. Hell, is it closing time already? Damn Dora. What a country! In Flanders at least one didn't have to get tight by the clock.'

Chapter Six

They spent an hour or two of the grey afternoon wandering about the streets of Gainsborough while Stephen made some rough sketches of gables and fluted roofs and the bridge over the Trent.

'I'm only giving Eliza her head about the idiotic "Mill" play because she's letting me do Richard,' he explained.

'You seem to be well in with the management,' said Clara.

'I am, my dear. I know which side my bread's buttered. Eliza's quite likely to take a London theatre next year.'

Clara asked suddenly:

'Did anything come out of your drinks with that man in London?'

'What man? When?'

'The night I went off. When you couldn't get to King's Cross.'

'Oh . . . *that* chap,' said Stephen heartily. 'I'd almost forgotten. No . . . the usual vague promises. Sheer waste of time.'

When dusk fell, they went back to Clara's lodgings. She had bought a few things to supplement the high tea of sausages, bread and butter and cake and bribed the landlady into giving them an extra scuttle of coal for the fire. Mrs Greaves, soothed by Stephen who went out of his way to charm her, became unusually gracious and produced not only her best china but two boiled eggs in woollen jackets.

When Clara came down with her windblown hair freshly

combed and wearing a soft green dress that Stephen had once said he liked, he gave her one of his most affectionate looks. At once the sense of disappointment that had haunted her all the afternoon vanished and her heart became as light as a bubble. The ugly shabby room, glorified by the firelight and the presence of Stephen, seemed suddenly delightful. She laughed from sheer happiness.

'Ah, that's better,' he said. 'Now you look like my old Clara. I fancied there was a kind of blight on you all the afternoon.'

'East wind, I expect.'

'Yes, indeed. And that terribly smug provincial town. This is the only way to enjoy the provinces. High tea, plush curtains drawn and a blazing fire. What superbly typical digs.'

'Were your Lincoln ones like this?'

'Actually I haven't been in digs for the last few weeks. I've been in loathsome provincial hotels.'

'On your beggarly screw?'

'Not exactly,' he said hesitantly. 'On the house, as it were. Miss Lane wanted to discuss things about the plays. She's very genteel. Doesn't like slumming.'

'I see,' said Clara in a slightly chilly voice.

He reached up his hand from where he sat with his long legs stretched out to the fire and pulled her hair.

'Don't look so fierce. I've had enough of disapproving women.'

'Is Miss Lane fierce?'

'A benevolent despot, shall we say? The company's one big family. But there's no doubt who's head of it. If she makes a suggestion, it's tactful to agree.'

'What are you? . . . The favourite son?'

He pulled her down so that she was kneeling between his knees.

'The prodigal, on this occasion.'

'And I am the husks and swine? Thanks.'

He smiled, stroking back her hair.

'A little pink and white obstinate pig,' he said kissing her gently. 'And the sweetest of nut kernels.' He stood up and drew her to her feet.

'Come along. I'm dying of hunger. It would be a shocking thing if I were tempted to eat you instead of the sausages.'

He ate ravenously, pausing every now and then to throw back his head and laugh.

'My God, I am enjoying this. I feel as if I were young again and nothing mattered.'

Clara was too excited to eat, but she talked and made silly jokes in an access of absurd happiness. She had never seen Stephen in quite this mood before. Perhaps it was because they were alone together in an illusion of intimacy they had never known in London. They had met in pubs and restaurants and at parties in other people's rooms; even when they snatched an occasional day in the country they had never shared a meal in a room by themselves. The plush curtains shut out all sounds but the hiss of the fire and the faint jangle of Sunday evening church bells. The lamplight softened the sharp lines of Stephen's face; he looked younger, almost boyish as he sat there drinking mahogany-coloured tea, eating everything from sausages to pink sugar cakes and making jokes even sillier than her own. At last Clara fell silent, content to do nothing but watch Stephen's face and hear his voice and laugh. For the first time she felt she could safely give herself up to the delight of being in love with him without always having to be on her guard. It was as if they were living together in a real house . . . almost as if they were married. She sighed with pure happiness.

'Stop smiling at the angels and attend to me,' he said. 'Give me some more tea. Black as you like.'

She poured it carefully from the pewter pot into the cup lavishly adorned with gilt and forget-me-nots, feeling his eyes on her.

'I like watching you pour out tea,' he said. 'So deliciously conscientious like a solemn child presiding at a doll's tea-party. You know, Clara, domestic life is vastly becoming to you. You oughtn't to be traipsing about with a troop of vagabonds. You ought to be married and have a home and all that sort of thing.'

Her hand shook as she handed him the cup.

'I nearly did get married once. As nearly as possible.'

'I'm exceedingly glad you didn't.'

'Any good reason?'

'Only that we probably shouldn't be having high tea together at this moment. Good enough?'

'Quite.'

'I've got a worse one. Pure dog-in-the-manger. I shall be absurdly jealous of the man you marry.'

There was a knock on the door, though it was not Mrs Greaves's habit to knock before she came in to clear the table. Evidently Stephen's presence put her on her best behaviour. Tonight she made an interminable business of removing the dishes, talking to Stephen to whom she had obviously taken a violent fancy and looking at the pair of them with benevolent curiosity.

When at last she had gone, they sat opposite each other by the fire, hardly speaking. The interruption had broken the spell. Stephen's mood of wild spirits had faded: he sat smoking and frowning at the fire. Clara became conscious of the ticking of the clock. Her sense of timelessness had gone; the precious day was running out. Impossible to recapture that mood; to reopen that conversation. Without meaning to, she sighed.

'Melancholy?' he asked without looking at her.

'A little.'

'So am I. Sunday evening. Now we've stopped talking one hears those infernal church bells. The tintinnabulation of despair. What were we talking about?'

'I forget,' lied Clara.

'I hate the autumn,' he said. 'Remember how we walked in the New Forest last June? You had a dress almost the same green you are wearing now. And the sun shone through the leaves on your hair. Remember that cottage in the clearing and the woman who asked us in to pick strawberries?'

Clara nodded. She wondered if he remembered that the woman had asked them if they were on their honeymoon.

Stephen threw his cigarette into the fire and sang softly in his thin tenor . . .

'And while I walked still to and fro
And from her company I could not go
But when I waked . . . it was not so
In youth is pleasure.'

Clara did not look at him. There was a terrible fluttering of hope
and fear in her heart.

He said, with a sigh, 'In youth is pleasure. Be thankful you are
young, my dear.'

'Why do you always talk as if you were old?'

He assumed his bitter smile.

'Because, as a man, I am finished. Henceforth I only exist as an
actor.'

'I can't bear it when you say things like that.'

'Because you're young and sweet and silly.'

'Silly, if you like.'

'You are also a considerable temptation to a middle-aged man
determined to do the right thing.'

She looked at him closely.

'Stephen . . . am I being very dense?'

'A little, my dear. It's one of your charms. But it makes things
infernally difficult sometimes.'

The sense of hope and fear became almost overpowering.

'Is there something you're trying to tell me?'

'Perhaps,' he said gloomily. 'It may, of course, be entirely
unnecessary. I was always rather a vain chap.'

'What do you mean?'

Suddenly he shook his shoulders and sat up.

'Nothing. Shall I read to you?'

'Yes, do,' said Clara with an eagerness she was far from
feeling.

'What shall it be? The old Shropshire Lad? It's in my pocket
as always.'

He pulled out of his pocket the small red battered copy she
knew so well and that had been with him all through the war.
The Shropshire Lad had been the background of all their summer
together. He had read it to her in pubs, declaimed it as they
paced the London streets in the dusk. All her life she would

associate it with Stephen and be unable to read a single line without hearing it mentally in his voice.

She watched him now as he read; his head thrown slightly back so that there was a wedge of shadow under his long thin jaw; his pale lashes dropped over his dark blue eyes. That foreshortened view of his face, so familiar to her since he had a passion for reading aloud, always struck her as masklike. Tonight when she longed for him to talk and not to read, it made him seem infinitely remote.

She glanced carefully at the clock. He had said that he would have to leave at ten and already it was nearly eight. At first she thought he was going to read her the whole sequence. Then, from the way he was turning over the pages, smiling and soundlessly shaping words with his lips, she saw that he was choosing the poems very carefully.

At last he looked across at her with a curious expression. She could not decide whether it was angry or appealing.

'Come and sit by me,' he said, indicating the floor at his feet. Then when she was about to move, he frowned and said, 'No . . . stay where you are . . .'

She sat down, beginning to be irritable herself from the strain.

'I don't know where you distract me more . . . over there or close beside me.'

Clara's nerves were so much on edge that she snapped at him.

'Perhaps I'd be less distracting if I went out of the room.'

'I'm sorry. I'm in an abominable mood. Sit wherever you like.'

'I'll stay here,' she said coldly, longing to go and sit with her cheek against his knee.

He shrugged his shoulders; his eyes on the little red book.

'As you prefer.'

She clasped her hands in her lap in an effort to be calm.

'Read to me, Stephen.'

He looked at her then.

'Oh, my dear, why is life so infernally difficult?'

'Is yours being infernally difficult?'

'Infernally.'

'Can't you tell me why?'

'Perhaps . . . at some point. Meanwhile . . . Shropshire Lad.'

He began to read, apparently at random. He always read beautifully but tonight there was a peculiar edge to his voice which gave each familiar poem a new poignancy. Listening to him Clara forgot all her resentment. She had been childish, she told herself. She was closer to him as he read these words he loved than through talk or even touch. Human contact was difficult for him as she knew; he shied off, suspicious or mocking, from any show of feeling. But the words built up a safe sphere where they could meet. She lay back in her chair, watching him through half-closed eyes, allowing herself the luxury of feeling all her love for him. When he came to 'Into my heart an air that kills,' he shut the book and repeated softly, staring into the fire:

'This is the land of lost content
I see it shining plain
Those happy highways where I went
And shall not come again.'

Clara, too, looked into the fire. It was the poem which always moved her most; taking her straight back to the summers of her childhood at Paget's Fold, to that Sussex landscape which she would always see in a peculiar light, at once homely and magical. The spires and farms would always be those of Bellhurst and the 'blue remembered hills' the downs. But, tonight, Stephen said the last lines with such finality that she came out of her nostalgic dream.

'Stephen.'

'Yes?' He kept his eyes averted.

'You read that . . . as if . . . as if you had lost something in particular.'

'Perhaps I have. Perhaps I never had it.'

'You wouldn't tell me what it was?'

He jerked himself round to face her.

'Some questions are better not asked. Let's have something more cheerful. Here's some good advice for you, Clara.' He pointed an admonishing finger at her as he read, smiling.

'When I was one-and-twenty.'

When he had finished, she smiled too.

'I wonder how many times you've given me *that* advice.'

'But have you taken it? *Have* you kept your fancy free?'

'You'd be the last to know if I hadn't?'

He looked at her curiously.

'Would I? I wonder.'

She shook her head.

'I *am* one-and-twenty. No use to talk to me.'

'Idiot girl. Can't you see I'm trying to be sensible? I don't want you to be miserable and full of regrets at twenty-two. And frankly, I don't want to have regrets myself. Of course I *shall*. Either way.'

Clara sighed.

'I wish you wouldn't always be quite so ambiguous.'

'I'm an ambiguous character. Dense as you are, you must have grasped *that*.'

'I never know what to believe about you. Least of all the things you say about yourself.'

'I'm an actor first and last. That's all there is to it.'

'Oh, *no*, Stephen. There's much more,' she said eagerly.

'I hoped you'd say that. You always rise so beautifully.' He held out his arms, 'Come over here.'

She knelt again between his knees. He turned up her face and looked into it.

'I like seeing my reflection in your eyes,' he said. Then, half smiling, he repeated:

> 'Oh, when I was in love with you
> Then I was clean and brave
> And miles around the wonder grew
> How well did I behave.'

'I *have* behaved well, haven't I, Clara?'

She tried to twist her face out of his hands, but he held it firm.

'How bright your eyes are tonight,' he said.

'All the better to see yourself in,' she said, forcing a smile.

'Clara . . . don't tell me those are tears.'

'Of course not.' She blinked them away before they fell.

He released her face and leant back in his chair. His face was troubled.

'Clara.'

'Yes, Stephen.'

'Is it just my middle-aged vanity? Or . . .' He scrutinized her face. 'Or do you really . . . are you really . . .?' The muttered unfinished question ended in a mere movement of his lips.

Clara's heart gave a violent lurch. Unable to meet Stephen's eyes, she stared down at her clasped hands. At last she said in a voice so rigorously controlled that it sounded impersonal.

'In love with you? Yes, I am.'

After the effort of saying it, she felt quite empty. She looked up dizzily, anywhere but at Stephen's face. Beyond his head the room swam out of focus. She became acutely aware of the cramp in her knees, the fire scorching her left cheek, the smell of Stephen's tweed jacket. She felt him take her hands and separate the clenched fingers; she heard him say softly:

'Dear child. Dear Clara. I want you terribly. But, sweetheart, it won't work. For either of us.'

One part of her longed only to give up completely, to throw herself into his arms and forget the long, tortuous game they had played for so many months. Desire, beyond anything she had believed herself capable of feeling, ran through her like an electric shock. Her flesh, her very bones, seemed to be melting. Yet her other part held her in such iron control that her voice sounded dry, almost cold as she asked:

'Why not?'

'I'm a rotten bet for any woman. Least of all, a child like you.'

'As if I cared,' she said fiercely. 'Do you think I'm afraid of being unhappy?'

'That proves what a child you are. You don't know what unhappiness means.'

'Of course.' Her voice was bitter. 'I've spent all my life in a pinafore picking daisies. I forgot. You're the only person who's ever suffered, aren't you?'

He loosened his hold on her hands and looked at her in such

surprise that she had an insane desire to laugh. She watched him trying to recover his old mocking look.

'You little Tartar,' he said. 'I'll begin to believe you *are* a woman in a moment. Having just said you love me, you proceed to glare at me as if you hated me.'

'I almost do at moments. But only because you won't see . . . And now you force me to admit . . .' Her lips went too dry to go on. She sat back on her heels, knotting her hands and swallowing hard.

Stephen turned very white. He said uncertainly:

'You frighten me a little. I do love you in my fashion, you know.'

'Do you?' she said sadly, feeling her sudden strength ebb away.

'I suppose I'm too old to have such violent emotions any more,' he said slowly. 'Perhaps I never did *feel* them. Only imagine them when I'm playing a part.'

'I could do with awfully little,' she said, managing a smile.

'That's what you think.' He risked a smile himself. 'But you ought to have a great deal. Oh, don't imagine I'm not tempted. I saw a cornflower in Flanders once, flowering away on the top of a parapet. I just had the decency not to pick it and to let it go on flowering away.'

'How do you know it mightn't have preferred to wither in your buttonhole?'

He laughed and pulled her hair.

'I'll remember you long after you've forgotten me. Young girls are always in and out of love.'

'I'm not a flapper. I've had silly flirtations and tried to persuade myself I was in love. But I never have been . . . before.'

'What about this chap you nearly married?'

She said after a pause,

'Archie? That was something quite different. I never even imagined I was in love with him.'

'Sorry for him . . . was that it?'

Clara frowned and said slowly: 'Partly that. It's so hard to explain. He'd been awfully good to me when something horrible happened. I was so absolutely numb and dead after that . . . that thing . . . I didn't think I could really feel anything again. We were both in it. He wanted very much to marry me. It seemed the only thing left . . . to try and give him at least . . .' she broke off. 'Oh, it sounds so disgustingly priggish.'

'I suspect you of a morbid streak of self-sacrifice,' said Stephen. 'Thank heavens you had the sense to break it off.'

'I'm glad now,' she said soberly, finding courage to look at him again.

'You strange child. I almost believe you when you say I'm the first. I'm a very weak character, my dear. When you look at me like that . . . I almost wonder . . .' He paused and shook his head. 'No, it wouldn't do. It wouldn't do at all. You must be firm with me, Clara. It would be sheer madness to ask you to marry me.'

'Would it?' Her heart was beating fast but she managed to speak as calmly as if they were discussing something quite impersonal.

He groaned: 'God knows. I don't. It might be the only sensible thing I ever did. I told you. Life's infernally difficult at the moment.'

'If you'd only tell me why.'

'Better not. Things work out if one leaves them alone. Put your nice little cold hand on my forehead.'

She passed her fingers very lightly over the dry skin stretched so tightly over the bone.

'Your head's very hot.'

He closed his eyes.

'Yes. Go on. It's like being stroked by a flower.'

He pulled down one of her hands and kissed the palm. 'To throw all this away,' he said as if to himself.

'You haven't – yet.'

He opened his eyes and smiled.

'Damn it, Clara. I'm no good at noble gestures. Put up with me a little longer . . . can you?'

'Of course.'

'Good. Come kiss me, sweet and twenty.'

The kiss was a gentle one. Clara's fever had subsided, leaving only tenderness. They sat in silence for a time, her head against his knee.

He said suddenly: 'You've no idea what hell it is being an artist.'

'I suppose not.'

'You're marvellously sensitive – marvellously responsive. That's why it's so refreshing to be with you. But you don't know what it is to feel a power in yourself that must be used or you might as well be dead. It's so damnable to be an actor. A poet or a painter creates his own material. But an actor's got to have a part. He's got to beg and grovel and push for the chance of getting one. Of all the frustrating, humiliating professions.'

She had never heard him speak with such violence. She said consolingly:

'At least you're going to play Richard.'

'I'm going to play Richard. And nothing is going to stop me from playing Richard.'

'Don't growl at me as if I were trying to.'

He kissed the top of her head.

'Silly child. What a pity you can't play my Queen. Delightful little part. And just right for you.'

'Oh . . . I wish I could.'

'No hope,' he said hastily. 'All cast down to the understudies.'

'Is Miss Lane playing it?'

'Good lord, no. The part's too light and her voice is too heavy. No. Some quite adequate young piece who played it at Stratford. Remember doing Katherine to my Henry V?'

'Of course. What ages ago that seems.'

'Very nice performance. Best thing you ever did. You've got something sometimes though you can be unspeakably bad. Your Mélisande . . . you know that was really rather exquisite. God knows why. You had no technique but at least you had no tricks. I suppose it was moving just because it was so naïve. There's something rather lost and ghostly about you sometimes, my sweet, though you look such a nice solid little milkmaid.'

'I expect the red hair and the white make-up helped,' said Clara, storing up her qualified compliment. 'Daddy didn't recognize me at first. It was the only part he ever liked seeing me in though he can't bear Maeterlinck.'

'Did he see us in *Henry V*?'

'Yes. He thought you were wonderful. But he's frightfully prejudiced. He can't bear seeing anyone kiss me on the stage.'

'Hmmm. Good old Freud.'

'Freud?'

'Some Viennese bore Eliza's got a bee in her bonnet about. Let it go.'

'I'm getting practically illiterate,' she sighed.

'Never mind. Intellectual women can be appallingly tiresome.'

'You do despise women, don't you? Women can't think. Women can't write. What *can* women do?'

He pulled her hair.

'I know one who can be rather endearing. Even when she's spitting like an angry kitten. How you hate being teased.'

'I might get broken in to it.'

'Then it would be no fun. Do you think I'm a heartless character, Clara?'

She said slowly: 'I *am* inclined to wonder sometimes. Not that it matters, I suppose.'

'If I laugh at you, don't I laugh at myself? If I torment you, don't I torment myself more?'

Something in his tone jarred on her. The words sounded like a line from a play. He spoke them as if listening to the sound of his own voice; almost as if he might repeat them, trying a different inflection. She glanced up at him without speaking.

'Why the cynical smile, Clara? Don't you believe me?'

'Not entirely.'

'Perhaps you're right. You're an honest wench. Could you make an honest man of me?'

'I'm not all that honest.'

He laughed, putting his arm round her. The clock on the mantelpiece, among the china dogs and knickknacks, began to strike.

'Good God . . . whatever's the time? It can't be ten already.' He stood up, almost pushing her away. 'I'll have to go. I've got to get this wretched car back to the garage in Lincoln by midnight. Otherwise there'll be the deuce to pay in every sense.'

Clara did not try to detain him. Painful as the wrench was, it

57

was also a relief. She was tired and on edge. At any moment her carefully sustained calm might collapse. She might cling to him; even burst into tears.

Instead, she became defiantly practical; finding his coat, putting his matches and cigarettes in the pocket.

'Don't forget your notes and sketches.'

'Wonderful girl. I nearly forgot what I was supposed to be doing in Gainsborough. Hope I've collected enough to impress the management.'

He stood over her, looking solid in the old trench coat which disguised his leanness, and gathered her to him.

'Dear child . . . dear Clara,' he said, with his thin cheek against her hair. 'So difficult to leave. So delicious to come back to. Be patient with me a little longer.'

'Oh Stephen . . . of course.' She pressed her face against his shoulder, trying to feel its warmth through the harsh, stiff material that smelt of benzine and tobacco.

He disengaged her gently and, holding her face in his hands, gave her a long intent look. 'I want to think of you in here . . . in this enchanting, appalling room. With your golden hair all tangled and one cheek as red as if someone had slapped it.'

He moved slowly away from her, singing under his breath.

> 'And from her company I could not go
> But when I waked . . . it was not so . . .
> In you-outh is pleasure
> In you-outh is pleasure.'

His voice cracked on the last note and he laughed.

'Ruined my exit.'

He sketched a mock salute and was gone, closing the door noiselessly behind him. Clara stood staring at the brown varnished panels and the strip of red rep, fringed with bobbles, which still trembled where Stephen's head had brushed them. When she heard the click of the front door, she knelt on the hearthrug in front of the chair where he had been sitting and buried her head in it, stuffing her fingers in her ears to deaden the sound of the starting up of the car.

Chapter Seven

Clara was not surprised to receive no letter from Stephen after that Sunday. He had warned her that *Richard II* was going into rehearsal at once and opened in Oxford in three weeks' time. She restrained herself from writing more than a note when she sent him back *The Shropshire Lad* he had left behind, determined not to intrude herself while he was concentrating on his part.

Refusing to allow herself to write to him only increased her obsession. She carried on incessant imaginary dialogues with him; she recalled every word, every look, every gesture in the attempt to interpret them honestly. Never did she suppose that he loved her as she loved him but she was convinced that she could put up with any suffering, any humiliation if only Stephen would allow her to marry him.

Maidie noticed her abstraction but mercifully made no comment for several days. At last she burst out:

'You're always up in the moon. What is it? That fellow that turned up in Gainsborough? I oughtn't to have left you without a chaperone.'

'I don't think a chaperone would have helped.'

'Hmmm,' said Maidie suspiciously. 'You were always vague, God knows. But ever since that Sunday you've been positively soupy. Almost mental, you look sometimes. Look here, Vere, I'm your pal. If you've got anything on your mind, old thing, you can spit it out to me.'

'It's sweet of you, Maidie. But I don't think anyone can help.'

Maidie looked at her anxiously.

'I say . . . you don't suspect the worst, do you?'

'What do you mean by the worst?'

'Come off it. Or didn't your famous education include the facts of life?'

Clara felt herself flush.

'Oh no . . . I've never . . .'

'Well, that's a weight off your mind, anyway. After all, even good Catholics have been known to fall. I always feel sorry for the ones that get caught. It's another mortal sin if they do anything about it. What *is* eating you then?'

'Wondering what he really feels, I suppose.'

'Is that all?' said Maidie contemptuously. 'I thought it was something serious. One of these days you'll come down to earth and give your fanny a nasty bump.'

The following week the company moved to Birmingham. One night, as Clara was changing for the third act, the stage doorkeeper handed in a card. It was Archie Hughes-Follett's. On the back was scribbled: 'Will you have supper with me after the show? Please say yes.'

'Can I tell the gentleman you'll see him, Miss?' asked the doorkeeper. He winked at Clara with the affability of one who has been well tipped. She said, after a moment's hesitation: 'Yes.'

'Not *him*, is it?' asked Maidie, dipping a hairpin in a heated spoon and carefully renewing a blob of black on one of her long lashes.

'No. Just someone I used to know ages ago.'

'Thought you didn't sound keen. What's wrong with this one?'

'Nothing. Only . . . we were once engaged and I haven't seen him since.'

Maidie swung round.

'What an old dark horse you are. *Two* fellows in your life.' She snatched the card and ran a finger over it.

'Classy card. Engraved, not just printed. If you've really done with him . . . you might pass him on. What a knut's name! *Is* he a knut?'

'Quite the reverse. You'd be awfully disappointed.'

'I don't believe a word you say these days, Vere. And I used to think you such a truthful little thing.'

All through the last act, Maidie was in her most mischievous mood. When they were upstage together for several minutes she did her best to dry Clara up by singing under her breath:

> 'I'm Archie the starchy
> The knut with a K
> Pride of Piccadilly
> The blasé roué.'

In the dressing-room she exclaimed with horror at Clara's crumpled skirt and the hole in her jumper.

'How often have I told you . . . be prepared. You look like something the cat's brought home.'

'The worse I look, the better.'

Maidie rolled her big blue eyes at the dresser and tapped her own forehead.

''Spathetic, isn't it, Millie? Almost normal to look at but Mary Rose isn't in it.'

She glanced approvingly at her own trim reflection.

'Now I could go out to supper anywhere and not disgrace a fellow. Instead of which I've got to go home to fish and chips all on my lonesome. I've a good mind to get in first with your Johnnie.'

'You can if you like.'

'Oh no,' said Maidie, pursing her small mouth, 'I never trespass. I'll go and get the boys to walk back with me. I don't like going home alone after dark in big cities. Ta ta.'

She went off singing:

> 'Mary Rose. Mary Rose
> No one ever found out where she goes
> Now she wears undies made of silk
> Comes home at daybreak with the milk.'

Clara had dawdled over her changing, partly because of her natural slowness, partly from reluctance to face Archie. Not that she felt embarrassed or even curious. Her only feeling was one of resentment that he was not Stephen. When at last she opened the dressing-room door, he was just outside, leaning patiently against the damp brick wall of the passage. The light was too dim for her to see his face clearly but his dark red hair was as untidy as ever. He swooped down at her from his immense height, seemed about to embrace her and then dropped his long arms to his sides with one of his old clumsy gestures that she remembered so well.

'Clara,' he said rather thickly, 'Lord, I'm glad you've come. I was afraid you'd given me the slip. I've got a taxi. We may as well go to the Midland. I'm staying there.'

He said little on the way beyond saying that he had seen the show and that it was out of the ark but that she had been simply topping. He seemed uneasy, almost bored; he frequently interrupted her to curse at the driver for not going faster.

'They'll be shut if the blighter doesn't hurry. I must have a drink.'

The Archie she had known four years ago had not been so desperately concerned with closing time. Even when they were seated opposite each other in the great padded dining-room that smelt of cigars, he did not so much as glance at her until he had caught the wine-waiter's eye.

'What do you want? Still like champagne? All right . . . a bottle of 35. But bring me a double whisky right away.'

While he ordered their drinks, she studied Archie's face. After the incisive modelling of Stephen's its bluntness was almost repellent. His features still had the oddly unfinished look they had had at nineteen. Nevertheless he had changed considerably in four years. There were grooves on either side of his mouth; both his skin and the dark red hair which fell more untidily than ever over his low forehead had a dusty look; the eyes she remembered as so clear were yellowish and slightly bloodshot. The hand which held the menu shook a little. It was the unexpectedly shapely hand she knew but the long fingers were deeply stained with nicotine and the nails dirty. Archie had always been untidy: now he looked almost dissolute. He had always treated his clothes brutally. Good though the ones he had on were, they produced an effect of forlorn shabbiness. However, catching sight of herself in a vast gold-framed mirror, Clara told herself she had no right to be critical.

'We look a pair,' she thought, surveying her untidy bunches of hair, her faded jumper with a streak of grease paint at the neck. The thought filled her with a peculiar dismay.

As if he guessed it he said: 'You're not furious with me for dragging you out like this without warning?'

'Of course not.'

'I thought it was the best way. Take you by surprise. I'm no good at writing letters anyway.'

His whisky arrived and he drained it as if it were medicine.

'God, I needed that. I didn't dare dash round the corner in case I missed you at the theatre.'

'Daddy told you where we were playing?'

'Yes, bless him. I thought you'd rather I turned up this week than . . . well . . . in Worcester.'

She glanced at him kindly for the first time. He averted his eyes and said hurriedly:

'What a nice chap your father is. My God, you're lucky, Clara. You should have known mine.'

She crumpled her roll. 'I was awfully sorry about your mother, Archie.'

He frowned.

'Sweet of you to write. Yes, I miss her a good bit. Of course her heart had been bad for a long time. She didn't tell me at first. But she knew even at Crickleham that it might suddenly give out.'

Clara wondered guiltily whether that had been another secret reason why both his mother and Lady Cressett had been so anxious for them to get married.

She said hastily: 'What exactly were you doing in South America? Did you like it?'

'Loathed it,' he said emphatically. 'What was I doing? Supposed to be learning the job from the bottom in some wretched business Papa had a lot of shares in. The bottom was bad enough but heaven help me from getting to the top. Can you see me in a bowler hat as a company director?'

She smiled naturally for the first time.

'Why ever did you go in for it?'

'No choice. My guardian just shipped me abroad.'

'Guardian? But you're over twenty-one.'

'Hell yes. Nearly twenty-three,' he said gloomily. 'Mamma's dying messed up everything. As long as she was alive, she had control of the money. She let me have all I wanted. But Papa left a frightful will. He hated me . . . Yes, even Mamma admitted it. So he tied up everything so that I can't touch it till I'm twenty-five. I get an allowance of £300 a year and not a penny more.'

'Not too bad for doing nothing. My salary's just half that,' said Clara, with the superiority of the wage-earner.

'It goes nowhere with the sort of things I *like* doing. And I can't get round my guardian. Papa chose my beastliest uncle because he shared his opinion of me. The idea was to drive me into some ghastly job.'

'Well, you'll soon be free of it all.'

'Only if I behave myself according to their ideas. If I borrow so much as a fiver on my prospects, they clamp on the guardian business till I'm thirty. *Thirty* . . . Might as well say till I'm dead.'

'I'm sure we oughtn't to be drinking champagne.'

'It's the first week of the month. Anyway I had a few quid left over from my South American screw when I landed. They gave me a month's salary instead of notice. I made enough at poker to pay for my drinks on the boat.'

'Were you sacked?' she asked diffidently.

'Certainly I was sacked. For being drunk, if you want to know. How the hell my uncle expects me to live on six quid a week with whisky at 12/6 a bottle.'

Still more diffidently, Clara said: 'Whisky's a necessity, is it?'

'It most definitely is.'

They ate and drank for some moments in silence. Never had champagne seemed less festive to Clara. Her parents were right: Archie had certainly changed. She remembered him as an odd creature, clumsy and kind, who did not fit into the grown-up world. Often he had sulked like a schoolboy but never had she seen him in this mood of aggressive bitterness. Tonight he had hardly smiled: in repose, his face was set in lines of angry discontent. She felt a pang of guilt.

'Go on, say it,' he muttered. 'You think I'm a pretty poor specimen, don't you? Well, you're probably right.'

She said uncomfortably: 'Of course I don't. I expect the war . . .'

'The war? Everyone blames the poor ruddy old war. *I* didn't mind the war. Apart from a couple of scratches I had a cushy time compared to most. Anyway, it took one's mind off things. Don't think I'm being sentimental when I say I jolly well wish I'd been killed.'

'Oh, Archie.'

'Don't worry, old thing. I was only explaining that it wasn't the war. Then I only used to drink in a cheery sort of way and get tight once in a while like anyone else. And afterwards, I chugged along somehow. Mamma was so bucked that I'd survived that she was quite happy to let me mess about in my own way. But since she died and they cut off my supplies and treated me like some sort of mental defective – well, can you wonder it's the only thing that makes me feel human?' He drained his glass of champagne. 'Chin-chin.'

'Chin-chin,' Clara echoed faintly, swallowing the flat remains of her own.

'Fill up. You're drinking like a sparrow.'

She shook her head.

'All girls on the stage I ever knew liked bubbly. But then you never were like anyone else. I can't get over your being an actress. Gosh, I envy you.'

'I always wonder why you didn't become a singer with that voice of yours.'

'Oh, I still sing sometimes. But I'd loathe to be a concert singer. The theatre's the only thing I'm keen on. Used to get up amateur shows in that beastly Santiago. I'm quite hot at lighting effects.'

'You were always brilliant at anything mechanical. Remember your model railway at Crickleham?'

'About all I'm good for,' said Archie gloomily. 'Fixing up models and playing with switchboards.' He sighed. 'Fancy your remembering the old railway. I was crazier about it than any kid when I first fixed *that* up. Then I came to hate the sight of it.'

Clara flushed with shame at her clumsiness. She was the first person to whom he had shown his treasure. He had always said that it was while they were playing with his toy trains that he had first fallen in love with her. And it was by the model railway, two days after Charles's death, that, having refused him once, she had told Archie she would marry him.

She said hastily:

'That very first day at Crickleham, you told me your great ambition was to go on the stage.'

'No one'd look at a great gawk of six foot four as an actor. That stage manager of yours, Lister, quite agreed.'

'Lister!' exclaimed Clara. 'Wherever did you meet him?'

'In the bar, in the first interval. Told him I was a friend of yours and stood him a couple. You don't mind, do you?'

'Why should I?'

Looking at him, she saw, for the first time that evening, the old puzzled, yet eager expression she remembered. Until that moment, she and Archie might almost have been old acquaintances who had met again by chance. He said hesitantly:

'Actually I wanted to have a word with him about you. Your career and all that. D'you know what he said? "If someone could back that kid in a good part that suits her, she might go far."' Archie suddenly banged his nicotine-stained fist on the table. 'Hell . . . when I think of all that cash lying there and I can't touch it for two bloody years. And here you are playing a rotten little part in a rotten old piece that'll pack up in a few weeks anyway. What happens then?'

Clara sighed.

'I've no idea. But if you *had* money, Archie, you don't think I'd let you throw it away on backing me? I'll never be a great actress.'

'I believe in you,' he said stubbornly. 'I believe you could do any ruddy thing if you were given a decent chance.' Suddenly he buried his head in his hands and groaned. 'What the hell's the good of talking? It's even more hopeless now than it was *then*.'

Until this moment Clara had almost convinced herself that he had forgotten their past. Now he raised his head and exposed a face so wretched that her heart sank.

'I swore to myself I wouldn't say a word tonight. But seeing you sitting there is too much. All these years I've been thinking: "What will it be like if I meet her again?" D'you know I almost wish I'd come back and found you were married? Then I'd have known there wasn't an earthly.'

'I hoped you'd got over it all,' she said in dismay. 'I'm sure you have really.'

He shook his head.

'Not a bit of it. Believe me, I've tried. I've gone around with plenty of girls. Damn pretty ones, some of them. But it's no good. There's only one Clara.' He leant across the table: 'I'll tell you something queer. Tonight when we came in here and I saw you properly for the first time I thought for one marvellous moment I was cured. I know I've changed the hell of a lot. But you've changed, too. On the stage, you looked just like the girl I used to know. But off . . . forgive me – you're not quite as pretty as you used to be. In fact, tonight you look a bit of a mess.'

'I know,' she said ruefully.

'But I'm not put off,' he went on. 'I realize now that it's as bad as ever – if not worse. I don't care what you look like. Wouldn't matter if you had smallpox. There can't be anyone else for me ever. It's a rum go, isn't it?'

Clara could only sigh. If Stephen had said those words, they would have meant joy beyond her wildest hopes. Coming from Archie they were meaningless. Yet she felt a deeper sympathy with Archie than she had ever felt before. She said at last:

'Oh, why can't things be simple? Why can't we fall in love with the people who love us?'

'*Are* you in love with someone, Clara?'

She nodded.

'You don't mean he's such an ass as not to love you?'

'He may be a little. Nothing like as much as I do,' she broke off, ashamed. 'It's beastly to talk to *you* like this.'

'Don't worry. It's almost a comfort, in a funny way, that you should be in the same boat.'

She felt a sudden kindness, almost warmth towards him. His shabbiness, his air of dissipation no longer seemed repellent. She saw them as the livery of his suffering.

'That's why you look different, perhaps,' he said. 'God, this man must be a fool. And here am I. Nothing in the world I wouldn't do to make you happy. I'm so crazy to marry you, I'd take you on any terms. I wouldn't expect you to love me now any more than I did then.'

'Dear Archie, it would be crazy.'

'For you, yes. Worse than before. At least I had some cash in those days.'

'That's not the reason.'

'No. But it would have sweetened the pill. We could have got around, done anything you fancied. Without it, I'd bore you to tears. D'you know I still enjoy playing kid games like we used to . . .' He broke off. 'God, what a clumsy swine. That shows you.'

'It's all right. I hardly ever think about that now.'

But as she spoke, she knew that she had begun to think about it again. When she had been Charles Cressett's governess and Archie used to come over to Maryhall on every possible occasion the three of them had spent their time acting out elaborate spy-games. It was in the course of one of them that Charles had been killed. They were silent for some moments and the silence brought them closer than any words.

'I've been to Maryhall since I came back,' Archie said at last. 'Theresa Cressett sent you her love.'

'How is she?' Clara asked eagerly.

'The same as ever. That woman's a saint. She talks about the boy quite happily now.'

Clara sighed.

'I don't think I could bear to go there again. Anyway it's out of the question.'

'Not with her. It's only Sir George and . . .'

'Nan? Is *she* still there?'

'Oh yes. For life. I found it jolly hard to be civil to her.' He glanced downwards. 'You still have a scar on your wrist.'

'She was hysterical. She didn't know what she was doing.' Clara paused, remembering the small, furious figure of Charles's nurse stabbing at her with the cutting-out shears. But for Archie, she might be maimed, even dead. 'It all seems so long ago. Like something in another life.'

'I thought that. Yet when I went back this time, it all seemed exactly the same. I suppose I oughtn't to say this. But Theresa still keeps harping on *us*.'

'You don't mean she still thinks we . . .'

'More than ever. You know what she's like. She never gets

away from religion for a moment . Thinks you might reform me and do your own soul no end of good.'

'As if I could reform anyone!'

'Well, no one else could. And I'm not going to give 'em a chance to try. I oughtn't to have told you. I'm probably a little tight. Which reminds me, I badly need another drink. You couldn't face coming up to my room? I've got a bottle of whisky there.'

She shook her head.

'It's awfully late. I must go soon.'

'O.K. I'll do without. That shows you how much I feel like going on talking and to hell with the consequences.'

'Say anything you like.'

'Maryhall,' he said slowly with his old puzzled look. 'Something rather queer about that. I said *it* hadn't changed. Of course you and I *have*. But up there I felt as if we *hadn't*. As if I was the old Archie coming chugging up on my motorbike to have tea in the schoolroom with you . . . and Charles. And you were the old Clara, rushing round playing the Schweinhund games with her hair tumbling down. It was so real that I used to find myself having long talks with you.'

He hit his forehead with his closed fist: − a gesture she remembered from those days.

'I'm hopeless at explaining. Always was. D'you know when I was telling you that I had that feeling again? You'll think I really am tight and seeing double. But it's as if I *were* double. You too − as if the two of us as we are *now* were here in this beastly dining-room in Brum *and* up there as we were then. Am I mad?'

She looked at him with startled interest.

'If so, I am too. I know that double feeling. I had it after Charles was killed. For months, off and on. I have it now sometimes.' She broke off, frowning. When she went on, her voice was a little out of control. 'I don't believe I've ever been quite real since. Not a whole person. As if some part of me died when Charles did. If I could only go back to before it happened.' She stopped, almost in tears, half frightened by what she had said: half wondering if she really meant it. Archie put his hand over hers and she did not draw it away.

For the first time they stared full in each other's eyes. At that moment, his struck her as beautiful. They seemed to have an independent life; as if another, unknown Archie existed in the darkness of those distended pupils.

It was he who glanced away first. Immediately she was seized with revulsion against herself and against Archie. It was as if by those words, by that look she had betrayed Stephen. Her whole body seemed to harden against the ugly young man who sat with his head bent forward, staring at the mess of cigarette ends among the crumbs of his roll. Coldly she noted every detail of his appearance that irritated her; the large, slightly inflamed nose that looked, from that angle, like a clown's; the flakes of scurf on his untidy red hair. When he raised his eyes to hers again, she saw only the discoloured whites and the film that drink had put over them. She drew her hand, which was still touching his, sharply away.

He made a grimace which deepened those new grooves beside his mouth.

'What's up? Now you're looking at me as if I were a leper or something.'

She bit her lip, ashamed of herself, yet all the more irritated with him for having noticed.

'O.K. You needn't tell me,' he said roughly. Some feeling she had never seen distorted his odd, unfinished face. For a moment she felt almost frightened of him.

'I'm no good to you,' she said. 'Or to anyone probably. It would be much better if you'd never set eyes on me.'

'Shut up.' His voice was cold with anger. 'We'd better be going. I'll see you back to your place.'

Walking by him in the darkness, almost in silence, she began to feel remorseful. As they turned into her street, she said:

'I'm sorry, Archie. It sounds so false, I know. But I do wish you could be happy.'

He gave a curious laugh.

'Happy! You're a nice one to talk.'

'Why?'

'Well, you're not exactly happy yourself, are you? Bloody *un*happy, it strikes me.'

Outside the house he stopped.

'Forget all about tonight. Except for one thing . . .'

'Yes, Archie?'

'If ever you want me . . . for anything . . . I'm always there. If you don't mind, I may stick around in this town for a few days. Not entirely because of you. I won't even speak to you if you'd rather not.'

'But that's ridiculous.'

'Everything's ridiculous if you ask me. I'd rather you married this chap whoever he is if it made *you* happy. And I'd rather marry you and be unhappy than marry anyone else. Doesn't make sense, does it?'

She said sadly:

'The second part makes sense to me.'

'Poor old darling. We seem to be in it together.'

He had used almost those very words four years ago. Tired and dazed as she was, they produced a peculiar effect. It was as if her mind were suddenly dislocated; as if the world consisted only of this dark doorstep and she and Archie were its only inhabitants. She swayed blindly towards him; he held her for a moment gently and, as gently, let her go.

Chapter Eight

For the rest of that week and all through the next, Archie haunted the theatre but made no attempt to see Clara alone. He left the Midland and took a room in the same house as Lister. When *A Clerical Error* moved on to Coventry, Archie moved with them and again shared Lister's digs. The two became so inseparable that Archie seemed like one of the company. He was backstage at every performance, chatting to the actors in their dressing-rooms or watching the electricians at the switchboard. Clara was amazed at the way he picked up not merely the language but the whole sense of the theatre. He learnt more in two days than she had learnt in two years. Every detail, from lighting to make-up, seemed to fascinate him. He studied each move of the play, the placing of each piece of furniture. Once, when Sam Brilliant was late, she saw him arranging the props table with great efficiency. At first she had thought that Lister regarded Archie mainly as a source of free drinks but, one night, she overheard the stage manager say to Merton Mordish:

'That boy's got something. I thought at first he was just a young ass who fancied himself stage-struck because he was keen on Clara.'

'I agree,' trumpeted Mordish. 'Pity he's so tall. I believe he might have some notion of acting if I had the coaching of him.'

'Can't see him as an actor,' said Lister. 'But I *can* see him being useful on production. Got the hang of the switchboard in no time. Made a damn sensible suggestion about the lighting at the end of Act II.'

He looked round, and, evidently not seeing Clara where she stood in a doorway, said so low that she only just caught it: 'I tell you, Merton, if we didn't look like packing up so soon, I'd sack that cocky idle yid Sam and give Archie a try-out as A.S.M.'

Overhearing this gave Clara a certain sense of guilt. All his life Archie had been looked on as an amiable fool. She asked herself what right she had to feel superior to him. What was she, after all, but a mediocre actress with the knack of writing advertisements and cheap short stories?

During the scene change in the second act she hunted him out and, beckoning him into a corner behind the backcloth, told him what she had heard.

His face lit up.

'You don't know how bucked I feel. Especially at your bothering to come and tell me. Two bits of luck in one day. It's almost too much.'

'What's the other?'

'Something I heard this morning. I've been dying to come and tell you. But I didn't want to make a nuisance of myself.'

The silence on the stage warned them that the curtain would be going up at any moment. She whispered:

'Come round to our dressing-room after the show.'

Maidie, like the rest of the company, had long ago accepted

72

Archie as almost one of them and no longer seemed to regard him as Clara's special concern. That night, however, she observed:

'Your Archie's always in Jimmy Lister's pocket these days. What's Jimmy up to? Trying to get him to put money into a show?'

'He hasn't got any money.'

'He'll have oodles one day, won't he? I guess Jimmy knows which side his bread's buttered even if you don't. Still, for once I think you showed a spot of sense turning him down. Mark you, I rather like old Starchy even if he does drink a lot more than is good for him.'

'Archie's dying to get into the theatre. I suppose he thinks Lister might help him.'

'Funny ambition for a *boy* of that class. I mean his uncle's got a title, hasn't he? Though . . . pardon my mentioning it, Vere, you'd hardly guess it, would you?'

'Archie was never a snob, if that's what you mean.'

'Snob! He goes a bit too far the other way, if you ask me. Honestly, sometimes you'd think he hadn't been as well brought up as Peter and Trev. You wouldn't think a real gentleman would want to hang round bars all day with a squirt like Lister.'

'I suppose he's always been rather a misfit in his own class. He hates the sort of conventional life he's expected to lead.'

'Unnatural, I call it,' said Maidie, sniffing delicately. 'I don't think you ought to let your own class down.'

She went on removing her make-up in silence for a few moments before asking:

'Is he still keen on you, Vere? It seems to me it's the company he's hanging round nowadays more than you.'

'I'm glad if it is.'

'Did you give him the bird completely?'

'I'll *never* marry Archie,' Clara assured her.

'Most men would go and console themselves. *I* think there's something queer about that boy.'

Clara asked rather coldly what she meant. However humble she felt towards Stephen, she did not altogether like the implication that Archie's fidelity was so surprising.

'For one thing I don't believe he really likes girls. Don't look so flabbergasted. I don't mean he's like Peter and Trev. But I bet you he's never really got going with one.'

'Well . . . after all . . . he's a Catholic. If you mean what I think you mean.'

'I do and I don't. Some Catholic boys are ever so naughty and some find it ever so hard to be good. But *I* don't believe Archie's ever been really tempted. I don't believe he's the least bit passionate.'

'Perhaps you'd like to try your Munroe act with him?' suggested Clara acidly.

'Miaow! Puss! Puss!' said Maidie, winking a large blue eye. 'I believe you're jealous. You don't want Starchy yourself but you like to keep the poor chap dangling.' She broke off to call: 'Come in,' as someone knocked at the door. 'Well, talk of the devil. How's our Tiny tonight?'

'Rather braced with life,' said Archie, stooping his tall limp body as he edged through the dressing-room door. He answered with equal affability to his public nickname of Tiny or to Maidie's private one.

'Why? Come into a fortune, old thing?'

'A fortune for me as things are.' He glanced at Clara and patted his breast pocket. 'Guess what I've got in here. A cheque for two thousand ruddy quid.'

'You're kidding,' said Maidie, dropping her hairbrush and staring at him almost respectfully.

'No. Cross my heart.' He turned to Clara. 'Had a letter from my beastly uncle this morning. Gosh, he hated having to part with it. But he had to. It's something under Mamma's will, not Papa's.'

'Archie, I'm *so* glad,' said Clara, trying hard not to be envious.

'Lucky pig. I should get him to give you a nice present, dear, before he blues the lot. My advice to you, old boy, is keep enough back to stand yourself a shave and haircut. You need 'em.'

'Spiteful little thing, aren't you?' He pulled one of the golden plaits Maidie was coiling up. 'As a matter of fact, I'm not going to blue it. Well, only a little anyway. God knows I need a bit of fun. And I must get myself some sort of a car. Haven't even a motorbike now.'

'Who gets the change – if any?'

'That's a secret at present.'

'Jimmy Lister, *I* bet,' said Maidie. 'Ba-aa! You ought to have a little blue ribbon round your neck, Tiny.'

'Jimmy's a good chap,' said Archie rather angrily. He glanced at Clara. '*He* doesn't think me such a bloody fool as Maidie does. If we go in together, he'll be in it as much as I will. Anyway I'm not talking . . . yet.'

'Since you're so thick with Lister,' said Maidie, suddenly serious. 'Any truth in this idea the "Error" may pack up after Worcester next week? Or s'only a rumour?'

'You'd better ask him yourself.'

Clara forgot all about Archie's mysterious projects. If the rumour were true, she would be free the week after next, the very week that *Richard II* opened. It would not cost much to get from Worcester to Oxford. She began to make hasty calculations. When she next became conscious of the others' conversation, she heard Archie saying:

'Well, it's my last week for the time being anyway. So I want to have a farewell party. Jimmy says we can have it on the stage. Everyone's coming, even Miss Cooke. You'll both come, won't you?'

Only when she saw Archie's expression of delighted surprise and the half-conscious movements he made towards her did Clara realize that she must, in her excitement, have smiled at him as if he were Stephen.

The party on the Saturday night had a noisy, slightly desperate gaiety. Their notices had gone up the night before. Though they were not entirely unexpected, most of the company had hoped that they might book up for a few weeks more. For many it would mean a time of acute anxiety wondering if and when they would get another job. Clara, with a home to go to and the prospect of seeing Stephen so much sooner than she had dared to hope, felt too guilty to enter into the 'eat and drink for tomorrow we die' spirit of it. All the others, even Archie himself who was already so much more part of the company than she had ever been, had something to lose. She was the only one to whom the end of the tour came as an unmitigated relief.

Though she talked and laughed and danced with all comers, she remained a little detached and felt the rest were aware of it. All round her old feuds were being forgotten in the common anxiety of the prospect of being out of a job. People who only a few hours before had been saying the most spiteful things about each other were exchanging addresses and recommending agents. She saw the astonishing spectacle of Maidie and James standing with their arms round each other's waists and overheard the even more astonishing tributes Merton Mordish was paying to Brett Wilding.

'You know, old man . . . and I'm weighing every word I say . . . it would be criminal if you gave up playing juvenile for ten years at least. *Anno domini* doesn't mean a thing when you've got the *touch*. Given the right part, you could knock spots off Gerald.'

She was conscious all the time of Archie's presence, more conscious than he seemed to be of hers. She even caught herself out feeling a childish pique because he was not paying her any particular attention. He danced with her only once and during the dance talked only company shop. It was almost impossible to believe that only ten days ago he had been imploring her to marry him on any terms. She had been touched by that devotion she could not return. Though for his own sake she wanted him cured of it, it had been a comfort to know that someone felt for her as she felt for Stephen. Had his outburst in Birmingham been no more than a mood of drunken self-pity? Since he had become so passionately interested in the theatre, though he spent so much time in bars, he was, in fact, drinking less. Tonight he looked more like the boy she remembered four years ago. Yet there was a difference. Perhaps because he was being the success of the evening, his odd, blunt features no longer gave the impression of being unfinished. Lit up with excitement, his face was amusing, even attractive. For the first time in her life she saw Archie as someone with whom other girls could conceivably fall in love.

Peter and Trevor came up to her as she was sitting momentarily alone on the canvas-covered steps of the set they used in the last act.

'Tst . . . fancy *you* being a wallflower, dear,' said Peter, putting his arm around her. 'You should have brought your knitting. *So* important to look as if you didn't care.'

'Tell us the facts, Clara,' said Trevor. '*Such* rumours are going round. They say Archie popped the question in Brum and you turned him down. And now he's come into a fortune and you're wishing you'd said "yes".'

Peter interrupted Clara's muddled attempt to explain.

'Of course she isn't. She's got other fish to fry. *I* saw you that Sunday in Gainsborough. Oo la la!'

'I didn't see you.'

'I know you didn't, dear. You were so occupied in gazing into somebody's eyes, you cut me dead. Don't blame you. The *most* marvellous-looking man.'

'*I* remember,' said Trevor. 'Peter raved about him. I got ever so jealous.'

'Too distinguished for words. That slightly hollow look.' He gave Trevor a malicious glance. 'A *real* blond, like that Norwegian chorus boy. Years older of course. But fearfully romantic-looking . . . that "I've got a secret sorrow" expression. Are you the secret sorrow, Clara?'

She said lightly, 'He looked just the same when I first met him.'

'I know the type,' said Trevor. 'Beware of them, Clara. They're absolute icicles, dear.'

'You got a touch of Norwegian frost-bite all right,' said Peter.

He began to sing, eyeing them alternately:

> 'The gipsy warned me
> The gipsy *warned* me
> He said to me "My child
> He's a bad man . . . a very *bad* man!"'

Clara laughed and joined in.

'But I just calmly smiled.'

'Stop it you ruddy amateurs,' shouted Jimmy Lister. 'Maidie's going to oblige with some *singing*.'

Maidie had seated herself at the piano and was playing chords on its tinny keys. People stopped shrieking and laughing and sat down on the furniture of the set or on the stage itself. Archie propped himself against the piano, whispering to Maidie. Clara heard her say:

'Don't be bashful, Tiny. After all, you're paying for the drinks.'

She nodded at him and went into the prelude of 'If you were the only girl'.

Clara had forgotten how astonishingly good Archie's voice was. It rang out true and rich, without a tremor or a hint of forcing, so that for some moments she was lost in the sheer beauty of the sound. When Maidie joined in the duet, her pure clear notes were like silver against the gold of Archie's. Clara was fascinated by these two voices, each perfect of its kind and each so unexpected in the singer. The voices, singing the absurd song with the utmost seriousness, seemed as remote from Archie and Maidie as two angels. Yet they belonged to these two strange creatures; they were perhaps more truly Archie and Maidie than the selves they presented to the world. All round her, people had assumed unfamiliar faces. Lister's coarse, shrewd features wore an expression of innocent yearning; Mordish had a look of inspired anger like an old priest reproving the devil; Trevor, pale as wax, seemed, with his closed eyes and lips parted in a faint smile, just to have died an edifying death. Everywhere faces perhaps unknown to the owners were revealed through the familiar masks.

She wondered what face she herself was assuming as she became, like the rest, involved in the dated, potent song. If 'Tipperary' would for ever call up the marching privates of '14–'18, 'The Only Girl' was the eternal theme song of the subaltern on leave. Innumerable 'only girls' had pressed their bobbed or piled-up hair against a khaki shoulder to the sound of it in the soft lights of Ciro's or the Four Hundred. Innumerable 'only boys' had played it over and over on scratched records in their dugouts. Clara could remember her father vamping it on the piano on Sunday mornings in Valetta Road; the only song he had learnt since he came down from Cambridge twenty years before the war. He had picked it up from his subaltern ex-pupils and sung it till so many of them had been killed that he could no longer bear the tune. She remembered how he had once liked to sing it to her, looking at her with a glint in his eyes that forced her to play up to him as she sang. Once, afterwards, he had sighed and said: 'Cheap sentiment, I grant you. Yet what, after all, but the universal aspiration of the human race? The garden of Eden. Plato's divided creatures eternally seeking their lost halves.'

Archie and Maidie, gazing into each other's eyes, slowed down to their last bars. Clara felt a double twinge of envy and jealousy. Envy of Archie for being able to do one thing supremely well was mean, but rational. It was harder to scold herself out of the jealousy which was not only mean but unreasonable. However, as the last notes thinned away, Archie turned his head and looked straight at her with such fervour that she knew his feelings had not changed. Her absurd relief made her more ashamed of herself than ever.

When the song was over, she made no attempt to join the people who rushed up to him, slapping him on the back and extravagantly praising his singing. Some minutes later Jimmy Lister came across to her.

'You know, Clara,' he said, pinching her bare arm. 'I think you're making a big mistake.'

'What about?'

'You needn't be upstage with me. Archie and me are pals. He's told me all. Damn nice chap, Archie.'

'I know.'

'What's more, he's got a bloody marvellous voice. Many a pro's making good money whose singing isn't a patch on it. He's dead keen to go into musical comedy or revue. But what manager's going to give a great hulk of six foot four a try-out even as a chorus boy? No, his only hope is to be in a position to put himself across in his own show.'

'But that's impossible.'

Lister laid a finger against his nose.

'I've got ideas. Long-term policy, you might call it. Here and now he's got a bit of cash. Don't look so sniffy, dear. I know, better than you, that two thousand quid doesn't go far in show business. But I might be able to get him in on the ground floor of something good. A real investment. I'd be prepared to go in with him though I couldn't put up any cash. Archie could work under me and be getting experience all the time. Then, when he comes into the big money, he could put on his own shows, and not as a ruddy amateur.'

Clara said doubtfully:

'I should have thought it was awfully risky.'

'You've got to take some risks in this business.' He gave her a truculent look. 'That's women all over. Bloody wet-blankets. No imagination. I was thinking of your good too, as it happens.'

'Mine?'

'Well, you want to get on, don't you? I'll be quite frank with you, my dear. You're quite promising and not bad-looking when you take a bit of trouble. But I don't see you going far unless you get a bit of a push. That poor mutt's crazy about you. If you've any sense, you'll stick around while the iron's hot.' He put his arm round her and breathed whisky into her face. 'I think you're quite a juicy piece myself. But what a ruddy little icicle! You'll never get on in the theatre if you're so stand-offish.'

Lister suddenly dropped his arm. Clara saw with relief that Archie was standing beside them. By now he was a little unsteady on his feet and his eyes were beginning to look glazed.

'No offence meant,' said Lister. 'Just telling this little girl she was a naughty, obstinate little girl who doesn't know what's good for her. Doesn't appreciate her Uncle Jimmy.'

'Doesn't appreciate me and never will,' said Archie, swaying slightly and propping himself on Lister's shoulder. 'Four bloody years I've been in love with that girl.'

'Trouble with you, old boy,' said Lister solemnly. 'You don't know how to handle women. Never let 'em get you down. Above all, never discuss business with 'em. Petty minds. No imagination. Can't see further than the ends of their silly little noses.'

Clara moved away. Archie made an attempt to follow her but Lister held him back. She felt a sudden disgust with the whole world of the theatre. Picking her way through the gabbling groups, she wondered how, only a few minutes ago, she could have found those tipsy faces touching, even beautiful. Now her only desire was to get away from them and be alone. The prospect of having to live with them for even one more week seemed suddenly unbearable. Then she thought that, at the end of that week, she would see Stephen and nothing mattered any more.

As she put on her coat in the dressing-room, she remembered that Stephen belonged, far more than Archie, to the world of the theatre. But he was working with people who cared only for their art; he was outside the vulgar scramble where people pushed and exploited and traded on others' love or trust to make big money, to have their name in lights. As she slipped behind the backcloth, on the way to the stage-door, Archie was singing 'The Only Girl' again. The wonderful voice sounded a little thickened and unsteady. She had forgotten, till that moment, that he had sung that song the first day she met him. Suddenly, almost like a hallucination, she saw that other Archie, slouching beside her in the park at Crickleham in his uniform slacks and a pair of unlaced tennis shoes, singing with impersonal fervour:

'I would say such – wonderful things to you
There would be such – wonderful things to do
If you were the only girl in the world
And I were the on-ly boy.'

Chapter Nine

It was a raw damp November morning when the company arrived at Worcester for the last week of the tour. Clara could not help recalling that golden afternoon, four years earlier when she had arrived there full of hope and excitement to begin her new life at Maryhall. As she stepped out on to the platform she glanced along it apprehensively as if she feared or expected to see some remembered figure. When a boy in a tweed overcoat dashed through the gates, she had a moment of panic. He was just sufficiently like Charles to bring up his image with painful sharpness.

She loitered at the bookstall, staring unseeingly at piles of magazines, to put off the moment of going out into those too-familiar streets and trying to replace Charles's image with Stephen's. But her mind was stuck in the past; she could barely conjure up Stephen's face.

She was interrupted by a painful dig in the ribs from Maidie.

'If you want to buy something, for goodness' sake buy it. I'm famished and it's miles to our digs.'

Clara hastily bought the *Saturday Westminster* she had forgotten to buy in Birmingham. As she picked it up, she had a feeling that there was something unusual about this particular number. But she was too frightened of Maidie even to glance at it.

As they tramped the half-mile to their digs, Maidie said unexpectedly:

'That green paper's the one you sent your tale to, isn't it? The one you were so coy about in Nuneaton.'

'Yes.'

'Ever hear any more about it?'

Clara shook her head: 'No. What's more, I never shall. I did something idiotic.'

'Would you believe it?' said Maidie sarcastically. 'What was it *this* time, may I ask?'

'I only put my address for that week.'

'Well, write, soppy. She'll forward letters.'

'There won't be a letter,' said Clara with gloomy certainty. 'Just the returned manuscript. Still, as it's my only copy . . .'

When they arrived at their digs, the paper slipped from under Clara's arm as she put down her suitcase. Maidie retrieved it, gave it a scornful glance, then suddenly whistled and thrust it under Clara's nose.

'Look at that, you silly Wurzit.'

Unable to believe her eyes, Clara stared at the list of contents and read: '*The Hill of Summer* – Clara Batchelor.'

Forgetting everything, she snatched the paper and standing there, still in her hat and coat, read every word of her story. Though she was used to the curious transformation effected by print, it appeared at first to have been written by a stranger. Convinced at last that it was hers, she found some parts far better and others far worse than she remembered. One paragraph drove her to a furious exclamation.

'What's biting you *now*?' Maidie asked.

'How *could* I?' Clara muttered. 'Of all the ghastly sentences!'

'Committed a spot of *faux pas* in your grammar? Well, they've printed it, haven't they? If this paper's so bloody educated . . .'

'Not the grammar. The adjectives!' wailed Clara.

'I shall use some adjectives about you in a minute. For heaven's sake, sit down and eat your kippers. Then you'd better write off straight away about that money. What'll they pay?'

'No idea. Two guineas perhaps.'

'Wish someone'd pay *me* two guineas for writing down my girlish thoughts. Nice work when you can get it, as the charwoman said to the tart.'

Clara floated through the remaining hours before the show in a state of bliss. For the first time in her life, she dared to think of herself as a writer. Even Stephen could hardly fail to be impressed by her appearing in a paper which published Coppard and De la Mare. She was planning to send him a marked copy when she remembered that she did not know where his company was that week.

There was no letter from him at the theatre. She told herself it was unreasonable to expect two miracles in one day. She reminded herself that each week of the *Richard* rehearsals would be more harassing than the last. Nevertheless, she was disappointed and vaguely disturbed. Not one sign had she had from him since their Sunday in Gainsborough.

That night in the dressing-room, Miss Cooke said with a sigh:

'There are some houses with such beautiful gardens in this neighbourhood. How much I wish I could see some of them. Crickleham Park, of course, is one of the show places of the county.'

'It's very impressive,' said Clara. 'I knew it when Archie and his mother lived there.'

'What . . . Archie Hughes-Follett who was with us in Birmingham and Coventry? How very interesting. What a pity he did not come on to Worcester. He might have been kind enough to get me permission to see the park.'

'I'm sure he would. If he knows the people who have it now.'

'Such a good-hearted boy I thought. Well, it can't be helped. Actually I prefer gardens not quite as grand and formal as the Crickleham ones must be. A friend of mine often talks of the most exquisite small place she once visited near Worcester. It belonged to a very old Catholic family – the Cressetts. I wish I could recollect its name.'

'Maryhall,' muttered Clara, feeling her skin contract under her make-up.

'*That* was it. Do you know that house too?'

Clara made a vague sound and concentrated on applying carmine to her lips.

'My friend told me,' went on Miss Cooke, deftly pencilling her crow's feet, 'about a dreadful tragedy there some years ago.'

'Go on, tell us,' said Maidie.

'I daresay Clara has heard about it.'

Clara said nothing. Her hand shook so that she could hardly hold the stick of grease-paint.

'*I* haven't,' said Maidie. 'I like a nice gruesome tale.'

'It's nothing to laugh about, my dear. The only child – the heir – was killed accidentally while playing some game. It was during the war. I know his poor mother had gone to London to meet Sir George Cressett who was coming home on leave. A governess, quite a young girl, was left in charge of the boy. People said that, instead of looking after the child properly, she was flirting with some young officer when it happened.'

Clara stared at her own reflection. Her crimson upper lip looked like a grotesque scar above the lower which had gone so white as to be almost invisible She said shakily:

'I don't think it happened quite like that. I . . . I knew the girl.'

'Clara dear, I'm sorry,' said Miss Cooke with concern. 'I had no idea. . . . I should never have referred to it if I'd dreamt . . . It should be a lesson to me not to listen to rumours. Poor young thing . . . she must have suffered dreadfully.'

Clara said nothing. She was aware of Maidie's eye on her; an eye that, propped open ready to have red spots planted in its corners, looked enormous and accusing like the painted eye that adorned a text at Paget's Fold. 'Thou God seest me.'

She remembered that she had told Maidie that she had once been a governess. But Maidie merely observed:

'Ever so sad for everyone. Still, accidents will happen. You know what kids are.'

That night Clara gave such a shocking performance that Lister told her roughly that if the tour were not finishing he would have sacked her. Back in their digs, Maidie said only:

'You'll never be an actress, old dear, if you let your private upsets interfere with your work.'

'I know,' said Clara meekly, feeling immense gratitude to Maidie for not asking the questions she was so obviously dying to ask. 'I'm beginning to wonder whether I ought to go on with the stage at all.'

'Heard from that fellow lately? The Gainsborough one.'

'Not a word.'

'Aren't men the giddy limit? Still, there are other fish in the sea.'

'There's only one person I'll ever want to marry.'

'We've all heard that one.' Maidie's voice was scornful but not unfriendly. 'It's like the measles. Better get it over while you're young. Trouble with you is you don't know the first thing about men.'

'I'm sick of being told that,' said Clara peevishly. 'When I was in my teens I had a friend called Patsy who used to keep saying the same thing.'

'And me thinking I was your first friend who had a spot of commonsense. Pity neither of us could pass it on.'

Clara said nothing. The evening had left her raw. Tears that were half anger, half nervous misery came into her eyes. She bit her lip savagely in the effort to stop them running over. Not for anything would she let herself break down in front of Maidie. But Maidie suddenly flung her arm round her shoulders.

'You're really hot and bothered, you poor old Wurzit, aren't you? Don't mind me. It's only my bit of fun. I know how it feels, believe it or not. That's why I prefer 'em bald and grateful nowadays.'

Clara had to laugh. Maidie gave her a friendly slap.

'That's better. Never say die, as the monkey said. Seriously, you should think twice before you chuck old Starchy out for good and all. He's a decent boy even if he does drink the hell of a lot. I wouldn't mind having a shot at reforming Mr Archibald Hughes-Follet Esquire myself.'

'Maidie . . . Why, only a week or two ago you were saying . . .'

'I can change my mind like anyone else, can't I! I hadn't heard him sing then. That voice does funny things to me.'

'Why don't you have a shot then? He likes you awfully.'

'Who cares?' said Maidie. 'He ought to be in a museum. Only living specimen of the boy who can only love one girl.'

'I hope you're wrong.'

'Sucks — I believe you get no end of a thrill out of Archie's soupy devotion. Still maybe there's a catch in it. I've never known there not to be.'

'What kind of a catch?'

Maidie turned her big blue eyes up to the ceiling.

'Something I'm too pew-er to mention let alone to try to find out.' She sang demurely:

86

'He's more to be pitied than censured
He's more to be helped than despised.

And don't forget it, Vere, next time the poor sap pops the
question.'

Chapter Ten

Two nights later, the stage doorkeeper produced a letter for
Clara. In her disappointment that it was not from Stephen, she
scarcely glanced at it. Tearing it open idly she was confronted
with an unmistakable handwriting, upright and impersonal as a
nun's. Intent, a little frightened, she read:

'My dear Clara,
    Archie is keeping me company for a few days while my
husband is away and Nan has gone off to nurse her sister in
Hereford. I do not know how you feel about coming to
Maryhall but it would give me so much pleasure to see
you again. Archie is driving into Worcester tomorrow
(Thursday) when, he tells me, you do not have a matinée. If
you would care to come over for lunch, he would pick you up
at the theatre at 12.30 and return you in plenty of time for the
evening performance. I shall understand perfectly if you do
not feel like coming but I hope very much that you will.
                                        Yours affectionately,
                                            Theresa Cressett.'

Clara slept little that night, trying to make up her mind
whether to go or not. She understood that tactful first sentence
too well. It would be painful to go to Maryhall again in any
circumstances, but to be smuggled into that household, to
which she had once had the illusion of belonging, would be
humiliating. She suspected that Lady Cressett was offering her a
kind of test. If she refused, it would be another proof of her

cowardice. She both longed and dreaded to see Charles's mother again. When at last she made up her mind to go, she knew, with a pang of self-contempt, that she could not have brought herself to face it without Archie.

He arrived next morning in the car she remembered so well. The sight of it brought back, not only Charles, but the whole background of Maryhall. Nothing could have been more typical of the Cressetts' orderly economy than that sober dark green Wolseley which had not been new in 1916 but whose paint and fittings shone with the patina of constant care. Even Archie himself looked well-groomed. He had had a shave and a hair cut; someone had evidently cleaned his shoes and pressed his clothes.

As he tucked the musquash rug round her knees (there was a new neat darn in its cloth border which she would have recognized anywhere as Nan's), he put his hand on hers for a moment.

'It's marvellous of you to come. Theresa's set her heart on it for some reason. Frankly I thought it was asking a bit too much of you.'

'What about you?' she asked gently.

He frowned, as he started the car with the expertness she had forgotten.

'Oh, I'm quite used to it now. But the first time, well, I guess you'd rather be on your own. Having me around might make it worse.'

She said truthfully:

'Without you, I couldn't have faced it at all.'

He said, with a look of such radiance that she turned her head away ashamed:

'That's the most wonderful thing you've ever said to me.'

She was grateful that he spoke little during the six-mile drive. It was almost exactly the same time of year as when they had driven along that road. The same wintry sun lit up the sallow fields and the pollarded willows by the Severn. That last day, they had driven in the other direction and she had been grateful for every milestone that took them further from Maryhall. Now, as the Malvern hills loomed larger and she began to recognize fields and houses, it was as if she were being drawn backwards through time as well as space. To avoid the landscape, she glanced at Archie's profile, set in lines of unusual resolution. That was how it had looked at the inquest. Against her will, she wondered whether Stephen Tye would have been so recklessly anxious to take all the blame on himself. To remind herself that Archie was inferior to Stephen she asked with a touch of patronage:

'Still stage-struck? Or have you thought better of Lister's great plans for your future?'

'By no means,' he said, keeping his eyes on the road. 'Going to look him up as soon as I get back to London. But the last day or two . . . Well, you know how it is at Maryhall. One gets talking to Theresa.'

Clara did not answer. She felt suddenly vulgar and diminished. It was Archie who next broke the silence which had become uneasy. Turning to her at last, he enquired:

'Have *you* any plans?'

'No. I suppose I only asked about yours because . . .'

He dropped one hand from the wheel and touched hers.

'I understand, old thing. You'll feel better once you've seen Theresa. *She's* just the same.'

She said wretchedly: 'I'm sure. But *I've* changed.'

'Hang it all, one expects people to at our age. What about me?'

Clara frowned.

'I don't believe you have. Not in yourself.'

'Theresa wouldn't agree. She used to think I was one hell of a good boy. Now I'm sure she believes I'm skidding down the road to ruin. Drink. Gambling. Won't stick to jobs. She probably suspects Women with a capital W too. There, for once, she'd be wrong. But it doesn't make the least difference to the way she treats me. So *you've* got nothing to worry about.'

'I'm not so sure. If you're different, it's only on the surface. But I feel I've changed deep down. Very much for the worse, too.'

'Can't say I've noticed it.'

'Probably hardly anybody would. But she might. She knows things about one before one knows them oneself. My badness –

or whatever it is – mayn't *show*. If it did, everyone might be so horrified that they'd run away from me.'

'Rot,' said Archie, slowing down so suddenly that Clara was flung forward. 'Sorry, darling. Even if it weren't rot, I know one person who wouldn't.'

Clara stared at the road and realized, with a thrill of terror, that they were less than a mile from the lodge. She wanted to cry out that she couldn't face it, but her lips twitched too much for her to make a sound.

Archie said suddenly:

'I've been reading *The Hill of Summer*. I liked it terribly.'

'You liked it?' she said, too astonished to be civil. 'I'd have thought it would have bored you stiff.'

'I bought the paper because I saw you reading it in Brum. Found most of the stuff too heavy going. But I read your story three times. Pleasure, not duty.'

Clara promptly decided that *The Hill of Summer* must be far worse than she supposed.

'Have you read any other stories of mine?'

'Rather. We had *London Mail* in the Club in Santiago. But – of course I don't know the first thing about writing – they didn't seem anywhere near the same class. Frightfully clever and all that. Can't think how you do 'em.'

'But "The Hill" seemed different?'

'Oh, absolutely.'

'Why? How?'

'Don't ask *me*. Hang it all, I'm not literary.'

'I'd *really* like to know.'

'Well . . . if you insist . . . I'd say anyone with the brains to do that sort of thing could have done the *London Mail* ones.'

'Perfectly true. And the other?'

'I'll only drop a brick.'

'*Please*, Archie.'

'Right. First, I thought no one but you could have written it. Second, I didn't think even you could write anything which got me so much.'

They were the first words of praise Clara had heard. She was so grateful that she was almost as pleased as if they had come from Stephen. Perhaps it was even more reassuring to know that she had impressed anyone as simple and honest as Archie. She looked at him with affection.

'*No* one could say anything handsomer than that.'

'Good egg. I'll tell you something rather odd. I used to be rather keen on poetry when I was at Beaumont. Don't suppose I've so much as opened a book of poems for years. But the other day I started rummaging in the Cressetts' library and found old Marvell. I used to like some of his stuff a lot.'

'Oh yes?' said Clara politely. She loved Marvell but, at that moment, she only wanted to talk about her own work. 'I don't suppose I shall ever write poems again. I used to write the usual rubbish at school of course.'

'Must be damn difficult. But it was reading "The Hill" that made me want to read some poetry again. Rather queer, eh?'

'Rather interesting.'

'You know, old thing, you ought always to write things like "The Hill". Sheer waste of time for you, that other stuff.'

Clara's pleasure gave way to panic. She muttered in a furious, jerky voice:

'You don't understand. One can't turn it on like a tap. That story was probably a fluke anyway. Also, you seem to forget *I* haven't got a private income.'

'Now I *have* put my foot in it. Sorry, darling.'

She said nothing, ashamed and a little frightened by her outburst. She was shaking all over as if she had been insulted or unfairly attacked. At last she managed to murmur grudgingly:

'*I'm* sorry. I'm developing a filthy temper.'

'Forget it. My fault. Bull in the china shop as usual.'

He slowed down the car almost to walking pace. They were within fifty yards of the gates of Maryhall. A woman was standing in the road outside the lodge, waving to them.

'Archie – look – it's Lady Cressett.'

A moment later, without knowing how, she found herself in Theresa Cressett's arms and being kissed on both cheeks as the nuns used to kiss her at Mount Hilary.

'My dear Clara . . . I'm so very, very glad you could come.'

The two of them walked up the drive together while Archie

went ahead in the car. However hard she tried not to glance at them, Clara could not help being aware of familiar landmarks; the rose-garden that had once been a cockpit and where a few late roses still bloomed; the blue-faced stable clock peering over the shoulder of the plum-coloured house. It was almost exactly the same time of year as when she had last seen Maryhall: she had, for a moment, the illusion that nothing had changed. She could have sworn Lady Cressett was wearing the identical grey-green tweed suit she remembered so well. Her hair was still piled above her pale, dim-eyed, Flemish-looking face in the elaborate way that had seemed old-fashioned in 1916. She talked gently as they walked, keeping the conversation to impersonal things. There had been a meet at Maryhall last week and the lawn had been rather cut up; the Severn had flooded badly last year; they had won six prizes at the flower show; they were thinking of putting up a new greenhouse.

As they approached the house, a collie advanced to meet them. Clara felt Lady Cressett's hand tighten for a moment on her arm as she said quietly:

'You remember Hero? He's quite a staid middle-aged gentleman now.'

Clara felt a catch in her throat and knew that the unavoidable moment had come. She remembered Charles's cherished and bullied Hero as barely full-grown. The illusion vanished. She put out her hand to the dog, almost expecting him to snarl at her.

'He's not forgotten you,' said Lady Cressett. 'Look – he's grinning. You remember Clara, don't you, old boy?'

Clara's eyes began to sting as Hero stood on his hind legs, pawing at her and trying to lick her face. Of all the things she had been so careful to steel herself against, she had forgotten Charles's dog.

'Down, Hero. Don't worry,' said Lady Cressett. 'And come along, my dear. You must be dying for some food.'

Chapter Eleven

A parlourmaid whose face Clara did not know waited on them. Otherwise nothing was different. Pine logs hissed on the open hearth; the dining-room still smelt of beeswax, herbs and woodsmoke. There had been a bowl of the same red dahlias the last time she had sat at that table with its patina of three centuries of polishing. Then she caught sight of the silver mug Charles had always used, standing on a sideboard among Sir George's trophies. After that, her eyes kept reverting to it and she found it hard to make conversation. Everything she thought of saying seemed to have some connection with Charles or to be so obvious an avoidance as to be worse. Lady Cressett came to her rescue.

'Fancy your acting in *A Clerical Error*. I took Charles to see it one Christmas when the y did it in Malvern. He thought the curate was a priest and was terribly shocked when he got engaged. Of course Nan's a Protestant but such a High one that Charles hadn't quite grasped the difference.'

Clara brought herself to enquire after Nan. Lady Cressett gave her that faint smile of approval she remembered so well.

'Very much the same outside,' Lady Cressett glanced over her shoulder and, seeing the parlourmaid was absent, went on: 'But *inside* there's a great struggle going on. You must pray for her. You know how . . . well . . . resolute Nan is in her loyalties.'

'Yes indeed,' said Clara. The face of Charles's nurse, thin and white under the smooth red hair, rose in her mind as she had last seen it, twisted in hysterical rage.

'Resolute is putting it mildly,' said Archie. 'She's the most obstinate woman I've ever met.'

'She has the defects of her qualities,' said Lady Cressett. 'That's what makes it so hard for her to take the final step. She feels it would be disloyal to her own Church.'

'Is she really thinking of becoming a Catholic?' Clara asked.

'It's only a question of time. Imagine how Charles must be praying for her in heaven. When you think she couldn't deny him anything on earth.'

Archie said:

'If there's one thing I can't imagine, it's Nan admitting she might have been wrong.'

'That's what my sister Monica used to say. She's dead, Clara, did you know? Of course she'll be praying for Nan too.'

'When she can spare time from arguing with St Paul about women's rights.'

'You're a very irreverent young man, Archie. If that's how the Jesuits brought you up, I'm glad we meant to send Charles to Downside. As to Nan, when she *does* come in, she'll put us all to shame. Those fierce, all-or-nothing people often turn into saints once they're converted. "God seeks and loves courageous souls." St Theresa said that. Nan's nothing if not courageous.'

Clara felt herself blush. She knew what St Theresa went on to say about cowardly souls and was painfully conscious of being one. Nor was she 'aided by humility', the only virtue in which cowards were likely to excel.

The three of them had their coffee in the drawing-room whose green panelled walls and gilt garlands Clara had admired on her first evening. Her eyes wandered nostalgically over the lute-backed chairs, the Sheraton tables tidily littered with snuff-boxes and porcelain, the miniatures of generations of Cressetts. When the heads of the other two were turned, she nerved herself to look into the bright impudent eyes of the page of Charles the First's court. Their likeness to those of his last descendent was too vivid to bear. She looked away and became aware of an unfamiliar frame on a table. Lady Cressett, catching her glance, said gently:

'It's a snapshot we had enlarged. We hated that stiff professional one with his hair plastered down and his tie straight.'

Clara had identified that snapshot. Now, the boy's upturned face grinned at nothing; the hand which had been clasped in her own had been retouched and furnished with a cricket ball. This wiping out of her image gave her such a sense of being utterly banished from Maryhall that her mouth went dry. She tried to say something and choked.

Lady Cressett said quickly:

'I like the original much better. It's in my Caussade that I read every night. Monica took the two of you without your knowing. Charles and his beloved "Spin" . . . Ah, Clara dear, don't.'

For Clara had burst into loud, blubbering tears like a child. Archie leant forward and put a hand on her heaving shoulder.

'My darling old thing . . . try not to.'

It was a minute or two before she could stop crying.

When she had recovered herself, Lady Cressett said:

'Shall you and I take a turn in the garden, Clara? It's such ages since I've seen you.'

Never would Clara have been gladder of Archie's presence. As she drew back at the door to let Lady Cressett pass first, she shot him a despairing look which he returned. Lady Cressett caught this interchange and smiled.

'You two,' she said. 'It's hard to realize you're officially grown-up. I'm only stealing her for a little while, Archie.'

Clara's tears had wholly restored her to the present. As she walked with Lady Cressett along the paths bordered by yew hedges and over lawns from which the day's fall of leaves had been swept into neat piles, she was aware of differences. Maryhall, however slowly, however minutely, had changed in four years; she saw it as a real place and no longer the fixed landscape of a dream. It was Lady Cressett now who kept reverting to the past.

'That tree really ought to come down but he did so love climbing it.'

Or: 'His rosebush only produced two roses this year. It's a miracle it ever produced any since he planted it practically upside down.'

They were skirting the wall of the kitchen garden when Theresa said hesitantly:

'Could you bear it if we went in? I couldn't for a long time. Now I've come to love it again. I come here every day to say my rosary.'

Clara had not the courage to refuse. After the first pang, she felt no more than a dull sadness as they paced between the box-edged beds.

'I thought it would help even if it hurt,' said Lady Cressett.

Clara made a vague sound.

The other went on: 'Of course *we* shall always feel it. The human loss. That's inevitable. But *he* is happy with God. Sometimes, you know, it is as if he were quite near me. Not whem I'm *trying* to feel it. But sometimes, when things are difficult and dark, quite unexpectedly, I have a flash of realizing what we know by faith – that the blessed do watch over us. After all, it's part of their joy in heaven to help the people they loved on earth.'

'Yes, indeed,' said Clara, embarrassed. It came over her how much she had lost that sense of commerce between heaven and earth which had seemed so natural at Mount Hilary and Maryhall.

'Clara,' Lady Cressett said after a pause. 'Do you mind if I'm very indiscreet?'

'Of course not.'

'Only because I'm very fond of you. For your own sake, not just because you were so devoted to Charles. I wonder so much what you are going to make of your life.'

'I wish I knew.'

'You're a changeable child, aren't you? The last time you and I had a talk, you were quite seriously considering becoming a nun. Now, here you are on the stage. So you feel you've found your vocation at last?'

Clara shook her head.

'I doubt if I'll ever be more than a bright amateur. If I were a real actress, I wouldn't mind drudging round the provinces for years.'

'But it's beginning to pall already? Ah well, perhaps one of these days you'll give it up and get married.'

Clara sighed.

'Perhaps.'

'Forgive me, my dear, but I'm afraid I've been plying Archie with questions. I've had so little news of you for years. I gather there is someone whom you care for very much.'

'Yes,' muttered Clara, as if confessing a fault. In the atmosphere of Maryhall, her love for Stephen seemed disordered, almost guilty. She laughed rather artificially. 'But I don't know if he does. Enough to risk marrying, that is.'

Lady Cressett asked gently:

'Supposing . . . just supposing . . . he didn't? Would that prevent you from marrying anyone else ever?'

'How can I tell? I just can't imagine wanting to.'

'No one can at the time. Yet, you know, Clara, I've seen girls who thought their hearts were broken make very happy marriages with someone else. Happier, often, than ones who have married men with whom they were very much in love.'

Clara said, rather irritably:

'You seem to take it for granted that I shan't.'

'No, no . . . of course I didn't mean that . . . I only said "suppose". If you've really found the right person this time and he feels the same . . . men are often slower than we are at making up their minds . . . I wish you all the joy in the world. Is he a Catholic, this man?'

'No.'

Lady Cressett sighed.

'My poor child. I've known some happy mixed marriages but not many. A man will promise anything when he's in love. But once married – I've seen it happen so often – he may object very strongly to carrying them out. That can lead to such terrible conflicts and bitterness. It's the Catholic wife who suffers most.'

'Isn't that looking rather far ahead?'

'Not too far surely, if you're so certain you'd say "Yes". And if he's holding back, isn't it very likely just because he's not willing to have his children brought up Catholics?'

Although – or perhaps because – these probings came nowhere near the heart of her trouble, Clara found them painful. Blind to everything but the dazzling hope of Stephen's allowing her to marry him, she had never even considered the religious side. Faced suddenly with these questions, she felt a chill deeper than the resentment of having her love treated like a legal abstraction. The fact that she had never faced them herself seemed to prove how frail her hope must be. Fear made her insolent. She said, with a particular smile and voice that always maddened her father:

'Even you could hardly expect me to ask quite such a leading question.'

Lady Cressett's pale, rather heavy face twitched for the first time in the nervous tic her sister used to call 'the tombstone of Tess's temper'.

'I expect I deserved that. Rushing in where angels fear to tread.'

'I'm sorry,' Clara said sincerely. 'It's sweet of you to bother about me at all.'

'Rubbish. I only hope it all comes out right. I'll pray for you. In the long run, it's the only thing any of us can do for each other, isn't it? And you must pray too. Of course I'm sure you do.'

They walked in silence for some moments. At last Clara said:

'I'm afraid I'm not very devout. I don't mean I've lost my faith.'

Lady Cressett squeezed her arm.

'Of course you haven't. Don't think I don't realize how difficult it must be for Catholic girls these days. When I think of the sheltered lives Monica and I led at your age! Even if we'd gone out and worked as you wonderful young things do, I'm sure things would have been easier then. The whole atmosphere seems to have changed since the war. It's no longer just a question of Catholic or Protestant. One hears more and more of people who believe in nothing.'

'Oh, I do believe. At least I go on taking it for granted that I do.'

'Now, now Clara,' said Lady Cressett with a touch of sharpness. 'None of that bad old habit of yours. Even in your teens you were much too introspective. Always questioning yourself and trying to analyse every little thought and emotion. Of course you believe.'

'But it all seems so remote. I don't seem to feel any fervour any more.'

'Feelings don't matter. There's probably much more merit in keeping up one's bare obligations when they've become a dry duty than in doing all sorts of extras because one's *feeling* pious. On the stage, I daresay it's difficult even to get to Sunday Mass.'

'Oh no. It's always been possible.'

'Splendid. I shall quote you to Archie as a good example.'

'Archie? Why?'

'You know what men are. They so easily get slack when there's no one to keep them up to it. It's not deliberate. Archie admits he sometimes just can't bring himself to get up in time. Of course, as you probably know, there's often a reason for that in poor Archie's case.'

'Yes. But I don't care what Archie does. He's a million times better than me in every way.'

Lady Cressett laughed.

'I believe you're a great deal fonder of Archie than you admit.'

'Of course I'm fond of him.'

'Just now, when we were in the drawing-room, you seemed so much of a couple that for the moment I forgot that all is supposed to be over between you.'

'It *is* over,' said Clara hastily.

'It seems such a pity,' Lady Cressett sighed. 'Of course you were both such babies *then*. It's obvious that the poor boy's fonder of you than ever, you naughty child.'

'It's not my fault. I didn't *want* to see him again. If Daddy hadn't put him on my track . . .'

'Your father likes him very much, doesn't he? And Archie seems devoted to him.'

'Oh yes. They dote on each other.'

'And what does Mr Batchelor think of the other one?'

Clara stiffened. Her father was the last person in the world to whom she could have admitted her feeling for Stephen.

'He thinks he's a very good actor. But he hasn't the least idea . . .'

'Oh . . . an *actor*.' Lady Cressett's voice was politely chill.

Clara said with a touch of malice:

'After all, Archie wants to go on the stage. Hasn't he told you?'

'I don't take that very seriously. It's just a notion he's got because you're on the stage at the moment. Also it's the one thing that would most annoy his uncle. You'll see . . . when he comes into his money in two years' time, he'll buy a nice place in the country and settle down sensibly. Let's hope he finds a nice girl to settle down with.' She pinched Clara's arm. 'Don't you hope he will?'

'Of course. Though I'm not sure that Archie *is* the settling down sort. Any more than I am.'

'Oh . . . oh,' said Lady Cressett. 'I knew a girl not so many years ago who longed for a place like Maryhall and a nursery full of children.'

Clara sighed.

'I know,' she said slowly. 'Back here with you, I could almost imagine wanting it again. You told me once I was like a chameleon. It's true. I change all the time according to where I am and the people I'm with.'

'Pity someone can't pick you up and put you on the right colour.'

They had arrived once again at the door of the walled garden. Lady Cressett stopped, with her hand at the latch, looking not at Clara but down the box-edged path. Clara knew by her expression that she was praying. It was not till they had closed the door behind them that she said:

'Charles was so fond of you both. You must forgive me if I can't help hoping that, in spite of everything . . . Yet I've no right to wish this or that. Nothing matters, does it, except that things should come out the way God wants them to?' She smiled. 'And that's so often just the opposite of the way *we* think best.'

Clara said nothing. She stared across the lawn with the cedar and the weeping-willow to the parti-coloured fields sloping down to the bend of the river, trying to replace them with the landlady's parlour where she had last seen Stephen. It was always hard for her to imagine life going on in any place other than the one she was in at the moment. Already it seemed unthinkable that, in a few hours, she would make up her face in a crowded dressing-room, prance and giggle through her silly part and eat sausages with Maidie over a gas fire.

Lady Cressett smiled:

'That was a long thought, Clara.'

'Not worth calling a thought,' said Clara, smiling too. 'Just a chameleon's automatic reflex. They have nervous breakdowns, don't they, if you change their backgrounds suddenly?'

'There's Archie coming to meet us. Poor boy. We've been out nearly an hour.'

Clara looked towards the soberly elegant plum-coloured house in its setting of clipped yews and flagged terrace. The sky, grey all the morning, had cleared in the west. The sun, already dipping towards the crescent of rising woods behind the house, warmed their last leaves to the cock-pheasant tints she remembered. Tree and lawn, brick and stone, were washed with soft colour and shadow in the muted light. Once again she saw Maryhall as the symbol of order and tradition; of a life oriented beyond time. As Archie's tall figure strode towards them, she saw his face, too, in a transfiguring light. For a moment she wondered whether, if she had never known Stephen, the two of them might not have been able to build up a Maryhall of their own.

Lady Cressett said softly:

'Whoever you marry, Clara, remember that the man and the woman are only the beginning. One doesn't always realize that when one's young. A Catholic, most of all, has to look beyond. To the children. To the family as a whole.'

Clara said nothing. Though it was only Stephen that she wanted, the words faintly stirred some part of her that seemed to have no connection with him.

Lady Cressett smiled.

'If you could love my boy so much, think what it will be when you have some of your own. You have so much capacity to love . . . too much to spend on just one person.'

Clara was startled.

'Capacity to love? No . . . no . . . I'm much too selfish. I mean . . . if I really had . . . it would be there all the time, wouldn't it? I'd be able to love *anyone*.'

Lady Cressett patted her cheek.

'Then you'd be a saint, my dear.'

Clara sighed. She knew more than the other suspected of what

Theresa Cressett's life had been. She knew that Charles's father, like Charles himself, turned cruel if he were thwarted in the least thing. Theresa had lost her only child and the fact that she could not have the others for which she longed had been turned into bitter reproach by the husband whose one passion was Maryhall itself and the carrying on of his name. What she had built up required qualities Clara did not even begin to possess. This home, this atmosphere whose spell Clara now felt again, was not something ready-made. It had been created and sustained by endless patience and daily small renunciations of self-will; by a love which expected no human return.

Clara said, almost with anguish:

'Oh . . . if only . . . only I could be like you.'

'Nonsense,' said Lady Cressett emphatically. 'Nobody's meant to be like anyone else. What's the point of God going to all the trouble of making every one of us unique if we go and spoil it all by trying to copy each other?'

The next moment, Archie was upon them. As he fell into step beside them, he gave Clara a quick questioning glance.

'Feeling all right now?'

She nodded.

'I was sent to tell you both tea was ready. Then I suppose I ought to be getting Clara back to Worcester.'

'I've arranged for Milburn to drive her,' said Lady Cressett.

'I say, Theresa. I thought I was going to,' protested Archie.

'I forgot to tell you. Lydia Coles phoned to say she was coming over after tea. She'll be so disappointed if you're not here. After all, she was one of your mother's best friends.'

'Oh, very well,' said Archie gloomily. 'Will you be going straight back to Valetta Road when the company packs up, Clara?'

Clara flushed.

'No. I'm going to Oxford.'

'For long?'

'I don't quite know. A week at the most.'

'Tell me the address. I'm getting a motorbike and sidecar in a day or two. I could easily pick you up there and run you back to London.'

Clara felt herself flush deeper still.

'I don't even know where I'll be staying.'

She forced herself to look up into his face. He had gone white and she knew that he had guessed.

He said with a strained smile:

'Well, that's napoo then. Have a good time in Oxford.'

On the drive back to Worcester, she could not shake off a weight of sadness. Revisiting Maryhall had aroused so many feelings she could not quite analyse. Sitting there in that familiar car, behind Milburn's rigid green back, she had an odd sense of being banished from that world even more definitely than four years ago. When she had first heard that Archie was not coming back with her, she had felt an irrational disappointment along with her relief. Now she began to wish he were there, if only to stop her from remembering his stricken face as he said 'Well, that's napoo then'.

She turned her mind with a definite effort to Stephen. Nearly three weeks had gone by without a sign from him. The fact that for the first time she did not know where he was playing this week gave her a feeling of panic. Never had she been so utterly cut off from him.

It was only four days now to his first night. If there were no letter for her that evening, she would risk sending him a note to say she was coming to Oxford – no more. She would have to send it to the theatre: he would be sure to be rehearsing there on Monday before the actual performance. But which theatre? Suddenly she remembered having seen an Oxford paper on the station bookstall when she had bought the *Saturday Westminster*. If there were no announcement of the play, at least it would give the names of all the theatres and she could send a note to each.

She asked Milburn to stop at the station and was just in time to buy the *Oxford Mail* before the bookstall closed. Back in the car, she opened it at random, searching for the theatre column. The first thing that caught her eye was a blotched photograph of Stephen himself. Beside it was one of a handsome, middle-aged woman with smooth dark hair and earnest eyes. Over the two pictures ran the heading – 'Stage romance'.

At first these words conveyed no meaning whatever to her.

Then she read the caption below the two smudged, smiling faces.

'An additional interest will be created in Mr Stephen Tye's performance of the title role of *Richard II*, which opens at the Playhouse next Monday, by the fact that he has just married Miss Elizabeth Lane, manager and leading lady of the company. Miss Lane is a firm favourite with Oxford audiences and we regret that she will not be personally appearing in *Richard II*. However, she and her husband plan to appear together in many future productions, including *Antony and Cleopatra* and a stage adaptation of *The Mill on the Floss*.'

PART TWO

Chapter One

On the morning of her wedding, Clara woke up with the sense of continuing a dream. She had refused overnight her mother's offer to help her to dress. When at last she forced herself to get out of bed, she pottered aimlessly about her untidy bedroom and was so reluctant to put on her white dress and veil that her father kept coming up to rap impatiently on the door.

In the end, it was he who nearly made her late for the ceremony. As they waited outside the Oratory, he discovered that one of his gloves was split. Before Clara could stop him, he leapt out of the hired car, hailed a taxi and disappeared. She sat there, as if in a trance, while strangers pressed their faces against the glass to stare at her and an agitated verger gesticulated from the steps. When at last he returned, he panted, as he pulled on his new gloves:

'Must think me mad. Thank God you're still here.' She wondered if he had really expected her to run away. Her will was too paralysed even to formulate the wish.

As they paced up the aisle, she was only hazily aware of organ music, turning heads and the candlelit altar at the foot of which stood a tall red-headed man, so unfamiliar in his formal clothes that at first she did not recognize him. She had dreamed so often in the last years that she was in a church, about to marry Archie Hughes-Follett, that this walk up the aisle might have been mere repetition. The only detail which made her suspect that, this time, it might be happening in fact was the trembling of her father's arm. As they advanced slowly towards the altar, it was she who seemed to be supporting him.

When she and Archie made their vows, she recovered enough sense of reality to feel awed. They stood side by side muttering, like children who have forgotten the answers in catechism class, while the old priest patiently prompted them. She heard the two of them make those tremendous promises which bound them for life and thought with panic: 'Do we really know what we are doing?'

She tried to follow the magnificent liturgy of the Nuptial Mass but the print swam before her eyes. All she could do was to pray distractedly that at least she would not make Archie unhappy. As she prayed, she was overcome by the sense of her own emptiness and fickleness. Only a few months ago it would have seemed impossible that she should ever stop loving Stephen. Now she could hardly remember what that love had felt like. She had soon reconciled herself to the first fierce pain of loss; what still came back in all its nakedness, often at the least expected moments, was her utter humiliation. This enduring sense of shame had become dissociated from Stephen himself. She no longer bore him any resentment; she had gone to see him play *Richard II* when the company had come to Croydon, only a few weeks before her wedding, and had critically admired his quite remarkable performance. Afterwards, she had accidentally run into him and his wife and had even felt a touch of cynical affection at his relief when she acted better than she had ever done on the stage. She had noted with amusement that Elizabeth Lane had watched him anxiously while they talked, with false heartiness, of old friends at the Garrick; she had even caught a covert glance of something warmer than gratitude from Stephen himself. But all this had done nothing to heal the deep hurt to her pride. That had remained and been gradually transformed into the conviction that, even if she could bring herself to take the risk of falling in love again, she would be quite incapable of doing so.

The great petitions of the Nuptial Mass brought home to her her utter inadequacy. What right had she to suppose that she could make Archie happy by marrying him? All she could do was to implore forgiveness for what suddenly seemed to her a shocking presumption as the priest prayed that she should be as pleasing to her husband as Rachel, as wise as Rebecca, as faithful as Sara. Only at the last blessing, when he prayed that they should see their children's children, did she lose the awful sense that she was treating a sacrament as if it were an empty formula. Though she dreaded the thought of Archie's making love to her almost as much as she dreaded the pain of having children, there, at least, was something real to which she had committed herself and where she was determined not to cheat. She gave an inward cry for grace to overcome her repugnance and cowardice and glanced upwards wanting, for the first time, to see Archie's face. But though she had often, during the ceremony, been aware of his eyes on her and avoided them, this time it was his that were averted. She saw only the kind red face of the old priest, smiling at them as he pronounced the words, as if adding a human blessing to the divine one.

Once the service was over, she relapsed into her dreamlike state. At the reception, she felt as if she were playing an unrehearsed part with surprising ease. Cousins ignored since childhood; friends whom she had not seen for years; unknown relatives of Archie's appeared like a well-drilled crowd on the stage. Only one person seemed not to be playing her part with conviction. Under her gay new hat, her mother's dark eyes were rimmed with red and her mouth drooped with a sadness more appropriate to a funeral.

While Clara was changing in the hotel bedroom, which gave her more than ever the sense of dressing for another act in a play, Isabel for a moment destroyed the illusion by bursting into genuine tears. Clasping Clara in her arms, she had sobbed: 'Darling . . . darling child . . . Oh, I hope . . . I pray everything will be all right.'

Arrived at Brevisham, the superbly inappropriate house which Archie's Aunt Sybilla had lent them for their honeymoon, they were once more involved in the ritual play. The butler and the housekeeper were waiting at the top of the steps to congratulate them; the house was full of white flowers. Later, when Clara descended the wide shallow staircase, in a new evening frock, aware of candlelight and slyly smiling servants behind the open door of the dining-room, the sense of being on the stage became overwhelming. It was a relief to her to see that Archie felt exactly the same. During dinner, while they ate out-of-season food and drank champagne, they tried to behave as if they had been married for years, under the eye of a butler who had known Archie as a schoolboy. When at last they were left alone, Archie blew out his cheeks with such a comic sigh that she laughed naturally for the first time that day. 'Gosh, I don't think I could go through all that again even for you, my sweet. I say . . . couldn't we bolt? Go to a pub or a nightclub or something?'

'We can't. Your aunt would never forgive us. After all she *has* been awfully kind.'

'That's the worst of Sybilla. When she's got a generous fit on, there's no holding her. When she hasn't, she wouldn't fork out so much as a dry biscuit. And of course she's only doing all this to spite Uncle Stanley. She hates him like poison.'

'Why?'

'Because he hates her, I suppose. For one thing because she's always taking up with weird religions and groups and so on.'

'But her husband . . . your uncle . . . was a Catholic, wasn't he?'

'Uncle Gerald? Gracious, yes. All the Hughes-Folletts are. I believe she used to go on at him a lot. Uncle Stan said she talked him into his grave. Gerald was the fool of the family of *that* generation but Uncle Stan had a weakness for him.' Archie frowned. 'Pity he hasn't transferred it to me.'

'I thought he was rather sweet at the wedding. I admit he looked formidable.'

'Well, as he couldn't actually stop me from getting married, he had to put a good face on it.'

'Did he want to stop you?'

'Naturally, he thinks I'm a young ass not to wait till I've got my cash or what *he* calls a decent job. But I wasn't going to risk losing you again. Suppose you'd changed your mind?'

He caught her left hand and kissed the ring on it.

'My wife. I simply can't believe it.'

'Neither can I.'

'Wish we could just have got into the old motorbike and sidecar and hopped off to nowhere without making plans. I can't stick Brevisham. These big houses bore me stiff.'

'I think it's quite fun for a little,' said Clara. 'You forget I'm not used to luxury.'

'You shall have as much as you like if you can stick me for two years. But you won't want a sort of ghastly formal life will you, darling? I thought it'd be fun to spend the cash on amusing things – *when* we get it. Not on servants and great boring houses and all that sort of rot. Still . . . if you want 'em . . .'

'I've no idea what I shall want in two years' time.'

Archie gave her an odd look.

'I know what I want now . . . this very minute,' he said in his most serious voice.

'What?'

'To dance with you.'

Clara had an obscure sensation that was partly relief, partly dismay. It lasted only a moment; by the time Archie had opened the gramophone and put on a record of *Avalon* it had gone.

Brevisham, built by a Hughes-Follett with a passion for Scott, was a fantastic example of nineteenth-century Gothic. From outside it presented a vast front of still raw pink brick and yellow stone adorned with crenellated towers, crossbow slits, ogives, iron grilles and huge oak doors studded with nails. The largest of these opened into a stone-flagged hall with stained glass windows and an organ loft. Sybilla Hughes-Follett had furnished it with huge chintz-covered chairs and sofas and strewn its chilly flags with white fur rugs. A concert-sized grand piano stood on a daïs at one end, banked by tubs of hydrangeas; a log-fire hissed in the carved stone fireplace. The general effect was that of a brand-new school chapel converted into the lounge of a luxury hotel. Archie rolled back some of the rugs and they began to dance, their feet rasping softly on the stone floor.

'I'm the least little bit tight,' he announced at one point. 'Hardly surprising when you consider how much champagne I must have swallowed today out of pure funk – Forgive?'

'Of course. It doesn't show, anyway. I feel slightly hazy myself.'

'It's all right as long as one stops there,' said Archie earnestly. 'And I'm going to, from now on.'

'You've been wonderful these last weeks.'

He held her closer.

'I wasn't going to take any risks. Don't even feel I want the stuff, now I've got you.'

The slight haziness seemed to disconnect Clara from her body. Her limbs moved smoothly and rhythmically, following Archie's lightest indication of their own accord.

'You're dancing marvellously,' he said. 'We've never gone so well together. Wish we could just go on dancing all night.'

'I wish so too,' she answered truthfully. 'Don't let's talk.' Dancing with him in this relaxed, dreamy state, she felt closer to him than she had ever thought possible. Never before had she been in close enough harmony with him to realize how well he danced. All his clumsiness vanished as soon as he moved to music; his subtle changes of step and rhythm, now that for once she could follow them instinctively, seemed to speak a language her body understood and which affected her almost as much as his singing.

When at last, suddenly exhausted after the long, glittering, unreal day, she said she wanted to go to bed, he looked, for a moment, almost angry. An odd expression, at once sullen and aggressive, clouded his face. Then he recovered his smile and kissed her.

'You must be almost dead. Run along, my darling old thing. I'll just go and have a nightcap. Positively only one.'

She had lain for some time in the great scrolled and gilded bed before she heard him moving about in the dressing-room. By the time she was aware that he had come into their bedroom, her eyes were closed and she was almost asleep with the lamp on. Rousing herself with an effort she saw him standing by the bed, looking more like an overgrown schoolboy than ever in his pyjamas. His red hair was tousled; his arms were so long that his lean wrists protruded from the sleeves as if he had outgrown them. But there was nothing boyish about his filmed, haggard eyes. He stood staring down at her so strangely, almost accusingly, that she sat up and asked:

'Is something wrong? Are you ill?'

'Ill?' he said vaguely and thickly. 'Not in the least ill. Perfectly all right. Didn't mean to wake you. Sorry.'

The next minute he lurched forward and fell on his knees by

the bed and buried his head in his hands. He stayed thus, without moving, for so long that Clara at last touched him on the shoulder. He lifted his head and stared at her blindly. His face was flushed and swollen.

'Archie,' she said gently, shaking him a little; 'What's the matter?'

'Nothing's matter. Only saying prayers. Must say prayers.'

She saw then that he was drunk. She did not feel angry, only helpless and a trifle frightened. With difficulty, she managed to persuade him to get up and helped him into the bed beside her. He lay heavily on his side, his head turned from her and buried in the pillow. But just as she bent across him to put out the light, catching the fumes of whisky from his half-open mouth, he looked at her, with a flash of recognition in his filmed eyes.

'Clara . . . darling Clara,' he whispered. 'Didn't mean . . . Couldn't . . .' The whisper became inaudible. He gave a grunting sigh, like a man in pain. The next moment he was fast asleep.

Chapter Two

After a while, Clara herself slept but lightly and uneasily. At intervals she woke, aware of the unfamiliar heat and weight of someone lying beside her. The darkness was already thinning, so that she could see the outlines of the furniture in the great three-windowed room, when she fell into a heavy doze. She dreamt that her father came and rapped impatiently at the door, exactly as he had done while she was dressing for her wedding. Just as she was going to call to him, she realized with horror that she was in bed with Archie. Overcome with shame and guilt, she crouched under the sheets, silent. The knocking grew more imperative; it sounded threatening. Then she remembered with relief that Archie was her husband. Her father had no right to be angry. She called nervously, 'Come in, Daddy,' and, in the effort of doing so, woke up. Someone was indeed knocking at the door, but softly and discreetly. Clara called more confidently, 'Come in' and a maid entered with a tea-tray.

'Good morning, Madam. Shall I draw the curtains? Mr Archie is still asleep, isn't he?'

'Good morning,' said Clara, smiling at the maid with passionate gratitude for not being her father. 'Yes, please draw them.'

The sight of the trees and a distant sunlit rise broke her wretched sense of isolation.

'It's nine o'clock, Madam,' said the maid, putting down the tray. 'Would you and Mr Archie like your breakfast in bed or downstairs?'

'I'll wait till he wakes up and ask him.'

The maid smiled slyly:

'Mr Archie's not usually an early riser, Madam. Will you ring when you want breakfast or your bath run?' On the tray was a letter in her father's writing. Seeing the words, 'Hughes-Follett,' she wondered what he could possibly want to say so urgently to Archie. Then she grasped that it was addressed to herself. She stared for some time at the envelope before she brought herself to open it. The small fact that her father would never again address her in her maiden name made her realize, for the first time, that she was actually married. Even when she had convinced herself that she was no longer Clara Batchelor but Mrs Hughes-Follett, she still hesitated to open her letter. When at last she did so, the 'Dearest Clara' dispelled the obscure anxiety that persisted from her dream. If he had been angry, it would have been only 'Dear'.

'Dearest Clara,

I had a childish fancy to be the first person to write to you in your married name. This is only to send my best love and all my blessings to you both.

I must apologize again for my absurd behaviour outside the church. I cannot think what possessed me. I knew, even at the time, that no one would have minded in the least, even if they had noticed it, the fact that the bride's father had a split in his glove! To think that, at such a moment, when you must have been nervous and overwrought, I should have distracted you and nearly made you late for the ceremony, fills me with shame. I can only say "mea culpa" and offer the feeble excuse that I was a little overwrought myself.

Let me say once more – to both of you – how delighted I am to have Archie for my son-in-law. How providentially it has turned out in the end! Bless you again, my dearest child . . . may I say, my dearest children?

Your affectionate father,
C.F.B.

She read the letter two or three times as she drank her tea. After the unreality of yesterday it seemed to link her once more to her old self. However disjointed her life might be, however much she was haunted by the sense that everything she undertook was doomed to failure, she remained Claude Batchelor's daughter. In marrying Archie she had perhaps made up to him for all the times she had disappointed him in the past.

The letter, she noticed, contained no reference whatever to her mother. This was so unusual that it brought home to her how deeply divided her parents were on the subject of her marriage. She tried to assure herself that her mother's disapproval meant nothing to her. Nevertheless it was faintly disturbing that anyone so vague and variable should have held firmly to the same opinion for four years. Even more disturbing had been Isabel's unusual silence. When, for the second time, she had announced that she was going to marry Archie, Clara had expected protests, even tears. There had been none. Her mother had merely said: 'I'm sure Daddy will be delighted. It's what *he* always wanted.' Only for that one moment yesterday had her unnatural calm broken down. She told herself that now it was positively her duty to ignore her mother. Henceforth only *he* mattered: her loving, admiring father who was so certain she had done the right thing. Forgetting that, only a few minutes ago, she had been reduced to guilty panic by his mere presence in a dream, she gave a satisfied smile.

As she sipped her delicious tea and looked out on sunlit lawns and trees in their fresh spring green, she felt a rush of gratitude that was almost like love to Archie, still heavily asleep. This marriage had restored her to her father; henceforth the three of them were bound in a new tie from which her mother was excluded. She thought how passionately Claude had wanted a son; how passionately she herself had wanted a brother.

She stared at Archie's flushed sleeping face and half-open mouth. What would her father have thought if he had known that her husband had been drunk on his wedding night? She turned back to that pathetic, rather pompous letter. Why was it so reassuring to her disturbed mind? Why did it seem like absolution for a sin she had forgotten to confess? What she had most dreaded in marrying Archie had not happened. She had dreaded it yet obscurely wanted it, as if that unknown, violent contact with another person would break down some barrier in herself. Suddenly she laid the letter against her hot forehead, as if it had some secret meaning which could only be communicated by touch.

Chapter Three

Four days later, Archie too had a letter. He glanced through it impatiently; then his face darkened.

'Whatever's the matter?' Clara asked.

'Hell,' he said without looking up. He was studying it carefully now and frowning with the effort to take it in.

'Bad news about the Lister thing?'

'Pretty grim,' he nodded.

Clara had long ago given up trying to follow the financial tangles of the enterprise in which Lister had persuaded Archie to invest three-quarters of his legacy. The idea was to found a club with a small theatre attached. Lister had not himself put any money into it but had agreed to run the theatrical side for a salary and a percentage of the takings. Archie, in return for his capital, was to be paid £400 a year for the vague job of 'General

Secretary' but would in fact spend most of his time working under Lister.

At first the plan had seemed fairly reasonable. She believed that Lister was too shrewd to be involved in something with no hope of success. But, after her only meeting with the man behind the scheme, she had begun to have doubts. She had met Bell in a bar with Lister and Archie and had asked him one or two questions. Bell's answers had been either evasive or patronizing. Later, Archie had told her apologetically that Bell was a temperamental chap and hated talking business to women. After that, she had only been able to gather from Archie the vaguest idea of what was going on. However, he was so happy and excited about the plan that she had kept her misgivings to herself. Less surprised than he, she was able to ask quite calmly:

'What's gone wrong?'

'Can't quite make out. Something about their not being able to get a theatre licence unless they make some structural alterations.'

'Surely Bell went into all that before he started the rebuilding?'

'Maybe they've changed the rules or something. He keeps saying "unforeseen circumstances". Anyway, what it boils down to is they need more cash. Everything's going to take a bit longer than they thought and they've got to find money for a mortgage instalment.'

'I thought they'd bought the place outright.'

'Well, it seems they had to do some wangling. Someone else who was coming in let them down and they had to borrow.'

'They can't have any more of yours.'

'They certainly can't,' he said quietly. 'I had a slight shock when I saw my bank manager the other day.'

'But, Archie,' she said aghast. 'It can't *all* have gone. Five hundred pounds is an *enormous* amount of money. You can't have spent it all in a few months.'

'Oh . . . there's a bit left,' he said hastily. 'Oh yes . . . quite a bit. Must be. But you know, even though I've mostly been staying with the family, it's damned hard to live on six quid a week if you're going to have any fun at all. Then there were odds and ends like the old motorbike and sidecar. Oh . . . and a quarter in advance on the Chelsea house.'

It was Clara's turn to feel guilty. During their engagement she had let him take her out and give her presents without worrying whether he could afford them as he could when his mother was alive.

'I ought to have restrained you,' she said. 'I'll be good from now on. I'm awful at managing money myself.'

'Don't worry, darling. As I say, there's a bit left. And I didn't fritter it all. That two hundred was really an investment.'

'*What* two hundred?' she asked, with sudden apprehension.

'I forked it out to buy the option on some play by a friend of Bell's.'

'You never told me.'

'I was going to. It only happened a week or two ago. Getting married put everything out of my head. Had to make up my mind in a hurry because Bell said there was another management keen as mustard to get it. Decent of him to tip me the wink. He swears it's an absolute winner and that I'd be mad to lose the chance.'

'Does Jimmy agree?'

'Actually, he hasn't read it yet. I've only glanced at it myself. I terribly want your expert opinion. It's translated from German by some foreign chap whose English struck me as a bit wonky. I thought maybe you might be an angel and knock it into shape a bit. We may make pots out of it some day.'

'Some day,' sighed Clara. 'But what's our situation now?'

'It certainly looks a bit critical, darling. Still I'm sure we can wangle something.'

'What's the worst that could happen?'

'It won't, of course. But if they can't raise any more cash, the whole thing may go phut. Including my job.'

'Have they any hopes?'

'Well, frankly no. They want me to approach Uncle Stanley.'

Clara's heart sank like a lift.

'Archie . . . you know he wouldn't. He loathes the idea of your having anything to do with the theatre.'

'He wouldn't in the ordinary way, the old swine. But Lister

says Bell's worked out a very hot notion. Something no chap with a head for business could resist. Hang it all, it's my money. Fairholm doesn't stand to lose a cent. Even he could hardly want to see everything I've put into the Club go down the drain.'

'You're jolly brave to tackle him.'

Clara tried to sound cheering but she had a foreboding that, even if Lord Fairholm agreed – and nothing could be more unlikely – the Club was doomed.

'Shouldn't dream of trying if we weren't right up against it . . . If it were just me alone, I'd probably say to hell with it all and cut my losses.'

Clara smiled at him across the breakfast table. The porcelain and fine linen seeemed suddenly to have become symbols of unattainable security. The Georgian silver winked smugly in the morning sun.

'Don't worry just because of me,' she said, her spirits rising as if in defiance of Aunt Sybilla's wealth. 'Even if the Club should fail, we'll manage somehow.'

Archie's angry, worried face relaxed for the first time.

'You're a wonder,' he said, reaching out a long arm and gripping her wrist. 'What a girl to have in a crisis.'

Clara felt a hypocrite. She knew very well that she was not being brave. She could smile, simply because the prospect of anything real, even a disaster, had revived her. The artificiality of Brevisham was beginning to get on her nerves. Something of Sybilla Hughes-Follett's own boredom had communicated itself to the place. Left a childless widow at forty, she had spent the last fifteen years fighting off this boredom by constantly changing houses, friends and religions. Brevisham was still a fairly new toy but, like all Sybilla's lavishly redecorated interiors, it suggested a stage set which might be demolished at any moment. Sometimes, when she and Archie came in to those restaurant-like meals, Clara was almost surprised to find the servants and the furniture still there.

'Some honeymoon,' said Archie, looking considerably less cheerful than Clara. 'The ghastly thing, darling, is that it looks as if I'll have to go up to London today. I've simply got to sort this out with Bell and Jimmy.'

'I'll come with you.'

'I say – will you?' His face lightened, then clouded again. 'But where can you go? I'll have to hang about in bars for hours. Probably have to stay the night if I'm to get hold of Uncle Stanley.'

'I shan't butt in on your conference. You seem to forget we've got a house of our own now.'

'Good Lord. I'd almost forgotten. At the worst, we've got a roof till June. But won't you be bored to tears all alone?'

'Not as bored as I would be here.'

'I say . . . I'm simply longing to get into our own place. What about you?'

'More than anything,' she said truthfully. 'I suppose we couldn't . . .'

They looked at each other questioningly. Then Clara shook her head.

'No. It would be too rude to your aunt. After all, she *has* been awfully kind.'

'Hang Sybilla. It's you I'm thinking of. I wanted you to have a bit of comfort.'

'I've had so much, I feel bloated. And if we are going to be ruined, it seems sillier than ever living in this sort of way.'

Archie groaned.

'When I think of all the things I'd like to give you . . . Lord, I hope I haven't really landed you in a mess. If this job *did* go phut we wouldn't have a penny. But it just *can't* happen. I'll get Fairholm to fork out some of my cash if I have to wring his neck to get it.'

'We've still got your three hundred a year. Lots of people haven't that.'

'Doesn't leave more than about a quid a week after the rent's paid.'

'I'll go back to doing advertisements. I made £250 one year. If I went on the regular staff instead of free-lancing, I might get quite a lot more.'

'Shut up,' said Archie fiercely. 'That's one thing I won't stand for. You're not going to slave at something you loathe just because I've let you down.'

She said, in sudden panic:

'We've got the house till June. Oh, Archie, I just couldn't bear to let it go. I'd do anything rather than lose my little house.' She added hastily, '*our* little house'.

He looked at her rather ruefully.

'You adore that place, don't you?'

'Yes, I do,' she admitted. 'Don't you?'

'Oh yes. Rather. Even if I do feel as if I'd bump my head on the ceiling. But then I'd adore any place where I could live with you. Theatrical digs – Tithe Place – Brevisham . . . it's all one to me.'

She wanted to say, 'To me too.' But before she could get the words out, he came over and kissed her.

'You shall have your precious house. Anywhere where you can put up with your ghastly husband a little longer.'

'Really, Archie. We haven't been married a week and you talk as if I were threatening to run away.'

'You'd be justified,' he said sadly. 'You know that, old thing.'

She kissed him with remorseful affection, saying softly what was almost the truth:

'I'm quite happy. I don't want things to be any different.'

Chapter Four

A few hours later, when Archie dropped her at the little box of a house in Tithe Place, Clara felt the first positive pleasure she had known since they danced together the first night at Brevisham.

She had discovered the house one afternoon in late February. She had been wandering about London on one of the many restless, discontented days of the interval between the tour and the wedding. During those early months of 1921, living once more in Valetta Road with her parents and her grandmother, she had felt like a traveller waiting to start on a journey. She had not particularly looked forward to it: there were moments when she would gladly have cancelled it. But she had committed herself and there had been nothing to do but idle about at home, neither inhabiting the present nor dreaming excitedly about the future.

Her preparations for her marriage had been sketchy and listless till the final rush of buying clothes. This time she had been able to afford only a minimum. Knowing that her father was short of money, she had felt guilty about his paying for the expensive wedding which neither she nor Archie wanted but which his pathetic pride demanded. He had been distressed when they had decided to take a small furnished house or flat to save trouble. To him it seemed almost immoral that a young couple should not begin life among their own furniture. But Clara and Archie had one trait in common; neither of them took the least interest in domestic details. All that they wanted was to walk straight into something ready-made that would give them the minimum of trouble.

That particular afternoon she had had no intention of house-hunting. She had been walking blindly, taking any turning at random, till she somehow found herself in the King's Road. She knew Chelsea hardly at all but she remembered that a friend of Stephen's called Clive Heron lived there. He had known Stephen in the army and Clara had been both amused and impressed by him when the three of them had occasionally spent an evening together in the Garrick School days. Wanting to forget everything connected with Stephen, she had not thought of Heron for months. Now, suddenly, she remembered his address and found her way to Paultons Square. She stood outside his house and was almost on the point of ringing the bell when she realized that, at this moment, he would almost certainly be at the Home Office. At once relieved and disappointed, she walked slowly through the square, charmed by the small Georgian houses. Suddenly it occurred to her how delightful it would be to live in Chelsea and she began to explore its back streets with a growing sense of excitement.

It was a mild afternoon with a foretaste of spring; crocuses were pushing up in paved gardens and window boxes; the pale sunlight made the cream and white and grey stucco-fronted houses look like an eighteenth-century print. One crooked row, where the houses changed colour and character at each bend, particularly charmed her. The variety was so utterly unlike the uniform terraces of West Kensington that she might have been in another town, almost another country.

She began to walk slowly and stealthily; peering in at windows. Even the curtains fascinated her after the dreary tiers of serge, brocade and lace in Valetta Road. Some were brightly coloured; orange, magenta or jade; some mere pieces of printed stuff carelessly draped. Now and then they were even of dirty yellow lace with an aspidistra behind them. The windows at which she stared longest had no curtains at all and through them she could make out dim shapes of easels, jars full of brushes and canvases piled anyhow against the wall. Through one such, which was open, she saw the back of a man actually engaged in painting a picture. The smell of turpentine affected her as once the smell of the theatre had done. Without stopping to think why, she stopped and stood, clutching the railings in a kind of ecstasy. At the same moment, further down the street, a piano burst out, firm and confident, in the first movement of a Mozart concerto in C major which she particularly loved. Hearing the piano, smelling simultaneously the turpentine and the damp earth of a window box and seeing an almond tree in flower at the corner of the street she had one of her rare timeless moments when everything came together and seemed to have a significance beyond itself. The moment passed; the tree, the music, the man painting the picture resumed their separate identities. But it had left her with a discovery. Chelsea was not merely charming or 'old-world' or unlike West Kensington: it was a place where people worked. If she could only live there, feel this atmosphere all round her, she might be able to begin to work properly herself. As if to confirm it, the pianist began patiently playing a phrase over and over again. Tears of joy came into her eyes: she found herself praying incoherently: 'Oh, God . . . let me work like that one day. Oh, God, don't let me be just a messy amateur.'

At the end of the street was an extremely small house with a 'To Let' board . . . Clara boldly rang the bell and interviewed the owners. To her disappointment, they were not artists but a young couple, slightly older than herself and Archie, to whom she took an instant dislike. The wife was harshly good-looking in a brassy way and the two of them conveyed a curious impression of being at once rather too smart and indefinably seedy. Clara was not yet expert at recognizing the peculiar stamp of those who live by small sharp practices.

She fell in love with the house at sight. The small rooms with their light distempered walls and sparse, gay furniture were as unlike Valetta Road as possible; indeed unlike any place in which she had ever lived. She was horrified to find that the rent was four and a half guineas a week – more than three-quarters of Archie's allowance. But Mrs Woods pointed out that there was a separate studio which she could easily let for a pound a week. Painters and sculptors, she asserted, were simply fighting for studios in Chelsea.

The 'studio' turned out to be a stone-floored wooden shed with a dirty, broken skylight. But Clara was in too ecstatic a state to notice details. She was so dazzled by the idea of possessing a studio, as well as a house in Chelsea, that she was already planning to use it herself as a work-room. She summoned just enough shreds of commonsense not to commit herself then and there. In spite of Mrs Woods's assurance that there were half a dozen people after it, 38 Tithe Place had still been to let in April.

Archie had signed the lease a fortnight before their wedding and during that time Clara had gone over to Tithe Place on every possible occasion. The pleasure of turning the key in her own front door was one that never failed, even though she had soon discovered certain flaws in her dream house.

The rooms were even smaller than she had fancied. An ingenious arrangement of mirrors gave a deceptive sense of space, as she found out when she tried to add a few objects of her own. There were no shelves and no room to put even the smallest bookcase; the fresh light covers concealed the hardest of cheap and ill-sprung chairs; the gay rush mats, strewn with apparent negligence, were calculated camouflage for holes in the carpets. The basement, which contained a dark little dining-room and a kitchen with a battered, rusty gas-stove and a cracked sink, smelt of mice and mildew.

However, the fact that the house was so tiny gave her a good excuse for leaving the bulk of their wedding presents at Valetta Road. Both she and Archie felt oppressed by those elaborate clocks, silver bowls, dinner services and cases of cutlery which they were sure they would never need even if there had been any room to put them. Since she was making yet one more new beginning, it was more fun to travel light; unencumbered by objects chosen by people of her parents' generation. Nevertheless, there was something about the atmosphere of 38 Tithe Place which faintly disturbed her. She decided that, since they were not yet actually living there, it must be because it still seemed to belong to the Woodses whom she disliked more each time she saw them.

Today, as Archie carried in their luggage, she thought she would really begin to inhabit the house and make it her own.

'Don't know when I'll be back, old thing,' he said as he kissed her goodbye in the hall that was so low that his head almost touched the ceiling. 'But you bet it will be the very first minute I can get away.'

As he reached the bottom of the steps, he turned, ran up again and caught her in his arms just as she was shutting the door.

'I just can't believe it,' he said. 'To think I'll come back tonight and find you here in our own house. Let's wash out Brevisham, shall we? After all, this is where we really begin.'

When he had gone, Clara wandered from room to room without attempting to unpack. All she wanted was to savour the intense pleasure of having, for the first time, a place where she could do as she chose. Even her father had no right to come here unless she invited him. At Valetta Road, though he had long ceased to be an alarming figure, her heart still jumped with the old apprehension when she heard his latchkey turn in the lock. Now, the click of a key could only be Archie's. Whatever she might come to feel about Archie, she was convinced that she could never be afraid of him.

Sitting in one of the Woodses broken-springed chairs, she closed her eyes in the effort to take in this enormous change in her life. It was Archie who had made all this possible. She felt again that glow of gratitude that was almost love. Her father had been so disturbed at the mere suggestion of her living alone or even sharing a flat with another girl that she had not had the courage to defy him. It occurred to her that, if she and Archie had been brother and sister, no one would have minded their setting up house. Slightly shocked at the thought which was so nearly a wish, she opened her eyes and stared at her wedding ring to remind herself that they were husband and wife.

In his remorse after that first night, she had had difficulty in persuading Archie to drink so much as a glass of sherry. Once convinced that he was forgiven, he had been as gay as a schoolboy let off a punishment. She had an odd sense that, in the last three days, she had grown older and Archie younger. There seemed a wilder disproportion than ever between the implications of the Nuptial Mass and their actual behaviour. They were like two children playing truant from school. At Brevisham, Archie had wanted to spend most of the day playing invented games such as they used to play with Charles at Maryhall. But though she tried hard to enter into the spirit of them, she easily grew bored. She had managed to hide her boredom but there were moments when she wondered how long she was going to have to keep up the part of Wendy to Archie's Peter Pan.

One tiny episode had shaken her far more than the tragi-comedy of their wedding night. For hours one morning she had fetched sticks and stones for Archie while he dammed a stream with the absorption with which he used to work his model railway. When at last he had finished his dam, he had turned to her with shining eyes.

'There, my girl,' he had said, holding her to him with a masterfulness unusual in him. 'You haven't married a dud after all. That dam will hold against the deluge.'

Suddenly, she had had to use all her self-control not to pull away some of the stones and release the imprisoned water. The impulse was so violent that for a second she had almost lost consciousness. And in that second she had had a kind of instantaneous dream in which she was a railway engine driven by Charles Cressett and Archie.

As if it were dangerous to think too much, she jumped up from the chair. Immediately she was conscious of the number of mirrors in the tiny space. Three different angles of her head and shoulders and one full length figure sprang towards her. The little room, with its holland covers and primrose walls and arty rush mats, seemed to close in on her. For a moment it was an effort to remember that this house was the symbol of her new-found freedom and not a room in a horrible story she had once heard where each day the walls of a prisoner's cell drew imperceptibly nearer together. She turned towards the window and looked out into the sunlit street. On the corner of the opposite pavement was a high oblong block of red brick which suggested a town hall. It had such a secular air from the outside that she had only recently discovered that it was a Catholic church. Now its uncompromising bulk, which interrupted the row of charming dwarf houses and partly blocked the light from her own, seemed both a relief and an irritation. It was like the intrusion of a firm Nannie into the nursery. The intrusion allays panic but it reduces the magic palace once again to toy bricks. She was about to turn away, like a sulky child, when she noticed a man walking along the stretch of pavement in front of the church.

He was tall and heavily built, with a rather impressive head which struck her as vaguely familiar, as if she had seen it photographed somewhere. There was something impressive too about the way he wore his shabby old jacket and torn, open-necked shirt. What interested her most was that he carried a large canvas under one arm and a frame over the other. Here was proof that she was really living in Chelsea where it was as natural to see painters walking about bareheaded carrying their pictures as to see bowler-hatted bank clerks carrying despatch cases in West Kensington.

She watched him reverently as he crossed over to her side of the street. Forgetting that she was visible, she gave an admiring smile. The smile was not for the man himself but for his profession and she was dismayed when he stopped dead under her window and smiled too. He was so tall that their eyes were almost on a level; his were grey and bright as a boy's though there were crow's feet round them and he was evidently much older than herself. There was an oddly youthful delicacy too about the features of his plump, full-moon face. His smile, which made dimples in his fleshy, but not flabby cheeks, was so unabashed and cheerful that she had to go on smiling herself. Then, suddenly, she turned away and hurried into the passage. The sitting-room was so small and the window so large that there was no hiding in it. She stayed for a minute or two in the dark, narrow hallway, half-excited, half-afraid. Perhaps in Chelsea people thought nothing of ringing strangers' door bells. It would not do to be stuffy and conventional as if one were still living in West Kensington.

She longed to meet this painter – any painter – but she wished she had not smiled at him like that. Something about him strongly suggested that he put only one interpretation on smiles from strange young women. After a few moments she ran upstairs to the bedroom and peered cautiously from behind the curtain. The man was still in the street, moving away very slowly and looking back hopefully over his shoulder at every other step.

When he was out of sight, she felt suddenly exhilarated. She decided she must stop mooning about from room to room and do something about organizing her new life. The house, though tidy, had an indefinable air of neglect. When she went to the dressing-table to take off her hat, she found an even film of dust on the mirror. Evidently the charwoman whom they had taken over from the Woods had not come in every day as she had been paid to do. There had been no time to warn her of their sudden return. Had she meant to leave everything to the last day, banking on their not finding her out?

Clara felt cheated and angry. Though she was aware of knowing little more about housekeeping than Dora Copperfield, she resented being treated like a fool. However, perhaps she was being unjust to Mrs Pritchard. Supposing she were ill – so ill that she would be unable to come back for weeks? Clara had no intention of sweeping and dusting and scrubbing. She decided she had better put on her hat and go round and see what had happened.

Congratulating herself on having been businesslike enough to have made a note of the address, she set out full of virtuous zeal. But by the time she found the house, which turned out to be nearly a mile from Tithe Place, she felt considerably less efficient. Mrs Pritchard, a youngish woman, with paste slides in her bobbed hair, who bore an odd resemblance to Mrs Woods, was smoking a cigarette in her open doorway. Mrs Pritchard assured her that she had been ever so poorly the last few days but would be round at nine sharp tomorrow though she wasn't really up to it. No one could have looked less like an invalid but Clara could not meet the challenge in those sharp green eyes. She thanked Mrs Pritchard meekly, dared not mention the money and walked away as fast as possible, aware of those sharp eyes boring into the back of her head.

Even when she was back again in Tithe Place, she was still conscious of Mrs Pritchard's contemptuous stare. Used to the friendly servants at Valetta Road, who thought nothing too much trouble for 'Miss Clara' and who were as honest as the day, it had not occurred to her that a daily help might become a tyrant. She could not get rid of her because the Woodses had made it a condition that she should be kept on. Indeed, she began to wonder whether the woman were not a kind of spy for their landlords.

To try and convince herself that the house was, after all, theirs for the time being and she was free to do as she liked, she unpacked and arranged her clothes and the few wedding presents they had brought over. She even daringly changed the position of some of the Woods's furniture and put away some of their ornaments, replacing them with her own books. By the time she had finished and gone out and bought some flowers, it was late in the afternoon and dusk was beginning to shadow the windows with blue. She began to look forward desperately to Archie's return.

She sat down, lit a cigarette, and her mind wandered back to the painter. How she envied that man, looking so happy and assured, not caring in the least that his jacket was old and shapeless and his shirt torn. How she wished she could be like that, really free, caring only for one's work and utterly absorbed in it. She had already convinced herself that he must be a very good painter. Why hadn't she had the courage to speak to him?

Perhaps at that very moment he had been looking for a studio. Hadn't she, after all, a studio to let? True, she had meant to use it herself for writing. But how stimulating it would be to have a real painter working just across their tiny courtyard. There was something, she was sure, about the smell of turpentine and linseed oil that would make her *want* to write – to work hard for hours every day like that pianist down the road, not just mess about with unfinished beginnings or bring off a fluke now and then like an amateur. She would put up a 'To let' notice tomorrow and see what happened.

Forgetting all about Archie, forgetting that she was tired and hungry, she ran out to the 'studio' to examine its possibilities. It was smaller than she had supposed at first and, now that the Woodses had piled empty crates of beer bottles and two tin trunks in one corner, one really could not think of it as anything but a large shed. Moreover, there were no means whatever of heating or lighting it. It had been a warm spring day but the 'studio' had a cellar-like chill and its stone floor numbed her feet through her thin shoes. Shivering as she walked through the small paved yard, bordered by a strip of earth in which grew a sooty laurel and three anaemic, fading hyacinths, her spirits sank again almost to zero. No one could paint there; no one could even write there. She made a final tour of the house, though she knew every detail of its three pairs of box-like rooms by heart. Where *had* she supposed she was going to write? The only solid table was in the basement dining-room, the one dark spot in the house. The sitting-room was unthinkable; the spare room too small to house even a school desk besides the bed; there was, in fact, nowhere but the bathroom that had enough floor space to put an extra table and chair. Ending her tour in the kitchen, she realized again that she was remarkably hungry. There was nothing in the larder and, if she and Archie were to have any breakfast, she must go out and hunt for some food.

By luck, she found a tiny shop, almost like a country grocer's, still open. As she walked back laden with tea, butter, bread, eggs and condensed milk, she remembered guiltily that she had not left a note for Archie. He had counted so much on finding her there when he got home. It was not till she turned into

Tithe Place, that she realized how much she herself was counting on finding him in. When she saw that the windows were dark, she could hardly bring herself to turn her key in the door.

Fumbling without success for the switch in the passage, she could have sworn she heard someone moving on the upper floor. She called weakly: 'Archie – is that you?' There was no answer. When at last she found the switch she was trembling all over. She forced herself to go upstairs but there was, of course, no one there. Afraid to pull the curtains, she turned on the lights in all the six rooms and installed herself in the little sitting-room staring out into the street and hoping that every male figure that moved into the circle of the lamp at the corner might be Archie. At last she could bear being alone no longer. Leaving all the lights on, she dashed out into the street and across to the church. She rattled vainly at the handle of the iron-studded door. It was locked. She stood with her cheek against the door, praying incoherently, trying to feel the presence of the Blessed Sacrament behind it. After a few minutes she grew a little calmer and found courage to cross the road again. A man was now standing where she herself had stood in the window. Unable to make out his face against the light, she had another rush of terror till she realized that it could be no one but Archie.

Chapter Five

Archie said thickly:

'Where the hell did you get to? Had the wind up. Lights on all over the show. No Clara. Whass it all mean?'

Clara tried to explain but he was too drunk to take it in. He collapsed heavily on to the tiny sofa and tried to pull her on to his knee. She avoided him and sat on a chair against the wall, as far away from him as was possible in the box of a room.

'Can't bear touch me, eh?' he said belligerently. 'Think I've had a few? An' why shouldn't I have a few? Bloody well needed them. Nice day I've had. Come home and what do I find? Wife gone. First money gone. Then wife gone.'

'I've not gone. Oh, do *try* and tell me what's happened.'

'Nothing's happened. Tha's the point. Ab-so-luly nothing – Napoo. Sunk.'

'You mean your uncle won't – '

He blinked at her, suddenly solemn.

'Not a bloody penny. There's a nice bloody uncle for you. Very offensive about my frien's – I took exception. Poor old Bell. Simply wouldn't listen proposition. *Water*-tight prop'sition. And my money, mark you. Who the hell else's? Eh? Tell me that if you can. It's free country, isn't it?' His voice rose aggressively again. 'Well go on . . . tell me . . . is it free country or not?'

'Yes . . . I suppose so.' She had never seen him in a state approaching this before.

'Glad you agree something I say. Think I'm a bloody fool, don' you? But you've got to admit chap's got right to his own money if it *is* free country. Jimmy agrees. Bell agrees. Nice chaps – absoluly dead right. And now where are we? Three poor sods . . . all . . . utterly . . . sunk.'

He rambled on incoherently. At moments he forgot who she was and argued angily with her as if she were his uncle or commiserated with her and invited her to drown it in a short one as if she were Lister or Bell. At others he would be conscious of her again, now remorseful, now resentful.

Sometimes it was:

'Only girl in the world. Married her on false pretenshes and now look at the bloody mess I've made. Went away and I don' blame her.'

Sometimes:

'How the hell d'you expect me to do anything when you think I'm utter dud? Don't argue – You know you do. Only got to look at your face. Never believed in me: never for one second. Old Jimmy was right. Never listen to a woman. Wet-blankets one and all.'

It was like a nightmare sitting there in the bright little room with this man who looked like Archie and spoke in Archie's voice but with whom she could make no contact. Anything she said, any questions she asked seemed to reach him in some form other than intelligible words, as puzzling or even threatening gestures. Sometimes when she spoke, he smiled at her foolishly: sometimes he put up his arm as if to ward off a blow. Once he lurched over to her, grabbed her by the shoulders and began to shake her. The pouring out of this incoherent talk seemed to fuddle him more and more. He was both more absurd and more frightening than Stephen had been at his worst. Stephen, even when he could hardly stand, had always retained a certain charm. He might no longer be able to identify Clara or anyone else but he created a kind of fantastic world and invited anyone who was with him to share it. If he was pugnacious, he behaved like Don Quixote riding at the windmills; if he was melancholy, he declaimed poetry or apostrophized the lamp-post, on which he proposed to hang himself, with articulate eloquence. Right up to the moment of his final collapse which was always sudden and silent, he remained recognizably the same person. Paler than ever, his eyes glittering, Stephen drunk had something of the air of a fallen angel. Archie drunk seemed almost sub-human. As he sat hunched up with his long arms dangling almost to the floor, his thick, low-growing hair falling forward over the big nose, now red and swollen, he suggested Caliban.

At last, after one of his long, mumbling tirades, she could bear it no longer. Her head was aching with the strain of trying to make any contact with him. She had eaten nothing since their breakfast at Brevisham and the fumes of stale whisky made her feel sick. She tried to make her escape but, before she could get to the door, he made a dash at her and wrapped her in his arms. He held her so tightly that she could make no movement beyond turning her head away. If he kissed her at the moment, she thought she really would be sick. Suddenly, he crumpled up, slithered to his knees, still clutching her fast round the waist and burst into loud, blubbering sobs.

'Don't go . . . Darling girl . . . Only girl in world . . . Don't leave me . . . Don't run away . . . Can't live . . . Absolutely can't live if you go.'

She managed at last to get him into the little spare room next door and heave him somehow on to the bed. He gave one or two deep grunting sighs and fell asleep, breathing heavily and painfully like a patient under an anaesthetic. She found rugs and blankets to cover him and put a jug of water beside him. These small practical tasks broke her sense of nightmare. He lay there so ugly, pitiful and defenceless that she could no longer feel frightened or even angry. She bent down and kissed his cold damp forehead and the half-open mouth twitched in a wry smile.

She went upstairs to their own bedroom where the light had been burning all those hours. As she went to the window to draw the curtains, she saw the great dark bulk of the church opposite against a sky full of stars. But now she no longer resented its presence. She leant her hot cheek against the glass. The tears prickled under her closed eyelids but she was too exhausted to cry. After some minutes, though her head throbbed and burned, she felt calmer. She forced herself to look for some sheets and made up one of the two beds. Tired as she was, it was some time before she fell asleep. She tried to put some order into her spinning thoughts. From what she had gathered from Archie, there could be little doubt that there was no hope for the Club. He had indeed talked wildly of new people who could be interested, even shouted once or twice that his uncle would be sorry for having missed a bloody wonderful chance, but she had no reasonable hope left. She must pull herself together, think of a plan, get some work before they were literally penniless. But her mind refused to bite on anything concrete. The future appeared only as a menacing, impenetrable wall. She gave up at last and let small jagged images project themselves on the screen of her closed eyelids; her father's agonized face when he had returned with his new gloves; Charles Cressett grinning at her in one of his fiendish moods; Archie drunk; Archie sober; Archie smiling as he left her twelve hours ago saying 'This is where we really begin'.

Chapter Six

Clara had been married for two months. Having for the first time no definite occupation, she could not establish any order in her life. The fact that Archie had none either, and was even more untidy and impractical then she was herself, was rapidly reducing her to a slattern. Day by day she grew more inert and apathetic, weighed down by a sense of guilt but too listless to pull herself together.

Archie had tried desperately to persuade some member of his family to put up the money to save the Theatre Club but everyone, including Aunt Sybilla, had firmly refused. Now that the scheme was dead and buried, he continued to spend most of his time in bars and drinking clubs with Lister and his friends. His excuse was that, if he 'hung around with the boys', sooner or later something would turn up. Sometimes he came back fairly sober: more often drunk. Twice she had had to bail him out of Vine Street. His moods varied between wild optimism and penitent pessimism. Already she was almost immune to both. Meanwhile another quarter's rent would soon be due for the house. She knew that Archie was spending far more than his allowance. The odd cheques they had been given as wedding presents had long ago been cashed and frittered away. For the past week or two she had been imploring Archie to tell her how much, if anything, still remained of his legacy. But he kept evading the question, saying that things were rather complicated at the moment and a lot of chaps owed him quite a bit of money and it would be time to start worrying when one of his cheques actually bounced.

This sense of insecurity, instead of bracing Clara to try and make some money herself, completely unnerved her. Once, when there was a chance that Lister might have been able to fix the two of them up in a touring company she was panic-stricken. Not only was she convinced that she would never be capable of acting again, but she could not face all the reorganization this would mean. They would have to give up the house which she clung to though there were times when she almost loathed it. Even the thought of packing her clothes was an intolerable burden. She was as relieved as Archie was disappointed when this scheme, too, came to nothing.

There was a positive reason, as well as sheer inertia, which conpelled her to try to stay on in Chelsea. At least she could wander about the streets and feel that people were working all about her. This was more often torture than comfort for, far from catching any infection of diligence, she became more and more incapable of writing anything, even the simplest letter. Original work was impossible. She told herself that, in any case, she had no right to attempt it until she had made some money. Her advertising firm was beginning to press her for some overdue pieces of copy. Day after day she sat down at the rickety dining-table in the basement, the only table big enough to work on, only to find herself at the end of an hour with two sentences begun and scratched out. Then she would take up the paper, hoping to warm herself up by reading other advertisements and find, at the end of another hour, that she had read everything in it down to the Stock Exchange prices till her mind was more fuddled and inert than ever.

Archie was out so much that she found herself more alone than she had ever been in her whole life. Yet she made no effort to seek out any of her old friends and took to putting off people at the last moment when they invited her out. She did not know what obscure impulse drove her to isolate herself in this way but, once she had formed the habit, she could not break it. The more she was alone, the more she became conscious of her own emptiness. Sometimes she even doubted whether she existed at all. Once this sense of non-existence was so acute that she ran up from the basement to the sitting-room full of mirrors almost expecting to find nothing reflected in them. But her face stared back at her anxiously from various angles and she was horrified to see how much she had changed in a few weeks. It was not merely that, in the sunlight, she had a dulled look as if there were a film of dust all over her skin and hair but that there was a vacancy in her expression that frightened her. She found herself addressing her reflection as she used to do when she was a child. 'Really, my dear,' she said severely, 'you look as if you weren't in your right mind.'

After that, Clara bought herself a stout black notebook exactly like the ones her father always used for writing his lecture notes, and began to keep a kind of diary. Writing in it gave her the illusion that she was at least producing something. If she was going to talk to herself, it was surely better to do so on paper. She might even discover something curious or useful in the process.

All sorts of odd things went into this secret book: reflections on her own character, severe exhortations to herself, scraps of conversation overheard in the street, descriptions of rooms or faces; dreams, speculations about religion and life, curious names which she might one day use in a story. She knew that the notebook was cheating. Sometimes she was so disgusted with the triteness or the flatulence of much that she wrote in it that she was tempted to destroy it. Suppose anyone who had ever credited her with a crumb of intelligence, let alone talent, were to read it? The thought was insupportable to her vanity. Nevertheless she continued to make entries at fairly regular intervals, offsetting the indulgence of this 'pretence' writing by refusing to allow herself to erase even the most shaming passages. It would do her good, she told herself savagely, to realize to what maundering idiocy she could descend.

Occasionally she and Archie lunched on Sundays at Valetta Road. When they did so, they made such an effort to appear a care-free modern couple that they almost deceived themselves. Clara, who might have been slouching about for days in the same crumpled frock, would dress and make up with as much care as if she were dressing for a stage part. Archie would shave, put on a clean shirt and only accept a second whisky after much pressing from her father. For an hour or two Clara would regain her sense of continuity enough to believe that the paralysed drifting of her days in Tithe Place would not go on for ever and that her life was not irremediably broken. Seeing Archie and her father's genuine affection for each other, her heart would warm to both of them. Stimulated by this and by the meaner wish not to let her mother have the satisfaction of knowing that her marriage looked like being even more of a failure than Isabel had predicted, she would behave to Archie with unusual sweetness. Archie, who never bore grudges, would respond at once so that by the time they left, arm-in-arm, Clara had almost convinced herself that, this coming week, things would definitely take a turn for the better. So far, however, they had not done so.

The last Sunday of June was Clara's twenty-second birthday: they were both invited to lunch at Valetta Road. That morning Archie was feeling so ill after a night out with Lister and the rest that he could barely open his eyes, let alone get up, by the time they were due to start. Reluctant, not to leave Archie to his hangover but to face her parents without him, Clara went alone. As she walked to the bus she thought rather bitterly of the difference between this birthday and her last. Her father, always punctilious about special anniversaries, had made an occasion of her twenty-first. There had been a dinner party of a dozen people with wines carefully chosen by Claude, including Château Yquem of her birth year, 1899, as well as the ritual champagne. He had also given her a cheque for fifty pounds. How much more she needed fifty pounds this year with the rent for Tithe Place due in a few days. What a fantastically large sum it had seemed at the time and how quickly it had melted, mostly on dinners and drinks for Stephen. She had not dared to ask Stephen to the party but she had asked his friend Clive Heron, the man who lived in Paultons Square and whom she had not run into since she came to Chelsea.

As she walked despondently along the King's Road wishing she could put the clock back a year, a man's voice said:

'Well, are you going to cut me dead?'

She looked up, only half-surprised and altogether pleased, to see Clive Heron himself. Her first reaction was relief that, for once, she was decently dressed and made up; her second that this was a good omen for a birthday which had begun so gloomily.

'How extraordinary,' she said, smiling up at him. 'I was just thinking about you.'

'*Most* extraordinary. *Very* queer,' he said in the mock

Bloomsbury voice he used except when he was unusually serious. 'Now *why*, may I asl.?'

Though Clara had only met Heron at intervals during the two years since she had first met him and he was reputed to be a 'difficult' person, she had always been completely at ease with him. In the intervals she was apt to forget his very existence but, as soon as she saw him again, she always felt a peculiar pleasure. She felt, too, as if they were resuming an interrupted conversation.

'Because it's my birthday.'

'Your birthday,' he said gravely. 'Dear me. Already? I have hardly recovered from your last birthday. Your father's wines completely metagrobolized me. Are you having another orgy?'

'No. It's all going to be rather dismal.'

'Come and have a drink. I was just taking a pre-prandial stroll to the Six Bells.'

'I'd love to but I daren't. I've got to lunch with my family and I'm late already.'

'Vexatious. Now I suppose I shall have to turn round and accompany you to your bus.'

'You needn't. I know it's agony for you to change your plans.'

'True. But I get an exquisite pleasure from occasionally mortifying myself. Besides, it appeases my eternal sense of guilt.'

As he turned and walked in her direction, Clara wondered why anybody who always appeared as gay and reasonable as Clive Heron should suffer from a sense of guilt. Probably it was only one of his amusing affectations. Looking up at him, she thought again how unlike anyone else he seemed. Dressed as usual with meticulous neatness and extreme conventionality, he always struck her as a creature who, in attempting to adopt a protective colouring which would make it invisible, merely emphasized its strangeness. Tall and preternaturally slender, there was something birdlike about the movement of his long legs and the quick turns of his small head that made his name oddly appropriate. He had a way, too, in talk of suddenly pouncing on something that interested him, like a heron spearing a fish.

'You are remarkably silent,' he said, after a moment. 'What have you been up to all this time?'

She told him that she was married.

'Yes, yes,' he said impatiently. 'I know. Stephen said something to that effect.'

'I didn't know he knew. Do you often see him?'

'Hardly ever. I can't stand that ghastly woman his wife. What a fool he was not to marry you. I told him so roundly. Of course it would have been disastrous.'

Clara laughed. 'How do you know?'

'I know everything. Surely you realize that by this time? Far more infallible than any of your Popes.'

'Are you speaking *ex cathedra*?'

'Certainly. However, no doubt you've married someone equally unsuitable.'

Since for some reason she was always compelled to be frank with Clive Heron, she answered:

'Yes.'

He darted her a look from the clear, light-lashed eyes which gleamed so intelligently behind his pince-nez. She could not imagine Heron's face without those pince-nez. Poised precisely on the bridge of his elegant nose – all his features were small and delicately finished – they seemed as much part of him as a bird's crest.

'I could have *told* you so. *Why* didn't you consult me?' he groaned.

'Because I can never bring myself to the point of ringing you up.'

'Precisely. Neither can I. That's the trouble with both of us. Hopeless neurotics. Yet I constantly get very near the point.'

'I got as far as your doorstep one day. In fact that's probably why I'm now living two streets away from you in Tithe Place.'

'Tithe Place.' He heaved a sigh. 'Really, then, there's no excuse for not doing something about it. Not that it *really* makes things any easier. I can't bear dropping in or being dropped in upon. I should still have to brace myself to use the telephone. Still, I am prepared to go to considerable lengths to see you. Ring me at the Home Office. *Yes-ss. You* ring *me*. We'll have a nice dinner together and moan about the *horrors* of the universe. The fair white scroll of the universe on which God so misguidedly scrabbled the history of mankind.'

'Here's my bus,' said Clara regretfully.

'Dear me, yes. A bus,' he said, looking at it over the tops of his pince-nez. '*Very* portentous. You had better mount it.'

As she did so, he gingerly raised the hat which looked so much too big for his small, shapely head, revealing the impeccably neat reddish gold hair which, she knew, caused him nervous misery to ruffle.

'All in perfect order,' she said reassuringly from the step. 'But *do* put it on again in case.'

'The *only* person who understands about my traumatic hair. Goodbye, now, goodbye. Write down all I said. And . . . oh, dear yes, remember me to your astonishing father. Has he any of the Château Yquem left?'

The bus started with a jerk.

'I'll bring you a bottle some day, if he has,' said Clara, almost falling off the step into Heron's arms. He pushed her upright.

'Don't titubate. I'm too frail to cope with titubating women.'

The bus suddenly stopped again. Heron said furiously:

'Why can't the beastly thing make up its mind? Machines have no right to be neurotic.'

The noise of the engine starting up again made it impossible for Clara to catch some admonition he called from the pavement. It began 'Why on *earth*' and ended with something which sounded remarkably like 'marry *me*'. But this, she decided, was impossible. One of the things about Clive Heron that made him seem to belong to a different species was the difficulty of envisaging him married to anyone. Not that he suggested a dried-up bachelor: on the contrary there was an extraordinary freshness about him which made him look considerably nearer twenty than thirty. He took, moreover, an ardent and analytical interest in the love-affairs of his friends. Stephen, who had known him first in the army and had a great affection for him, said he was too much like a cat ever to attach himself to anyone. Stephen had also been unflatteringly surprised that Clive Heron had apparently taken a fancy to Clara at their first meeting. Clara knew that he liked her and that something about her – she had no idea what it could be – seemed to please and amuse him. But never, in her wildest moments, had she ever considered the possibility of his falling in love with her or she with him. Even if he had used the words 'marry me', they could not conceivably have any personal reference. Next time she saw him, she would ask him exactly what he had said. Knowing Heron's habit of vanishing, though he seldom left London, as completely as if he had gone on a world tour, it might be months before she had the opportunity. The fact that he lived only three minutes from her own house made it almost more unlikely that she would run into him by chance. Not that he would consciously avoid her now that they were near neighbours, but he hated unexpected meetings so much that she could almost fancy that he had the power of making himself invisible to avoid them.

She realized, when she almost overran the point where she had to change on to the West Kensington bus, that she had been thinking about Clive Heron longer than she had ever thought about him before. She realised, too, that these thoughts had been curiously comforting. When at last she rang the bell in Valetta Road, she felt more lighthearted than she had done for months.

Chapter Seven

Inevitably the birthday lunch was strained. Old Mrs Batchelor kept enquiring curiously what was the matter with Archie and would not let the subject alone. Finally, Isabel lost her temper and said:

'Probably Archie was drunk last night and Clara is too loyal to say so. After your own experiences one would suppose you might have learnt a little tact.'

There was a painful silence. Claude, always hurt by any reference to the fact that his adored father had at one time been a heavy drinker, turned white with anger. Clara's grandmother laid down her knife and fork, sniffed and fumbled for her handkerchief. Only her mother, with ostentatious calm, went on eating.

'Really Isabel,' Clause said at last. 'That seems to me quite unjustified.' He turned to Clara. 'Please tell Archie how *very* sorry I am he could not come. You might add how much I appreciate his unselfishness in letting you desert him when he is feeling so ill. You must go back and look after him as soon as possible. But, before you go, my dear, could you spare me just a minute or two in the study?'

Though no painful interview had taken place in the study for several years, Clara's heart still sank at those works. Back among the shelves of old books and neatly labelled black files, sitting in the huge faded green armchair her father had used at Cambridge and staring at the dusty casts of Plato and Athene, she felt once more an apprehensive child. It was the first time she had been alone with him since her marriage. Though she no longer feared his disapproval more than anything else in the world; though, ever since her re-engagement to Archie, he had treated her with the utmost gentleness; something of her old sense of guilt returned as he seated himself at his desk, sucking at his pipe and absently jabbing a fountain-pen in and out of a bowl of shot as he often did when worried.

For a moment she thought he was indeed angry. He was frowning and his jaw thrust forward in the way she had always taken as a storm signal. Only once before had she known him angry on her birthday. That was an occasion at Mount Hilary which she could still hardly bear to remember.

The nuns had confiscated the beginning of a novel she had been writing in secret. They had given her no chance to explain that she had made her characters behave as badly as possible in those opening chapters because she meant to convert them all sensationally in the last. Without telling her, they had sent the manuscript to her father and even threatened to expel her. The day he came down to deal with this situation happened to be her birthday. Summoned to the parlour at an unusual time, she thought his visit was a delightful birthday surprise. But, as she was sliding excitedly over the slippery parquet to greet him, she saw the expression on his face. It was so thunderous that she had stopped dead; her knees trembling so much that she could not take another step. He had been in no mood to listen to explanations even if she had not been too paralysed to attempt them. The things he had said to her that day had been so terrible that there was a blank in her mind about the end of the interview. She could not remember his going away; she had nothing but a confused recollection of sobbing in the chapel all through Benediction and being put to bed in the infirmary. The next time she saw him, he had been quite genial and had made no reference to the object of that terrible visit. Neither of them had ever mentioned it since.

As she sat there now, waiting for him to speak, she realized that it was the eighth anniversary of that incident. She had a sudden absurd notion when he cleared his throat, rather portentously, to speak, that he was going, at last, to refer to it. Suppose he were going to give her, after all these years, a chance to explain? Suppose he were actually to forgive her for what had outraged him in what she had written, in all innocence, at fourteen? Might that relieve the appalling guilt and self-mistrust which overcame her every time she tried to write anything which was not merely confected? In the last two months, this guilt and impotence had spread to anything she wrote at all: to advertising copy, even to letters; to anything, in fact, designed to be read by others. Only the black notebook, though it contained much that might make her reasonably feel guilty, was exempt from the blight, simply because it was secret.

All her father said, however, when he spoke at last, was:

'Forgive me, my dear . . . you have every right to be offended if I am wrong . . . but was there any grain of truth in what your mother suggested just now?'

Clara's mind had wandered so far that she could not at once bring it into focus. She frowned, trying to remember precisely what it was that Isabel had suggested.

'Oh . . . about Archie, you mean? As a matter of fact she guessed perfectly right. But I didn't want her to know.'

'I appreciate that. I admire your loyalty very much. Very much indeed. You can be sure, Clara, that nothing you choose to say will go beyond this room.'

'I'm sure it won't. Still I don't think there's much point in saying anything.'

'Perhaps you're right. And I respect your silence. Yet would you mind my asking one thing?'

'Of course not.'

'Then is today exceptional? Let us say last night rather. That sort of thing happens now and then to any young man. I'm afraid it happened to me quite frequently at Cambridge. And, I regret to say, occasionally even after I was married.'

'It happens a good deal, yes.'

He sighed and bit the stem of his pipe.

'I can't tell you how sorry I am to hear that. My own impression was that Archie had taken himself in hand quite remarkably. All through your engagement . . . and on the few occasions when he's been here since your marriage . . . I've never seen him anything but perfectly sober.'

'He was wonderful for months before we got married. It's only since . . .' she stopped suddenly.

He gave a half-smile.

'Come, come. Let's hope there's no connection! But seriously, my dear, don't you think that it's time Archie got a proper job? It seems to me obvious that these shady theatrical people he goes about with – I wish to God he'd never heard of that infernal club – are doing him no good at all. Isn't it time you used your influence to keep him away from that crowd?'

'I couldn't if I tried. Archie *likes* those people. And he's determined to get into the theatre by hook or by crook.'

He said, eyeing her rather sternly:

'The last thing I want to do is to hit you when you are down. And I have nothing but admiration for the pluck with which you have taken this blow. I have never heard you reproach Archie, though I believe you were sceptical from the first about this disastrous business. All the same, Clara, I must point out that it was through you he met these people. Also, if you hadn't gone on the stage, I doubt if he would ever have had this insane idea of becoming an actor.'

She said with some heat:

'That's absolutely untrue. He talked about it years ago. The very first time I ever met him, in fact. Long before it ever entered my head to be an actress. I suppose you'll blame me for his drinking next.'

'Nonsense. I know very well it began in South America. I attribute it entirely to the shock of his mother's death and finding himself alone in the world.' He paused and glanced tenderly at the photograph of the distinguished-looking, white-bearded old man who had once been an unsuccessful village grocer. 'My poor beloved father . . . *his* trouble began with the shock of my sister's death as a baby. And no doubt with Archie . . . the shock of losing nearly all his capital – not to mention the salary those swine promised him . . . accounts for this relapse.'

He broke off, as if not quite convinced by his own words. Clara, darting a sidelong glance at her father, intercepted an equally hasty one from him. Averting their eyes, they both spoke at once.

'I'm sorry, Clara . . . what were you saying?'

'No . . . no . . . go on. Nothing at all important. I mean . . . I daresay you're right.'

He squared his shoulders and pulled fiercely at his pipe which had almost gone out.

'Things can't go on like this. Archie must pull himself together and make a fresh start. And you must help him.'

'But how?'

'I am sure Lord Fairholm would do everything possible to find him another post.'

'What . . . abroad?' she said aghast.

'Not necessarily. Nor would it matter if the salary was not very impressive. He has, after all, his allowance. The great thing is that he should have a regular job.'

'Nothing would induce Archie to ask his uncle for anything. He's definitely quarrelled with him. Anyhow, Archie would refuse point blank to work in an office. And I absolutely see his point of view.'

'Then may I ask how the two of you propose to manage? His private income barely covers this preposterous rent you are paying. That house was an absurd extravagance even when

Archie supposed his income would be more than double what it is. Now, it is sheer folly to keep it on.'

Conscious that her father was perfectly right, she bristled defensively.

'Oh, we'll manage somehow. You seem to forget that I'm quite capable of making money. I made £250 the year before I went on tour. I could probably make even more if I set my mind to it.'

'I don't deny it. But I should like to point out two things. First . . . that I never expected you to contribute one penny of anything you made to the household expenses here and you never saved one penny of it for the future. You had all that to spend on anything you fancied and I am afraid it gave you very unrealistic ideas about money. Your mother and I had exactly £250 to live on – for everything – the first year we were married.'

'Yes, I know,' said Clara peevishly. 'What was the other thing?'

'That I am sure Archie is far too fundamentally decent to wish to depend on his wife's earnings. Moreover . . .' He hesitated and cleared his throat. 'There might come a time when, even if you were contributing something, you might no longer be able to go on working.'

'Isn't that looking rather far ahead?' she asked flippantly. 'After all it's not much more than eighteen months till Archie comes into his money. Presumably I shan't be entirely decrepit at twenty-three.'

He stiffened.

'A good many things can happen in eighteen months in the life a young married couple. Particularly if they are Catholics, as, thank God, you both are. That is why it is so essential that you should not dip into whatever is left of Archie's capital.'

Clara felt her face assume the supercilious little smile he hated. She said pertly:

'Why don't you give all these awful warnings to Archie? After all, it's really up to him, isn't it?'

He flushed a little.

'I'm sorry if you think I'm prying into your private affairs.

After all, you are my only child. It's only natural that I shouldn't want to see you make a mess of your life.'

'Have I complained?' she asked coldly.

'Never for one instant. I can't say how much I admire your loyalty.'

It was Clara's turn to flush.

'I'm sorry, Daddy, I'm being rather beastly. I know you're only trying to be helpful.'

He sighed:

'If only there were some way that I could be of some help.'

On a reckless impulse, she took him up.

'Actually you could. Only I expect it might be rather a nuisance for you.'

His face brightened . . . 'Yes?'

'Well, as a matter of fact, we *are* awfully hard up at the moment. I've got various things on hand not quite finished. Even when they are, it'll be some time before I get paid and it comes in in driblets. You couldn't possibly lend me the money for this next quarter's rent? I'll pay you back, I promise.'

The moment she had said it, she realized her folly. To cover up the blunder, she launched on a lie.

'I mean . . . I'm sure Archie has all that and . . . much more in the bank still. But after what you said about not dipping in . . . I agree . . . it would be *much* more sensible not to.'

Her voice trailed away. She was quaking inside in case he challenged her. Never before had she tried to deceive him on such a scale as this. She watched his face anxiously but could not immediately read his expression. He scratched some figures on his blotting-paper, then shook his head.

'I'm very sorry indeed, my dear child, but I am afraid it's quite impossible. By my reckoning, you are asking me to lend you something over sixty pounds. I have to admit that I don't possess such a sum or anything like it. I don't get this term's salary from St Mark's for another three weeks and every farthing of that is earmarked.' He smiled ruefully. 'Now you see the results of mismanaging money. Having never managed to save anything myself, I am a shocking example for you to avoid.'

Clara felt ashamed. She knew very well that, all his life, he had given away money and helped his many poor relations so that, though he made a good deal by his coaching and his classical text-books, he had constant anxieties about money. Her mother was extravagant and he himself loved occasional outbursts of entertaining or present-giving. If he was hard up at the moment, Clara knew that it was because he had spent considerably more than he could afford on her wedding. Yet, though she was ashamed, she also felt obscurely and unfairly resentful.

She said, none too graciously.

'Forget it. I'm sorry I suggested it. But you did ask if there was anything you could do.'

'And I meant it. But, my dear child, I honestly don't think it would be helping you to encourage you to go on living in that furnished house. You could get an unfurnished place for a quarter of what you are paying now.'

'I daresay. But we haven't any furniture.'

'I'm sure we could spare you quite a lot. And I think Archie would be wise to break into the nest-egg for that. It would be a real economy in the end.'

Clara said quickly: 'Moving's out of the question. We have to give the Woods three months' notice.'

Though already she half hated Tithe Place, the thought of leaving it, still more the idea of having to take any definite action, threw her into a panic.

'You could sub-let. Incidentally there's a very pleasant little maisonette going in Baron's Court Road for £40 a year.'

'I'm sorry, Daddy. I simply couldnt *bear* to live in West Kensington. I'd rather live in a *garret* in Chelsea.'

This time he was really angry. He said sarcastically:

'I'm sorry you were forced to live for so many years in the slum that was good enough for your parents.'

'I didn't mean that.'

'Hmm. I presume you mean you prefer the atmosphere of art for art's sake and all that rot? I'm beginning to wonder whether you're not considerably more to blame than poor Archie. I can assure you this isn't at all the life I envisaged for both of you. What's more, I'm sure Archie detests it as much as I do. The boy's a gentleman and is probably longing for a quiet, decent life. No doubt you fill the place with short-haired women and long-haired men. Archie has all my sympathy if he prefers the public house.'

Through her own resentment, Clara dimly guessed that there was pain as well as anger behind this outburst. But she could make no allowances for this. She broke out almost hysterically:

'If I'd known you were going to do nothing but carp at me and criticize me, I wouldn't have come here at all today. All my life, you've wanted me to think as you thought and do what you wanted and made me feel guilty if I didn't. Why shouldn't I live as I want to? I'm not asking *you* for anything.'

Oblivious of the fact that she had just asked him for sixty pounds, Clara felt possessed by a glow of righteous fury. She felt she was defending something immensely precious almost at the risk of her life. Never had she spoken to her father like this. Yet, even as she raged, she was conscious that she had no idea what it was that she was defending with such vehemence. He turned and stared at her with his jaw dropped and his face working. At that moment, the study door opened and her mother looked in smiling.

'Clara, darling Zillah's made you such a charming birthday cake. She'll be so hurt if you don't come and look at it before she goes out for her afternoon off.'

She looked at their two faces.

'Whatever is the matter with you two? I could hear your voices all along the passage. Really, Claude, you look as if we were back in the old days and you had been scolding Clara for not doing her homework properly. You must remember she's a married woman now.'

Profoundly grateful for the interruption, Clara jumped up and followed her mother.

Outside, Isabel whispered to her:

'Darling . . . was that a rescue in the nick of time? Was Daddy being horrid and unsympathetic? He *can* be when he talks about duty and all that. Men so seldom understand what women feel.'

Clara said offhandedly:

'We were only having a rather boring discussion about houses and so on. Nothing in the least dramatic.'

Chapter Eight

The next day Archie was penitent. Instead of going off at midday as usual to meet Lister, he took Clara to lunch at a cheap little restaurant in the King's Road where the waitresses wore orange smocks and there were check cloths and earthenware pitchers on the tables.

'You can't be more fed up with me than I am,' he said. 'I didn't even give you a present. Not because I forgot. A temporary breeze at the bank.'

'Do tell me the worst. Have we *anything* left?'

'I haven't blued the lot, if that's what you mean. Things need a bit of wangling at the moment, that's all. Thank heaven, the old pittance is due this week.'

'So's our next quarter's rent.'

He started.

'Hell. It *can't* be. Thought we had ages yet. The Woodses will jolly well have to wait. Serve 'em right. They're bloodsuckers anyway.'

'I tried to borrow the money from Daddy yesterday. He hadn't got it.'

'Gosh, I wish you hadn't done that. I can hardly look him in the eye as it is. When I think of my own beastly relations – rolling in money and too mean even to lend one a fiver . . .'

Clara, still resentful from the day before, said:

'He wouldn't either in his present mood. Not to *me* at any rate.'

'What do you mean?' he asked suspiciously.

'Oh – you've entirely cut me out with Daddy. You're the blue-eyed boy and I'm the unscrupulous woman who's ruined you.'

'Don't be so sarcastic.'

'I'm not.'

'Then you're just pulling my leg. I feel rather awful because I touched him for a fiver myself last time we were over. Of course I'll pay him back. Did he say anything about it?'

She shook her head.

'He *wouldn't*,' said Archie. 'He's too damn nice. Greatest sport I ever met except one of the J's at Beaumont, old Sam Sissons.'

'He isn't always as nice as you think. He can be beastly sometimes. And very unjust, too.'

'That I simply can't believe.'

'It's perfectly true. As true as the fact that the rent's due and we owe the laundry over four pounds, not to mention various other bills. Also we still haven't paid Mrs Pritchard for last week.'

'Go on. Rub it in. You've every right to, I suppose. But . . .'

'But what?'

'I can't bear it when you look like that and use that acid sort of voice. It's not like you. You used to be so sweet.'

'I've always told you I wasn't sweet. And even if I ever had been . . .'

'You'd be as sour as a lemon after being married to me for two months? Thanks.'

'Archie, truly I don't *want* to be a beast. But things are getting me down. I just don't seem to know where I am any more.'

'They're getting me down too. And one of the things that's getting me down most is seeing you look so utterly miserable most of the time. I feel such a guilty swine that the only thing seems to be to go out and get blind.'

He looked so wretched that she said remorsefully:

'I expect it's my fault too, being miserable. I don't know what's come over me lately. I feel as if everything had got jammed up inside and out. I can't get up the energy to do anything . . . even to write my silly stuff for Rapson's. I'm tired and depressed and irritable all the time – for no reason.'

'Plenty of reason.' His low forehead, under the untidy red hair, crinkled into a deep frown. 'The way things have turned out, you must wish I'd never come barging back into your life.'

Almost frightened, since she had fought hard against the thought for weeks, reminding herself constantly about 'for better, for worse', she stretched across the table and touched his long, nicotine-stained fingers. Trying to puzzle out something, she herself frowned as she said gently:

'No, I don't. It's just that I don't seem to be able to fit things together any more. Or perhaps because *we* don't seem to fit in anywhere. Do you remember years ago – we'd only known each other a few weeks then – saying you and I were two of a kind?'

'I remember all right. The day I gave you my revolver and you didn't want to take it. God knows what I thought I meant . . . if anything.' He sighed. Clara could find nothing to say. She took one of the cigarettes from his crumpled packet of Gold Flakes and asked him for a light. Mechanically, he struck a match but, instead of lighting her cigarette, let the flame burn itself out. He took her left hand, absently removed the cigarette she held and began to twist the wedding ring on her finger.

Almost accusingly, he said:

'It's getting too tight. At Brevisham, it was so loose it nearly fell off.'

'I know. I've been getting steadily fatter for weeks. All my skirts are getting tight too.'

He dropped her hand, as suddenly as he had taken it, and lit the cigarette he had removed from her fingers. After a puff or two he said, as if to himself:

'I wonder. If we could have gone to Maryhall instead of to that beastly Brevisham . . .'

Clare said nothing. Her mind shot off on one of its tangents. They could not have gone to Maryhall because Charles's father could not have endured her being there. Yet, if Charles had not been killed, would there ever have been any question of her marrying Archie? Where did any chain of circumstances begin? What had led her, step by step, from that afternoon in the walled garden to be sitting here, facing Archie across a check tablecloth littered with crumbs and cigarette ash and bound to him for life?

She looked into his eyes as if she could find the answer there. They still recovered their clearness almost at once if he kept off drink for a day or two. The lids were still pink and puffy from his last bout but, once again, she saw in the eyes themselves that extraordinary beauty she had noticed in Birmingham. She could only describe it to herself as 'unfallen'. The contrast between that innocence and her own growing sense of being somehow inwardly corrupt was so painful that she had to look away.

'Buck up, my darling old thing,' he said. 'Our luck's bound to change sooner or later. Actually I met quite a useful bloke in Mooney's on Saturday.'

'Chance of a job?' She tried to sound hopeful.

'Well, no immediate prospect. Actually we weren't discussing jobs. Though this chap's well in with the Craven and Ellis management. No, the main thing at the moment is he's got a friend who wants to buy an Indian and sidecar. I'm meeting them both for a drink tomorrow.'

Though Archie had used his mororbike, the first thing he had bought out of his two thousand, very little lately, Clara knew how he treasured it. She realized things must be desperate.

'Archie . . . must you really sell her? Isn't there any other way to raise the rent?'

'Blast the rent. I certainly wouldn't sell her for that. No, I'm going to buy you a decent birthday present. I meant it to be a surprise but I thought even the prospect might cheer you up a bit.'

'Dear Archie . . . Truly I don't want one. I'd far rather . . .'

'But *I* want to. And I shall,' he said doggedly. 'You mayn't believe it and most people might think I've a damn queer way of showing it. The fact remains that I happen to love you.'

She stared at the fading marigolds in the mock peasant jug.

'I don't deserve to be loved,' she sighed. 'I really believe I'm a kind of monster. Not a real person at all.'

'Shut up. I can't stand it when you talk like that.'

'It's true,' she persisted, finding a curious relief in attacking herself. 'Look at the way I've let people down all my life. Look at the people I've disappointed . . . and worse than disappointed. My father. Lady Cressett. Now you.'

'Me?' He stared. 'How do you make that out? Surely it's the other way round. I've let you down good and hard, haven't I?'

'I *don't* make it out,' she said. 'Yet I believe somehow it's my fault. I believe Daddy was right. Perhaps that's why I blazed out at him.'

'Absolute rot,' he said. 'I don't even see what you're getting at. I'm right out of my depth. All these heartsearchings are too subtle for me. I used to have the hell of a time at Beaumont when we were supposed to examine our consciences every night. Easy enough if I'd had a fight or passed round sweets in chapel. But how the hell was I to know if I'd been "diligent in setting my neighbour a good example" or provoked another to sin?'

Clara laughed for the first time.

'We used to have that one. I expect we took it straight from you. I used to drive myself nearly mad with scruples. My bugbear was "Have I wasted time in idle day-dreaming?" I used to wonder if thinking up stories counted.'

'My God, it's good to hear you laugh again,' he said. 'Talking of stories, that's something I *have* got on my conscience. I don't believe you've done any of your own writing for ages. I know you've been hammering away at some of those beastly advertisements again.'

'Well, we need the money, don't we? As a matter of fact, I've gone so stupid I can't even do *them* now. I ought to be hammering at them this very minute instead of sitting here.'

He groaned. 'And you say you've let *me* down. That's just the one thing I didn't want — that you should have to go on drudging away at that wretched stuff. To think I've got two hundred quid tied up in that play. I'd sell the option tomorrow though Jimmy swears I could make a packet if I held on. Just a question of smartening up the script a little.'

'You wanted me to do that, didn't you?'

'My darling old thing . . . I just haven't had the face to ask you . . .'

On an impulse, she said:

'I'll read it as soon as you like. And I'll gladly do some tinkering if it would give you a better chance of selling it.'

His face became radiant.

'Would you really? My God, you're a sport, Clarita. I know it's like putting a race horse in a coal cart. When I think of that marvellous story of yours . . .'

She broke in morosely:

'Forget it. I'll never write anything decent again. I know that for certain.'

'Don't say that. Believe it or not, it hurts.'

In the bitterness that swept over her almost like physical nausea at any reference to her writing, Clara hardly heard him. She muttered as if to herself:

'Amateur's luck. Exactly what Stephen said about my bringing off Katherine and Mélisande.'

Archie said jealously:

'You were in love with him when you wrote it.'

'What on earth has that got to do with it?'

'*He* let you down all right.' He flushed darkly. 'My God, there are moments when I could almost kill that man.'

'Don't be absurd. I've told you over and over again he doesn't mean anything to me now. I've seen him. I've proved it.'

'I believed you when you told me you'd go on loving him whatever happened.'

'I believed it too. That ought to show you how absolutely unreliable I am.'

'For once *you* don't see what *I* mean. It's not just jealousy. I hate him because he's done something to you. You're not the same person.'

'I'm not *any* person. That's the point. I never was and never will be. The sooner you realize that, the better.'

The anger left his face.

'Talk all the nonsense you like about yourself. Won't make the slightest difference to me. I'm quite content with what little bit of you I've got.'

The orange-smocked waitress who had been hovering impatiently for some time approached with the bill. Archie fumbled desperately in all his pockets and produced two shillings and a threepenny bit.

'I say, old thing. Frightfully sorry but can you come to the rescue? Thought I had lots more than this on me. I cashed a cheque at Mooney's only the night before last.'

Luckily Clara had a pound note that her mother had given her for her birthday. It was all the money she had.

'Pay you back tonight, cross my heart,' he said. 'Means I'll have to nip up to Mooney's though to cash another cheque. If I take a taxi, I'll just get there before closing-time.'

'Why Mooney's and a taxi? Your bank's just along the road.'

'Yep. Only it *might* be safer to postdate it a bit. The barman at Mooney's knows me.'

Clara could not help saying:

'He certainly ought to by now.'

Chapter Nine

For the next fortnight Clara forced herself to work several hours a day. By some extraordinary stroke of luck, the rent account did not arrive. What was almost as great a relief, Mrs Pritchard, who had been coming more and more irregularly, disappeared altogether. The fact that Archie's cigarette case and Clara's silver brushes disappeared too seemed to guarantee that she would not return. They were both delighted to get rid of those hard, prying green eyes and of the difficulty of scraping together fifteen shillings every Saturday. Grateful for these respites, Clara resolved to make a fresh start. Perhaps if she tackled what was to hand without fussing and fretting, heaven would take pity on her and Archie. She polished off six long overdue pieces of copy for the advertising agents and plunged into the revision of *A Night in Vienna*.

It was difficult to imagine why anyone should want to produce such a stale, feeble, back-broken play as it turned out to be. Nevertheless, turning it into recognizable English demanded just enough ingenuity to give her the illusion of working. It even gave her a certain satisfaction of the kind she used to feel when she had produced a passable Latin prose for her father. Having something concrete to do gave some shape to her days and restored her sense of continuity enough to keep her from slipping back into inertia. She locked the black notebook in a drawer and felt no need to write in it.

The change in Archie was startling. He paid only short occasional visits to the Leicester Square bars and when he did, drank only beer. With excited optimism he began to build a model stage in the 'studio' and to design sets and lighting effects. Instead of wandering about the house in his pyjamas most of the morning, unshaved and chain-smoking cigarettes, he was often at work on his models before breakfast. Sometimes Clara could almost pretend to herself they were two struggling artists; the fact that they couldn't pay the rent when the demand did arrive and that lately they had lived mainly on buns and chocolate, now seemed rather romantic. When they walked down King's Road, hatless and untidy, she thought they looked a typical Chelsea couple.

Once she caught sight of Clive Heron, carrying a neat despatch case and evidently on his way back from the Home Office. She waved from the other side of the road but he appeared not to notice. However, she was quite sure that he had when he promptly reversed his direction and darted up a side street.

'What made you think you knew that man?' Archie enquired. 'You gave him the fright of his life.'

'I do know him. His name's Clive Heron. He's a civil servant.'

'He looked that type,' said Archie, with contempt. 'Why the hell did he cut you? Thought we looked too disreputable, I suppose.'

He squeezed her arm affectionately.

'Good heavens, no. He'll have some fantastic reason of his own. If you think he's just a conventional bore, you're absolutely wrong. He's about the most amusing and original person I've ever met. I like him immensely.'

'You do, do you? I'm not exactly conventional myself. But I call that little exhibition just now plain bloody bad manners.'

'It wasn't. It was extremely funny. All the funnier as the last time I saw him – it was only on my birthday – he was imploring me to ring him up.'

'Was he indeed?' Archie did not sound at all amused. 'And are you going to?'

'Probably not. We hardly ever do meet in fact, though I've known him since my second year at the Garrick. It's become a kind of joke. We keep saying we must do something about it but we can't make the effort.'

'Hmm.' Archie's voice was still suspicious. 'Sure it wasn't me he was running away from? Is he an old flame?'

Clara laughed.

'If you knew how funny that was! Even as an *idea*!'

'It doesn't strike *me* as so uproariously funny,' said Archie stiffly. 'Anyway I don't think I much care for this precious Pelican or whatever his ruddy name is.'

In spite of the heat, which showed no signs of breaking, Clara managed to keep going fairly hard on *A Night in Vienna*. Even in the basement dining-room, the coolest room in the tiny house, the rest of which was like a slow oven, her hand sweated so much that it stuck to the paper. It was so hot that the water from the cold taps ran permanently tepid; the grass between the flags in the yard was as dry and yellow as old cornstalks: the leaves of the parched laurel drooped motionless, like strips of painted tin. Tired and limp as she was, Clara worked on with a persistence which surprised her. She felt that, if once she stopped, she would never get up the energy to start again. She managed to suppress the knowledge that what she was doing was not only futile in itself but unlikely to bring them back any fraction of the two hundred pounds Archie had spent on the option. In spite of everything she drove herself on, determined to finish it as a point of honour. At least, her working produced an extraordinary effect on Archie. If she were to give up, she was sure he would relapse too.

One afternoon, when she was halfway through the last act, the two of them went into one of the little shops that sold painting materials. While Archie was choosing some odds and ends he needed for his model stage, the tall heavily-built man who had smiled at her through the window on that first afternoon in Tithe Place, came into the shop. Archie was standing at the far end of the counter, with his back turned. The stranger gave Clara a quick smile of recognition, followed by a long, brooding stare. He was evidently about to speak when Archie called to her:

'Come and give me some advice, darling.'

At the same moment, the owner of the shop, deserting Archie, bustled up to the newcomer and said deferentially:

'Ah . . . Mr Marcus Gundry, sir. It's a long time since I had the pleasure of seeing you here. Thought you'd given us up.'

Trying to place the name, which, like his face seemed vaguely familiar, she remembered she had seen it on a poster of an exhibition of pictures by Duncan Grant, Matthew Smith, Mark Gertler and other painters the mere mention of whom made her father fulminate.

Forgetting Archie's appeal for advice, she stayed to listen reverently while Marcus Gundry joked with the proprietor and ordered some tubes of paint ('Viridian' . . . she must remember that for her notebook), three brushes and a gallon of turpentine.

The painter had a rich voice which matched his size and his ample gestures. The proprietor asked if he were exhibiting with the London Group and he answered that he was sending in three pictures. When it came to adding up the bill, he laughed; 'I'm broke. Put it down to me, will you, Mr Steen?' and the other laughed back: 'I quite understand, Mr Gundry. Only too pleased to oblige you again.'

Clara had crept up so close, in order not to miss a word, that when Gundry swung round t o leave, he knocked into her and dropped some of his tubes. As they both bent down to pick them up, he whispered: 'Third time lucky, perhaps?' Eyeing Archie's back, he added: 'Husband?' Clara nodded. He smiled. Two round dimples appeared in his firmly padded cheeks, making him look like the conventional jolly monk of Victorian pictures. He muttered 'Damn' under his breath and said aloud:

'I say, *please* don't bother. Awfully kind of you. Entirely my beastly clumsiness.'

Archie had turned round to see what was happening. Gundry stood up and included all three in a sweeping mischievous glance. As he opened the shop door, booming 'au revoir', he dropped his eyelids and fixed Clara once more with that intent, brooding stare. This sudden change of expression transformed the whole aspect of his face. The jolly monk vanished: there appeared instead a mask, at once sensual and sad and curiously Napoleonic in cast.

On the way back to Tithe Place, Archie said:

'Do you know *him* too? That chap who was throwing his weight about in Steen's?'

'Marcus Gundry?' Clara spoke the name with proprietary pride. 'Of course not. He's an *extremely* well-known modern painter.'

'Never heard of him.'

'I don't suppose you've ever heard of Sickert or Duncan Grant.'

'Right as usual. But I wouldn't care if he was Michaelangelo. I didn't like the way he looked at you.'

'The other day you were complaining because someone *didn't* look at me.'

'This is entirely different. Civil servants are harmless. But all these Chelsea painters are bad lots.'

Clara said irritably, 'Do stop talking like Daddy. "*All* Chelsea painters . . . *All* modern poets . . . *All* Russian novelists". I hate to hear people sneering at artists. Especially when they know nothing and care less about art.'

'I'm not concerned with his ruddy art. But when I see a hulking middle-aged swine, who presumably paints naked women, leering at my wife as if he were guessing what she'd look like without her clothes, I feel like punching his fat face.'

'Now you're merely being disgusting.' Furiously, she tried to march ahead of him but could not outdistance his long stride. He clutched her arm, though she tried violently to shake him off.

'I'm sorry. I just can't help it sometimes. I keep cursing myself and fighting like hell not to be jealous. But every now and then something just blows up inside me. Can't you make just a bit of allowance for me?'

Muttering 'Oh, I suppose so', she let her arm stay limply in his for the rest of the walk home.

When they got back to the house he fussed about remorsefully in the kitchen, making tea on the rusty gas-stove. Clara sat there without offering to help, her face sullen with the effort of trying to reason herself out of her irritation.

He said with his rueful smile:

'God, I must bore you stiff sometimes. You ought to have married a poet or something.'

She made herself smile too.

'Poets probably prefer barmaids.'

'I'd do anything. Swat through books . . . go round cricking my neck in art galleries . . . if I thought it would be any use. But I'd only rile you more than if I kept off it altogether.'

Penitently, she put her arms round him.

'You will keep up this legend about my being intelligent. I daresay it was even true once. My mind's been going off steadily since I was fifteen. Look at me. I don't even *read* any more.'

He pushed back her hair and kissed her hot forehead.

'It's all there, still. You need people you can talk your kind of shop to.'

She said nothing. They sat down at the chipped kitchen table, drinking their tea black: the milk had, as usual, turned in the heat.

'Bet I'm right,' he went on. 'I know I can talk theatre shop for hours. I don't hang around with those boys *just* to get blind.'

Clara sighed.

'No, I'm sure. If you knew how I envy you, knowing exactly what you want to do.'

'Precious little hope of doing it. When you think of all the old pros who can't get a shop. Why, even Jimmy's not had any work since the "Error" tour.'

'What ages ago that seems. I wonder what's happened to Maidie and all of them.'

'Heard some rumour that she was doing cabaret. Peter and Trev are booked for the "Aunt" again. Don't you ever hanker to go back, Clara? When we lost that chance, you seemed almost relieved.'

Clara sighed.

'I just don't feel capable of doing anything. Even if I had the chance of a marvellous part, I couldn't face an audition. Lost my nerve, I suppose.'

He said eagerly:

'That's the fatal moment to stop. They all say that. I met a chap the other day who's casting for a lot of really good tours.

Put on your best bib and tucker and we'll go along together tomorrow. I haven't an earthly but maybe I could tag along as baggage man or something. If *you* could only get something decent . . .'

She interrupted in panic.

'No, Archie. Please. You don't understand. I can't do . . . anything at all.'

'Nonsense. Look at the marvellous job you're making of this play. Oh, I know it's donkey work for you and you should never have had to do it. But I almost thought you were getting a kind of kick out of it.'

'It's about all I'm fit for,' she said bitterly.

'What's made you suddenly so depressed again? Only this morning you were as cheery as possible.'

'Oh, don't use that loathsome word,' she exploded.

'Sorry, old thing. Every time I open my mouth, I seem to drop a brick. I'd better shut up.'

'I'm sorry, Archie,' she said wearily. 'I'd better get back to the grindstone.'

'Oh no, you don't. I've let you slave at that wretched thing till you're worn out. All my fault, like everything else.'

He looked so wretched that she said hastily:

'Let's blame the weather. I believe it's hotter than ever today.'

She stared through the dusty kitchen window at the little courtyard. The sun blazed on the flags and struck spots of light like the reflections of a burning-glass on the stiff shining leaves of the laurel.

'Some English summer!' said Archie. 'London's almost as hot as Santiago. That blue sky and that sun scorching on the stone makes me think of a rather decent house I lived in. About the only thing that *was* decent in that beastly job. White . . . with a *patio*. And an orange tree instead of that sooty old shrub.'

Clara fingered her damp forehead and nodded without answering. She was thinking how seldom she ever considered Archie's life except where it touched her own.

She said:

'I always meant to do something about that bed. But I put it off like everything else. Now it's too late.'

'Doubt if much would grow there. Soil's too sour. Might be fun to fix up a fountain like the one I had in Santiago. But the Woods might raise hell.'

Clara thought: 'Sour soil where nothing will grow. That's what I am!' Aloud she said:

'I suppose they'll throw us out if we can't pay the rent.'

'Something will turn up. It *must*. You'd really hate to leave here, wouldn't you?'

She asked suspiciously:

'Has Daddy been getting at you too?'

'You know the line he's always taken. But much as I love your Papa, I'd never let him talk me into doing anything you didn't want. What you say, goes. And *you* love the place.'

'It's Chelsea, more than the actual house. I can't think why now I've proved it's no earthly use.'

'Don't follow.'

'I had an idiotic idea that if I lived in Chelsea, I'd be able to write. All it's done is to show me up for an utter sham.'

Archie said after a moment:

'You've been in this black mood ever since you ran into that painter chap. Any connection?'

She felt herself flush and said quickly:

'I feel like that underneath all the time. Forget it. I'd better go and get on with the "Night".'

'No. You're worn out with that wretched thing. Have another cup of tea.'

He took up the kettle to fill the teapot: it slipped in his grasp and sent a spurt of nearly-boiling water over his left hand. Clara cried out, but Archie merely swore and then grinned.

'Oh, my dear,' she said anxiously. 'What can we do? I'm sure there must be something one does . . .'

'No need,' he said. 'I'm tough. You know I'm always damaging myself.'

She had forgotten his extraordinary proneness to accidents. The first time she had met him he had been recovering from the effects of nearly blowing himself up with a hand grenade.

'It must hurt horribly.' The sight of the red swollen fingers afflicted her.

'Like hell for the moment. But pain can be almost a relief sometimes.'

She looked at him in surprise.

'Do you feel that too?'

'Yep.'

Clara said almost angrily:

'Why do I never know how other people feel? Why do I take it for granted I'm different from everyone else?'

'So you are. I thought that the first time I saw you. That's why I always felt I'd got to get you at any price. Like the chap in the parable about the pearl.'

'Oh, *don't*,' she implored. 'If you only knew what an absolute, utter sham you've got.'

'Rubbish,' he said sombrely. 'The pearl's genuine all right. Unfortunately it's cast itself before a swine.'

'Archie, please,' her voice was anguished. 'I can't bear it. I could *prove* to you that what you think a pearl is the cheapest, most rotten fake.'

'I'd like to see you try.'

She said hesitantly:

'I put down things in a notebook sometimes. About myself mostly. They show me up so that I can hardly bear to read them myself. I never thought I could bring myself to read them to anyone. But I think you should see that notebook. It's only fair.'

He shook his head.

'No, darling. I'm terribly touched that you'd trust me that much. But better not. You need some place where you can feel private.'

Clara felt rebuffed. Once again she perceived in Archie a fineness which made her ashamed. She said with a slightly false bitterness:

'The grave's a fine and private place.'

He muttered under his breath:

'But none I think do there embrace.'

She stared at him; then covered her surprise clumsily.

'I forgot. You love Marvell, don't you?'

'Dog on its hind legs,' he said with his rueful smile. 'There was a moment of difficult silence; then Archie fumbled unconvincingly in his pockets.

'Not a fag left,' he declared. 'Mind if I pop out and buy some?'

Suddenly solicitous she said:

'When you're out, *do* get something to put on your poor hand. It might be dangerous . . . such a bad scald.'

He seemed not to be listening. She babbled on urgently.

'You're always using your hands making those models. If the skin came off and you got some dirt in it, you might get a poisoned finger. You might even . . .' she broke off, suddenly aware that her voice sounded as high pitched and ridiculous as when one realizes one is addressing an empty room. Archie however was still there. He gave an odd laugh.

'Even have to have it cut off; is that it? Thanks for the jolly suggestion.'

Instead of kissing her as he usually did whenever he left the house, he went out abruptly, slamming the kitchen door.

Chapter Ten

Two or three nights later, Archie said:

'Feel like coming dancing tonight? There's a little club just opened off the King's Road. I know a chap who plays the sax there who could wangle us in.'

Clara's instant reaction was that they couldn't afford it but Archie assured her it was a cheap place and they need only drink beer. He added: 'Lots of Chelsea artists and models go there. Thought it might amuse you.'

'It's too hot to dance,' she began, but, seeing his disappointed face, said quickly: 'Let's go all the same.'

The small subterranean nightclub was hot and smoky. The floor was so crowded that they spent the first half-hour sitting at a rickety table, lit by a candle stuck in a Chianti flask, watching the other people. Archie had put on one of the tropical suits he had worn in Santiago and Clara, also for coolness, an old gauzy black evening frock. In the fashion of that year it was cut very low, leaving her arms and shoulders bare save for two narrow black velvet straps.

'I wore this in the last act of the "Error",' she said, as Archie dealt clumsily with the straining hooks. 'I *can't* have got so much fatter in a few months.'

'Who cares? You look lovely tonight, anyway. What stunning shoulders you have.' He kissed them when he had managed to fasten her into the dress saying, as judicially as if he were praising her handwriting, 'I'd be prepared to bet you have one of the softest skins in the world.'

Now as she looked round the room she seemed to be the only woman in an ordinary evening frock. There were women draped entirely in Spanish shawls; women in Augustus John frocks with tight square-cut bodices and long full skirts; women in crumpled cotton frocks that looked as if they were made out of curtains; one or two even in shirts and trousers. When at last they stepped on to the packed dance-floor, she felt self-conscious. Archie, with his loose shock of red hair and his creased shantung suit, looked far less out of place. She was glad when the dim lights were turned down and a cabaret was announced. People who could not find chairs sat huddled together on cushions at the edge of the dance-floor. A shaft of greenish limelight struck across the room: a young Jew dressed as a matador began to play the concertina. She turned her head away to study the groups. Here and there the harsh light picked out a striking head; a woman with smooth black hair coiled like a Russian dancer's; a crop-haired girl who looked like a sulky boy; a sad Indian face under a turban. Suddenly, leaning against the opposite wall, in the shadow, she saw Marcus Gundry. A tepid clapping announced the end of the concertina player. Then came a burst of louder claps. The band struck up 'Here comes Tootsie'. Archie gripped her shoulder and whispered:

'Would you believe it? Look who's here.'

For a moment she thought he meant Gundry. Then she saw that he was staring at the plumed and spangled dancer who had just appeared in the green shaft of limelight. He began to clap like a machine gun and she realized that the dancer was Maidie.

Forgetting all about Gundry, Clara clapped and called excitedly. As the slim, glittering figure spun and leapt and high-kicked with amazing speed and precision, she remembered that evening in Nuneaton and Maidie, in her pink chemise, scandalizing the unhappy Munroe. She must have been working hard since then; there was no doubt now as to whether she could 'manage to get up on her points'. Maidie looked as neat and demure as ever. Not a hair strayed from the coiled flaxen plaits, the rosebud mouth was fixed in a conventional roguish smile. She must have caught sight of them, for, as she whirled into her final curtsy, she managed to wink in their direction without disturbing another muscle of her dancer's expression.

'Let's go behind and dig her out,' said Archie when Maidie had vanished after loud applause. The dancers surged back to the floor, hemming them in. Before they could move, Maidie herself appeared through a dusty curtain and made straight for their table.

'Fancy finding you two dear old Wurzits,' she cried, flinging a slim, wet-whited arm round each of them. 'I'm breaking every rule of the house by coming out in my make-up but it's my last night, so who cares?'

'What'll you have, Maidie?'

'A Guinness for old times' sake, Starchy dear.'

While Archie was getting drinks at the small besieged bar, Maidie kept up an excited stream of chatter. After *A Clerical Error* she had been working hard at her dancing and taking cabaret jobs in obscure nightclubs 'just to get warmed up'.

'But now,' she finished, 'I've got something ever so good coming off. I'll hold it till Starchy comes back.'

When he returned with the drinks, she said:

'Listen, you love-birds. This'll make you sit up. I've got a part in the West End.'

'You lucky little so-and-so. Here's to it!' said Archie.

'Well, you deserve it.' Clara drank too. 'What in?'

'Big new musical show. "My Girl Billie" at the Summer Palace. Half a dozen speaking lines, two speciality dances, and one singing bit in a sextet. Pray that I get over all right.'

'Of course you will. Knock 'em cold, won't she, Clara?' Archie drank to her again, then heaved a sigh.

'And how's life treating you two?' she asked, looking at them shrewdly. 'Did you sigh, Starchy, or was it the wind? I see Clara doesn't press your trousers for you.' She ran her hand through his untidy hair. 'Honestly, Starchy, I wouldn't be seen out with you if I were her.' She turned to Clara. 'Seeing you in that dress, I could almost fancy we were back in the dear old "Error": Act III, Scene II. It always suited you, dear. But you've put on weight, haven't you? Now I come to look, you've got black circles under your eyes, too.' She pursed her pink mouth and began to count on her fingers. 'How long since the happy day? I only make it three months. You didn't waste much time.'

Clara said hastily:

'Three months and poor Archie still hasn't got a job. Did you hear about Lister and that club?'

'Heard rumours that something Jimmy and Archie were in had gone bust. I don't want to rub it in and say I told you so, old dears. Still stage-struck, Starchy?'

'Yep. Afraid so. But my hopes are getting pretty blighted. Run myself right on the rocks now. And Clara too.'

Maidie frowned.

'Seriously? As bad as that?'

He nodded.

'I wonder now. With that voice . . . Trouble is you've had no experience.' Maidie assumed the expression Clara remembered so well in crises over landladies' bills, damp beds and lost luggage. They both studied her face anxiously. Suddenly, it relaxed and she said: 'Chance in a thousand but it *might* work.'

'If it were one in a million, I'd take it,' said Archie eagerly.

'This show I start rehearsing on Monday. Nothing in it for Vere. She doesn't dance or sing and there are no straight parts. But . . .' she paused and frowned. 'No . . . it's so unlikely to come off. Might be cruel to raise your hopes, Starchy.'

'Go *on*,' he implored.

Clara could see his eyes shining in the dim light. He clutched her hand under the table.

'There's one tiny part not filled yet. A singing footman. He's got one quite good scene with Sherry Blane who's playing the comic lead. Of course all the chorus boys are after it. But they thought it would be funnier if they could get an awfully tall man. You know what a funny little knee-high Wurzit Sherry is. I bet Starchy could do it. Can you dance a bit, Starchy?'

'He dances beautifully,' Clara assured her.

'*You* wouldn't know,' said Maidie with her old asperity. 'But come to think of it, he can shake a hoof. Remember that adagio we guyed at your party at Coventry? It was after you'd gone off in high dudgeon for some reason, Vere.'

'D'you mean you might be able to get me an audition?' Archie was gripping Clara's hand so hard that her wedding ring was grinding into the flesh.

'I'll try. Come round on the off-chance. Ten o'clock at the Summer Palace. I'll meet you at the stage door. Bring a song with you. I'll spin them a yarn . . . say you were in Number 2 company of *The Maid of the Mountains* with me. There's no one from that lot in this show.'

Archie flung his arms round Maidie and kissed her heartily.

'Mind my feathers, old boy. This costume belongs to the management. I must go and change or Percy'll have kittens.'

As she stood up, she waved to someone on the far side of the room, pointed to her spangles, shook her head and beckoned.

'It's old Marcus Gundry,' she explained. 'Mind if I get him to come over? I daren't cross the floor in this outfit.'

'You know him?' said Clara, avoiding Archie's eye. 'How exciting.'

'I did a bit of modelling once for a chap he shared a studio with. *Not* what you think, Starchy. Ballet poses for illustrations complete with tights and *tutu*.'

The next minute Gundry's tall, heavy figure loomed beside their table.

'Mr Gundry, meet Miss Clara Batchelor,' Maidie giggled. 'Pardon me. Mrs Hughes-Follett I *should* say. This great gawk's her husband.'

Gundry bowed gravely.

'Mrs Hughes-Follett and I have quite literally bumped into each other before.' He turned to the scowling Archie. 'I'm afraid

168

I interrupted your shopping. Sorry. I have to put on rather an act with Steen. Otherwise he mightn't let me have things on tick.'

'Clara's artistic,' said Maidie proudly. 'She writes tales. *And* gets 'em printed.'

Clara flinched. Gundry looked at her under half-closed lids and said non-committally: 'Indeed?'

'And he'll have his name in lights one of these days. Shut up, Starchy. You will.'

'And I paint a little. Oils and watercolours. All done by hand,' said Gundry solemnly.

When Maidie had skipped away to change, Gundry focused all his attention on Archie. The one or two covert glances he darted at Clara were so swift as to be almost imperceptible. Archie was sullen at first but Gundry's manner was so easy and deprecating that they were soon laughing together. When Maidie returned, having exchanged her spangles for a schoolgirlish blue linen frock, she cried:

'What are you boys sniggering about? Swapping dirty ones, I'll bet. Time you broke it up. Come on, Tiny, let's dance.'

Left alone with Clara, Gundry's face assumed its mischievous, dimpled smile.

'Now we've been formally introduced, will you risk dancing with me? I'm heavy, but women tell me I don't actually trample on them.'

As he danced monotonously, but rhythmically, his face resumed the brooding Napoleonic look. At intervals, almost without moving his lips and gazing over her head, he spoke to her in a low abrupt voice.

'At least, dancing's an excuse for holding you in my arms. I've wanted to since the first day I saw you. At the window. You smiled. Remember?'

Clara fenced.

'I didn't really mean to.'

'Should be more careful, then. Grossly unfair to male sex. Raises hopes.'

'Actually,' Clara explained, 'I smiled at you because you were a painter.'

'Do you smile at all painters on principle? Bad habit in Chelsea.'

'Of course, if I'd known you were Marcus Gundry . . .' she began rashly.

He interrupted. 'Ever seen a picture of mine?'

She floundered.

'Well . . . I'm not actually quite sure. But I know . . .'

He said out loud and rather fiercely:

'You obviously *don't* know.'

'You'll think me awfully stupid . . .' she fumbled.

He held her closer.

'With shoulders like that, you can afford to be stupid.'

Clara felt humbled. She tried vainly to think of something intelligent to say. They danced for some moments in silence. Gundry muttered very low:

'Beautiful woman.'

Flattered but nervous, Clara said:

'Not *beautiful*, surely. No one's ever even suggested that.'

'I didn't mean your face. Women always assume one does, for some extraordinary reason. Don't look so deflated. I haven't really paid much attention to yours. Let's have a look.'

He stooped his head, examining her face with half-closed eyes.

'Nothing wrong with it. Rather a good phiz really.' He went on, with detached interest. 'Quite amusing to draw. I like the way the lower part pinches in to the chin just a fraction too late.' He removed his hand from her back to thumb a line in the air. '*So*. There's a woman in the National Gallery with that same pinched-in jaw. In pink. Cosima someone. But her forehead's too low. You've got the whole of a brow under those curls. Definite likeness, though. But you're better looking.'

Clara listened greedily, her vanity more than appeased. No one had ever talked of her face in that way. She made a mental note to go and look at 'Cosima someone' as soon as possible.

'I'd quite like to do a drawing of it,' he went on. 'But I'd make you shove back those bangs or whatever they are. They mess up the shape. When could you come along to my place?'

The thought of being drawn by Marcus Gundry sent her off

into an excited dream. She had visions of being admitted to the charmed circle that seemed so inaccessible. He must know other painters, perhaps musicians, even writers. The very idea of being allowed to watch and listen to these enchanted beings was so intoxicating that she forgot to answer his question.

'Well?' he pressed. 'Or don't you want to?'

'Oh, I *want* to,' she said ardently. 'But . . .'

'But what?'

She sighed: 'Perhaps I oughtn't to. Archie might be . . .' she was going to say 'angry' but substituted 'unreasonable'.

'Married long?'

'Only a few months.'

'You're not as much in love as he is, are you?'

'That's an unfair question.'

'Not a question. A statement.'

Again she could think of nothing to say.

Gundry laughed.

'He'd be perfectly justified, I suppose. But I imagine you usually get your own way. The point is, have you made up your mind?'

There was something about the man she could not help liking. She looked up into his face as if to reassure herself that he was not dangerous. Seeing her anxious face, he gave his rich laugh again. There was something so solid and genial about him that she had to laugh too.

'I must seem such an idiot. But things are rather complicated.'

He said kindly:

'You're very young, aren't you?'

'I suppose twenty-two *is* officially young. But I don't feel young any more.'

'Sure sign that you are. I'm nearly forty and I feel far younger than when I was your age. I was very earnest in those days.'

'Of course forty's not old,' said Clara reassuringly. Actually it seemed an immense age to her. It was a shock to realize that he practically belonged to her parents' generation.

'When you get to my age, you'll find life's much simpler than you supposed. You want something and you get it. Or you don't get it. Or you get it and lose it. Let's sit down, shall we?'

Clara was more at ease without his arms round her. Held close against that heavy, yet lithe body; feeling the hairy sleeve of his jacket against her bare back, it had been an effort not to relax unthinkingly into his embrace. Nevertheless, she was glad to see that Archie and Maidie were clapping for an encore of their dance.

'They're quite happy,' said Gundry with a chuckle. 'However did you come to know Maidie? You're not exactly each other's types.'

'We were on tour together. I got awfully fond of her in the end.'

'I adore Maidie myself. Quite dispassionately, though. I could be safely left on a desert island with her. At least till I'd made quite sure there wasn't some lovely brown-skinned Woman Friday about. What are you smiling at?'

'The thought of you and Maidie on a desert island. She'd keep you in order all right. I shared a room with her for five months.'

'Lucky Maidie.'

Clara said hastily:

'She is the most astonishing character, isn't she? I've enough material to do a whole book of Maidie's *obiter dicta*.'

'I see you're what she calls "bloody educated".'

'Do you get accused of that too?'

'I get accused of a great many things.' He glanced down at her bare shoulders and his face took on its heavy, brooding look. He said in a low, almost angry voice: 'Don't you *know* what a lovely body you have? Or what a marvellous texture of skin?'

'I'm getting fat. Maidie's just been warning me.'

'Rubbish. You're like one of those delicious Renoir girls – the early ones before the old man started blowing them up like air-cushions. Pneumatic bliss with a vengeance.' He smiled. 'I assure you, you could be twice as pneumatic as you are and still remain most disturbing. To me at any rate.'

Once again Clara could think of nothing to say.

'Don't look so alarmed. Surely you're used to being a disturbing influence.'

She said, without thinking:

'I can't imagine being an influence of any kind. You see I

don't feel as if I existed at all. So when someone talks as if I did, my mind just goes blank.'

He stared at her.

'What an extraordinary statement from a creature like you. I can assure you that four of my five senses affirm that you do exist and in no uncertain manner. I admit I don't know exactly how you'd taste but I've a shrewd idea. You're talking nonsense, my dear.'

She said, frowning:

'I'm sure it sounds nonsense. But I do mean something by it. Someone on a desert island might feel like that when they got back to ordinary life, don't you think?'

He laughed.

'Maidie might, I grant you. But if you'd been marooned with me . . .' he began. Catching sight of her face, he broke off. 'Sorry. Forgive obvious joke. What is it, my dear? You look as if something were really worrying you.'

She smiled. 'I'm sorry. I'm being very heavy on the hand.'

He smiled too and gave her wrist a quick pressure.

'Not on this hand. I assure you it's strong enough to support the entire weight of a non-existent young woman.'

She said impulsively:

'I almost wish I didn't like you so much.'

He shook his head.

'I suppose there must be some connection between your various remarkable observations. I'm blest if I know what it is.'

She laughed. 'I'm blest if I do either.'

The band had stopped. Half-relieved, half-disappointed, Clara watched Archie and Maidie elbowing their way towards them. As he turned his face towards them, flashing an exaggerated smile of welcome, he said without looking at her:

'No need to pull the alarm cord. Here come the guard and the engine driver.' Turning off the smile, he added quickly: 'In case I don't get another chance – 100 Rosehill Gardens. Know it? Long dull street running up to Fulham Road. I'm in every day. Don't come till sevenish. I need all the decent light for painting.'

'If I come, will you let me see some of your pictures? Though I probably won't understand them.'

He answered in a gruff, almost hostile voice:

'Don't pretend to if you don't. I'll show you some if I feel like it. You needn't make remarks about 'em. I'll do the talking. If I think there's any point.'

He stayed only a short while after Archie and Maidie had returned to the table. During that time he conducted a fantastic dialogue with Maidie in alternate broad Lancashire and stage French. They were so absurd that the other two simply sat back and enjoyed the turn.

When Gundry had gone, barely acknowledging Clara in his goodbyes, Archie said:

'I must say he's damn funny, that man. I've seen far worse acts in quite good revues.'

'Old Marcus does a spot of acting now and then. Highbrow Sunday night shows. He's a great pal of that Russian producer – Kirillov. Lives in the same house, I believe.'

Clara's heart soared.

'Kirillov who did that wonderful production of *The Cherry Orchard* last year? I'd give anything to meet him.'

'You'd better get Marcus to introduce you. K. might give you some work. That sort of arty stuff's probably more in your line than the "Error" and suchlike.'

Clara shook her head.

'Oh, no. I'm not good enough even to walk on for Kirillov. I've practically given up all ideas of acting, anyhow.'

'In favour of domestic bliss? Congratulations, Starchy.'

Archie said:

'It's not my idea. I think it would do her good to act again. I'm sure she'd be jolly fine, given a chance.'

Clara sighed.

'I'd rather have written *The Cherry Orchard* than be Duse and Sarah Bernhardt combined.'

'Never heard of it,' said Maidie. 'Wait a minute though. It's not that awful thing about V.D. by Ibsen, is it? I know there was a line about cherries in that because it's the only line I remember.' She said to Archie in a pansy voice '"Mother, my brain is turning to cherry-coloured velvet." Cue for laugh, wouldn't you say? My dear, not a soul in the house even tittered but me.'

'If I'd been there, I'd have backed you up,' said Archie, when Clara had assured her that *The Cherry Orchard* was not the same play.

'Glad to hear it,' said Maidie severely. 'The other was ever so dirty. If something's dirty it's really a bit much if it's dull as ditchwater too. I'd have buzzed off after Act I only the boy who gave me the free pass was on in Act III.'

'That man Gundry,' said Archie. 'What sort of pictures does he paint?'

'Nothing spicy, if that's what you mean. At least *I* never saw anything in the "September Morn" or "Bath of Psyche" line. Ever so boring, I thought. Just old trees and things and he can't even get the colours right. Oh . . . and plates of fruit on the most shockingly crumpled serviettes. My dear, some of the apples were blue instead of red. I said "You're colour-blind, old boy." And he had the cheek to say "Perhaps you are, old girl." I ask you!'

'Clara says he's supposed to be famous.'

'Don't you believe it. He's never had one picture in the Academy. I know, because I asked him. And he's been at it for donkey's years. Tried to kid me he didn't want to. "Sour grapes, dear," I told him. "Sour pink grapes with orange knobs on to you."'

She glanced at the clock.

'Well, you dear old Wurzits, I must love you and leave you. Got to get all the way to Golders Green and it's Sunday tomorrow.'

'Have another Guinness,' Archie begged her.

'What, after midnight and break my fast? I'm shocked at you, Starchy.'

'You're wonderful,' said Clara. 'When I think we live right opposite a church. Archie and I never seem to get there before eleven.'

Maidie said severely:

'Then you both promise me to get up tomorrow, you bloody

old slackers. Otherwise I'm damned if I'll even try and get that audition for you, Starchy. If you don't do the decent thing by God, you can't expect Him to do the decent thing by you. Now, come on, promise.'

Archie said sheepishly: 'All right, Maidie.'

'That's better. If you don't believe in answers to prayer, look at me. Two dozen candles, St Joseph's going to get the first night of "My Girl Billie". If I do a prat-fall, I've warned him he'll only get one.'

'Monday . . . ten . . . Summer Palace?' said Archie anxiously.

'That's right. Cheerio. If you can't be good, be careful.'

'Oh, Maidie, you haven't changed a bit,' Clara laughed, as they kissed each other.

Maidie darted her a shrewd look:

'Hmm. More than one can say of some people. Still, it'll all come out in the wash, as the monkey said.'

'Dance, darling?' Archie said, when she had gone. They took a few turns on the crowded floor. But tonight Clara could not follow his steps.

'What's up with you?' he asked. 'Tired, old thing.'

'I'm sorry. I'm dancing abominably. It must be worse than ever for you after dancing with Maidie.'

'Maidie's a pro. I'd a million times rather dance with you and you know it.'

'Not the way I'm dancing tonight.'

'You managed well enough with that great lout Gundry. I was watching you.'

'All right,' she sighed. 'Let's say I'm tired and leave it at that.'

'Like to give up?'

'Yes. I'm getting more out of step with you with every bar.'

Chapter Eleven

On the Monday morning, Archie went off in high spirits to the Summer Palace. Even though the demand for the rent arrived just before he left the house, nothing could damp his optimism. Clara, watching his tall figure almost dancing away down the street, dreaded the thought of another disappointment more for him than for herself. Since that Saturday at the nightclub, she had been aware of a sense of returning life which made it easy to share Archie's excitement. On the Sunday morning, for the first time since they had lived in Tithe Place, she found herself humming as she washed up the breakfast dishes. Later she had bought an armful of flowers from a coster's barrow and filled every vase and jug in the house. Archie had for once reproached her for extravagance.

'Mustn't count our chickens before they are hatched, darling. If I don't bring this off, our prospects are slightly grim.' She had answered, with most unusual lightheartedness:

'If we're going to be ruined, five shillings won't matter either way. Anyhow, I've got a feeling that our luck's going to change.'

As soon as he had left for the theatre, she slipped across into the church to pray for his success. It was a big, bare place, coldly lit with plain glass windows. There were no shadowy side-chapels; no stands of guttering candles. It did not even smell of incense but of damp stone and carbolic soap. The whole of the wall behind the altar was covered with a vast dull canvas of the Crucifixion. She had never know a Catholic church whose atmosphere was so chill and formal. This morning, coming in from the gay, sunny street and finding it empty but for herself, it seemed drearier than ever. However much she reminded herself that the atmosphere of a church was irrelevant, that all that mattered was the presence of the Blessed Sacrament, she could not help being depressed by it. It emphasized her growing sense of religion as something remote from her real preoccupations.

Staring at the huge painting with its three conventional, lifeless figures and its pallid neutral colours, she felt such a longing for warmth, for mere human life however untidy and painful, that she could hardly remain on her knees. It seemed almost irreverent to pray for anything so worldly as Archie's getting a part in a musical comedy. Nevertheless she forced herself to stay for a few minutes with her face buried in her hands, adding rather guiltily to her petition 'Make me a better wife.'

It occurred to her that her sense of being chilled and rebuffed might be her own fault. What right had she to approach God like a confident child? She performed only the bare minimum of her religious duties and carelessly at that. Moreover, since Saturday night, her conscience was not altogether easy. The sun-shafts, pouring through the dusty greenish glass, were transformed into a cold glare like searchlights. They reminded her at once of the nightclub and of the beam of a policeman's lantern searching for suspects. That sudden spurt of lightheartedness and hope – which had vanished the moment she entered the church – was certainly connected with Marcus Gundry.

Partly to appease her conscience, partly to prove to God that she was willing to make some sacrifice for Archie's success, she made a mental promise not to go to Gundry's studio; not, at any rate, during that week.

Back in the little house, she did some penitential tidying up in the effort to carry out her resolution of being a better wife. She was horrified to find how much mess and dirt had accumulated now that Mrs Pritchard no longer came to give the place even a sketchy cleaning. Untidy herself, Clara had long ago given up the effort to cope with Archie's quite astonishing capacity for reducing any room to chaos. Every carpet was littered with ash and cigarette butts; half-empty cups and glasses lurked behind chairs and even under the beds. His clothes were invariably thrown on the floor and, as he had a habit of wandering from room to room as he undressed, she would often find dirty collars, socks and underclothes strewn all over the house and even on the stairs. This morning, in his frantic search for a clean shirt, he had emptied the entire contents of a chest of drawers on the unmade bed. As she put them back, she noticed again how brutally he treated his clothes. Everything was torn, stained and frayed like a schoolboy's.

Finding that he had taken his last clean shirt, she rang up the laundry to know why their things had not been delivered for a fortnight. She received a curt answer that they would be delivered when the bill, now amounting to over five pounds, was paid.

Suddenly dispirited, she abandoned the hopeless task of trying to make the house presentable, went down to the kitchen and made herself some tea. Then, sitting at the chipped table, she tried to work out their financial situation. She found, to her horror, that it would take nearly a hundred pounds to clear the rent and the various small debts they had accumulated. Telephone, gas and light were threatening to be cut off; two crumpled bills she had never seen had fallen out of a jacket of Archie's when she hung it up: both for bottles of whisky. Till that moment she had believed that he drank only in bars.

She sat staring hopelessly at her accounts and gnawing her pencil. There was no way of knowing how much, if anything, she could put on the credit side. The most she could hope was that Archie had not yet spent the whole of this month's allowance. In her own purse she had exactly nine shillings and eightpence, the remains of the fifteen guineas the agents had paid for her last set of advertisements. Most of that Archie had borrowed in small loans, with ardent promises of repayment. Even if he were to get the part, it would be months before they would be able to save up enough to pay all they owed. Even saving up, in the unlikely event of their being able to save, would not solve the problem of the rent. The enormous sum of £61 8s. 6d. had somehow to be paid in a few days. The only faint hope was that Archie might sell his motorbike. She clutched her head, trying to think of some way out. Should she approach the advertising agents and ask them to give her a regular free-lance contract again as they had done before she went on tour? Their last letter had not been encouraging. They 'needed no more copy at the moment but would communicate with her in the event of their envisaging future plans involving her possible co-operation'. She knew that she had lost the light touch that had once made them so eager for her work. Should she grovel to them, offer to work at lower rates? Three years ago, they had offered her a good salary to join their permanent staff but her dreary year at the Ministry of Pensions had made her loathe the idea of working all day in an office.

Suddenly, on a desperate impulse, without thinking what she was going to say, she ran upstairs and phoned Rapson's number. She almost hoped to find it engaged, but by an extraordinary chance, she was put straight through to Rapson himself.

A rather irritated voice said:

'Rapson here. Who is that?'

She mumbled, 'Miss Batch . . . I mean Mrs Hughes-Follett.'

'Speak up. Can't get the name. Is it something urgent? My secretary will be back in ten minutes.'

She managed to convey to him who she was and his voice became more genial.

'Yes . . . yes . . . of course. How's married life going, eh?'

Clara had meant to do no more than ask for an appointment. Instead, she lost her head completely. She began to babble nervously:

'Things are a little difficult at the moment. I was wondering whether . . . Do you remember you offered me a staff job some years ago? I wasn't willing to take it then but I've changed my mind.'

The geniality vanished from Rapson's voice.

'Steady on, dear lady. A lot of water's flowed under the bridge since then. I'm not contemplating making any additions to my staff at the moment.'

Clara was trembling all over. She could retrieve neither her self-control nor her commonsense. She went on in a high, almost hysterical voice.

'But it's rather different in my case surely. I mean I've free-lanced for you for years. You always said my copy was in a class by itself.'

'*Was*, my dear, certainly. You've done some very nice work for us, I admit. Incidentally, we've paid you more for it than we've paid any free-lance in my time. I don't want to hurt your feelings, but your stuff's deteriorated very considerably since you got married. Too busy looking after hubby to put your mind on it, I daresay.'

'I've been worried,' Clara babbled on insanely. 'I haven't been awfully well. My husband's lost his job. I'm sure, Mr Rapson, that if you'd give me a chance, I'd manage to . . .'

He cut in:

'Sorry, my dear. Nothing doing. I've built up this business *as* a business, not a charity institution. Sorry to hear you're not feeling fit. You'd better see a doctor. Excuse me if I ring off. Got a lot of work on. Drop in any time you're up our way and have a chat. Might have a few captions or suchlike you could have a bat at at home. Afraid I can't promise anything though. So long.'

Clara collected herself just enough to say coldly:

'Thank you. I'm sorry I bothered you. Goodbye,' before she hung up the receiver.

She knew that she had made an utter fool of herself; nevertheless she was as shaken as if Rapson had slapped her face. She remembered his effusiveness in the days when he had been only too anxious to have as much copy as she was willing to do for him. It was useless to tell herself that she hated the idea of working in Rapson's office, of being subject to that absurd little man with his patent-leather hair and his diamond tiepin in the shape of a fox's mask. The fact that he should have spoken to her like that was far more humiliating than a snub from someone she respected. She felt like an old actress, once a star, who has been refused a walking-on part. It seemed the measure of her utter failure that she could no longer succeed even at work she despised.

Catching sight of herself in the mirrors of the tiny room whose holland covers had long lost their freshness and whose carpet showed islands of stains in the merciless sunlight, she thought she looked as battered as the room. There were faint creases round her eyes and mouth and a dusty look about her face and hair. Words slipped into her mind . . . 'Abstinence sows sand all over the ruddy limbs and flaming hair.' She checked herself from finishing the verse. Against her crumpled blue dress, her arms still had the milky whiteness they showed in hot weather or when she was warm from sleep. She touched the inner side of her elbow, noticing the pure blue and violet of the veins and marvelling at the softness of this sheltered area of skin. Such softness, which meant nothing to herself, must surely be meant for some purpose, like the soft breast-feathers of a bird. All at once the memory of Gundry, overlaid since she had left the church, returned with violence. Forgetting her resolution, she would have set out then and there to find him, if she had not remembered his warning not to go before seven. With a pang of conscience, she brought her mind back to Archie. It was after noon. He had promised to telephone her the moment he had news. The fact that he had not done so yet might be a good sign. Though the house, tawdry and unkempt as an actress waking up with last night's make-up still on her face, oppressed her more every minute, she must stay in till he called up.

The paralysed lethargy she had managed to fend off for the last weeks began to creep over her. At all costs, the day which had begun so hopefully must not turn into one of those terrible ones when she wandered aimlessly about the house, stopping now and then to stare for long spells at an old newspaper whose meaning she could not take in, smoking cigarettes, mechanically combing her hair and eating, if she ate at all, with a strange compulsive greed; stuffing herself with anything she could find; sponge cakes, chocolates, old heels of bread and cheese, like a ravenous child. She must do something, anything, at once while she still had enough will to make herself act.

She went out into the glare of the courtyard feeling the flags hot through her shoes as she crossed it and went into the shed Archie now used as his workshop. There was no purpose in her mind beyond wanting to get out of the house and look at any objects which she did not know by heart in the effort to stave off inertia. The stone floor was littered with Archie's half-finished models for the play that she was sure would never be produced. Probably even the models would never be finished; Archie had only worked on them desultorily the last few days. She could not blame him. She had not finished her own part. Since that day when they had run into Marcus Gundry in the art shop, she had not been able to force herself to do another line of the wretched piece, though she was within twenty pages of the end.

Looking at Archie's sets, though the designs were banal and the colours crude, she had to admire the neatness of their construction. It was astonishing that anyone so clumsy in handling ordinary objects should be able to make such delicate adjustments of fine wires and tiny pieces of wood. She picked up one of the miniature stages with care, thinking what an enchanting toy it would make for a child. A child of hers and Archie's was something she could no longer even imagine. Staring out at the strip of parched earth at the edge of the courtyard, she thought again: 'Sour soil where nothing will grow.' Suppose things had been different between them, could her numbed body have produced a living creature any more than her numbed mind could produce even a fragment of living work?

Stooping to replace the models, she saw for the first time the cluster of empty whisky bottles it had screened. It was true, then, that he had been drinking secretly at home. She wondered how long it had been going on. All the bottles but one were thickly covered with dust. That one was almost clean and still had some whisky in it. She guessed he must have bought it the day he scalded his hand.

Standing there, holding the bottle, she thought how hopeless their situation was becoming. Was it her fault or his that they seemed to be slowly destroying each other? He had begun to drink long before their marriage; she could hardly be blamed for that. But was it her fault that it was becoming more and more of a habit? She wondered what compelled him to drink: was he, too, sometimes overwhelmed by that sense of being utterly cut off from life, gasping for air inside a bell-jar? If so, did drink lift the bell-jar? On an impulse, she uncorked the bottle and gulped a large mouthful of whisky. A fiery heat ran through her: she had the feeling that someone had switched on a light inside her skull. At that moment the telephone rang inside the house. The bell sounded insistent and accusing. She started guiltily, hastily corked the whisky bottle, and ran across the courtyard to answer it. It must be Archie. Anxiously she picked up the receiver, only to hear a stranger's voice asking for a quite different number.

The gulp of neat whisky on an empty stomach had made her head swim. Nevertheless, she felt better. The creeping paralysis was arrested. She could actually feel it move some steps away, as a circle of wolves is said to do when the menaced traveller throws a firebrand at them. Nothing, indeed, seemed to press on her quite so heavily any more. The unpaid bills, even her humiliating conversation with Rapson, retreated into a kind of fog where they became blurred and unreal.

Almost lighthearted again, she decided to finish the correcting of *A Night in Vienna*. As she worked, the play no longer seemed quite so idiotic. Perhaps it was not impossible after all that someone would want to produce it. Even if they could only sell the option outright for what Archie had given for it, two hundred pounds would clear all their debts and leave them a hundred in hand. And if Archie got this part . . . why shouldn't he get it after all? . . . one of their nagging worries at least would be removed. She finished Act III in a state of slightly drowsy exhilaration. By then, she was so sleepy that she went and lay down on her still unmade bed.

When she awoke, it was nearly four o'clock. The effects of the whisky had entirely worn off. The late afternoon sun poured through the window, hurting her eyes and pitilessly showing up every detail of the disordered bedroom. There was a sour taste in her dry mouth: the oppression had returned in full force. Each anxiety was like an actual weight on her diaphragm pinning her down on the rumpled bed: the bills, Archie's drinking, her own impotence to write, the impossibility of going either backwards or forwards in any direction. But more crushing than any of these was an overall sense of guilt, not localized, as if all these were a punishment for some mysterious sin she did not remember having committed.

The pink walls and blue check curtains mocked her with their arch brightness. They gave the untidy bedroom the air of a night nursery inhabited by two undisciplined children. Those pink distempered walls had the texture of sugar icing: she was reminded of the sugar house in which Hansel and Gretel were trapped. Archie and she were trapped too. But by whom? No wicked witch had lured them in to destroy them. Through the window, she could see part of the dark brick wall of the church where she had tried to pray that morning. Stern, heavy, uncompromising, it reminded her that, for her and Archie, there could be no escape.

Her mind wandered back to her wedding morning, to the Nuptial Mass and those tremendous petitions which seemed to have so little relevance for them. She remembered her father, fussing over his split glove and how his arm had trembled as he escorted her up the aisle. It was strange how little she thought of him nowadays when once her whole preoccupation had been to please him. Since her birthday, she had avoided Valetta Road. Suddenly his face came sharply into her mind, angry and disapproving as she had last seen it in the study. What would he say if he were to walk at this moment into the room and find her lying in broad daylight on the unmade bed? Her old fear of him, which she thought had been dispersed for ever except in dreams, rushed over her with new force. What would he think if he had overheard the things Marcus Gundry had said to her in the nightclub? At that moment she heard a latchkey click in the lock downstairs. Such a thrill of terror went through her whole body that she hardly dared to breathe. She forgot where she was: she was convinced that it could be no one but her father coming to accuse her. She shut her eyes and clutched the sheet with both hands. Then her spinning head cleared. She let out her breath on a great sigh of relief. Before he had banged the door and called to her, she realized it could be no one but Archie.

She ran down to meet him. He was smiling triumphantly. Under his arm he carried a bulky parcel. For the moment, Clara was so dazed that she forgot to ask him what his news was. He pushed her into the front room, put down his heavy parcel, and clasped her in his arms.

'I've got it, darling,' he said. 'I've got it!' At first she could only stare at him. 'You look as if you didn't believe me. I can hardly believe it myself. But look – here's my contract.'

She collected herself enough to exclaim excitedly and ask for details.

'It's my lucky day,' he exulted. 'Maidie fixed an audition, bless her, and I did my stuff. And here I am with an actual part *and* an understudy and eight quid a week. What do you think of that?'

'Wonderful,' she said.

'You don't sound awfully excited.'

'Of course I am.' She had taken it in but her relief and pleasure were soured by an obscure resentment. 'Why didn't you ring me up? I've been waiting indoors all day for you to ring.'

'Sorry, darling. I wanted to give you a surprise. Besides, that's not all my news.'

She persisted, hating herself for taking the edge off his triumph.

'What time did you know about the part?'

'Round about two.'

'It's half past five now.'

'Late as that?'

She said meanly: 'No doubt you went straight to Mooney's to celebrate.'

'Right as usual. But don't look so peeved. I didn't go just to have a drink. Naturally I wanted to tell old Jimmy. I don't say we didn't have a round or two. But the real reason was that I'd arranged to meet that chap there. And he turned up all right.'

'Which particular chap?'

'The motorbike and sidecar one, of course. He's bought it. For cash.'

She asked anxiously: 'How much?'

'Sixty quid . . . well fifty-five actually . . . I had to give the chap who introduced me a rake-off.'

Penitent in her relief, she said:

'Poor Archie. I know you hated selling her. But it means we've nearly enough for the rent.'

His jaw dropped.

'Oh, damn. I forgot the bally old rent. But I'm sure we can wangle something. Hang it all . . . £8 a week plus my rotten allowance . . . that's not too bad? You're being a bit of a killjoy, aren't you, darling?'

'I'm sorry. It's all wonderful, of course. But we do owe quite a lot besides the rent. I've been going into our bills.'

'Forget 'em. Our luck's turned, that's the great thing.'

She only just checked herself from saying meanly: '*Yours* has turned' and asked instead 'Whatever have you got in that vast parcel?'

'Aha! I was waiting for you to ask that. It's something for you.'

'For me?'

'Yep. Belated birthday present.'

'Oh, Archie . . . you shouldn't have . . .'

'Rubbish. I've been planning it for ages but I couldn't raise the wind. But now I've sold the motorbike . . . Gosh, it was marvellous to have a bundle of fivers again . . . I couldn't wait to get it for you.'

She asked anxiously:

'Oh darling. It's not something terribly expensive?'

'Hang the expense. Anyway I've bought it now. Thought you'd be pleased. But you don't even seem to want to see what it is.'

He looked so hurt that she said quickly:

'I'm *longing* to see it. May I open it?'

He revived at once.

'No, you mayn't. You stay where you are and keep your eyes tight shut. Promise not to open them till I give the word.'

She shut her eyes and promised.

'I warn you, you may have to keep them shut quite a time. Rather go out of the room?'

'No . . . no . . . I'll stay. But *do* be quick.' She made her voice sound as eager and impatient as possible.

'Better put your fingers in your ears too. I want it to be a big surprise.'

She sat patiently, wondering whatever it could be, trying to identify certain strange noises which penetrated her stopped ears. It was like Archie to rush off and buy her an extravagant present the moment he had some money in his pocket. She thought, remorsefully, how churlish she had been. Whatever the present was, she must seem delighted. As she sat there for what seemed a very long time, with her eyes squeezed conscientiously tight, she realized that her prayer of the morning had been answered. Archie had got his job and she had not even had the grace to be thankful. She made a hasty mental equivalent of Maidie's 'Sorry, God'.

'Now!' said Archie, in a tone of immense satisfaction.

She opened her eyes. Spread out on the floor were two magnificent Bassett-Lowke model engines; a tail of coaches for each; stations, signal boxes and a glittering heap of rails. She could do nothing but stare, open-mouthed.

'Thought that would knock you flat,' said Archie, grinning with pleasure. Ignoring her silence, he went on:

'I'd planned to try and sneak into the workshop tonight when you were asleep and put it all up. It makes a grand big circuit – double track – when it's assembled. All electric. We'll have to start on an accumulator – there's a whacking big one being delivered tomorrow. Too heavy to bring home. But I'm sure I could fix a wire off the house and we could run it off the mains. I got two locomotives. No nonsense about one of them being mine. They're both yours. Only it's more fun with two. We can have races . . . crashes if you like. We've got the most marvellous points system you ever saw. Think it's too late to start fixing her up now? . . . You see . . . I've got to rehearse all day tomorrow and I'm dying to show you how it works so you can have fun with it on your own. I'll have to leave you alone such a lot till we open and you can amuse yourself for hours with it . . . Darling . . . whatever is the matter?'

For Clara had burst into a fit of uncontrollable sobs.

He held her close, questioning her anxiously.

'My pet . . . my little love . . . Are you ill? . . . Don't you like it?'

After some moments she managed to control herself to say that she wasn't ill and that it was the most wonderful model railway she had ever seen.

'It's not as big as the one at Crickleham . . . but it's a far better model. The latest and best. Remember my railway at Crickleham? I always connect it with you. We played with it the first time I ever set eyes on you. I believe I fell in love with you that moment.'

She remembered it as well as he. She remembered how he staged a crash and a tiny engine fell down a bank which seemed as steep as a precipice. She wondered, as her tears dried leaving her exhausted and gentle, if he remembered the second time she had seen him with his model railway – two days after Charles's death. His face, as he looked up at her with a toy locomotive in each hand, had been blind with misery. It was then, simply to wipe away that hopeless look that matched her own sense of numb despair, she had, for the first time, said that she would marry him.

Chapter Twelve

Some days later Clara received a patronizing letter from Rapson offering her half a dozen pieces of copy at less than her usual rates. She sighed and said:

'I'd like to refuse. But I daren't.'

Archie looked up from the typewritten part he was studying.

'Refuse what, Clarita?'

She showed him the letter:

'Damn cheek. Send him a snorter. Turn him down flat.' He returned to his part and began to gabble another line under his breath.

'Archie . . . how can I? It means twelve guineas. Think of all our bills.'

'Let 'em wait. We can start sending them dollops once the show's running.'

'But they're urgent. They won't wait. We haven't even done anything about the rent yet.'

'I sent the Woods twenty quid. Absolutely all I could raise. That should keep them quiet.'

'You know it won't. We're supposed to pay a quarter in advance. That leaves £41 8s. 6d.'

'What a head for figures you have.'

'It's as well someone in this house has. And what are we going to do about the others? We haven't had clean sheets for a fortnight and the gas and phone are threatening to cut us off.'

'Let 'em. I'll send them postdated cheques. Stop fussing, old thing.'

'Postdated cheques on what? The date of the opening night isn't even fixed yet. You're only getting paid £2 a week for rehearsals. You don't seem to realize we've got to find something like sixty pounds as well as keeping going from day to day.'

'I realize I may lose this part if I'm not word-perfect at rehearsal this morning.'

'It's all very well for you,' she flared. 'You don't have to sit about here all day worrying about how to find money. You've got what you want. You don't care what happens to me.'

'Steady on, old thing. I daresay we are in a bit of a tight spot but there's no need to go off the deep end. Things will sort themselves out somehow.'

'That's what you keep saying. You just won't face facts. About money or anything else.'

He turned rather white.

'I happen to care a good deal about what happens to you. Actually, I phoned Sybilla on the strength of having landed this part and tried to touch her for a hundred quid. But she was in one of her cheeseparing moods. So that was napoo.'

'Just as well. How could we ever have paid her back?'

'Sybilla could have afforded to wait. Hang it all, it's only just over a year till I come into my money.'

'A year! When you think of the mess we've got into in less than four months.'

'How about the old "Night"? Now you've smartened it up, I might take it along to the Summer Palace. Maidie's well in with the management.'

She almost screamed:

'Oh, stop, Archie. Of all the fantastic pipe-dreams! A child of six would have more sense. If someone gave you two pounds for that idiotic thing, lock, stock and barrel, you'd be lucky.'

'All right. I'll shut up then. Must be hell being married to a child of six.'

'I'm sorry, Archie. But you don't seem to grasp that something's got to be done here and now.'

He jumped to his feet, still angry, and thrust the script into his pocket.

'What I've got to do here and now is to get to rehearsal on time. So long.'

He strode out without kissing her and she heard him bang the front door.

She sat, staring down at the smeared plates and the cups full of dregs, with tears of irritation in her eyes. Archie had as usual spilt his tea, adding another spreading stain to the various brown blots on the cloth. Until they paid the laundry, they could not have a clean one. Untidy though she was, she hated dirty linen. Archie was no more perturbed than a schoolboy by wearing the same grimy shirt day after day but Clara loved the look and feel of fresh, clean clothes and felt demoralized without them. If the gas were cut off, they would not even be able to have baths.

She felt for some moments such a rage of resentment against Archie that she felt like walking out of the house and never returning. But where could she go except back to Valetta Road? That would be too humiliating. Anything was better than having to face her father's pained questions and her mother's triumphant sympathy. However exasperated she might be with Archie, she would rather be with him than with her family. The mere thought of having to live in Valetta Road again, having to appear punctually at boring meals, to listen to the bickering of her mother and her grandmother, to be asked where she was going and when she expected to be back, oppressed her more than their debts. The sugar house might be a prison but at least she and Archie were their own gaolers.

Still bitter against Archie, she pulled herself together. If he was utterly feckless, she must find some way out. She got up and washed the breakfast things with self-righteous indignation. Then, reflecting that in a day or two she might not even be able to boil a kettle, she went upstairs, turned on the geyser and washed clothes and table linen till her back ached and her hands were sore. For the rest of the day, she sat in the gloomy little dining-room, determined to earn her twelve guineas before nightfall. Anger sharpened her wits. With ironic enthusiasm, which developed almost into ironic conviction, she wrote six variations on the 'selling angle' of Glintex shampoo. 'Maybe you thought your hair was just "ordinary". Then you've never tried Glintex. You've never known what sunny glints, what hidden glories Glintex can reveal. Maybe you thought you were just "ordinary" too – that success, fulfilment, all that a woman hopes and dreams might never come your way. But Glintex affects your whole personality. New confidence . . . new charm . . . a subtle magnetism you suspected no more than that hidden radiance in your hair – that is what Glintex releases in you. In that little green packet is not "just another shampoo" but the key to a richer, more thrilling life. Let the rare, secret ingredients of Glintex reveal the rare, secret, dazzling *you*.'

The agents had enclosed a packet of Glintex shampoo. She washed her hair with it, assuring herself that this was merely a practical measure in case the gas was cut off. Nevertheless, as she rubbed it dry, she found herself hopefully watching for some astonishing change in its appearance. She even felt obscurely cheated when she combed it out and found it looked exactly the same as after any other shampoo.

Just as she had finished, the telephone rang. It was Archie, to say that he would not be home till late. Maidie had offered to coach him in his dance routine and he was going back to Golders Green with her after the rehearsal. He sounded brisk and cheerful; she could hear giggles and chattering going on in the background. Evidently he was phoning from the theatre. Suddenly the sense of isolation which she had managed to fight off all day came flooding over her. She felt as if even Archie had abandoned her. Fear and resentment put a cold edge on her voice. He appeared not to notice it.

'You'd better go and have a bite at the Three Cornered Hat. Do you good to get out of the house.'

She answered bitterly:

'No doubt. Only I happen to have exactly sevenpence halfpenny.'

'Oh well, that's napoo. But there are two eggs and a slice of cake in the larder.'

'So there are,' she said with savage brightness. 'And then I can have a nice game of trains.'

'That's the idea,' came Archie's heartiest voice. 'Mind the acid from the accumulator though. Cheerio.'

She hung up the receiver, furious and aggrieved. Here she was, having drudged away all day writing advertisements and washing clothes as a result of Archie's fecklessness, and he showed not the least sign of penitence or even concern. In justice, she had to admit that it was an excellent thing that Archie was making such efforts to succeed in his part. Nevertheless, she felt envious and neglected. Archie had got what he wanted: he was launched on something real. She saw herself desperately trying to scrape up money to patch up a life which was not really a life at all. As Archie became more and more absorbed in that intense private life of a theatre company, which she remembered from the 'Error' days, she would grow lonelier and duller. Tonight would be merely a sample of the endless stretch of blank evenings which would begin when 'My Girl Billie' opened in a few weeks' time. She thought bitterly how a real writer would have welcomed those uninterrupted hours. But she no longer had the confidence nor the will even to try any more. Even reading had become painful. It was weeks since she had so much as made an entry in the black notebook. The last time she had looked at it, one or two patches that seemed goodish, even to her jaundiced eye, had depressed her more than the morass of nonsense in which they were imbedded since they were a reminder of what she could never hope to do and yet obscurely longed to attempt. It would have been a relief to be able to tell herself that she had no aptitude whatever for the real thing and had better concentrate cynically on slick nonsense which might at least earn some money.

Money, she thought bitterly, that was the first necessity now. Well, with luck, she had made twelve guineas today but it was only a fraction of what they needed. It would take ten of her *London Mail* stories – and she hadn't the wits to concoct one of the wretched things – to make the thirty guineas still due on the rent. She seized a bunch of her newly washed hair in each hand, as if to tug some idea for raising money out of her skull by sheer force. Nothing occurred to her but the remote possibility of inducing Bassett-Lowke to take back the model railway. Until this moment, she would not have even considered it for fear of hurting Archie's feelings. Now she no longer cared; it even gave her a kind of pleasure to revenge herself on him.

She went out into the shed and stared at the shining, half-assembled network of rails and the two miniature trains still uncoupled to their engines. At first Archie had rushed to experiment with the railway the moment he came back from rehearsal and she had not had the heart to refuse to help him. But, in the last day or two, he had almost abandoned it: all his interest had been switched over on to studying his part. She picked up the two scale-model engines. They were so perfectly made that she could not resist a feeling of pleasure in them and even a pang of regret at the thought of parting with them. But, turning them over to examine their fine detail, she saw that already a great patch of the glossy paint on each boiler had peeled away, exposing the metal. Then she remembered that, the last time they had been running them, some of the acid from the accumulator had spilt on them. They were too spoilt for anyone to consider buying them now.

Her first reaction was to want to damage them still further. She stood with one in each hand, half-meaning to dash them down on the stone floor. Then she relented. Bending, she laid them down gently on a pile of shavings as if they must at all costs be preserved from even a single further scratch. For some reason, this gesture calmed her resentment. She stood up, with the oddest sense of having released herself from some pressing obligation. Even their debts no longer weighed on her so heavily; a space seemed to have cleared itself round her in which she was free to act on her own. Locking the shed door quietly and deliberately as if she had locked away some anxiety with it, she began to think how she should spend her evening. The first thought that occurred to her was to go and see Gundry. She had an odd sense of having somehow earned the right to do so. Nevertheless, her conscience was not quite at ease. Then she remembered Clive Heron, to whom she had not given a thought since the day he had avoided her in King's Road. Now, the idea of seeing him seemed not only blameless but almost as pleasurable as going to Gundry's studio. She would just be in time to catch him at the Home Office if she rang him at once. As she asked for the number, she told herself that, even if he were not available, she would put off going to see Gundry at least till she could tell Archie that she intended to go.

A secretary informed her that Mr Heron had just gone abroad on three weeks' leave. It was not yet six o'clock. Without stopping to question herself further, Clara went upstairs, dressed herself with more care than she had done since the night they had danced at the club and, as seven o'clock struck, set out, trying to make herself walk slowly, in the direction of Rosehill Gardens.

Chapter Thirteen

It seemed to Clara, after she had been sitting in Gundry's room for two hours, that she had known it for years. Curled up on the broken-springed bed, she watched his tall, heavy figure moving with surprising deftness among stacks of frames and drawing boards as if it were as familiar a sight as her father sitting at his desk correcting Greek proses.

He had made two or three rough drawings of her head, sometimes making jerky conversation, sometimes leaving her last remark unanswered while he worked for a spell with frowning concentration. Clara was not at all disconcerted by these intervals of silence. Provided she kept her head still, her eyes were free to wander round the room. It was not a studio but merely a large ground-floor room in a house which, from the outside, looked very much like the one in which her parents lived. It amused her to see how many features it had in common with the dining-room at Valetta Road; the marble mantelpiece, the Edwardian wallpaper, dingy serge curtains, a gas fire surrounded by hideous tiles. There, however, the resemblance ended. Except for one ancient armchair, a couple of battered chests of drawers, a deal table and the iron bed with its cheap Indian cotton bedspread, there was no ordinary furniture in the room. The paint-splashed boards were bare except for a rag rug. Everywhere, in a kind of orderly confusion, were Gundry's working materials; rolls of canvas, heavy palettes, a tin tea-tray full of tubes of colour, a zinc bucket holding a great bouquet of meticulously clean brushes. It gave her such extraordinary pleasure to look at these things that, at intervals, she would forget she was sitting to him, lose the pose and be barked at to keep still.

When he had finished his drawings, she was glad she had resisted the temptation to ask to see them.

'You're the first woman who hasn't rushed to the easel and said "Do I *really* look like that?" the moment I put down the charcoal.'

'Of course it's exactly what I'm longing to do,' she admitted, watching him as he sprayed the drawings to fix them. 'Only I'm too vain.'

'Are you? You strike me as rather a modest young woman.'

'Oh, this is mental vanity. Fear-of-giving-myself-away disease. I'd be sure to say the wrong thing. Have you forgotten how you warned me not to ask to look at your pictures?'

'No. But I'm flattered – and rather impressed – that you've remembered. Look if you like. You don't have to make any comment. They'll probably give you a shock.'

He passed the drawings to her one by one and she examined them in silence. They were done in free sweeping strokes; some almost as black and hard as the leading of stained glass; some mere indications, almost as delicate as pencil. He had simplified and slightly distorted her face, exaggerating the weight of her forehead and the fullness of her lips; minimizing her eyes and treating her hair merely as a shape suggested by a few broken curves. It gave her a strange sensation to see herself presented in this brusque, unfamiliar way. When she had absorbed the shock to her vanity, she found the sensation exhilarating.

'Well?' Gundry asked at last. 'What's making you look so pleased all of a sudden, after knitting your brows for about five minutes? One would think you had just found the answer to a sum you'd given up as hopeless. Or have you thought of something intelligently non-committal to say?'

'I wish I had,' she laughed. 'No, I can't *think* at all at the moment. And what I'm feeling is so personal and vague that it would infuriate you if I tried to put it into words.'

'Risk it,' he said affably. 'I won't eat you.' Then he added, with his jolly monk's smile: 'Actually, there's nothing I would like better than to eat you. You're looking quite exceptionally appetizing at this moment.' He advanced a step towards her and she instinctively stiffened. There had been some rather difficult moments before he settled down to draw her.

'All right,' he said. 'I'll retreat in good order. Go on. I'd be amused to hear these highly personal reactions.'

She summoned up her courage.

'Well . . . can you remember as a child tasting for the first time something grown-up people like? Hock for example. Or olives. You don't immediately like the taste, even if you pretend you do out of pride. But if it's something you are really going to like one day, I believe you recognize it in advance.'

'Rather prettily put, if I may say so. Let's have some more of your subjective art criticism.'

Emboldened, she said:

'I can't judge your drawings as drawings. But I know you've drawn the lines you meant to draw. You can make that bit of charcoal do exactly what you want. That's always terribly exciting to me. Just the mere expert handling of anything, whether it's a man controlling a horse or a comedian timing a gag.' She added apologetically: 'I know it's nothing to with art.'

'Nonsense. Obviously it's not the whole story. But one's got to have technique. One's got to have it all there . . . and yet be able to forget it. One can get so damned expert that it turns to tricks. Goes off and turns its private somersaults just for the sake of showing off. Doesn't wait on the eye or the mind . . . or, to use a word I loathe but I can't think of another . . . on one's vision.'

'Yes, of course,' she said excitedly. 'But that's what I want to know . . . which comes first . . . the hen or the egg. The vision or the technique. How does one know that one is . . . I hate that word too . . . an artist? I suppose everyone at some time wants to be one . . . not necessarily a painter of course – or even imagines one may be. But how does one know that one has the *right*?'

'That's a rum question. You talk as if it were a case of conscience.'

'Perhaps I think of most things like that. I expect it's the result of my convent education.'

He gave her a shrewd, considering glance.

'Oh . . . you went to a convent school, did you? That explains a lot. Still believe it all?'

'Certainly.'

He smiled.

'It doesn't explain everything. I've known a great many women who went to convent schools and who would have been extremely offended if one had suggested they weren't *croyantes* and even *pratiquantes*. But they weren't as difficult as you are. Or are Catholics more puritanical in England?'

'I've no idea. Anyhow I'm not going to follow your red herring. I want to know how people . . . you yourself for example . . . *know* that they are artists.'

'What a formidable creature you are. When you stick your chin out like that, you look like a little bulldog. Don't do it. It ruins that nice pinched-in line.'

'I won't . . . if you'll tell me.'

He sat down in the battered armchair which creaked under his weight and placed a hand on each of his knees.

'I've never really considered it. Obviously I was always what's called "good at drawing". Rather too good in fact. There wasn't a style I couldn't imitate like a monkey. Scholarships. The white-headed boy of the Art Class. When I was in my twenties, I made over a thousand a year copying Old Masters. Absolutely indistinguishable. Like a Chinese tailor who reproduces even the patches and the frayed buttonholes on a coat. I was a wow at getting the famous patina without stopping to think it was only dirty varnish. When I painted pictures myself, they looked so like Old Masters – patina and all – that everyone foresaw a highly successful future for me. Provincial art galleries and collectors bought Gundrys as a safe bet. One year I even made two thousand. I'd like to get hold of every one of the beastly things and burn 'em.'

'What happened to change everything?'

'I suppose it all started with seeing a Cézanne. He knocked me flat. Hated it at first. Colours, drawing, everything seemed to me all wrong. Heretical, as you'd say. But the beastly thing haunted me. I even tried copying it to get it out of my system. Oh yes, I imitated it all right, down to the last brush-stroke. All the time, I kept asking myself why the hell does he do this or that? Hasn't he ever heard of perspective? Why treat the sky like a solid? What's that damn white spot where he hasn't even covered the canvas? Then I came to love that wretched picture as much as I'd hated it. Call it a religious conversion. I saw every Cézanne I could. I was excited by Pisarro and Monet too, but it was always that old boy I came back to. I painted a lot of sham Cézannes, trying to work out from the outside what his game was: such and such a palette, such and such relations of forms. I even fancied I'd worked out an underlying theory of his proportions – a mathematical rule of thumb. So I became a promising "modern" painter. I didn't make so much money but I sold my pictures. Now I looked a safe bet to the cautious *avant garde* collector.'

'And then?' asked Clara, leaning forward with clasped hands and gazing reverently at his averted head.

'Don't quite know,' he said slowly. 'I suppose I gradually began to look at things. Really look at them off my own bat. Cézanne and some of the others had shown me that they really saw what they saw. My eye had got all cluttered up with other people's images of things and I had this damn facility for reproducing those in any style, ancient or modern. So I started right off from the very beginning, merely trying to see. I even did silly things like drawing with my left hand so that I wouldn't go off into tricks.'

'How wonderful,' Clara breathed ardently.

He turned and glanced at her.

'You odd creature. Anyone would think all this desperately concerned you.'

'Oh, forget about me. Please go on.'

'Not much more to tell. Still experimenting. Half the things I do, I don't finish. Half the ones I finish, I destroy. I paint things that people find uninteresting or even ugly. I don't paint what people call beautiful objects or scenery because I don't *think* they're beautiful. I do. But I'm trying to clear away all the accumulated mass of associations and expectations they arouse. I want to keep my eye clear . . . look at a thing with detachment . . . for itself . . . not because of any feelings I've got about it. At the moment I'm deliberately painting things which don't in themselves excite me. Exercises, really, in simple *seeing* with all the concentration I'm capable of. Now the critics wonder what the hell's happened to me; the collectors fight shy and I'm lucky if I sell two pictures a year for a quarter of what I got for muck.'

Clara said softly:

'If thy eye be single, thy whole body shall be full of light.'

'That's good,' he said. 'Blake?'

'It's in the Gospel. Christ says it somewhere.'

'Does he indeed? Good for Jesus Christ. But he'd be scandalized at having it applied to painting, though.'

'I wonder,' said Clara. 'It's one of the things that's always nagging me . . . the connection between art and religion.'

'No connection at all, if you ask me. Old Cézanne was a pious Catholic. He also had a beard. One's as irrelevant as the other. He'd have been just as great a painter if he'd been an atheist. If I believed in the devil, he could have my soul tonight for the price of five good pictures before I die. That shocks you, doesn't it?'

'I don't know. I suppose it would if you *did* believe in the devil. Anyway no one could call you worldly.' She looked round at the uncarpeted room, furnished with only the barest necessities besides his painter's equipment. 'I wonder how many people would give up as much for their religion as you have for your work. I'm sure plenty of monks and nuns who've made a vow of holy poverty live in far more comfort than this.'

He laughed.

'I don't think there's any virtue in poverty. It's a damn nuisance. I assure you I have no scruples about getting money by any other means, however frowned-on. Often I haven't got the money to buy paints and canvases. I go round to different art shops that knew me in palmier days getting stuff on tick and trusting to be able to pay some day.'

'Oh . . . if only I had some money,' Clara said earnestly. 'I'd be so awfully happy and proud to help you.'

'What a nice creature you are. I warn you I'd have no hesitation in taking it if you could afford it.'

She burst out:

'Oh . . . I feel so ashamed of myself. It's true we haven't any money at the moment: we're up to our ears in debt. But it's all my fault . . . if I hadn't wanted to live in that absurd, pretentious doll's house.' Twisting her hands, almost in tears, hardly caring whether he listened or not, she poured out an incoherent stream of self-accusation. 'And not only now,' she ended. 'To think I used to make quite a lot before I married and spend it on idiotic things like clothes and taking people out to restaurants and here were you . . . *needing* even tubes of paint . . . and I could have bought them for you. I'll never, never be able to do anything myself but I could have helped someone who can.'

She was aware of Gundry staring at her with a strange expression almost as if he were angry. When at last she stopped, he said nothing. They sat for some moments in silence while she stared miserably at the rag rug, not daring to look at him. Then he stood up, padded over the bare boards and, sitting beside her on the bed, took her very gently in his arms, saying gruffly:

'You absurd creature. You quite preposterously absurd creature.'

She said with relief.

'Laugh at me, if you like. I thought you were furious.'

'Silly one. I'm only laughing in self-defence. Otherwise I might cry.'

'What nonsense.'

'Nonsense, indeed. Look at me!'

She turned her head in the crook of his arm and looked up at his face. It had relaxed again into his mischievous, dimpled smile but his eyes were wet. He put up his forefinger to them and solemnly showed her a glistening streak.

'There, doubting Thomas. Have you got a tear-bottle handy? These authentic specimens are rare.'

She said, imitating his smile rather shakily:

'If I let myself go now, I'd never stop. I'd fill buckets. I don't know what's come over me. I just want to howl and bellow. And I've no idea why.'

'Howl and bellow by all means. But for God's sake don't sniff. Here . . .' He offered her an enormous handkerchief. 'I've wiped my brushes on it but there's a clean space in the middle.'

She blew her nose obediently.

'Well, what do you want us to do now?' he asked. 'Have a good weep over our overdrafts? I daresay I could pump up another tear or two to keep you company.'

Suddenly, for no reason at all, she felt so violently happy that she had to laugh. She said, trying to get her breath between the gusts . . .

'Two walking baths, two weeping motions
Portable and com . . . compendious oceans.'

He laughed too. Then suddenly the laugh broke off; his face made its sudden switch to the brooding mask. He clutched her close against him and muttered:

'There's something much better for us to do than crying. Isn't there, my sweet, my lovely one.'

He put his mouth against hers, gently at first, then as she half-willingly yielded, with a fiercer and fiercer pressure as if he were trying to suck the blood from her lips. Crushed against his great body, she was aware only of a blank darkness in her mind and a sense of suffocation. He shifted her weight expertly, holding her tight in the hollow of one arm, while his free hand caught her under her knees and lifted her so that she lay on the bed. Still with his lips fastened on hers so that she could hardly breathe, he leant over her and began, gently but urgently to pull her dress off one shoulder. Under the weight of his body, she could not move. She had lost all sense of his identity or her own; she was only aware of a desperate need to get her breath. When at last he raised his head and buried his face in the hollow of her bare shoulder, the relief was so great that she could not think connectedly enough to protest. She lay for a moment with closed eyes, gasping between her stiff, swollen lips, feeling the unexpected softness of the hair on the hard round head under her chin. Then, as suddenly as he had closed on her, he let her go, walked across to the window and drew the curtains. The room, already dusky, became completely dark.

She sat up, pulled her dress straight and groped along the wall.

'Marcus . . . please . . . put the light on . . . I can't find the switch.'

He did not answer. She heard him stepping carefully over the bare boards. Then he struck a match and lit some candles stuck in saucers on the mantelpiece. The room immediately took on a mysterious beauty, full of monumental shapes and wavering shadows. Some crumpled brown paper, torn and showing patches of the white canvas it covered, became a pile of rocks with rifts of snow; a naked mirror propped against the wall, reflecting tubes and brushes at an odd angle, became an aquarium with silver fish and spiky plants glimmering through dusky water.

Gundry's face, too, as he stood at the mantelpiece, putting a taper to the candles with the slow, careful movements of an acolyte, had changed its aspect in the soft, transforming glow. His profile was grave and intent; modelled in clear light and shadow, the broad, simple planes of cheek and brow, the full jaw, the small straight nose reminded her no longer of Napoleon or a jolly monk, but of a Buddha.

Now, removed from her and condensed once more into a human being, she could hardly connect him with that blind force, impersonal as an avalanche, which a few moments ago had threatened to crush her. The silence during which she watched him methodically light and foster each little tongue of flame, cupping it from the draught with his large, sure hand, seemed to spin out for ever. Somewhere at the back of her mind was a nagging sense that there was something she ought to say or do, but she could only sit there on the edge of the bed, intent as an animal on his every movement.

Suddenly he crouched down and lit the gas fire; the small explosion shattered the silence which had become so intense that it was like a third presence in the room. The air, which she could have fancied congealing in solid layers under its pressure, moved again. She shook herself out of her almost hypnotic state and said uncertainly:

'Marcus . . .'

He turned at once and came towards her. The next moment his arms were wrapped round her again, this time gently.

'What is it? Why do you look so frightened? You like me, don't you?'

'Oh I do . . . I do . . .'

'Well then,' he laughed softly. 'What's all the trouble about?' He held her closer, still gently, but as she tried to recoil, more insistently. He put his mouth against her ear, saying in jerky whispers: 'I've wanted you for so long. I want you so terribly. No one ever wanted you more.'

She turned her head away, trying to loosen the hand that was once more busy with her dress, saying miserably:

'Oh . . . please let me go . . . It's all my fault . . . I feel such a cheat . . . I should never have come here . . .'

He raised his face which he had buried in the hollow of her neck, gripped her by the shoulders and looked at her under his heavy lids.

'You don't want me? Is that it?'

'Even if I did . . . oh, how can I make you understand . . . I can't . . . I mustn't . . .'

'What is it? . . . scruples of conscience? . . . This infernal religion of yours? You're not a fool. You can't seriously believe that there's anything wrong in something so natural. Do you think it wrong to eat when you're hungry and drink when you're thirsty?'

She hedged:

'Do remember that I'm married.' She realized, as she said it, that it was she who had forgotten.

'Of course you're married,' he said impatiently. 'I'm not a barbarian. I don't seduce virgins. If you find me repulsive, that's another matter. But I don't believe you do.' He caught her in his arms again; kissing her neck, her ears, her eyelids, very gently and murmuring: 'You silly, adorable creature. There's nothing to be afraid of. Just forget everything and let's be happy.'

In spite of herself, Clara could not help yielding to the comfort of his warm, solid embrace. Her strained nerves relaxed, her mind grew numb and drowsy. She nestled against him, feeling small as a child in his powerful arms. Without thinking she began to return his gentle, reassuring kisses. But, as his became more urgent and his heavy body pressed closer against her, she tautened again and tried to push him away.

'No . . . no, my girl. Enough of that,' he said between his clenched teeth, leaning down over her so that she could hardly move. Suddenly, he let her go and started to his feet. She caught a glimpse of his face set in a strange, blind look; lips parted and forehead damp with sweat, before he turned away, tore off his jacket and began to drag at his shirt.

'Take your clothes off,' he said abruptly. 'I can't make love to you like that.'

Her mind went blank. She could only utter an incoherent sound. He turned about and faced her with his shirt hanging out; half his heavy torso, smooth and padded as a wrestler's, bare; the flesh almost golden in the candlelight. Even in her dismay, she was struck by something at once ludicrous and impressive in his appearance. He said more gently, with a twitch of his old mischievous smile that made his face recognizable through the mask of desire.

'Don't be shy, my sweet. There's not a line of your body I don't know by heart already. I'll put the candles out if you insist. Anything you want. Oh . . . for God's sake, woman, what is it now?'

For Clara had burst into hysterical tears. She crouched on the edge of the bed, her face clutched in both hands, giving great gulping sobs as uncontrollable as hiccups. She could hear him moving about the room, muttering under his breath; then came the noise of a door opening and shutting. When at last she raised her head, she found herself alone.

She had pulled herself together enough to get up and begin to grope for her coat among a jumble of objects, in the deep shadows beyond the range of the candles when Gundry returned. He had put on his jacket again; his face was still pale and glistening but composed in a distant, almost severe expression. For a moment she thought he did not see her where she stood in the dark patch behind his easel. He opened a cupboard, took out a saucepan, a tin and two chipped enamel mugs.

'I'll make some coffee,' he said over his shoulder.

'No. Please. I must go.'

'Sit down. In the chair.'

As she still hesitated, he said irritably:

'You needn't be alarmed. I can take a broad hint.'

She obeyed meekly.

'Shove the chair back, can't you? I want to get at the gas ring.' She watched him as he crouched at her feet, heating up his saucepan and putting on his kettle. He seemed so absorbed as to be quite unaware of her. Once again she could not help admiring the deft way he handled objects. His mood had changed so completely that she felt rebuffed. She wanted to restore the intimacy she had felt with him before that violent interruption. It was as if she would lose something precious, hardly acquired yet already indispensable, if she did not at once make some effort to retain it. Tentatively she put our her hand and touched the silky dark hair at the nape of his neck. He started as if she had burnt him and swore.

'None of that. Or this time you'll bloody well take the consequences my girl. Here . . .' he swung round and thrust a saucepan into her still outstretched hand . . . 'Put that damned little paw to some practical use.'

As he turned, he glanced at her face and his severe expression relaxed into a grin. He snatched the saucepan back.

'No . . . better use it to comb your hair. There's a bit of looking glass on the mantelpiece.'

In the glimmer of the now guttering candles, she saw that her face was blotched and swollen beyond recognition under her wildly disordered hair. She set to work almost savagely with comb and powder puff.

He sat back on his heels, mocking her.

'What is this fetish women have about plastering their faces? I believe even you would rather be seen naked than with your nose unpowdered. There . . . stop dabbing. Come and drink your coffee.'

He thrust one chipped mug at her and returned on to the bed with the other.

She sipped the sweet strong coffee in silence, feeling herself revive with every sip. He drank his without looking at her, in three long gulps, put the mug down with his usual care and lit a cigarette.

'Well,' he said at last. 'That was rather a violent reaction, wasn't it? One might almost have supposed no one had ever attempted to make love to you before. Or do you find me as repulsive as all that?'

'Oh, not you . . . Not you yourself.'

'Then what? I can't believe that outburst was entirely due to moral indignation. It was a little too primitive.'

She said nothing. He looked at her questioningly.

'You've got a very odd expression on your face. As if there were something you wanted to say and couldn't quite bring out.'

'Yes . . . perhaps,' she said slowly.

He gave his reassuring smile.

'Come now. We've both given ourselves away pretty thoroughly tonight, haven't we? I think it's your turn.'

She shook her head.

'If it were only myself, I would gladly. But this involves someone else.'

He stared at her for a moment; then said abruptly:

'Look here . . . Something quite fantastic has just occurred to me.' He broke off, frowning. 'No. It's inconceivable.'

'Is it so fantastic? I've no means of knowing. Perhaps it's quite usual.'

'Quite usual?' he said fiercely. 'You can sit there calmly and talk about "quite usual" . . . Why, it's the most monstrous, unnatural thing I ever heard. A woman like you. No . . . I can't believe it.'

'It's true. But I wish I hadn't told you.'

'You've told me nothing. But, my dear girl, this is serious. I've got to get this clear . . . for your sake as well as mine.'

Seeing his face almost angry with concern, she could only tell him the truth. He did not look at her as she spoke. When she had said the little there was to say, he continued to smoke for some moments in silence. Then he threw away his cigarette, crushed it out with his heel and asked shortly:

'Well, what are you going to do about it?'

'Do? What can I do?'

'You're not seriously proposing to go on with this farce of a marriage?'

She stared at him.

'But I have to go on. We're both Catholics. We have to go on whatever happens. Even if I were ever to leave Archie, there's no question of divorce for either of us.'

'I'm not talking of divorce. Even that hidebound institution, your Church, recognizes one or two basic facts of human nature. If things are as you say . . . Yes, yes, I believe you now . . . then you've got a clear, foolproof case. The sooner you start consulting your priests and lawyers the better.'

It was Clara's turn to be incredulous.

'But are you sure?'

'Of course I'm sure,' he said impatiently. 'I knew someone else in that situation. Hers was more complicated because she'd had a lover before she married this man. I take it you haven't.'

She shook her head.

'Then it's simple. Mere matter of routine. I believe it takes the hell of a time though. You ought to get going at once.'

She said in sudden panic:

'Oh . . . no. It's such a huge decision. I'd have to think it over. I still can't take it in properly.'

He said grimly:

'You'd better start thinking quickly. You've very young, presumably normal, and uncomfortably desirable. Have you thought of the alternatives? Sooner or later, you'll land yourself in an intolerable position. If you take a lover, you'll be overcome with guilt and incidentally block your way of escape. If you don't you'll do yourself incalculable harm, physically and mentally. Either way, that young man will suffer less in the end if you make the break now.'

Her mind was in such confusion that he seemed to be remorselessly attacking her.

She pleaded wildly:

'Oh please. Don't be so cruel. Give me time to take it in.'

He said more gently:

'You really mean you hadn't the least idea?'

'No . . . Not the remotest . . . I never even dared imagine . . .' She could not go on. Her throat had gone dry and her head was swimming. The shadows in the dim room suddenly thickened and seemed to have swallowed up the last glimmer of the candles. She became conscious for the first time of the heat and smell of the gas fire and the rasping wheeze of a broken jet. The smell of the gas, the growing darkness seemed to mix together in her head, blowing it up like a balloon. From very far away she heard a minute, authoritative voice, which she could just recognize as Gundry's saying:

'Put your head down . . . No . . . right down between your knees.'

She tried to obey but the balloon head seemed to be floating up to the ceiling. Before she could establish any connection with it a heavy weight fell on the back of her neck. Gradually the balloon descended, and shrank back into a normal head again and now she found it was nearly touching the floor and that someone's hand was forcing it down. She had just grasped the fact that the hand was Gundry's when his voice muttered close in her ear: 'All right now?'

When at last she raised her head, she found he was sitting on the arm of the chair. He threw one hand across the back and, with the other, gently pulled her back so that she lay in the crook of his arm.

'Lie quiet,' he said, almost in a whisper. 'Keep your eyes shut. Don't be afraid. We've given each other enough shocks for one night.'

She lay back obediently, exhausted and relaxed. Gradually, an extraordinary sense of contentment crept over her. When at last she forced herself to open her drowsy eyes, she glanced up and saw him sitting above her solid as a statue, his face in profile. She watched him for a moment, thinking that he looked older and sadder than she had seen him yet. The glow of the gas fire caught his jaw, showing the just-slackening line of the chin, the creases by his mouth and in front of his ear. She felt such a wave of warmth towards him that she wanted to speak, but dared not, for fear of breaking the spell. Lying there in quiet bliss, she let the warmth flow out of her to embrace everything in the room, from the candles buring low and crooked in their wax clotted saucers to the gigantic shadow of the bunch of paintbrushes which half covered the ceiling. She said at last, on a long sigh: 'I could stay like this for ever.'

At once her started, and, turning his face to her, switched on his jolly monk's smile and said:

'I couldn't. I've got pins and needles in my left arm.'

She sat bolt upright.

'Oh . . . I'm so sorry . . . I never thought . . .'

'Don't apologize.' He flexed his stiff arm, heaved himself off the chair and pulled her to her feet.

'You'd better go now, my dear, if you're feeling up to it. Want me to see you home?'

'No, of course not.'

She felt extraordinarily forlorn as she watched him pick up her coat, shake off a paint rag that had clung to it, and hold it up for her to put on.

As she slipped her arms into the sleeves, he kept his hands on her shoulders and turned her to face him.

'Well, young woman, I hope you're grateful to me.'

'Oh I am . . . I am . . . You'll never know how much.'

'There's a charming irony about my situation, you must admit,' he said drily. 'That I of all people should be the one to point the way out of yours. And in doing so, effectively spike my own guns.'

She said fervently:

'Marcus . . . dear Marcus . . . it's not just that. You don't know what it's meant to me. Being here with you . . . watching you work . . . hearing you talk . . . It's been like coming to life after being dead for months . . .'

He caught her chin in one hand and turned her face into the light.

'What's come over you?' he asked. 'You look entirely different.' Suddenly he slapped her cheek lightly and pushed her away. 'Out with you. That face gives me ideas I've been sternly repressing. It's how I imagined you'd look if . . .'

'If?'

'If I hadn't behaved so bloody well. Now be off with you, you baggage.'

'All right. I'm going.' But she still lingered, looking round the room. 'I suppose I'll never see this place again.'

'Not in these circumstances you won't, my good girl. You can't have your cake and eat it too.'

'Goodbye then, Marcus.'

She made a step towards him and he put his arms round her. He kissed her eyes and said with his reassuring laugh:

'Portable and compendious oceans.'

'Don't,' she said, managing to smile. 'I'll begin again if you're not careful.'

'Heaven defend,' he said, loosening his hold. 'I, at least, have the sense to come in out of the rain.' He gave her one mocking kiss and marched her firmly to the door.

Chapter Fourteen

The air struck chilly after the heat of Gundry's room. She had no idea what the time was but she suspected it must be very late. The long lamp-lit street was empty but for two cats, alternately crouching motionless in the gutter, then darting across the road in pursuit of each other. She stood, for some moments, watching them while the damp wind played on her face. At last, she began to walk very slowly in the direction of King's Road.

So many new and confusing ideas were fighting in her head that she hardly knew which to try and follow up. Like the cats, now one, now another would start up and chase the rest away: then her mind would freeze again and she would be aware only of the sound of her own footsteps. It seemed so long since she had set out from Tithe Place that it was difficult to remember the chain of small events that had led to her going to Gundry's room. When she did manage to reconstruct them, they seemed to belong to another time; almost to another dimension from the one in which she had been living for the last hours. It was as if she had undergone an operation and were trying to force herself back to normal consciousness.

Gradually, as her mind cleared enough to focus it on Archie, she had to make an effort to remember how he looked and spoke. Having recovered his image, she was seized with such terror that she stopped dead in the street. If what Gundry had said were true, how could she ever bring herself to suggest that possibility to Archie? Almost she wished that she had never heard of it. The more she concealed it, the more false and constrained she would become with him. If she told him, even with no idea of taking action, he would always be conscious of a threat. Either way, their old freedom and frankness had gone for good.

She walked on again, this time as fast as possible, treading with deliberate noisiness in the effort to drown any attempt at thought by the clatter of her heels on the pavement. As she turned into the King's Road, the sound of passing cars and of other footsteps muffled her own. The sounds and the brighter lights brought her back to the immediate. She realized it could not be as late as she supposed. A headlight lit up the clock on the town hall. It was only a few minutes after midnight.

She crossed the road and almost ran down the turnings that led to Tithe Place. If she hurried, she might get back in time to be in bed, with the light off, before Archie returned from Maidie's. When he did come in, she would pretend to be asleep. There was only one thought in her mind now. At all costs she must avoid any conversation with Archie tonight.

As she turned the corner by the dark bulk of the church, her latchkey already in her hand to save even a moment's delay, she saw there was light in their sitting-room.

He came out into the passage as she opened the door, saying fervently and without a tinge of reproach:

'Thank God, you're back. I had a fright when I got in just now.'

He put his arm round her, kissing her so affectionately that she felt as much remorse as if she had betrayed him. She could not quite bring herself to return his kiss.

He drew her into the sitting-room, still keeping his arm round her. After the dark streets and the hours in the dim, candlelit studio, her eyes hurt, as if suddenly exposed to limelight. The tiny room was like a brightly-lit box; wherever she turned her head to avoid the glare, Archie's face and her own confronted her from the ruthless mirrors.

'Still fed up with me, old thing?' he asked. 'Sorry I was snooty at breakfast. I didn't mean to be.'

She frowned, trying to take in the fact that he was apologizing to her when she expected questions, even accusations.

'Ah, come on, Clarita,' he pleaded. 'Can't you forgive a chap? Hang it all, you've punished me enough, haven't you? I rang up from Maidie's just to say "Hullo". I thought you sounded peeved when I said I wasn't coming straight back after rehearsal. No answer. Then I tried Valetta Road. Napoo too. Of course I didn't really think it was likely you'd be there. Nothing matters except that you're here now.'

Freeing herself gently from his arm, Clara sat down, shading her dazzled eyes.

She said in a stifled voice:

'I'm the one who ought to say I'm sorry. Of course your part's the most important thing at the moment. How was Maidie?'

'Oh, in terrific form,' he said heartily.

'Have you got the hang of your dance now?'

He nodded.

'Maidie's some teacher. Ruthless but damned efficient. Could do it in my sleep now.'

'Did she take you through your song, too?'

'Rather. Played my accompaniment by ear and sang all Sherry's part. Word perfect too.'

'And you've got your own lines right at last?' Feeling they could go on like this indefinitely, she removed the shading hand from her eyes and looked at him for the first time. His face was radiant. Was it a trifle too consciously radiant as her questions were too consciously eager?

Over his shoulder she caught the reflection of her own, looking so extraordinary that she was amazed he seemed to notice nothing. For a moment she forgot his presence; the face in the glass bore such a startling resemblance to the drawing Gundry had made of her that it was as if her features had imitated it. Her hair, blown back by the wind, revealed the broad, high forehead that was normally hidden by a fringe; her lips were still swollen and her eyes almost invisible from that violent burst of tears; the high collar of the dark coat emphasized, almost to caricature, the pinched-in line of the jaw. Suddenly, she realized that the woman who had been in Marcus's studio and the woman who sat in this doll's house room were the same person. This came as such a shock that, though she could hear Archie talking excitedly, she did not take in a word of what he said.

Focusing sharply on him again, she heard him say:

'. . . and they've asked us to do a stunt for this first night party. Jolly decent of Maidie to let me do a turn with her . . . she could have asked practically anyone in the cast. I'm not risking a dance, you bet. Just pantomime stuff. But the song's an absolute ringer for our two voices. Maidie's got a friend in this new show "Sally" that's just gone into rehearsal and she's bagged a top-hole number from her. No one's heard it in London yet.'

Clara asked, with the attentive stare of one whose mind is on something else:

'Won't this other management mind?'

'No. It's O.K. We've got permission because it'll be a private audience, not a public one. You see this party's being kept absolutely to the members of the "Billie" company. I won't even be able to wangle you in, old thing. I swear I did my best. But they're not even letting Sherry's wife come though she's raising hell. Understand?'

'Of course,' she said brightly. 'Anyway, one feels out of a first-night party if one isn't in the cast.'

'Don't mind my going?'

'No, no. Of course not.'

'You're a sport. I'd back out like a shot only it would be letting Maidie down after she's been so decent. You see she thinks it'll be a chance for me to show off the old voice. My little bit of nonsense with Sherry is really only burlesque. He keeps interrupting and guying me every bar or two. But I can really let the old vocal cords rip in this number.' He began to hum. 'Can't get the words of the verse right yet – but this is the refrain. Don't look so frightened . . . I'll do it pianissimo so as not to wake the neighbourhood. Pity you can't sing the girl's part: you need the harmonies to get the real effect. Listen.'

He stood up and, eyeing an imaginary partner, sang softly:

'Dear little, dear little church round the corner
Where so many lives have begun
Where folks without money
See nothing that's funny
In two living cheaper than one.'

He broke off looking slightly offended.

'What's the matter?'

'Nothing – why?'

'You put on such an odd expression.'

'Did I?'

Suddenly he smiled. 'I've got it. Why, it's just like us. I never noticed that.'

'Do go on.'

He picked it up again.

'She's a girl, so it's no use to warn her . . .
He's busted, but what does he care . . .
"I'll be dressed all in white" . . .

that's Maidie's solo line of course –

'"I'll by dying of fright" . . .

yours truly solo.' He took a few prancing steps, holding one arm out to his invisible girl.

'We go into a little routine here but this damn room's too

small to demonstrate; then both together, all out, rather showy harmony . . .

> '"At that church round the corner
> It's just round the *corner*
> The *corner* of Mad-i-son Square."

There! Catchy don't you think?'

Clara had pulled out her handkerchief and was holding it to her lips. She nodded violently.

Archie broke off a dance step he was tentatively trying and stared at her.

'I say . . . you're not crying are you?'

she shook her head.

'N . . . no,' she said unsteadily through the handkerchief. 'Laughing.'

'It's not meant to be a really comic number,' he said doubtfully. 'The way Maidie and I work it, it's more like "the Only Girl".'

She removed the handkerchief and twisted it in her fingers. Seeing there was a spot of blood on it, she tried to hide it and hastily licked her lower lip where she had bitten it.

'I say, what's the matter?' he asked, staring at her. 'You've hurt your lip or something. Clarita, darling whatever is it?'

'Nothing. Nothing at all. I'm sure it'll be a great success. You'll both do it beautifully. So sorry I can't see it,' she gabbled.

In one stride he was kneeling beside her and had clutched both her hands.

'What's upset you so? You're shaking all over.'

'Nothing. Really nothing,' she repeated feverishly, looking wildly round the room to avoid his troubled eyes.

'You know, Clarita, I'm worried about you. You're getting a bundle of nerves, old thing. You don't look like yourself tonight. Anything wrong?'

She said nothing. He went on after a moment, in a hesitant, rather strained voice.

'Maidie said she was quite worried about you that Saturday at the nightclub. She said you looked queer. As if you'd been ill or were going to be.'

'Well, I'm not ill, am I?'

He frowned.

'N . . . no. I hope not. I don't think she meant just ordinary illness.'

Clara said, with the sharpness of one who has something to hide:

'Maidie's usually pretty explicit. She's said something you don't want to tell me.'

He stared down at the arty raffia rug and nodded. There was a dull flush all over his face, extending even to the back of his neck.

'So you and she have been discussing us?'

He said wretchedly:

'I didn't mean to. But Maidie started pitching into me a bit. Somehow I blurted out a lot more than I meant to. It seemed quite natural at the time. Maidie being a pal of yours and so on. But on the way back I felt absolutely hellish. And when I got home and found you gone, I felt it bloody well served me right.'

She said gently:

'You shouldn't have felt hellish. Perhaps there comes a point where one *has* to talk.'

'There's something I haven't told you,' he said, still with his eyes fixed on the rug. 'Maybe I ought to. But there's also something I haven't asked you. Perhaps that evens things out.'

It was Clara's turn to stare at the floor. She longed to be able to tell him the truth but dared not. If she so much as mentioned Gundry, she was terrified that she would say everything that was on her mind. She sat there, feeling so mean and treacherous that she could hardly endure to be silent any longer, when Archie said abruptly:

'After all, you've had to put up with pretty good hell one way and another, Clarita.'

She passed a hand over his untidy red hair.

'So have you.'

He turned his face up to her sharply.

'Maybe. But *you* weren't to blame.'

She frowned, staring out through the uncurtained window at the lamp on the opposite corner of the street. He sat there at her feet, leaning his head against her knee and staring out of the window too, for what seemed a long time. The cone of misty light cut across a section of the unadorned brick wall of the church. She said at last, as slowly as if she were making out words written on that wall:

'I haven't told you where I went tonight.'

He gave her hand a convulsive clutch.

'You don't have to tell me. I know.'

'You mean you knew when I came in?' she asked, startled.

He shook his untidy head.

'I wasn't quite sure. Only in these last few minutes.' After another pause he said: 'It had to come sooner or later, I suppose.' He added with bitterness: 'I wish it had been anyone but that man.'

She told him, very quietly, only enough to reassure him. He listened without comment, only removing his head from where it rested against her knee and dropping it forward on his chest. Suddenly he straightened his body and turned towards her a face so stricken and distorted that she thought for a second he had not understood.

'My God,' he said savagely. 'I almost wish it had happened. Then at least you could never marry anyone else.' His body collapsed as suddenly as it had stiffened. He buried his face in his hands and his shoulders heaved once or twice. When he spoke again, his voice was low and almost steady.

'Clarita,' he said, pulling one of her hands forward over his shoulder and pressing it against his cheek, as he sat there with his head averted and his face lifted towards the window. 'There's something I've known quite a long time but hadn't the guts to tell you. I kept hoping . . . no, never mind.'

'Yes?' she said softly.

'Well . . . I thought by some miracle things might come right. Or . . . even if they didn't . . . perhaps it wouldn't matter so much. That we two . . . forgive me, dear . . . might be alike in some queer way. Not wanting exactly what everyone else wants.

Oh, I know you've had the rawest possible deal with me. No money. And my going off and getting tight like a hog.'

'Only because you were miserable,' she urged, feeling a desperate need to comfort him. 'Now that you've got your job . . .'

He interrupted: 'Yep. I kidded myself like that. It's even true up to a point. Theresa Cressett thought that, if we got married, everything would come right. But there are some things even Theresa doesn't understand about people.'

Clara said despondently:

'If I'd been what Theresa thought I might be . . . something that, when I'm with her, I almost fool myself I could be . . .'

'Rubbish. You're all right, Clarita. Or could be. Only not with me . . . see? I suppose I never could admit it till tonight.'

'What was it you said you'd known a long time?'

He hesitated.

'You've heard me speak of Sammy Sissons?'

'The Jesuit you liked so much at Beaumont?'

'Yes. Well . . . oh, long ago now . . . it was in the days when I was around with Lister and Bell and Co. I ran into him in a pub and I went back with him to Farm Street. And we talked about this and that.'

'Yes?' she pressed him, feeling a weight begin to lift from her heart.

He muttered: 'Well . . . he said that if things went on like this . . . naturally he kept saying "give yourselves a chance" . . . that you'd got a way out.'

She gave a sigh of relief. He asked sharply:

'Did you know about this? Lots of Catholics don't.'

'I knew vaguely that some people . . . Nothing definite.'

'I know I should have told you. Maidie went for me about that and I knew she was right. But I'd made all sorts of excuses. How beastly it would all be for you. It *is* beastly. Father Sammy admitted that. Told myself that if you could hold on till I came into my money, I could give you everything you fancied. Travel. Time to concentrate on your writing. We could have adopted some children. Only if you'd wanted them too, of course.'

She interrupted:

'Oh, don't, don't. All the time it's you who've been thinking of me. What *I* might feel. What *I* might want . . .'

He said simply:

'Well, I loved you, didn't I? It was up to me.'

'But when did I think what *you* wanted? I've been nothing but a beastly spoilt child.' She looked round the bright room, smirking still in its shabbiness. '*You* never wanted this house. Now I hate it every bit as much as you do.'

'This house?' he said wonderingly. 'You were so keen on it. I admit I wasn't so keen myself. Not that I really care much where I live. Still, this is a bit like living in a box of sweets. Bit of a strain for a great clumsy gawk like me. I admit it looks pretty. Or did before I started messing it up. Everything in it's so damn flimsy that it breaks off in your hand like barley sugar.'

'Exactly. A sugar house. Hansel and Gretel's sugar house.'

Suddenly he stood up and pulled her to her feet facing him.

'My darling old thing,' he said. His eyes were haggard and bloodshot. Every touch of warmth and tenderness and gratitude she had ever felt for him came flooding over her and with it a terror of the unknown. She flung herself into his arms seeing, in a wild jumble of images, herself returning to Valetta Road alone; an endless, featureless stretch of living again with her parents; interviews with priests and lawyers; prying questions; gloating pity; humiliation of every kind. She said wildly:

'Archie . . . I can't. I *can't* face it . . . let's go on as we are.'

'No, Clarita.' His voice was quiet, almost stern.

She began to plead with him, trying to force him back into the Archie she could dominate.

'We don't have to decide at once. Let's wait at least till after your first night. That's the only thing that matters here and now. Only a few minutes ago you were thinking of nothing else. Let's forget all this for the moment.'

He said, his voice sounding angry with pain:

'Now it's come up, do you suppose we could forget? It'd be hanging over us like a knife. I'd rather it came down short and sharp.'

In panic she went on appealing to him, saying disjointedly anything that came into her head, in a desperate attempt to gain time. She chattered on feverishly, her voice rising shriller and shriller till it broke on a cry of 'Archie' that was almost a scream. He remained absolutely still and silent. Frantic at her impotence to reach him by words, she began to claw at his coat.

He said roughly:

'Stop it. I'm not made of iron.'

Suddenly all his firmness crumbled. His shoulders drooped, he moved his head slowly from side to side with a gesture of such exhaustion that she thought he was going to fall. She stepped close to him, and felt him lean almost his whole weight against her as she put her arms round him.

'I've gone as far as I can. It's up to you now, Clara.'

They clung together, feeling each other's cheeks wet yet hardly conscious that they were crying. Archie jerked his head up at last and said, with a caricature of his old smile.

'The bloody silly things one remembers.'

She sobbed: 'Oh, don't, Archie . . . don't. Isn't there anything else we can do?'

He said gently:

'We'd better face it, old thing. The sooner, the better.'

She swallowed hard and said, as steadily as she could manage:

'Is there anything . . . anything at all I could do to make it easier for you?'

He nodded.

'Let me go off now, at once. Before I lose my nerve.'

'But where?'

'Doesn't matter. I'll find somewhere. Can't face coming back here again and finding you gone.' He was making absurd grimaces in the effort to control himself.

She had to call up every drop of her strength to gasp:

'Yes.'

'That's bloody good of you. Goodbye, my darling dear.'

She said incoherently:

'Not in here . . . don't let's say goodbye in here. Not in this house.'

Hand in hand they went out into the empty street. In the patch of darkness by the locked railings of the church they held each other close and long without a word. When their arms dropped at last, he moved away quickly, without looking back. For a moment his tall figure stood out under the street-lamp at the corner as clearly as if he had stepped into a spotlight; the next he was gone. She stood clutching the railings to stop herself from running after him until the sound of his footsteps died away. Letting go her hold, she turned towards the church, too exhausted to offer any prayer, only some wordless cry for pity for him and courage for herself. Then, very quickly, she crossed the road and let herself in to spend her last night in the sugar house.

Beyond the Glass

To
KATHERINE GURLEY, M.D.
*of Jersey City, whose friendship I value
so much and without whose encouragement
this book might never have been written*

PART ONE

Chapter 1

Usually, Claude Batchelor was so eager to get down to Sussex for his annual three weeks' holiday that, the moment the prizegiving was over, he changed hurriedly into tweeds and was on his way within an hour. This year, for the first time, he had decided to take things more easily and go down the following day. Perhaps because, at fifty, he was feeling the strain of having consistently overworked since he came down from Cambridge, he was wearier than he could remember ever having been in his life.

On the morning of the day he and his wife were to travel down to Paget's Fold he awoke with no joyful anticipation. On the contrary, his mood was curiously oppressed. A nightmare, whose details were already fogged, had left him with a confused sense of guilt and apprehension which he could not dispel. Normally, his dreams were rare, vivid and recountable. Of last night's he could remember nothing except that they had been of a kind he could have told no one and that they had concerned his daughter, Clara.

He had reason enough to be anxious about Clara. She had been married only a few months and it was obvious that things were not going well. Archie Hughes-Follett had begun to drink again and he suspected they were getting into debt. What troubled him far more was the swift and violent change in Clara herself. The last time he had seen her, there had been a defiance, even a coarseness in her looks and manner which had shocked him. Any real or fancied defect in his fiercely loved only child had always caused him such pain that his first reaction was to be angry with her. He had been so angry with her that day that, though several weeks had passed, he had felt none of his usual desire to placate her. He had deliberately tried to put her out of his mind and had almost convinced himself that, if she chose to ruin her life, it was no concern of his.

His disturbing dream had made him sharply conscious of her again. As he dressed, he remembered that his son-in-law had rung him up late the night before, asking if Clara was there. At the time, he had been not worried but annoyed. It was one more black mark against Clara that her husband, drunk or sober, should not have found her at home when he returned. No doubt she had gone to some horrible Bohemian party. He had always disapproved of their living in Chelsea, a quarter about which he had lurid ideas. It was useless for his wife to assure him that it was Archie's drinking which had made Clara hard, insolent and slatternly. Since he was extremely fond of Archie and had been strongly in favour of the marriage, he preferred to think that it was the deplorable effect of Chelsea on Clara that had driven his son-in-law back to the bars and drinking-clubs. Nevertheless, as he came downstairs, he found himself feeling vaguely guilty that he had not mentioned that telephone-call to Isabel. He would ring up after breakfast and make sure that Clara had come safely home.

In his anxious mood he had taken longer than usual to dress. His mother was waiting for him at the table where the bacon and eggs were already congealing on their dish. As usual, she had refused to help herself to so much as a cup of tea before his appearance. Breakfast was the one meal old Mrs Batchelor really enjoyed. At all others she was cowed by her daughter-in-law's exasperated glances. This morning she had looked forward to a deliciously prolonged chat with Claude who would be able, for once, to eat without his eye on the clock. The prospect of his holiday would make him not only cheerful but extra attentive to her as he always was before a parting.

To her dismay, Claude looked sombre and preoccupied. She tried several openings with no more response than a polite 'Yes, Mother' or 'Really?' Finally, she risked mentioning her granddaughter. Even a rebuff would be better than indifference.

'What a pity Clara won't be going down to Paget's Fold with you this year. You'll miss her, won't you? You were always so

232

happy together there. Summer after summer, ever since she was four years old.'

Claude said, none too amiably:

'She wasn't there last year either.'

'Dear me . . . fancy my forgetting. My memory's getting as bad as my hearing. Of course, *last* year she went off on that theatrical tour, didn't she? I daresay she little realized that by the next summer she'd be a married woman.'

'Probably not.' Claude's eye wandered furtively towards *The Times.* Mrs Batchelor said in a suffering voice:

'If you want to read the paper, don't mind *me*, dear.'

'No, no, of course not, Mother. I'm sorry.'

'I thought you'd want to save it for the train. But if my chatting vexes you . . .'

'Now, Mother, please. You know it doesn't. I'm afraid I'm a little absent-minded this morning.'

'You're overtired,' she purred. 'I'm sure nobody at St Mark's works as hard as you do. It must be bad for your health taking all those private pupils as well as all your other teaching. I wonder Isabel doesn't stop you.'

'She couldn't if she tried. How often have I told you I *like* work.'

'You overdrive yourself, Claude. You can't go on working day in, day out, even in the school holidays, and never taking a proper rest.'

'My dear, good Mother . . . I'm just about to take three whole weeks off.'

'It's not enough. What's three weeks in a year? You're not as young as you were, dear. I don't like to say it, but you've aged quite a lot in the last few months.'

'Thank you!'

'I only say it for your good, dear. I'm sure Clara would be upset if she saw how tired you look. She's devoted to her Daddy.'

'Hmm.' His mouth tightened.

'Oh, but she *is* . . . It's true she doesn't come over and see us as often as she did when she was first married. I know *I* haven't set eyes on her since she lunched here on her birthday.'

'Neither have I.'

Mrs Batchelor's dull onyx eyes brightened with curiosity.

'Fancy! I was sure *you* had. Even though you hadn't mentioned it. Though *you* usually tell me things even if Isabel doesn't. And so often I don't hear when she does. She speaks so fast and she gets impatient if I ask her to repeat something. Yet I can always hear *you* quite plain, Claude. Well, you do surprise me! Not since her birthday! Why, that was in June.'

'Yes.'

'You don't think she's poorly? No, I'm sure Archie would have told you. Still I didn't think her looking at all well that day. In spite of her having got so much plumper since she married. Of course *I* think putting all that stuff on her face makes her look older. I'm sure anyone who didn't know would have taken her for more than twenty-two. It seems such a pity when you think of the lovely natural complexion she used to have.'

'I entirely agree with you.'

'I wonder you don't say something to her.'

'It's no longer any business of mine. If Archie doesn't object . . .'

'I can't see Archie objecting to anything Clara does. He's so very devoted, isn't he? By the way, I hope *he's* better.'

Claude frowned and asked rather sharply:

'Better? I hadn't heard that he was ill.'

'I was only thinking that he wasn't well on Clara's birthday and couldn't come to lunch.'

Claude's face relaxed.

'Ah yes. I remember. Couldn't have been anything serious.'

'A bilious attack, I daresay. He doesn't look as if he had a good digestion. He's so painfully thin and his nose is always rather red. They say that's a sign of chronic indigestion.'

'Very unpleasant thing, dyspepsia.'

'I wonder if Clara gives him proper food. She's not had much experience of cooking, has she? I could have taught her for I've had to cook all my life. Until I came to live with you and Isabel, that is. But I didn't want to interfere. Still, it's not Clara's fault that she's always expected to have servants to do everything.'

234

'I'm sure Archie's extremely sorry that she hasn't. In a year of two they'll be able to afford as many servants as they like.'

'When he comes into his father's money? Dear me, they'll be a very rich young couple then, won't they? I must say Archie's wonderfully unspoilt when you think he was brought up in luxury. I know Isabel has never cared for him but I've got a very soft spot for Archie. He's so jolly and unaffected. And always so very pleasant to his old granny-in-law.'

'I'm very fond of him myself.'

'I know you are. Though he's not clever like you. Anyhow Clara has enough brains for two, I always say. She looks rather discontented sometimes. I suppose it's because of all that bad luck Archie had about that Theatrical Club. I never did understand the right of it all.'

'There were no rights. The whole thing was a disastrous, foolhardy speculation. I wish to goodness Archie had never got interested in anything to do with the stage. However, I suppose now that he's got this acting job, it's better than nothing.'

'I didn't know he *had* a job. A part in a play?'

'In some wretched musical comedy or other.'

Mrs Batchelor sniffed.

'I *do* think you might have told me, Claude. You might have known I'd be interested.'

He said unguardedly:

'I didn't know myself till last night. Archie rang up.'

His mother exclaimed eagerly:

'So it was *Archie* telephoning! Why, it was nearly midnight! I had my light on because I couldn't get to sleep and was having a little read. I thought "Whoever could be ringing up so late . . . how *very* inconsiderate!" Then I thought it must be one of those tiresome wrong numbers. Archie, well, fancy that! It must have given you quite a shock, him ringing up at that hour. I expect you thought at first something must be wrong.'

He said stiffly:

'He apologized for ringing up so late. He had been rehearsing.'

'I suppose he was so excited about getting the job. Still, you'd think he could have waited till the morning.'

At that moment the telephone bell sounded from the study next door. Claude leapt to his feet.

'Did you ever?' said his mother. 'Now whoever can it be this time? Surely not Archie again! Claude, there's no need for you to dash off like that. Why not let one of the servants answer?'

But Claude had already thrown down his napkin and hurried out of the dining-room. His unusual eagerness to answer the call made Mrs Batchelor wonder whether he had been expecting it. All through breakfast he had seemed to have something on his mind. Was something going on about which, as so often, she had not been told? Could there be some mysterious and interesting trouble connected with Archie and Clara?

The minutes went by. Normally, Claude's telephone conversations were brief. Old Mrs Batchelor's devouring passion, curiosity, had grown with her increasing deafness. More and more, the exciting scraps of gossip she longed to hear seemed to be deliberately muttered in an inaudible whisper. The telephone was in the adjoining room. In his hurry to answer it, Claude might have forgotten to shut the study door. On the pretext of looking for letters, she went out into the hall. To her annoyance, the study door was closed. Pausing outside, she listened. Her son was the one person whose words she could usually make out even when he did not raise his voice. All she could hear was an indistinct murmur, punctuated by long silences. Since he had only recently acquired a telephone, Claude tended to shout into it. This morning he was evidently keeping his voice deliberately low. Mrs Batchelor's curiosity began to itch like chilblains before the fire. She had to use all her considerable will-power to move away from the door in the direction of the letter-box. She was only just in time. Barely had she reached the hall table when the study door flew open and Claude emerged. She said, without looking at him:

'I just came out in case there were any letters. The postman's often late at this time of year. I'm getting so deaf I don't always hear his knock.'

'The post came ages ago. Mother, for goodness' sake go and finish your breakfast.' Claude's voice was so irritable that she wondered if he guessed she had been trying to eavesdrop. She peered up anxiously into his face. In the dim light, it looked not accusing but distraught. She said timidly:

'Something's upset you, Claude? Not bad news, I hope?'

'No, no. Just some trouble about a pupil. I'll have to go out and deal with it at once.'

'But, dear, you haven't even finished breakfast . . .'

'I've had all I want.'

He was already taking his bowler hat from the peg on the hall-stand and picking up his chamois gloves. His mother was now quite certain that he was lying. The itch of her curiosity became unbearable.

'As urgent as all that? A *pupil*? Why, you're supposed to be away on holiday.'

Claude did not answer. He was mechanically selecting a stick from the yellow drainpipe-like receptacle that stood just inside the front door.

'You're not going out without going up to say goodbye to Isabel? I've never known you do that all the years I've lived here!'

Claude was already opening the door. She went up to him quickly.

'Not even time to give your old mother a kiss?'

He stooped and kissed her flaccid cheek.

'I'll go up and tell Isabel you had to go out,' she said importantly. 'Have you any idea when you'll be back?'

'Long before lunch, probably. There's no need to tell Isabel.'

The door slammed behind him. His mother decided to ignore the last words. She could always pretend she was too deaf to hear them or had misheard them as 'Do tell Isabel'. Since her own curiosity had been so cruelly frustrated, there would be a certain pleasure in arousing her daughter-in-law's. True, Isabel was not particularly inquisitive but she would be annoyed that Claude had gone out without saying goodbye. Old Mrs Batchelor wondered whether she dared risk implying that she knew more than she did. Her mauve lips, with the mole on the upper one that so revolted her daughter-in-law, rehearsed soundlessly:

'I'm sure Claude will tell you all in good time, dear. I know you wouldn't wish me to break my promise.'

Shaking her large head on which the dark wig, curled in an Alexandra fringe, sat slightly askew, letting a few wisps of her own white hair escape, she decided it was too dangerous. For a moment, she wondered it if was really worth climbing the six flights to Isabel's bedroom. She was heavily built and her short neck and tight stays made it necessary to pause and pant a great deal when going upstairs. Then she remembered a remark she had not been intended to hear but which had pierced her capricious deafness.

'If you really want to know, dearest, why I insist on going on having my breakfast in bed, it's simply that I cannot face the sight of your mother before lunch.'

The mauve lips tightened. Picking up her long, heavy black skirts with one hand and clutching the banisters with the other, old Mrs Batchelor planted her velvet-slippered foot firmly on the first stair.

Chapter 2

When Claude returned home some three hours later, his wife came quickly down the stairs as he opened the front door.

'I've been listening for your key. Wherever have you been all this time? I was getting anxious.'

'I'll tell you in a moment,' he said hurriedly. 'Come into the study, Isabel. I must talk to you.'

It had been too dim in the hall for her to see his face. When the light from the study window revealed it, she exclaimed:

'Dearest, whatever's the matter? You look ghastly. Are you ill?'

'No . . . no.' He shook his head impatiently. 'We'd better sit down. This is going to take some time.'

He settled her in the big faded green armchair that had been in his rooms at Cambridge and, from force of habit, seated himself at his desk. Taking one of the fountain-pens from the bowl of shot in which he always stuck them, he began to screw and unscrew its cap, frowning as he did so. Well as Isabel knew his expressions, she could not decipher that frown. Did it mean anger or pain? He was silent for so long that she began to examine her conscience. If it were anger, it must be over something much graver than her latest filching from the housekeeping money. Only once or twice in their married life had she seen his face drained of its usual fresh colour to that ashy yellow. In the hard light of the window by the desk his few lines showed up as if they had been pencilled in. She began to be frightened. There was only one secret of hers whose discovery could possibly have made him look like that.

Unable to bear the suspense, she probed him gently:

'Your mother came up all those stairs to tell me you'd rushed out. She said something about an urgent phone call from a pupil. But her manner was so odd, I wondered if . . .'

'I told her a lie,' he interrupted. 'It was Clara who rang up. I've been over in Chelsea all this time.'

'Clara!' Isabel was so relieved that she forgot to be surprised. Confidently, she raised her head and looked straight at him. He too had been avoiding her eyes but now he had met them. The misery in his made her gasp:

'She's ill . . . She's had an accident?'

'No, no. Not exactly ill.'

'Is it that wretched Archie? Has he done something dreadful?'

He said sharply:

'You're always ready to think the worst of Archie, aren't you? In this case you're wrong.'

'You don't mean it's Clara who's done something?'

'She proposes to do something that distresses me more than I can say.'

Isabel's frightened face relaxed. She was almost smiling as she said:

'She's going to leave him? I'm not surprised. I only wonder she's stood it as long as she has.'

Claude's blue eyes, which had gone so dull, snapped with some of their old brightness.

'Really, Isabel!' he exclaimed. 'You *expect* your daughter to desert her husband after being married barely three months?

Have you forgotten that they're both Catholics? And, incidentally, that we are?'

Isabel's large brown eyes opened wider under their almost invisible eyebrows.

'Why shout at me, Claude? Because I've guessed right?'

He dug the fountain-pen viciously into the shot.

'It would be nothing to be complacent about if you had. As it happens, your guess is far from accurate. Even Clara is not quite as irresponsible as that. Isabel, this is a very serious matter indeed.'

'I wish you'd tell me straight out what it is instead of lecturing me.'

He stretched out a hand towards her but could not reach her across the desk. Withdrawing the hand again, he propped his head on it and said wearily:

'I'm sorry, my dear. I didn't mean to be angry. I'm rather tired and bewildered. It's not an easy thing to tell, even to you. Mind if I smoke?'

She waited while he went through the familiar movements of finding his pipe and stuffing it. It took longer than usual. The short white fingers were visibly shaking as they pressed the tobacco into the bowl.

'Poor dearest,' she said. 'Whatever it is, it's obviously given you a terrible shock.'

He nodded. Then he cleared his throat and said in a dry voice:

'I'd better begin at the beginning. After I'd spoken to Clara on the phone, I decided I'd better go over there at once. She was so incoherent, I couldn't really make out what she was trying to say. In fact I could hardly believe it was her voice – she sounded so strained and unlike her normal self.'

Isabel muttered under her breath:

'She's been unlike her normal self ever since she married.'

'Yes . . . yes, I daresay. I'm not denying that she's changed rather disturbingly in the last few month. But I've never seen her look as she looked this morning. If I hadn't known it was Clara who opened the door to me, for a moment I could have imagined it was some stranger twice her age.'

'She's gone off quite alarmingly lately,' sighed Isabel.

'I'm not referring merely to her looks. Though goodness knows she was slatternly and unkempt enough. No, it was something in her expression. A kind of distortion . . . rigidity. I can't describe it. Absurd, I know. I can only say it reminded me horribly of my father's face after that first stroke.'

'Claude, you're frightening me . . .'

He said quickly:

'I don't want to do that. I admit the most appalling ideas came into my mind. God knows the sort of thing that goes on in Chelsea at these parties one reads about. I wondered if she might have taken some horrible drug. She'd talked so wildly on the phone. But now her voice was perfectly clear and calm. We went into that little box of a sitting-room with those beastly yellow walls and gimcrack furniture and all those confounded mirrors . . . Lord, how I loathe that house . . .'

'I think it's very charming and artistic,' Isabel murmured.

'I doubt if you'd have thought it either this morning. I can't pretend to describe the mess it was in. We sat down and she talked, as I say, quite calmly. From her eyes, I should say she'd been crying. She didn't shed a single tear in front of me. It would have been a relief if she had. There was something unnatural in the way she sat there talking in a perfectly matter-of-fact voice as if she were discussing something quite impersonal.'

'But that's how she always talks when she's terribly unhappy. Her self-control's frightening at times . . . just like yours. But what did she say?'

'In a nut-shell, that she and Archie were thinking of separating.'

'And you told me I was wrong!'

'Wait. It's not just a question of leaving him for a time because things were difficult. Heaven knows I should have disapproved. But that would have been trivial compared to this.'

'You mean she wants to get a divorce?'

'You know perfectly well the Church doesn't permit divorce.'

'Haven't I always said the Church was inhuman? Oh, it's too cruel. Poor darling child. To be tied to a drunkard for life. I don't see how anyone could blame her if she . . .'

'My dear,' he interrupted, 'before abusing the Church, will you let me finish what I am trying to say?'

She sighed and closed her eyes.

'Very well. Go on.'

'There *are* grounds on which the Church can annul a marriage. If Clara is right . . . and she seems to have gone into this very distressing subject very thoroughly . . . there are such grounds in their case.'

Isabel's eyes flew open again.

'You mean there's a hope that she can get out of it?' she said eagerly. 'Be really free . . . as if she'd never married at all? But that's the most wonderful news!'

He stared back at her.

'Wonderful news, you call it? I'm afraid I hardly agree.'

'Why ever not, Claude? You've seen for yourself what a few months of this ghastly marriage have done to her. Now that some miraculous loophole has appeared . . .'

'You haven't heard the nature of the loophole.'

'I don't care, as long as it exists. Oh, all right! What is it then?'

'To put it crudely, the marriage has never been consummated.'

Her arched, slightly wrinkled eyelids fluttered.

'You mean Archie has never . . .'

He averted his head and sucked nervously at his still unlit pipe.

'So I understand,' he said stiffly.

There was a pause. Isabel gave one of her deep sighs. She said at last, as if talking to herself:

'What a relief! When I've tormented myself imagining what she might have gone through. *That* . . . with a man the worse for drink. Even if she's not as sensitive as I am . . .' She gave an expressive shudder and added in a stronger voice:

'The last time she came here, I was so terrified. Of course, I wasn't tactless enough to ask her.'

'What do you mean, terrified? Terrified of what?'

'Why, that there might be a child on the way, of course. Her face, her figure, that nerviness . . . even *you* must have noticed them. It seemed the only reasonable explanation. And when you and she were closeted together in the study and it was obvious she'd said something that upset you, I naturally supposed it was *that*. Thank heaven, I was wrong!'

He stared at her as she sat there, a charming, incongruous figure in the sternly masculine room. She had got up late, as usual, and was still wearing a primrose silk kimono, feathered slippers and a boudoir cap. The lace lappets covered her hair and framed her face, enphasizing the beauty of the full-lidded brown eyes and narrow, elegant nose while the ribbons tied under her chin hid the little loose fold that was beginning to form in spite of her careful massage. Fresh from her bath and newly powdered, she exhaled a sweet, troubling scent into the atmosphere of dusty books and stale tobacco. There was a mixture of disapproval and unwilling admiration in his gaze.

'For a Catholic, you say the most extraordinary things. Surely a child is precisely what you and I should have been hoping for.'

'A child by a drunkard? *Our* grandchild . . . *Thank* you,' she said bitterly.

'You talk as if Archie were a chronic dipsomaniac. He only began to drink after his mother's death. When he and Clara were engaged, he practically gave it up.'

'And took to it again as soon as they were married.'

'He'd had another severe shock, losing practically everything in that wretched theatre club. To get that sort of news on one's honeymoon!'

'Excuses!' she broke in. 'Always excuses for Archie! Haven't you any sympathy with your own daughter?'

'Most certainly I have. But there is such a thing as justice. There's also such a thing as a Catholic marriage for better or for worse. It's not something to be broken up lightly. A little patience and things might change.'

'Of course, Archie's trying to persuade her to stay?'

'As it happens, you're wrong. According to Clara, he's the one who's so convinced that they ought to take this drastic step. For *her* sake. She says he's talked to a priest about it.'

'That's the best thing I've heard of Archie yet. Naturally, *you* tried to argue him out of it?'

'I didn't have the opportunity. For the simple reason he wasn't there. He left last night.'

'You mean he's *deserted* Clara?'

'Call it that if you like. It must have taken something like heroism on his part. Clara said she was quite incapable of making any decision. He thought, if he went away, it would make it easier for her to make up her mind to take action . . . I think he acted far too impulsively. But it was an act of pure unselfishness.'

Isabel said slowly:

'Yes. He *does* love her in his queer way. It's rather pathetic he should have been so faithfully devoted all these years. The moth and the star, I suppose. All the same, how Clara could *ever* . . .'

'Is it so surprising? After all, brains aren't everything . . . Such absolute, faithful devotion for so many years. I fancy it's pretty rare in any young man. And in these days . . .'

'I can't think of Archie as a *man*. He's the same overgrown schoolboy he was four years ago. Except that now he's a dissipated and degenerate one. He looked more *like* a man *then*.'

She glanced towards the black marble chimneypiece where the photograph of Archie stood among the ranks of photographs of other young men in uniform. Already they were beginning to look more dated than Isabel in her wedding-dress. Claude's eyes followed the direction of hers.

'Schoolboys, yes.' He sighed. 'Schoolboys, the whole lot of them.'

'Dearest, it was all dreadfully tragic,' she said, seeing an older cloud settle on his face. 'But you mustn't let it become an obsession. At least Archie wasn't killed.'

'He was wounded more than once. I wonder . . .' He paused and frowned, sucking at the pipe which he had eventually lit but which was drawing badly.

'What do you wonder?'

'Whether there might be some connection? . . . It's hardly a subject one can discuss with one's daughter . . . Perhaps if Archie saw a doctor . . .'

'You seem determined this tragic farce should go on. Archie's being ten times more reasonable and humane than you are. Do you *want* to drive Clara to a nervous breakdown?'

He looked alarmed.

'You don't think that's a serious possibility?'

'Of course I do. Think of the way you described her this morning. *I* shouldn't have dared to leave her alone in such a state. Of course *I* wasn't even consulted. Not even so much as told my own daughter had rung up . . . so hysterical that even *you* were frightened.'

'It was precisely because I was frightened that I didn't tell you. I didn't want to upset you till I'd discovered the facts. And I'm not quite such a heartless brute as you think. I suggested she should come down with us to Paget's Fold for a rest.'

'She's coming?' Isabel asked eagerly.

'Yes. I sent the aunts a telegram on the way home. I told Clara to meet us at Victoria, not here. I don't want to have to enter on long explanations to Mother.'

'Of course she guesses there's something up. You never saw anything so portentous as her manner when she came up to my room. Obviously she wanted to make me think she knew more than she said. *Does* she?'

'Certainly not. I'm afraid I didn't tell her it was Clara who rang up.'

'Thank goodness for that. Her curiosity is becoming a perfect mania.'

'Could you criticize my mother another time? We're discussing Clara.'

'I thought we'd finished with that. What more is there to discuss? If they've made up their minds . . .'

'Not finally, I hope.'

'Dearest, that terrible conscience of yours! Why not leave well alone?'

'*Well*, you call it! When they've been married only a few months?'

'They should never have got married at all.'

He said acidly:

'This time even you made no attempt to stop them.'

'What would have been the use? This time she was determined to go through with it. The other time she was too dazed with shock after that little boy's death to realize what she was doing. Of course she was no more in love with Archie than before. Sorry for him, yes. Oh, all right . . . fond of him in a queer kind of way.'

'I should have said she cared for him more genuinly than four years ago. This time, there was no money to dazzle her. Not in the immediate future, anyway.'

'He'll run through it when he does come into it. No, you're the one who's more dazzled by all that than Clara. You've always been obsessed by the idea of her marrying Archie Hughes-Follett. Because it's an old Catholic family and so on. My family's just as old though they haven't got a penny. But thank goodness we Maules haven't degenerated through inbreeding.'

'I don't deny his background appeals to me. Being a convert . . . and a lower middle-class one at that . . .'

'Don't say that,' she broke in. '*You're* not lower middle-class, whatever *some* of your family may be . . .'

'Let's leave that old question, shall we, my dear? You don't have to remind me you married beneath you . . .'

'You're saying it, not I . . .' she murmured.

'I don't deny,' he went on, ignoring her, 'that it was the background I'd dreamed of for Clara. Ever since I sent her to Mount Hilary.'

'That *absurdly* expensive convent,' she put in.

He continued steadily:

'I happen to like Archie for himself. His faults are obvious but they're all on the surface.'

Isabel gave a faint yawn.

'Yes, dearest. So you're always saying. The point is, you wanted it so much that Clara knew she'd please *you*.'

He swung round in his chair.

'If you're suggesting I influenced her . . .'

'Oh, not directly! But she hates it when you don't approve of her . . .'

'That, my dear, is arrant nonsense. For some years Clara

seems to have gone out of her way to do things of which I most thoroughly disapprove. Going on the stage, for example.'

'Oh, she may *do* things you don't like. But she has fearful pangs of conscience after.'

'Hmm,' he said bitterly. 'I can't say I've seen any signs of that. The last time she came here, she treated me with open contempt. And this morning, she refused even to consider any suggestion of *mine*. To suggest she renewed her engagement in order to please *me* . . .'

'Don't be so angry. I never said it was the *only* reason. Obviously the main one was a rebound from some other shock.'

'Shock?' he asked irritably. 'What shock?'

'Oh, I can only guess. Clara's only really confided in me once in her life. *You've* always been the only parent who counted.'

'Don't imagine I count *now* . . . If I ever did! As to confiding . . . I can assure you, my dear, there was no confiding, even this morning. She merely stated the facts and calmly informed me what she proposed to do. May I ask the nature of this supposed shock?'

'Ten to one, an unhappy love-affair.'

'Really, Isabel . . . all these novels you read must have gone to your head. Unobservant as I am . . . I ask you . . . is it likely? Oh, there were plenty of young men around. But even you never suggested that any of the ones who came here . . .'

'I don't suppose he ever did come here.' She paused and shook her head. 'No, I'm sure it *wasn't* Clive Heron.'

'My dear . . . these are wild speculations. Can't we come back to facts? At this moment, Clara is a Catholic wife married to a Catholic husband . . .'

'Don't say it all again,' Isabel burst out, putting her hands up to her lace-covered ears.

'Very well, my dear,' he said in a hurt voice. 'I suppose I should have known better than to expect you to see my point of view.'

She rose and went over to him, laying her hands on his forehead.

'Poor dearest. How hot your head is. It's the fires of that remorseless conscience.'

He dropped his dead pipe and put his hands up to cover hers.

'Am I being absurd?' he said wearily. 'I only want to act as a Catholic father should.'

'You seem to forget I'm a Catholic too. Oh, I know I'm nothing like such a good one as you. But I *do* believe, all the same. And *I* don't think God expects people to be tortured beyond what they can bear. And, in this case, the Church seems to agree with me. You say yourself the Church allows this . . . annulment . . . is that right?'

'Yes. Provided the authorities in Rome are satisfied with the evidence. I understand it's a very long, slow process.'

'Then the sooner it starts, the better.'

'You realize that it would be quite extraordinarily unpleasant for Clara herself? To begin with, it would go through the English civil courts. That means she would have to go into the witness-box and give the most embarrassing kind of evidence in public. These cases aren't, unfortunately, heard *in camera*.'

'But it should be Archie, not Clara, who should have to do all these horrid things. After all it's *his* fault.'

'Precisely because it's what you call "his fault" Clara would be the plaintiff. He wouldn't have to appear since he doesn't propose to defend.'

'But that's barbarous! *He* gets off scot free and *she* has to be dragged through the mud. As usual, it's the woman who pays. Still, *anything*'s better than letting this tragic farce trail on.'

'You honestly don't think that, with a little patience . . . a fresh start . . .?'

'Of course not. How *can* you be so blind? When even Archie . . . It would be the cruellest cat and mouse game. Rest . . . then start the torture all over again like those poor suffragettes in prison. Don't you *realize* what would happen?'

'You really fear she might have a breakdown?'

'Yes. Or run off with another man.'

He jerked violently away from her.

'Isabel! Of all the monstrous suggestions! Are you forgetting the child's a Catholic?'

'Don't Catholics ever give way to temptation? They aren't all such paragons of virtue as you, Claude.'

He was silent for a moment, staring at the dusty cast of Pallas Athene on the bookshelf full of neatly labelled black files that stood against the far wall. Looking down at his face, Isabel saw a slow, patchy flush invade it.

'God knows *I'm* no paragon of virtue,' he said at last. 'But Clara . . . so young . . . and . . .' He paused again, painfully. 'She's headstrong and self-willed . . . but one thing we definitely know . . . otherwise she wouldn't dare . . .'

'Just *because* of that. Because she hasn't had any . . . any experience, she'd be all the more likely to do something she'd regret all her life. You know how impulsive she is when she's unhappy. Why, when little Charles was killed, her first idea was to become a nun.'

He said with a wry smile:

'Hardly the same as committing adultery.'

'Make me out a perfect fool as usual,' she said angrily. 'You don't *want* to see my point. When a woman's at the end of her tether . . . she'll do something she wouldn't *dream* of doing otherwise. Don't *men* ever . . .'

He made no reply. Instead, he glanced at the faded green armchair where she had been sitting and said mildly, as if he had not heard her:

'Will you go and sit down again, Isabel? I can't see you standing there behind me. I don't feel so utterly confused when I can look at you.'

'Poor dearest,' she said, kissing the bald patch in the middle of the brindled grey and gold hair.

She relaxed into the big chair again and, for some moments, neither of them spoke. Isabel said at last:

'It's terribly shabby but *so* comfortable. I don't wonder you can't bear to part with it.'

For the first time that morning, he smiled naturally.

'The old Duke of Norfolk? Far too comfortable I used to find it at Cambridge. Larry said that was why he gave it me . . . as a temptation to idleness. I most certainly yielded to it.'

'The only time in your life when you did. A very good thing too.'

He shook his head, but the smile was still there.

'That chair's to blame for my getting a second. Well, partly to blame, anyhow. But I fear I'd be as bad if we had our time over again.'

He glanced at one of the few non-military photographs on the mantelpiece. In thirty years it had faded so much that little could be seen beyond a pair of eyes that looked at once sad and amused, a thick, drooping moustache hiding a long upper lip and a pair of braided lapels in one of which was a white blot that had once been a gardenia.

'Larry O'Sullivan,' she said softly, following his gaze. 'No one ever took his place for you, did they?'

He shook his head. 'No one.'

'I remember him so well, after all these years . . . However many is it now?'

'Nineteen, almost to a day.'

'You're very faithful, aren't you? But I can understand. Once one's known that extraordinary Irish charm . . .' She broke off, biting her lip.

'Yes, indeed. That Irishman who was a temporary master at the school during the war . . . Callaghan . . . He reminded me just a trifle of Larry. You never met him. An odd fellow. Very intelligent but not very presentable. I'm afraid he drank. He went off to the front and was carried off by pneumonia.'

Isabel was staring fixedly at the photographs. She said in a carefully neutral voice.

'Yes. I've heard you mention him.'

Claude nodded.

She ran the tip of her tongue over her lower lip and said, more easily:

'He didn't sound very like Larry to me. I always remember Larry's exquisite manners.'

'He admired you immensely, my dear,' Claude added, with a certain restraint: 'He worshipped beauty in any form.'

'Strange that he never married.'

Claude seemed about to say something then suddenly compressed his lips under the clipped, still golden moustache. When he did speak he merely observed:

'After all, he died at only thirty-three.'

'I'd forgotten he was so young. Of course, it was before we became Catholics. Strange that the reason he couldn't be Clara's godfather was because he was a Catholic and we weren't then. But it was you and he who insisted on her being called Clara because you both had such a passion for *The Egoist*. *I* wanted Cynthia.'

'You don't still mind?' he asked.

'No, of course not.' She sighed. 'Poor pet, she's not awfully like Clara Middleton at the moment, is she? Don't look so miserable, darling. She'll blossom out again when this is all over.'

He said sadly:

'Even for *that* . . . God knows how much I'd like to see it . . . But unless this is really the *right* thing for her to do . . .'

'Claude . . . dearest . . .' She twisted her hands together. 'Oh, if only Larry were still alive . . . He'd have agreed with me. *He* was the human, understanding kind of Catholic. Aren't converts *plus catholique que le pape?*'

'Perhaps . . . perhaps . . . *He* took it easily . . . as he took everything in life. As I've never been able to do, except at moments. But don't get the idea he was lax when it came to fundamentals. Whatever he might say or do, the faith was in his bones. I've been surprised sometimes . . .' He broke off again and added after a moment: 'He made a good end. I've never doubted that.'

'I'm sure he did. They do, that kind.'

He looked at her with a puzzled expression.

'Odd,' he said. 'Something in your voice when you said that . . . Quite suddenly I remembered another time you sat in that chair. It was years ago . . . You looked very different . . . So utterly worn out. You'd been walking about the streets in a bitter wind. Do you remember?'

'I . . . I think so,' she said cautiously.

'It was my fault. I'd made you very unhappy.'

'Had you?'

'It was you who were right that time. About Clara.'

'Clara? Ah yes, Clara!' She added, with more certainty: 'No, I haven't forgotten *that* morning.'

'I'd behaved like a brute to you. But for you, I'd have behaved like a brute to *her*.'

'Then, dearest, *dearest* . . .' she urged, suddenly alive and eager. 'Don't make things hard for her now. *Don't* interfere . . . leave it to her . . . all right, to *them*.'

'You may be right . . . you may be right,' he sighed and fell silent again. His eyes returned to the photographs until they came to rest on one. 'Look at her *then* . . . Only six years ago . . . And to think of the face I saw this morning . . .'

Isabel looked at the photograph of Clara at sixteen. Her fair hair was neatly tied back with a black bow and she wore a white, embroidered blouse with a V neck so modest that it barely revealed the base of her smooth neck. Her lips were pressed together in the effort to conceal their fullness of which she had always been rather ashamed; her eyes looked out, clear and unconfident.

'Poor pet . . . looking so desperately innocent. But much too serious. Still, she wasn't at her *best* at that age,' said Isabel critically. 'The photograph *I* love is that charming Elwin Neame of her at eighteen.'

'I infinitely prefer this one,' he said stubbornly.

'Clara loathes it herself. She says it has "convent girl" written all over it.'

'Perhaps that's why I like it.'

'*And* she says,' went on Isabel, 'and I must say I agree – she looks as if she can't make up her mind whether to become a schoolmistress or a nun.'

He said in voice half hurt, half angry:

'After all, there are worse alternatives.'

Chapter Three

When her father had gone, Clara Hughes-Follett stood at the window watching his stocky, upright figure retreat. She watched till, without once slackening his pace or glancing back, he vanished round the corner of Oakley Street. Then, with an effort, she turned to face the empty room.

All the time they had been talking, she had been aware of his eyes consciously avoiding the stains on the carpet, the littered cigarette butts, the pool on the painted table where Archie had slopped over his last glass of whisky. Clara knew how her father loathed the room even when it was tidy. During the last few weeks, she had come to loathe it herself along with all the other speciously gay little boxes with their fondant-coloured walls and brittle furniture. 'A sugar house,' she had said to herself only a few days ago, lying upstairs on the crumpled bed and staring at the pink distemper. 'Hansel and Gretel's sugar house. And we're trapped in it.'

Now that the trap had been sprung, she felt a perverse desire to remain in it. Instead of going upstairs to pack, she began to tidy the dishevelled room. She paused in front of the armchair where her father had sat so upright on the orange cushion which concealed its broken springs. There was a dent where Archie's untidy red head rested, less than twelve hours ago. Hesitating to smooth it out, she found herself suddenly confronted with her image in one of the mirrors artfully disposed to make the room seem larger. She was as startled as if she had discovered a stranger spying on her.

Like herself, the other had fair, wildly disordered hair and wore a creased tussore dress but its face was almost unrecognizable. The eyes were dull and parched between the reddened lids; a pocket of shadow, dark as a bruise, lay under each. The features were rigid and distorted as if they had been melted down and reset in a coarser mould. She forced herself to smile, half-hoping the mask in the mirror would remain unchanged. But its pale swollen lips parted, grotesquely dinting one cheek with the dimple she hated.

Not since she was a child had she had this sense of another person staring back at her from the glass. In those days, she had often held long conversations with the reflection. Usually the other was friendly: a twin sister who thought and felt exactly like herself. Occasionally she became mocking, even menacing. Clara would smile placatingly and the other would return a sneering grin. Gradually the other would take charge, twisting its features into grimaces she was compelled to imitate. Clara would try to turn away but the tyrant in the looking-glass held her hypnotized. When, at last, she wrenched herself free, she was weak and giddy. For days after, she would hurry past mirrors with her eyes shut.

Now, staring at the other, she felt the old spell beginning to work. The dull stony eyes fixed her; the teeth bared slowly in a grin. In spite of herself, she felt the muscles of her own cheeks twitch and lift. As if something were pulling her over an invisible line, she took a reluctant step forward. Suddenly the telephone-bell shattered the silence like an alarm-clock. She broke off her tranced stare and picked up the receiver. Her mind was blank. If someone had asked 'Who is that speaking?' she could not have replied. But at the sound of Archie's voice she recovered her identity.

'Clarita?'

'Archie! Oh, thank God!'

'I just had to ring up. I say, are you all right?'

'Well . . . I'm here. Where are *you*?'

'Call-box at the theatre. Only this minute got away from rehearsal.'

'Where did you go? Where did you sleep?'

'Nowhere. Did *you* sleep?'

'A little, I expect. I don't really know.'

'Darling, you sound all in.'

'You must be too.'

'Oh, I'll survive.'

'Have you found somewhere to go tonight?'

'Yep. Maidie's fixed me up with a room. What about you?'

'I'm supposed to be going down to Paget's Fold this afternoon. With the family.'

'Best thing you could possibly do. I've been worried sick in case you just hung on *there*.'

'I'd much rather. I don't want to go *anywhere*.'

'Darling old thing, you *must* go. I can't bear the thought of you there all alone. At least I've got the show to take my mind off things a bit.'

'Yes.'

'Darling, *don't*. You sound so utterly wretched. For two pins I'd chuck everything and come rushing round.'

'I wish you would,' she said frantically.

'Clarita . . . I'm trying like hell to be sensible.'

'Sorry. I'll try to be too.'

'You said "with the family". That means you've talked to your people?'

'Daddy's been here. He's only just gone.'

'Did you tell him the whole thing?'

'I told him the brute facts.'

'Must have been pretty bloody for you. Was he awfully cut up?'

'Yes.'

'But he does see it's the only thing to do?'

'No. He says we oughtn't even to think of it yet.'

'Well, for once he's wrong. Did you try and convince him?'

'Oh yes. I talked and talked. I don't remember what I said. It didn't seem to have any connection with *us*. He was shocked.'

'Because of our being Catholics?'

'Mainly, I suppose. But . . .'

'I can convince him about that. Or rather I'll put him on to someone who can.'

'Archie, it wasn't just the Catholic thing. It was *me*.'

'Darling, you're fancying things. Or you've got the wrong end of the stick. Hang it all, I'm the one to be shocked with. He could only have been bloody sorry for *you*.'

'Oh . . . if I'd cried or something. But I didn't. I was as hard as nails. It was like someone else saying it all for me. Perhaps I *wanted* to shock him. You should have seen how he looked at me. Archie, I *frightened* him.'

'Hold on, darling. You frighten *me* when your voice goes like that.'

'He looked at me as if I were some kind of monster. Or *mad*.'

'Clarita!'

With an effort she brought her voice down to normal pitch.

'You don't think he might be right?'

'Of *course* you're not a monster. *Or* off your head. Just dead beat.'

'I mean right about our putting it off.'

'Darling old thing, the longer we wait, the worse hell it'll be. Specially for you. We've *got* to go through with it.'

Clara was struck by the firmness in his tone. She had been too relieved to hear his voice to pay much attention to what he said. Now she realized there was no hope. The thought of going on alone, of being forced to take action, filled her with a fury of panic. She almost screamed:

'Of course, if you're so anxious to get rid of me!'

'Shut *up*! That's bloody unfair and you know it. It's not what *I* think or *I* want. It's what's got to be done. That's what Sammy Sissons said this morning.'

'This morning? You've been talking to Father Sissons this morning? You *said* you'd been rehearsing.'

'So I have. Will you listen without snapping my head off? Honest, Clarita, I can't take much more at the moment.'

'Neither can I.'

'Rather I rang off?'

'No . . . Don't, *don't*,' she implored. 'I'll be sensible. I swear I will. Tell me about seeing him.'

'It's a long story. Rather queer, too.'

'Begin at the beginning.'

'Well , last night after we'd . . . well, after I'd gone off I just walked and walked . . .'

She broke in plaintively:

'I kept *wondering* where you could be . . . all night I kept wondering . . . Where *did* you go?'

'Don't ask *me*. Don't remember much except just walking and now and then sitting down on a doorstep. Anyway, somewhere about six I came to in the neighbourhood of Farm Street. I was bloody tired so I thought I'd go into the church and sit down. I suppose I dozed off for the next thing I remember was someone tapping me on the shoulder.'

'Father Sissons?'

'No. But some old boy saying Father Sissons had seen me in the church and would I serve his Mass please? Well, I didn't like to refuse though I haven't served Mass more than two or three times since I left Beaumont. And I was so damn sleepy, I thought I'd make some ghastly muddle. Well, I went up and met Sammy coming out of the sacristy and just had the presence of mind to tell him not to give me Communion because I'd cut Mass last Sunday. Guess what he did.'

'Asked if you'd like to go to Confession?'

'Dead right. He put everything down, took off his vestments and into the box we went. Hadn't been to Confession since Easter and there was a good bit to tell. I was so sleepy I probably left out half. When he'd given me absolution, he said, just as if it were quite *normal* for me to be at Mass on a weekday: "Ten minutes for our thanksgiving and then your breakfast with me, my boy. And for goodness' sake don't do your old trick of not leaving enough water over for the ablutions." Fancy his remembering that from school . . . all those years ago.'

She said, humbled:

'You went to Communion. And I didn't even *think* of going to Mass. With a church bang opposite.'

'*I* didn't mean to. It just happened.'

'Did it make things better?'

'I *feel* just as bloody about it all. But, in a way, yes. Can't explain *how*. Rather as if you were in the hell of panic on the way to an operation and knew somehow you'd just manage not to get off the trolley.'

For the first time since they had parted, Clara gave a smile that was not a grimace.

'And I haven't the guts to get *on* the trolley.'

'You will, darling. D'you know you said that just like *you*? Oh, Clarita!'

She asked hurriedly:

'What happened over breakfast with Father Sissons?'

'He made me come clean about everything from A to Z. Including the drink, naturally. Of course that had already come up in Confession. I didn't mind talking about *me* so much. What I jibbed at was being made to talk about *you*. But he said he couldn't give any sensible advice unless he'd got the whole picture.'

'What did you tell him about me?'

'Oh, that you'd put up a marvellous show but your nerves were getting all shot to pieces.'

'I *haven't* put up a marvellous show. Nothing else?'

Archie said reluctantly:

'Well, about last night and that beastly painter.'

'You might have spared me *that*.'

'I tell you, he dragged it out of me.'

'He'd no right. It has no bearing *whatever*.'

'Try not to be so furious. And, actually, it *has*. That was what clinched it for Sammy. I was beginning to hope he'd say "Wait and see", like your father. But when I told him that . . .'

'What did he say?'

'That you might have resisted temptation once but another time you mightn't. And I'd no right to go on exposing you to . . .'

She interrupted savagely:

'What does he think I am. A whore?'

'Clarita, be *reasonable*.'

'I *am* reasonable. I wasn't tempted. I was revolted . . . And you two have the impression . . .'

'Darling, we *haven't*,' he said wearily. 'Do try and understand. After all, you're a normal human being. Or *were* until I messed everything up for you.'

'*You* didn't,' she said, softening again. 'I've messed things up for myself.'

'I made you damned unhappy.'

'It wasn't your fault. I've forgotten *how* to be happy. Oh, long before we got married. I can't even remember what it feels like.'

'You'd be happy all right if . . .' Archie stopped for a moment, then brought it out with an obvious effort, 'if you married a real chap. Someone you could fall in love with.'

'Archie, don't,' she implored. 'I don't *want* to marry. As to falling in love . . . I don't believe I could.'

'Sammy's quite sure you will.'

'How does *he* know? A priest!'

'He knows a damn lot. After all, you did once.' Archie's voice sounded almost exhausted.

'So you even told him that,' she said bitterly.

'Darling, he wanted to know everything.'

'Oh, all right. Well, what did he say?'

'I didn't understand half of it. Anyway, it boiled down to the sooner the better. It's up to you now. Darling I *do* wish it was me that had to do all the beastly part. Sammy says he'll help you in any way he can. He'd awfully like to see you.'

'Don't think I want to, thanks.'

'Honestly I believe it might help. You don't know how terribly decent he was. I don't mind admitting I cracked up completely and made a bloody fool of myself. I told him I was an ass and a boozing swine but I truly did love you.'

'Oh darling,' said Clara wretchedly. 'You're not . . . you're worth a million of me. I don't know why you . . .'

'Know what he said? "I think she does too. Only not the sort of love for people to marry on."'

'Archie . . . I do. As much as I can *anyone*, I believe. But I suppose . . .'

He interrupted her again.

'And then he said: "You don't have to stop loving her." Funny, but that bucked me up more than anything else he said.'

'Oh, Archie, *dear* . . . Now you're making *me* . . . Well, what else *did* he say?'

'Oh, a lot of stuff right above my head. Holy talk, you know, must have forgotten who I was and thought he was talking to some budding J. in the novitiate.'

'What sort of holy talk?'

'Oh, all about acceptance and loving another person's good even if it happens to be the opposite of what *you* want. Then he suddenly remembered it was *me* and came down to earth. Said we were a couple of young fools . . . I mean *I* was . . . and you were lucky to have a hope of getting rid of me with the approval of Holy Church. Also that you'd better hurry up because the law's delays were greased lightning compared to Rome's.'

'Hearty Catholic humour,' said Clara. 'Afraid I've never appreciated it.'

'He had to make me laugh or I'd have maundered off again. Then he gave me a whisky, just one but a good stiff one, and packed me off to rehearsal.'

'And you got through all right?'

'Not too bad. Thank God I didn't have to sing. I'm as hoarse as a crow. I say, darling, I'll have to ring off in a minute. There's another chap in the company who's been waiting ages to make a call. He's beginning to bang on the window.'

'We'd better say goodbye then.'

'Not goodbye, please. It sounds so beastly final. He can wait another minute. Just tell me you're all right.'

'I'm all right,' she said obediently.

'Promise?'

'Yes.'

'And you'll go away and get a good rest?'

'Yes.'

'I'll be so much less worried about you if I can think of you down in the country with your people tonight. Just clear out and leave everything. I'll fix things with the Woodses. I'll come over some time and collect my stuff. Oh . . . one other thing . . .'

'Yes?'

'The railway. It's yours you know. Absolutely and entirely yours.'

'Archie, *please*. I'd feel awful . . . Every time I looked at it . . . No, *please* . . .' She was almost in tears.

'Same here. All right, darling. Shall we give it to Sammy for his ruddy boys' club?'

'Yes, do.'

'Well, good luck, my darling old thing.'

'Good luck, dear, *dear* Archie.' She mastered her rising tears. 'Your first night . . . Just think of nothing but your first night . . . It's *got* to be a success.'

'Bless you.'

'Bless *you*.'

He muttered almost inaudibly: 'Pray for us' and rang off.

She paused a moment before hanging up the receiver. Talking to Archie had half brought her back to reality. Nevertheless she still could not bring herself to take any action. She slumped down in a chair and fished out a flattened packet of cigarettes that protruded from the crevice where Archie must have thrust it last night. As she stared helplessly round for the matches, the Angelus began to clang from the church opposite. Dropping the yellow packet, she stood up and joined her hands. For the first time for many years, she said the Angelus aloud and slowly, as she used to do at school, making a careful genuflection instead of her usual hurried bob at 'The Word was made flesh'. After the bell had stopped she stood a few moments longer, with her hands still clasped, making a silent, confused petition for Archie.

Saying the Angelus calmed her and gave her just enough strength to face doing what had to be done. Its bell, announcing it was already midday, had restored her sense of time. She wound up her watch, reckoning that she must leave the house in less than three hours. With one of her sudden switches from listlessness to activity, she ran down to the kitchen. She had eaten nothing since about six the day before. She stared at the cup, at the oilcloth spotted with burns from Archie's cigarettes. It was unimaginable that it was only yesterday she had made that cup of tea. She clutched the table, looking fixedly at her own hands, trying to convince herself that they belonged to the same person who on a sudden, excited impulse had gone to see this painter whom she barely knew. If she had not yielded to that impulse, she and Archie would still be together. She had had no time to reflect on that strange, violent evening. It was all there, in her mind, with every detail vivid; the hiss of the broken gas fire, the shadow of the brushes on the ceiling, the weight of the man's body on hers, the suffocating panic, his ironic kindness after her rebuff. But it was there unconnected with real life; a scene she had once acted in a play. She shifted her stare back to the tea-cup, frowning with the effort to think. It had not been a scene in a play. It belonged to the same realm as the dregs in the cup and the jug half-full of sour milk. It was because of something Gundry had said that the situation between herself and Archie had flared up to its crisis. When she had made that cup of tea, when she had yielded to that impulse to go to Gundry, she had lit the fuse which had exploded the Sugar House and all it stood for. Feeling suddenly weak and sick, she sat down at the kitchen table and drank up the cold, scummy dregs. She found that she was shaking all over with a slight, but uncontrollable tremor. All at once, though she was still exhausted and trembling, she was invaded by a kind of ruthless energy. She rushed upstairs, flung open cupboards and drawers and began to pack. As she did so, she had the odd impression that it was not she who was stripping hangers and throwing armfuls of clothes into suitcases but some callous, efficient stranger. She herself was lying on the unmade bed, staring blankly at the cracks in the sugar-pink ceiling.

Chapter Four

In two years, nothing seemed to have changed at Paget's Fold. The old aunts were wearing the same clothes and looked as Clara remembered them from her childhood. Aunt Leah's silver hair fell in the same soft fringe above her narrow, dead-white face: Aunt Sophy's, which must have been as golden as her own in youth, was still the same indeterminate brown and pinned up in the same thin coil, from which soft, damp wisps were always escaping. Her face was still like a plump, shrivelled yellow apple with streaks of pink below her faded pansy-blue eyes. Clara had always thought of her great-aunt Leah, whose stiff manner matched her thin, bleached appearance, as an old lady; Aunt Sophy, only two years younger, had never seemed to her like a real grown-up. She was so short that she looked like a plump, prematurely-aged child and she still had a child's impulsiveness and soon-forgotten spurts of temper.

The rooms were the same in their odd medley of furniture which ranged from plain, solid, worm-eaten pieces made by village carpenters a century and more ago, through Victorian horsehair and mahogany to throw-outs from Valetta Road and objects ingeniously constructed by the aunts themselves out of tea-chests and packing cases. The Misses Sayers had never resented their poverty or been crushed by it. Paget's Fold was a monument to their diligence and independence. Everything that could be done by human hand they had done to their house, from covering its oak beams with whitewash and its ancient wood and plaster walls with layer on layer of sprigged wallpaper to making it cushions from Isabel's old silk dresses and curtains from Clara's discarded muslins.

As a child, she had never considered the effect quaint, pathetic or ugly. She admired every button-trimmed hair-tidy and wool mat. The 'real' furniture at Paget's Fold interested her no more than that at Valetta Road: what fascinated her were the aunts' wonderful contrivances that made Paget's Fold like a large home-made doll's house. She loved the red blinds, with their crochet lace edging, that had to be rolled up with infinite care for their pulleys were only cotton-reels; she loved the dadoes and picture-frames of varnished corrugated paper; the pillows stuffed with goose-feathers collected from the green outside; the little stools and sofas and dressing-tables, which, when you lifted their chintz skirts, revealed a skeleton of old trunks or hatboxes. Most of all, she loved to trace some forgotten, once-familiar object magically transformed and given a new life: scraps of an evening dress of her mother's inlaid in a patchwork quilt; a hair-ribbon of her own tying back a curtain; a child's bead necklace unstrung and patiently stitched, bead by bead, into the initials I.B. on Isabel's state pincushion.

Everything was the same, but she could not recover the old blissful security. Her parents tried hard to keep up the illusion, both for her and for themselves, that this was just one more family holiday, no different from innumerable others. But sudden silences would fall at mealtimes and Clara was often aware of puzzled, hastily averted glances. Claude's decision that the aunts must, on no account, be told the real reason for her being there created an atmosphere of constraint.

The aunts, incapable of the most innocent deceit, had swallowed the story unquestioningly. Clara was tired from the unusually hot summer in London and, as Archie was rehearsing for the next three weeks, what more natural than that she should take a holiday with her parents? Had they suspected anything was wrong, they would have said nothing. As it was, they were always making innocent comments until keeping up the pretence became a nervous strain, especially as Isabel, who could see no need for pretending, was always on the point of giving the secret away.

Aunt Leah, though delighted to see Clara, was a trifle shocked and wondered how poor Archie would manage with no one to get his meals. One of those awkward silences fell when she hesitantly suggested that he might like to come down at week-ends. It was easier to deal with Aunt Leah's faint censoriousness than with Aunt Sophy's constant desire to send Archie boxes of fruit and vegetables. One morning she came in so triumphantly with an apronful of the second crop of peas she had nursed for Claude and Isabel that Clara felt she could hardly bear to discourage her. She turned red and stammered:

'You see, Aunt Sophy, he gets all his meals out. It would be a shame to waste them.'

'Yes, dear. I forgot. Of course a man wouldn't cook for himself. Suppose Leah made him one of her fruit cakes you always enjoy so much?'

'No, *please* don't bother. They're such a trouble to make. And well . . . he hardly ever *eats* cake, you know.'

Two days later Aunt Sophy appeared at breakfast with a basket of plums, her face pink with pleasure and exertion.

'There, I've got the very thing. They don't have to be cooked and everyone finds fruit refreshing in this weather. I've picked them just at the right moment, with the dew on them. I'll wipe them and pack each one in tissue paper. Then they'll travel perfectly.'

Clara was searching for some new excuse when she caught a frantic signal from her father's eye. She said hastily:

'I'm sure he'd love them, Aunt Sophy. I'll help you pack them, shall I?'

'No, no, my dear. I'll do them myself. I've got my own little fads about packing fruit . . . not that I'm sure you wouldn't do it beautifully. Besides, I'd like them to be a little present from his old great-aunt-in-law whom he's never seen. We were so very disappointed that we couldn't come to your wedding.'

'*You* could perfectly well have gone, Sophy,' said Miss Leah. 'You know that I urged you to do so.'

'And leave you here alone with that dreadful attack of bronchitis?'

'I could have managed very well. Clara, your Aunt Sophy is just making excuses. The fact is she was too shy to go without me.'

'Stuff and nonsense, Leah. I don't deny I should have been shy with or without you. Clara's wedding was such a grand affair. But, if Clara wanted me there, I wouldn't have minded how queer and old-fashioned I looked. London scares me but I'd have gone to Timbuctoo to see her married. No, Leah, you're being very wrong, trying to put it on me. How could I have left you . . . my own sister . . . gasping for breath and no more fit to look after yourself than a baby?'

'Really, Sophy. I trust I have a little commonsense.'

'Not when it comes to managing oil-stoves and creosote kettles. And you forget how often that cough used to make you sick.'

Aunt Leah said with dignity:

'*Please*, Sophy. I'm sure no one wishes to hear people's ailments discussed at table. Let's talk of something else. I've so often wondered what can be the origin of that expression "go to Timbuctoo". No doubt you can tell us, Claude.'

'I'm afraid not, Aunt.'

'What about you, Clara? You were at school more recently than any of us.'

Clara shook her head regretfully. She knew how Aunt Leah treasured miscellaneous scraps of information.

Isabel, always irritated when Aunt Leah scolded or patronized her favourite Aunt Sophy, said mischievously:

'I wish I were a cassowary
On the plains of Timbuctoo
I would eat a Missionary
Prayer book, bible, hymnboook too.'

Aunt Sophy gave a delighted giggle but Aunt Leah looked genuinely hurt. She said quietly:

'I may seem very old-fashioned, my dear. I hope I can enjoy a joke as much as anyone. But when one thinks of the heroism of our missionaries and the dreadful things they had to suffer . . . It seems a little unkind . . . perhaps almost irreverent . . .'

Claude frowned at his wife. There was a painful silence during which all three of the Batchelors remembered that Aunt Leah's secret, passionate wish had been to be a missionary. Aunt Sophy broke the silence with her usual kindliness:

'There, there, Leah. You know Isabel meant no harm. And if there's any joke you *can* enjoy, I've yet to hear it. I don't count those old riddle-me-rees and conundrums you get out of *Beeton's Annual* and *Enquire Within*. They're too clever for me. Now I must go and see about Archie's parcel.'

'It's too kind of you, Aunt,' said Claude miserably. 'You shouldn't take so much trouble.' He hated deception at any time. Deceiving the aunts, who had such boundless trust in him, made him feel as if he were committing a sin. He added, with a forced heartiness which could hardly have convinced the most guileless:

'How delighted Archie will be. Won't he, Clara?'

'Oh, yes. He *adores* plums.'

Aunt Sophy's faded blue eyes brightened.

'Now isn't that lucky? They don't agree with some people. And isn't it lucky we always save boxes? That one you sent us at Christmas, Claude, with those beautiful biscuits in it, will be just the thing.'

She bustled off happily. Her tiny cottage-loaf figure was so short that she had to stand on tiptoe to reach the string latch of the door to the stairs. On the same impulse, Clara and her father stood up from the table.

Aunt Leah exclaimed anxiously:

'But you've eaten hardly any breakfast, either of you. Isn't the bacon done to your liking?'

'It's delicious, like all your cooking, Aunt. I'm just not very hungry. And the garden looks so extraordinarily tempting this morning.'

'Your appetite isn't as good as usual this year, Claude. Sophy and I have both noticed it.'

Isabel said calmly:

'Mine is. You give us such lovely food that I get quite reckless about my figure. Even the garden isn't going to tempt *me* from your home-made marmalade.' She picked up the yellow rose by her plate and smelt it. 'Darling Aunt Sophy. She's put a flower there for me every morning ever since we first started coming down here. I daren't think *how* many years ago now.' She helped herself to butter and marmalade and looked mischievously at her husband and daughter standing there, mute and stiff.

'If you're going, why don't you *go*? I hate being stared at while I eat. I'll come out when I feel like it.'

There was nothing for Clara to do but to leave the room with her father. Unlike the old days, she was furious with her mother for not accompanying them. Ever since they had come down to the cottage, she had done her best to avoid being alone with either of her parents, particularly with her father.

They walked in silence along the tangled, dew-wet paths, making instinctively for somewhere out of earshot of the house. In the orchard, where the grass was so long that they stumbled nearly knee-deep in it, they came to a standstill. Clara looked unhappily at a tree whose branches were nearly breaking under the weight of fast ripening plums.

'Daddy, we can't let her send them. Why didn't you let me stop her?'

'We can't hurt her feelings again. As a matter of fact, I'm going up to London tomorrow. I'll take the plums myself.'

'Going to London? But you *never* do that in the holidays! Well, then why ever didn't you tell Aunt Sophy?'

'Because, I haven't had a chance to tell your mother yet. I met the postman on the green and took the letters. There was one for me from Archie.'

Clara frowned. It was the first time he had spoken of Archie except in the aunts' presence. She had not been consciously trying to forget Archie but each day at Paget's Fold, without restoring the past, had successively deadened her sense of the present. Now it was as if the real Archie, not the lay-figure they referred to in public, had suddenly intruded into this orchard he had never seen.

She asked nervously:

'What did he say?'

'It was a very touching letter. He wants very much to see me. I shall wire him that I'll come up tomorrow.'

'Does he mention me at all?' she said, with an absurd pang of resentment that he should have written to her father and not to herself.

'Most certainly he does. In the most pathetically affectionate way.' Claude sighed. 'Poor boy, poor boy. What a tragedy it all is. I believe you're very fond of him yourself, in spite of everything . . . If only . . .'

Clara broke in: 'It's no good, Daddy. Of course I'm fond of him. But I can't explain. I couldn't begin to explain to you or anyone about me and Archie. But we can't go on. Not either of us . . .'

He looked at her with a kindly puzzled expression.

'My dear . . . I do realize you've suffered very much . . . Perhaps I see life too much in terms of rules. This is something where I'm out of my depth.' It was still an effort for him to smile but he managed to do so. 'Anyhow, it seems the rules are in your favour. Do you know this Jesuit Archie speaks of . . . Father Sissons, I think?'

'I've never met him. He was one of his masters at Beaumont.'

'He wants me to talk to him too. It seems I'm in a minority of one. If this priest thinks it's for the best, as well as Archie and yourself and your mother . . . I suppose I'd hoped that, now you've had a little time to think things over . . .'

All Clara could think of at the moment was what Archie or Father Sissons might say about her. Suppose they were to mention Stephen Tye or the fact that she had gone to Gundry's studio? Her old terror of her father's disapproval revived sharply. It was in this very orchard, years ago, on the day of her grandfather's funeral that he had abused her so bitterly for having let a distant cousin, a shy young farmer, kiss her. She said desperately:

'Daddy, why *need* you waste a whole precious day in London? Why not just write to Archie? The thing's decided. We've got to tell the aunts sooner or later. Why not get it over now and stop all these beastly deceptions?'

'I hate them as much as you do. But nothing will stop me going to London tomorrow, quite apart from the question of the plums. I very much want to *see* Archie.'

She sighed.

'Oh, well, if you've made up your mind . . . But *can't* we tell the aunts the truth?'

'My dear child, it's unthinkable. Can you imagine attempting to explain such a thing to them? Even if they understood, it would come as the most appalling shock.'

'Claude, how *absurdly* you exaggerate.'

They started at hearing Isabel's voice. She was walking slowly up the overgrown path between the flower beds and the vegetable plot, picking her way delicately through the wet grass and twirling a rose-coloured sunshade over her shoulder.

Claude put his finger to his mouth. As she came up to them, he asked in a low voice:

'Was I talking very loud?'

'You forget I have ears like a cat's.' Isabel smiled. 'How guilty you both look. Like two conspirators. Well, *have* you conspired something about poor Aunt Sophy's plums?'

Claude told her about Archie's letter, adding:

'Of course I shall have to make some excuse to the aunts about going to London tomorrow. A pupil or something . . .'

'All these complicated fibs. What's the *point* of them? I'm sure the aunts would much rather be told straight out than find out some day that you've been deceiving them. Oh, I know how prim and proper Aunt Leah is. But if *you* think it's right, she'll accept it. She won't understand what you're talking about but she'll be too proud to admit it. As for darling little Sophy, all *she*'ll care about is that Clara's going to be happy again.'

'Happy!' said Clara rather bitterly. 'Really, Mother, it's not quite as simple as that.'

'Darling, I didn't mean all at once. But till you're free, you haven't even a chance of being happy.'

'I'm afraid I haven't any rosy dreams about the future. I haven't even thought about it.'

'My child, you're probably wise,' Claude sighed. 'In any case, is happiness so *very* important in this life?'

'Really, Claude!' said Isabel. 'All right, *you* don't think happiness is important. But I don't see that's any reason to make other people miserable.'

'Certainly not. But have I done so? And, if so, whom?'

'The aunts, of course. They see something's wrong and, being the aunts, they think it's *their* fault. They imagine they've offended you or aren't looking after us as well as usual or some such rubbish.'

'Good heavens, Isabel, you don't seriously suggest that?'

'I'm not *suggesting* it. I'm saying what is perfectly obvious. Clara knows it as well as I do.'

He looked stricken.

'But this is appalling.'

'It's my fault,' said Clara wretchedly. 'I've ruined your holiday by coming down here. I'd better go to London with Daddy tomorrow and stay there.'

'No, no, darling. That's the last thing we want. Isn't it, Claude?'

'God knows it is. You're looking a different person . . . almost like your old self . . . already. Isabel, is there nothing I can do?'

'Either tell them straight out or behave, both of you, as you used to do. If *I* can make silly jokes and over-eat so as not to hurt their feelings, why can't you?'

'Your mother's right, Clara. But when one has a guilty secret . . .'

'One should swallow one's own smoke. It's part of the penalty of having a guilty secret. What you're doing is keeping the secret and making *them* feel the guilt . . . And if you won't tell them . . .'

'No. There I stand firm. Otherwise, you're perfectly right, my dear. You have the natural human approach in these things. Why is it the more I try not to hurt people, the more I seem to do so?'

'I'm just the same,' put in Clara. For the first time for months, she slipped her arm through his.

Isabel took a step back and surveyed them both, smiling and twirling her sunshade.

'How like each other you look at the moment,' she said.

Claude looked at the rosy reflections playing over her pale oval face and her scarcely marred neck and smiled.

'You're unflattering to Clara. She should look like *you*.'

'One beauty in a family's enough. Anyway, I've lost interest in my looks,' said Clara.

'That's a silly thing for any woman to say. Especially my clever daughter. What you mean is, you're afraid of being foolish and frivolous like your poor *maman*.'

'You make me sound the most revolting prig. Am I a prig?'

'Only in spots, darling.' Isabel slowly furled her pink sunshade.

'The sun's gone in. Do either of you feel frivolous enough to play a game of croquet?'

'Why, certainly, my dear,' said Claude with alacrity.

'Good. Then I'll go in and ask the aunts if they'd like to come and watch. Of course they'll say they're too busy but they adore to be asked.'

'You would think of that,' he said admiringly. 'And, if you *are* going in, Isabel . . .'

'Yes?'

'I wondered if . . . You don't think perhaps it might be better if *you* told Aunt Sophy about my going to London tomorrow.'

She laughed and tapped him with the ferrule of her sunshade.

'Oh, dearest, you'd go to the stake for truth in the abstract, wouldn't you? But if a fib's *got* to be told . . . and *your* fib too . . . let a woman tell it. I believe you're a Mahomedan at heart and think women have no souls.'

He laughed too.

'And I'd say I was a moral coward, as all men have been since Adam.'

'A moral coward is the last thing you are, Daddy,' said Clara hotly.

When Isabel had gone, Claude turned to Clara.

'I wish you appreciated your mother more. I'd give a great deal to have some of her intuition . . . that simple, impulsive way of dealing with things.'

'I prefer you as you are,' said Clara. For the first time for months she gave him a quick, spontaneous kiss. He looked almost startled as he muttered 'Thank you . . . thank you, my dear.'

Chapter Five

The next morning, after her father had left for London, Clara invented every possible pretext to avoid being alone with her mother. But when, after lunch, Isabel insisted on going for a walk instead of dozing as usual in the hammock, she could hardly refuse to accompany her. As Clara had expected, the walk was a short one. No sooner had they crossed two or three fields than her mother sat down under a hedge and patted the parched grass beside her.

'It's too hot to be energetic,' she said.

Reluctantly, Clara sat down too. For a time, neither of them spoke. Clara fidgeted and stared moodily across the fields which sloped gently down to the disused canal which wound like a narrow river between pastures that still showed green though the higher meadows were baked almost to the colour of stubble. No barges had come up it for a century and its surface was almost solid with weed and lilies. On the further bank was an old pink brick, slate-roofed farmhouse flanked by a poplar on either side. That farmhouse, whose poplars never seemed to be stirred by the wind, always had a peculiar magic for Clara. Though so near, she had never visited it and it seemed part of an eternal landscape which never varied, year after year. Other fields and farms changed with the summers; pasture would be ploughed up, clover be planted instead of corn, a harsh blue-white corrugated roof replace the mellow thatch on a barn. But this farm – it was called Hollow Land and was associated in her mind with a poem of William Morris's which she had loved as a child – never altered. The poplars were always the same bluish green, the single hayrick beside them the same faded gold, as if they were painted in a picture and impervious to change. The sight of Hollow Land, more still and dreamlike than ever on this golden August afternoon, softened her sullen mood.

'How lovely and peaceful it is,' said Isabel. 'Why can't life be like that exquisite landscape instead of being so sad and complicated?'

Clara said nothing and her mother went on:

'When I was a girl, I really used to believe that the future would *be* like that. I suppose I was hopelessly romantic.'

'Aren't you still?' asked Clara, patronizing but indulgent.

'Perhaps. You always try to make out that you're so cynical and disillusioned. I don't believe you are really.'

'I'm not sentimental, that's all.' Honesty compelled her to add: 'At least, I hope not.'

Her mother sighed.

'You hate admitting you have *any* feelings, don't you? At any rate to me.'

Clara flushed angrily. She could hardly tell her mother that she had a dread of being like her; emotional, impulsive and greedy for praise and affection. The dread was all the more acute because, however sternly she tried to repress or disown it, one side of her was constantly betraying her into behaving exactly like Isabel. At moments she could hear the echoes of her mother's high, straying tones in her own. Pitching her voice deliberately low, she said coldly:

'We can't all be the emotional type.'

'Still, with two such emotional parents . . .'

'*Daddy*'s not emotional,' Clara cut in.

'Really, darling! Considering how clever you are, you do say the most absurd things. I've known very few men with such violent feelings as Daddy.'

'Well, at least he controls them. He thinks everything out logically.'

'Not when he's angry or upset. I can assure you there have been plenty of times when it's your silly, illogical mother who's stopped him from doing something he would have regretted afterwards.'

Clara said fiercely:

'Why don't you come to the point and say "I told you so"? I've been waiting for that ever since we came down here. Well, now's your chance. Say it and have done with it. I'd rather be crowed over than pitied.'

'My darling child, the last thing I want is to crow over you.'

'You've every right. I always wondered why you didn't try and stop me the second time.'

'From marrying Archie? You know perfectly well you wouldn't have listened to me.'

'No. But I'm surprised you didn't try. After all, you brought it off the first time.'

'That's a very unfair way of putting it. You know that you were longing to get out of it yourself, only you couldn't face disappointing Daddy and all the rest of the fuss. You were grateful enough at the time. And it was I who had to do all the horrid part, explaining to Archie's mother and sending back the presents.'

'Yes. I admit you were very good about all that,' said Clara, grudgingly.

'I'd have done anything for your happiness. I always would. You don't know how many battles I've fought on your behalf. Yes, with Daddy. He adores you but he can be terribly hard and unreasonable just *because* he adores you.'

Clara was perfectly aware that her father could be violent to the point of cruelty when she did anything of which he disapproved. But nothing would induce her to admit the least imperfection in him to her mother. She said drily:

'Let's get back to the point. I'd simply like to know – out of pure curiosity – why you didn't try and stop me this time.'

'Because things were different. *You* were different. Oh, not just that you were older. Or because you didn't confide in me. I

274

don't believe you ever *have* confided in me except that once when you were seventeen. If you knew how wonderful that was for me! But you'll never understand that, unless some day you have a daughter of your own.'

'That's rather improbable, isn't it?' said Clara with a grimace.

'Of course it isn't. Some day, when this horrible business is over, you'll marry again and have children.'

Clara shook her head.

'You're quite wrong there. If there's one thing I'm certain of, I shall never, never get married again.'

Her mother smiled.

'That shows how young you still are. You think your life's come to an end because you've had a terrible experience.'

'You exaggerate. I've survived one or two quite . . . well . . . uncomfortable experiences. I'm surviving this one. In fact I'm beginning to wonder what all the fuss is about.' She tugged out another grass stalk. 'Oh, I admit I worked myself up into rather a hysterical state. I'm disgusted when I think of it. Thank goodness, I'm perfectly reasonable now. Just rather flat and bored, if you want to know. I assure you it's a great relief not to have any feelings. I'm certainly not going to risk getting involved with anyone again. In any case, it's unimaginable.'

'Is it, my poor pet? And what *do* you propose to do with your life?'

'I haven't the remotest idea,' said Clara, contriving a yawn.

Isabel sighed. After a moment, she said hesitantly:

'You won't believe me. But *I* think you're just numb from shock. You were the same after that time when . . . when that dreadful thing happened up in Worcestershire.'

'When Charles was killed? You needn't be so awfully delicate. I've quite got over that. Thank goodness, Archie and I can talk about Charles quite naturally now.' She added, less cocksurely . . . 'Could, I mean.'

'It was so understandable your wanting to marry Archie *then*,' said her mother. 'He stood by you so splendidly at that terrible time. Of course *I* knew you weren't to blame for the poor child's jumping off the wall and breaking his neck. But you had the morbid idea that you were. And that nurse was so shockingly jealous and told such dreadful lies about you at the inquest. You even tried to convince Daddy it was your fault. In fact you did convince him. I only just stopped him from writing you the most cruel, unjust letter.'

'*You* did? I thought it was Patsy Cohen. I must have written *her* a crazy letter. I knew she went round to see him. She said she didn't know he *could* be so angry.'

'She did come round. I never approved of your little Jewish friend, as you know, but I thought it was nice of her to try and plead for you. But I can assure you, darling, it wasn't Patsy who made Daddy see reason. It was your poor foolish mother.'

'It's all ancient history, isn't it? I expect no one remembers exactly what happened.'

'I remember very exactly indeed,' said Isabel. She compressed her lips. 'I've good reason to remember every detail of that morning.'

Clara said carelessly:

'I've quite lost sight of Patsy. I wonder what's happened to her.'

'Married, let's hope,' said Isabel tartly. 'If I'd had a daughter as . . . well, flirtatious is putting it kindly . . . as that . . . my mind wouldn't be at rest till she was safely married.'

'Really, Mother!' Clara laughed for the first time. 'I don't think she could help it. She was so soft-hearted. And so desperately attractive to men.'

'I suppose so. I've never admired that flashy sort of prettiness. And her methods were so obvious. Always rolling those enormous eyes . . . beautiful eyes, I admit but so *empty* . . . at any man in sight . . .'

'I believe you're jealous.'

'Jealous! Of a chit of a girl with ugly hands and no profile?'

'I didn't mean of her looks. But she adored Daddy. She told me once that, if only he were free, she'd like to marry him.'

Isabel smiled.

'Then she has better taste than I supposed.'

'All right, you win. Anyway, you know you're safe. I believe Daddy would be just as moral even if he weren't a Catholic. If Patsy had *really* made up her mind . . . even for fun . . .'

'Daddy has plenty of experience in fending off young women,' said Isabel. 'I know several of his girl pupils have fallen in love with him.'

Clara looked surprised, even shocked.

'How extraordinary. Well, I suppose, for a *man* he's not so old.' Her expression became thoughtful. 'I wonder how they *dared*.'

'You can't stop yourself falling in love. People fall in love against all reason and commonsense. At *any* age.' Isabel's expression, too, was thoughtful.

'Of course, Patsy was only joking,' said Clara hastily. 'But she did admire him enormously. And he disapproved of her much less than you did.' Her faint smile gave way to a slightly puzzled look. 'Funny. I've just remembered something.'

'What's that?' asked Isabel.

'Oh, nothing. Just that whenever I saw Patsy after that, she never mentioned Daddy. Before that, she was always talking about him and asking after him.'

'Perhaps he was cross with her for trying to interfere on your behalf. He was cross enough with *me*.'

'Yes, I daresay,' said Clara. 'People usually are when other people butt in, even with the best intentions. I don't blame them.'

'I'm sure *you* were cross enough,' said her mother reminiscently. 'You said the most dreadful things to me when I "butted in" as you call it.'

'About my marrying Archie that other time? Did I? I don't remember after all these years. Was *that* why you didn't risk it again?'

'No. Because this time nothing would have stopped you. And I think I know why. That other man must have hurt you very much.'

Clara was so startled that she said, without thinking:

'How could *you* know? I'll swear *Archie* never . . .'

'No one told me. But I'm right?'

'Oh, very well,' said Clara sullenly. 'But it was utterly and completely over. By the time I got married, I'd practically forgotten his existence.'

'Were you very much in love with him at the time?' Isabel asked in her dreamiest voice.

'Oh, I thought so, of course,' said Clara contemptuously. 'Yes, I had all the symptoms you read about in your Mudie novels. Now I can't even remember what it felt like. So much for grand romantic passion.' She turned her head away to avoid her mother's scrutiny.

'Poor darling. You needn't pretend with me. I'm sure it went very deep.'

'I assure you I'm not pretending. Sorry to disillusion you if you think I'm nursing a secret sorrow or keeping a stiff upper lip. What's more I can prove it. Before I married Archie, I deliberately went to see the man *and* his wife, just to make sure I *didn't* still feel anything. And I didn't. Not a tremor.'

'Ah, so he was married!' said Isabel. 'I daresay that came as a terrible shock to you. Men are so unscrupulous when they're attracted to a young girl.'

'You're wrong again. For one thing he was unattached when I met him. For another, he wasn't in the least a wicked seducer. On the contrary, it was all "I'd never forgive myself" and "You're only a child." *That* line.'

'He sounds like a philanderer,' said Isabel thoughtfully. 'I believe they're the most dangerous of all. My poor darling. When they marry, it's usually for money.'

'Very sensible. Actually, it was someone who could give him good parts.'

Isabel said after a pause:

'Do you think you'll ever go back to the stage?'

Clara shook her head.

'I'd never be more than third-rate. That's one thing I found out by going on tour.'

'You were very good in one of those student shows . . . no, two. Not in all of them, I agree. A little stiff and self-conscious. And your voice is like mine . . . too light to carry far.'

'Which two?' asked Clara in spite of herself.

'Such very different ones. Mélisande . . . and that little French princess in Henry V.'

Furious with herself for having fished for praise, especially from her mother, Clara said rudely:

'Any idiot can drift about the stage in a long wig, saying "*Je ne suis pas heureuse.*"'

'Not as you did,' said Isabel romantically. 'You made me think of Undine . . . *wasn't* it Undine . . . the water-nymph searching for a soul?'

'I've no idea,' said Clara.

'*Je ne suis pas heureuse,*' murmured Isabel. 'You brought tears to my eyes. Perhaps I felt it was an omen. Oh dear, how pathetically it's been fulfilled. And the other little princess showed how gay and charming you were *meant* to be. Let's hope *that* will come true one day.'

'Kate didn't take any acting either. It was just a question of playing up to Stephen. *He* carried the whole scene.' To her dismay, Clara felt her skin tingle. She averted her head in case she was visibly flushing.

'He was the one, wasn't he?' said her mother softly.

'Let's drop the subject, shall we? Unless you want to discuss him as an actor. He's going to be quite astonishingly good. His Richard II for example . . . particularly the deposition scene . . .'

'Of course I've always thought *your* real gift was writing.'

'Writing! Mother, please. Please don't be funny!'

'What is there funny about it? I'm not talking about your advertisements and clever little stories . . . though they're very good of their kind. Lots of people would be only too glad to be able to do them as well. But that other story . . . the one in the *Saturday Westminster* . . . "The Hill of Summer" . . . why, it was quite exquisite.'

'Fluke,' said Clara furiously. She clawed a pebble out of the dry grass and threw it viciously and aimlessly. 'If there's one thing I *do* know, it's that I'll never be able to produce anything but slick nonsense. If you knew how I loathed the very *mention* of writing. Can't we talk about something else? I'd rather discuss even love-affairs than *that*.'

Her mother sighed.

'I wonder if you're as fierce and defiant with *anyone* but me.'

'Oh, I expect so. Do *you* like being probed about your private life?'

'It depends who does the probing. Of course, if it's no concern of theirs and they're just doing it out of curiosity . . . But I suppose *you* think a mother has no right . . . even with her only child . . .'

Isabel sounded so unhappy that Clara felt a little ashamed.

'Sorry, Mother. I'm afraid I'm an awful failure as a daughter. Bad luck for you none of the others survived. They'd probably have been much nicer.' It was the first time for years that she had mentioned or even thought of those three younger sisters who had died at birth. She waited apprehensively for Isabel's outburst of melancholy reminiscence. To her surprise, it did not come. Instead, her mother said:

'I don't grieve about them any more. After all, they're in paradise, aren't they? And I never *knew* them. No, darling, it's the *real* daughter I care about. And if I could have them back, all three . . . as model little angels of daughters . . . I wouldn't, if it meant losing my real one. Even if she *is* rather difficult sometimes.'

Clara felt guilty. She wished she were capable of making some sweet impulsive gesture. All she could do was to mutter:

'I don't *mean* to be beastly to you. It's something in *me*, not you. I really admire you in lots of ways.'

'No one's fonder of admiration than I am,' said Isabel. 'It's my besetting sin. Yet I'd almost rather be plain if you could . . .'

'I should hate you to be plain,' Clara cut in. 'I expect the truth is I'm jealous of your looks.'

'Nonsense. You're very attractive yourself when you're well and happy. Anyway, mine won't last much longer. Perhaps it's just as well.'

Clara accepted the topic eagerly. She was most at ease with her mother when she could tease her about her fatal beauty.

'You've always been a menace, haven't you? All those men who used to follow you in the streets and slip notes into your hand at church. Really, I wonder Daddy didn't keep you under lock and key.'

Isabel smiled thoughtfully.

'Yes, peculiar things used to happen. It's very naughty of me . . . but I'm afraid I *did* enjoy it a little.'

'Used to,' mocked Clara. 'You know perfectly well they still do . . .'

'Perhaps. But I don't enjoy it any more. Oh, not that I'm not as vain as ever . . .'

'When did you suddenly become so virtuously detached?'

'I don't know about virtuously,' said Isabel slowly. 'Oh, several years ago.'

'Was it about the time I was first engaged to Archie? I remember you suddenly had a tremendous burst of piety. You took to going to the Oratory every afternoon.'

It was Isabel's turn to avert her head. Her pale skin never flushed but tiny broken veins were suddenly visible under the powder.

'Yes . . . about that time . . . yes.'

'Sorry, Mother. I only meant it as a joke. You sound as if I'd really upset you.'

'No . . . no . . . It's just that I've tried not to think about it.'

'Why, was it something horrible?'

'No . . . no . . . Not horrible at all . . . A little frightening, perhaps.'

Clara suddenly recalled the evening in Marcus Gundry's studio. She said sympathetically, almost as if Isabel were a contemporary.

'*I* know how frightening a man can be. Even someone you like very much.'

Her mother looked at her curiously.

'I wonder how much you *do* know . . . No, there's something more frightening still. Discovering feelings in yourself . . . violent feelings you never even suspected you had . . . Feelings that would make you throw up everything . . . yes, even your religion . . . just to be with a particular person . . .'

'You mean *you've* felt that . . . Only a few years ago?'

Isabel said with agitation:

'Nothing wrong happened. I swear it didn't. Call it a tremendous temptation. I've never told Daddy. I never meant to tell *anyone*.'

Clara frowned, but said nothing.

'Now you'll despise and condemn me. Oh, why was I such a fool as to tell you of all people? As if you weren't critical enough of me already! As if you could possibly understand! Now, all your life you'll have something against me.'

'Why rush to these wild conclusions? I haven't uttered a word.'

'But that frown . . .'

'It's not a thing you can take in all at once. One doesn't somehow imagine one's own *mother* . . . I've always supposed you loved Daddy . . .'

'But I do . . . I do . . .' said Isabel vehemently. 'Only just for the time this blotted everything else out. Call it a fever . . . call it insanity . . .'

'Well, at least you got over it . . . That's one good thing.'

'Getting over it's hardly the word. I tore it out of myself. Oh, I'm not a good Catholic, like Daddy. But for those weeks I was . . . I *had* to be . . . I couldn't have done it if I hadn't prayed and prayed . . . for *him* too.'

Clara was embarrassed by her mother's mention of religion. In spite of herself, she was shocked though she could not tell exactly why. She was convinced that her mother was speaking the truth; that she had, indeed, behaved almost heroically. Nevertheless she felt an unreasoning resentment which she could not entirely control . . . She wanted simultaneously to forget what she had heard and to press for every detail. She stared ahead at the landscape which seemed no longer peaceful but sinister; a dream on the edge of becoming a nightmare.

'This man. Did Daddy know him?'

'Yes. But he didn't know that I did.'

'You used to meet him secretly?' Clara's voice hardened. She was glad of the excuse for righteous disapproval.

'I only met him twice. The first time was pure accident. Then I avoided him. I wouldn't see him. I wouldn't answer letters . . .'

'Very correct,' said Clara drily. 'All the same you did see him again.'

'Once, yes. And even that wasn't deliberate. It was that awful morning your letter came about the little boy being killed.'

Clara pounced on it.

'You said just now you remembered every detail of that morning. I was conceited enough to think it was because of *me* . . . Well, one lives and learns.'

'And it *was* because of you. All the things were connected up together . . . You . . . and Daddy being so terribly angry with you . . . Oh, darling, it would be hopeless to try and make you understand . . . I'm sorry I spoke of it at all.'

Clara remembered something.

'That night you came into my room . . . about the Archie thing . . . after we'd run into each other in the Oratory. Was that what you meant? When you said there was something you might tell me some day.'

'Did I? Well, now I've told you.'

Clara said nothing for some moments. Then she muttered:

'And I supposed it would be something wonderful and mysterious. So it was nothing but a love-affair.'

'How contemptuously you say it. Wait till something of that kind happens to you.'

'I shall take jolly good care it doesn't. Do you know what became of him?'

'He's dead,' said Isabel quietly. 'He joined up. He didn't have to.'

'And got killed at the front?'

'He got pneumonia in those dreadful trenches. He'd been drinking too much for years. He didn't have a chance. He died in a few days. I wouldn't have known if Daddy hadn't told me. I had to pretend to be just conventionally sorry.'

'He *drank*?' said Clara, astonished. 'But you've always pretended to have such a horror of men who drink. Look how you've always raged about Archie's drinking. And you've never let us forget about that one solitary time Daddy came home tight. You still harp on it though it was before I was born. Mother, I simply don't understand you.'

'It's not pretence. I loathe the sight of a drunken man. I don't understand myself. I can only say that even that wouldn't have mattered.'

Clara stared at her mother. Though puzzled and shocked, she

was conscious of a reluctant admiration. In the sunlight Isabel's face seemed suddenly to have aged. It was as if the carefully preserved bloom had withered, showing another face with a still, haggard beauty of a different order. Isabel seemed unconscious of her daughter's eyes. Her own were almost closed. With a strange pang, Clara thought 'She'll look like that when she's dead.'

Abruptly, she stood up and gave herself a violent shake as if throwing off something heavy and clinging.

'I'm afraid all this is rather out of my depth,' she said. 'Let's go back, shall we? It must be getting on for tea-time.'

Shortly before dinner, her father arrived back, looking extremely tired. However, during the meal, he roused himself enough to give a convincing account of his day and to dwell elaborately on Archie's gratitude for Aunt Sophy's plums.

'He'll be writing to thank you, in a day or two.'

'I'm sure I wouldn't wish him to go to all that trouble,' said Aunt Sophy, obviously delighted. 'And you shouldn't call them my plums, since everything here is yours, Claude. All I did was pick them.'

'Now, Aunt dear,' Claude insisted. 'How many more times am I to remind you both that you're to look on this place as yours?'

'We know how kindly you mean,' said Aunt Leah. 'But you know we shall never do that. It wouldn't be right.'

'I warn you . . . One of these days, if you aren't careful, I shall make it over to you legally, lock, stock and barrel.'

'Oh please, Claude,' said Aunt Leah in genuine distress. 'Of course, you know we wouldn't accept it. But I don't like your so much as suggesting it. Your mother deprived herself of it to make it over to you as a twenty-first birthday gift.'

'A present is hardly a present if you can't do what you like with it,' said Isabel. 'If Claude want to . . .'

Aunt Leah's eyes filled with tears.

'Isabel . . . I beg you . . . Oh, pray don't refer to it again. We are so happy as things are . . . Please, never so much as mention such an idea.'

'Now Leah, don't make such a fuss . . .' said Aunt Sophy

briskly. 'Of course it was just one of Claude's jokes . . . You never could take a joke, you know . . . As if he weren't worn out with his tiring day! You must have a glass of my parsnip wine, Claude.'

When he had finished eating and had drunk some of the home-made wine, strong as a liqueur, which the aunts never touched except in illness, Claude suggested that Isabel and Clara should take a turn with him out-of-doors. Normally, however lovely the night, they sat with the aunts round the lamplit table while Aunt Sophy mended and gossiped and Aunt Leah tried to give the conversation a more serious turn. Luckily, the aunts saw nothing strange in this break from the ritual routine.

'I was just going to suggest that myself,' said Aunt Sophy. 'I'm sure you need a breath of air, poor boy, after being up in that nasty dusty London all day.'

As the three of them strolled up the road almost in silence, Claude told them in a resigned voice of his interviews with Archie and Father Sissons.

'There is really no point in further discussion, I suppose,' he ended. 'Father Sissons seems quite convinced that Clara should begin proceedings as soon as we get back to London. Actually, he used some of the arguments you used yourself, Isabel.'

'And, because he was a man, you listened to them,' said Isabel.

'Not because he was a man, because he was a priest. Frankly . . . I had hardly expected some of the things he said . . . Well, obviously his knowledge of human nature is far more extensive than mine.'

'What sort of things?' asked Isabel.

'Oh well . . . we needn't go into them. The less we talk about this painful subject the better. I'm sure Clara will agree.'

'Yes,' said Clara vehemently. She could guess all too clearly the line Father Sissons would have taken. To her relief, there seemed no sign of disapproval of *her* in her father's voice, only the flat, tired tones of a man too weary to fight any more.

'Amazingly competent, the Jesuits,' he said after a pause. 'He had got it all worked out for you, Clara. He even put me on to an excellent solicitor . . . not a Catholic . . . to handle the civil side. Ramsden, I think the name is. The ecclesiastical side can run concurrently but, of course, you will need separate evidence. Also they have to get permission from Rome before the Church proceedings over here can even begin.'

'What appalling complications and red tape,' said Isabel. 'When you think how easy it is to *get* married.'

But she, too, sounded weary and did not pursue the subject. Clara listened abstractedly while her father talked on about technical details. Once he said rather sharply:

'After all, this concerns *you*, Clara. You hardly seem to be listening.'

'I'm sorry. Yes, I heard. But I can't *do* anything till we get back, can I?'

Gradually, all three fell silent. Clara found herself thinking of what her mother had said that afternoon. The darkness, the steady beat of their steps on the road produced a hypnotic effect. It was as if the three of them were walking in a dream. It began to get on her nerves. She had an insane desire to shatter the trance by screaming out: 'I know something about her that you don't know.' The impulse was so strong that she had to press her lips together. The small effort restored her to reality. She relaxed her lips and let out a quick breath as if she had only just avoided some imminent danger. To her relief, Isabel spoke.

'It's been such a worrying day for you, dearest. But what a heavenly night it is. It seems a shame to go in.'

He said, as if startled from a dream of his own:

'What's that? I had almost forgotten where we were . . . Yes . . . we must get back . . .'

They turned about and, relapsing once more into silence, retraced the road to Paget's Fold. The smell of wild peppermint in the ditches gave place to the smell of camomile as they crushed the flowers on the green underfoot, climbing the gentle slope up to the house. They paused at the gate to take a last breath of the soft night air. Over the house the walnut tree stood like a rounded black cloud against a sky full of stars.

'A bat,' said Isabel, almost in a whisper. She always heard the high squeak a moment before Clara. Claude could never hear it at all.

The aunts had left the curtains of the living-room undrawn so that the light should shine out on the uneven brick path where tufts of musk grew in the cracks. Clara and her parents had approached so quietly that the two old faces bent towards the lamp did not look up. Aunt Sophy was sewing; Aunt Leah reading her bible. Clara forgot everything in the absorption of watching them. This was their real life. Night after night, when the Batchelors were not there: Aunt Sophy still making those dresses for farmer's wives, as carefully and hardly less elaborately than when Clara was a child; Aunt Leah reading her daily chapter of scripture before she allowed herself to pass on to anything secular. The sewing would be whisked out of sight as soon as the Batchelors entered for Aunt Sophy feared that, if Claude knew that they needed the money, he would increase their yearly present. The bible would be slipped under the table on to Aunt Leah's lap, not because she was ashamed of her devotion to scripture but because she felt they might be embarrassed. One of the notions most firmly lodged in Aunt Leah's head was that Roman Catholics were not allowed to read the bible: she felt it might wound them to be reminded of their loss.

Clara waited in terror for her parents to spoil a moment which, for her, was becoming enchanted. But they stood as silent as herself, not unfastening the gate, the click of whose rusty latch would have instantly disturbed the calm of the two old, intent faces. The night scent of stocks and nicotine came up intoxicatingly from the bed under the lighted window; it was so still that she could hear the whirr of the moths' wings round the lamp. It was the smell of all the summer holiday nights of her childhood. Something in her blank, stony heart melted as it had not melted for a long time: it felt swollen, yet lightened as if it had expanded to take in sorrow and joy, others' as well as her own. She was aware of her father and mother having moved imperceptibly away from her and standing close together. She did not resent it. She wanted to savour this sense of being apart from these two pairs of human beings; each pair so dissimilar, yet so deeply united. For a moment she felt neither old nor young, as if some part of herself were as unchangeable as the rest was amorphous and unpredictable. That part seemed to have no other desire than to stand outside, watching, observing, registering every shift of shadow on the two old women's faces, every sound and scent in the clear darkness outside. Then, all at once, without warning, the smell of stocks and nicotine and trodden grass awakened an overpowering longing in her . . . a longing not to be alone but to be loved, to share her whole life, her whole being with someone else. It was so overwhelming, so violent that she would have burst into tears had she not broken the spell, by flinging open the gate and stumbling up the path to tap on the window.

In the moment of fright on the ladies' faces before they realized who was tapping, she experienced a third sensation . . . a touch of pure panic. She had an instantaneous vision of herself as someone forever outside, forever looking in through glass at the bright human world which had no place for her and where the mere sight of her produced terror.

PART TWO

Chapter One

It was the first time Clara had been in a solicitor's office. While the youngish man on the other side of the desk slowly wrote her answers to his questions on thick blue foolscap with a quill pen whose squeak set her teeth on edge, she stared round the dreary room.

Behind Mr Ramsden the wall was lined with black japanned boxes lettered in white 'Estate of Mr X' or 'Executors of Mrs Y'. Depressed as she was already, the place had such a mortuary air that she could almost believe the boxes contained the ashes of the people commemorated on them. Mr Ramsden's appearance and manner increased the funereal atmosphere. Not only did his black coat and tie suggest an undertaker's but he asked his questions in a hushed, considerate voice as if in the presence of the corpse.

'Your husband's name is Archibald James Hughes-Follett – is that correct?'

'Yes.'

Only once before had Clara heard Archie referred to as Archibald James. She glanced aside through the grimy window at the plane trees shedding their leaves in the courtyard of Gray's Inn. It seemed impossible to connect the present moment with a morning, only last April, when she had stood before the candle-lit altar and accepted him 'till death do us part'.

'Now residing at?' urged Mr Ramsden gently.

She recalled herself with an effort and told him. As he carefully formed the letters on the blue paper with the squeaking quill, she absently traced her old initials C.B. in the dust on the mahogany desk.

To her dismay, Mr Ramsden noticed the gesture.

'I must apologize for the really disgraceful state of my office.

It is not a very attractive place for a lady at the best of times but, with our cleaner away ill, I fear it is quite shocking. I do trust you have not soiled your glove beyond repair.'

Clara flushed and shook her head. She tucked the wandering hand into her muff and clutched it firmly with the other to restrain it. She was finding it extraordinarily difficult to control her thoughts as well as her movements. At one minute her mind was an utter blank; the next it was off on some irrelevant, even frivolous tangent. At that very moment she had an absurd desire to ask Mr Ramsden how, in the room where dust lay thick on everything, he himself remained as immaculate as if wrapped in invisible cellophane. His black hair shone with the same discreet lustre as his black boots; his black coat seemed to have been newly sponged and pressed; his stiff collar gleamed so startlingly white that it made the handsome teeth he bared in that restrained, commiserating smile seem dingy by contrast.

'Your marriage took place at the Brompton Oratory in April of this year 1921?'

'Yes.'

Mr Ramsden's smile became a trifle more relaxed.

'I'm sure a lady as young as yourself will not mind telling me her age.'

'I'm twenty-two.'

For a moment, the solicitor looked ever so faintly incredulous. Then, looking at her with quite human curiosity, he said:

'Really! As young as all that!'

Clara smiled for the first time.

'I know I look much older. But I honestly was twenty-two last June.'

'Please, please Mrs Hughes-Follett, do not think I would doubt your word for one moment. Now that you are smiling, one could well believe you were even younger,' said Mr Ramsden gallantly. 'It is only natural that the severe nervous strain of your . . . ahem . . . peculiarly distressing marriage should have left some temporary traces. I am sure they are *purely* temporary. Once this ordeal is over . . .'

'How long is it going to take?' Clara interrupted.

Mr Ramsden laid down his quill, pressed the tips of his well-shaped, well-groomed fingers together and looked at her through his shining glasses. The brown eyes behind the glasses looked in such excellent condition that Clara could not help wondering if Mr Ramsden's spectacles were merely part of his professional make-up. Or were they simply a protective device, like the glass in front of a book-case, to preserve those handsome eyes, so correctly drawn and coloured yet so uninteresting, from dimming or fading?

'We-ell, it is not possible to say exactly. I am afraid you will have to exercise a certain amount of patience. The law's delays, you know. I doubt if there is any hope of our getting your case into the present session – the lists are very full. But say . . . mind you, I am not committing myself . . . say February or March. Presuming we get a favourable decision and allowing six months for the decree to be made absolute . . . then there is a reasonable possibility of your being a free woman in slightly less than one year from now.'

'It seems a long time,' sighed Clara.

'At your age, I am sure it does,' said Mr Ramsden. ' At my considerably more advanced one, I assure you a year seems negligible. Forgive my asking, but are you by any chance entertaining another matrimonial project?'

'Oh dear, no,' said Clara emphatically. 'I'm quite certain I shall never marry again.'

'There, let us hope, you are mistaken. But, in the present circumstances, I am glad of your assurance. You understand, Mrs Hughes-Follett, that in the case of a petition for nullity, it is desirable that the plaintiff should be most particularly . . . ahem . . . discreet in his or her behaviour. I understand you have returned to live under your parents' roof.'

'Yes . . . The day after we . . . separated.'

She frowned. 'Separated' did not seem the right word. It suggested something quiet and painless. But she could not visualize Mr Ramsden writing anything as violent as 'tore apart'.

'Very proper. Very proper indeed,' said Mr Ramsden, squeaking off another sentence on the blue foolscap. 'And have you seen Mr Hughes-Follett on any subsequent occasion?'

'Only once. He came back to Tithe Place to collect his things and I was there packing up mine.'

Clara clenched her hands together inside her muff and stared at the black deed-boxes, trying to fight down a memory that had suddenly become vivid. The dusty office, the law books, Mr Ramsden squeaking away with his quill pen were the reality now. At all costs she must forget that afternoon in the Chelsea house when Archie had walked in as she was miserably tidying up. In spite of herself, Archie's dishevelled red head, the flushed unhappy face above the collar rimmed with grease-paint obtruded itself between her and the impeccably neat, flawlessly respectable person of Mr Ramsden.

The solicitor looked up. She forced herself to see those brown eyes, that looked as if they were as meticulously cleaned and polished as their protecting glasses, instead of a pair of blue ones, bloodshot with drink and weeping.

'On that occasion, did Mr Hughes-Follett try to force you to continue living with him as his wife?'

Clara said in a flat voice:

'He would never force anyone. He did want it, yes.'

She could hear Archie's tormented voice. 'I know it's just bloody weakness, Clarita. But the last weeks have been such hell. Worse than the first days even. Couldn't you give me one more chance? I swear I wouldn't have asked you . . . But actually finding you here . . .'

'And you very properly refused?' asked Mr Ramsden.

Clara looked down at her muff. It was a recent gift from her father and Archie had never seen it.

'I said no. I don't know about "very properly". I felt an utter beast. I still do.'

'Your sentiments do you credit, Mrs Hughes-Follett. The fact remains that you have undoubtedly taken the wisest course in seeking to annul this exceedingly unfortunate, one might almost say disastrous marriage.'

'I suppose so,' Clara said almost inaudibly. At that moment she wanted nothing but to bolt from that room and never set eyes on Mr Ramsden again. As if he guessed her feelings, he addressed her almost sharply.

'Come, come, Mrs Hughes-Follett. You should allow yourself to be guided by those who have your best interests at heart. Still, you are a free agent. If you do not wish me to proceed with the preparation of your petition . . .'

'I'm sorry,' said Clara wretchedly. 'I know I'm being tiresome. I realize I've got to go through with it.'

Mr Ramsden awarded her the commiserating smile.

'My dear young lady, pray do not think I am unsympathetic. I fully realize the painful nature of your ordeal. As your legal adviser, I warn you that I shall have to ask you questions of an exceedingly delicate, even distressing nature. But you must regard me as a surgeon, who is forced to inflict pain for the ultimate benefit of his patient.'

'Yes, I see that.'

'You are looking somewhat overwrought. Perhaps you would like to defer further questioning to another interview.'

'I'd rather go on now and get it over.'

'Excellent.'

Mr Ramsden beamed at her through his glasses, drew in his breath and grasped the quill pen with renewed vigour.

'We will proceed then. And pray remember that these questions which must seem to you so embarrassingly personal are utterly *impersonal* to me. In my profession, we learn to be strictly detached.'

The questions proceeded. They were far more searching, far more intimate than anything Clara could have imagined. Mr Ramsden's hushed voice and tactful circumlocutions embarrassed her more than any brutal frankness. There was nothing to do but harden herself and reply coldly and candidly. There were moments when she realized that her composure was slightly shocking to Mr Ramsden. It was he who occasionally cast down his eyes and faltered while her own face and voice remained stiff and aloof. Her detachment was not entirely assumed. It was impossible to connect these questions with those two living human beings, who had once laughed and quarrelled and wept together. The questions concerned two puppets A and B and had only one object: to discover whether those puppets had or had not performed a particular mechanical gesture.

'Had you any reason, Mrs Hughes-Follet, during the period of your engagement, to suppose that your future husband was incapable of . . . er . . . consummating the marriage?'

'No. It's hardly the sort of thing one discusses, is it?'

Mr Ramsden's dark lashes drooped modestly behind his glasses.

'Pray forgive me . . . But in these days when young people are often so remarkably frank . . . let me pass on . . . may I enquire, had you known of such a disability, would you have refused to marry Mr Hughes-Follett?'

For the first time, Clara felt herself flush. Her reasons for marrying Archie had been too complex for the question to have any relevance. She could only stammer foolishly:

'I don't know.'

'Yet I take it you were willing yourself to have the . . . er . . . normal conjugal relations?'

She could not say 'I don't know' again. She could not admit that, in the abstract, the idea terrified her. How could she explain that something which would have seemed quite natural with Stephen seemed unnatural with Archie? She would have submitted, she would have tried to play fair, but she could not conceal from herself that it was a relief that the demand had never been made.

Misinterpreting her blush and her silence, Mr Ramsden said kindly:

'Let me put it in a way which is perhaps less embarrassing for a lady to answer. You hoped that there would be children as a result of the marriage?'

'Yes. Oh, yes.' She was surprised how emphatically she said it. That was another odd thing. She did not want children in the abstract yet she would have liked to have had Archie's. If she had married Stephen, she would not have wanted them. He would have found them a bore and she herself wanted nothing but Stephen.

Mr Ramsden looked relieved. He permitted himself an almost sly smile.

'Ah, that is better. For legal purposes we can assume: *Qui veut la fin veut les moyens*, as the French say.'

He wrote a long sentence with the quill pen. As he did so, Clara thought the aphorism was not true in her case. Mr Ramsden's writing was so clear that she was able to read it upside down.

'The Petitioner was at all times ready and willing to consummate the marriage and expressed herself keenly desirous of having offspring. The frustrations of her natural hopes, through no fault of her own, caused the Petitioner such grievous distress and such damage to her nervous health that, on her parents' advice, she decided to seek the annulment of her marriage.'

Clara had to bite her lip to avoid smiling. She wondered what Mr Ramsden would say if he knew that not only the advice but the very knowledge that a Catholic marriage could be annulled had come from a middle-aged painter who had tried to seduce her?

When the solicitor read the statement over to her and said: 'I think that puts the case correctly, does it not?' she answered vaguely:

'Oh yes, I expect so.'

He looked slightly hurt.

'Of course, if there is anything you feel could be added or more strongly put? I am open to suggestions . . . though I fancy that, from the legal point of view, no alteration is necessary.'

It occurred to her that he wanted her to praise his style. She said politely:

'Oh no. I'm sure it's most impressively put.'

Mr Ramsden brightened again.

'There is a little touch of . . . what shall we say? . . . that one likes to give even to these dry-as-dust formalities. I understand you are a young lady of some literary ability.'

'Whoever told you that nonsense?' Clara asked rudely.

'Nonsense?' Mr Ramsden looked pained. 'My dear Mrs Hughes-Follet, Father Samuel Sissons is one of the last people who talk nonsense. He mentioned something of yours that had impressed him in some periodical.' He gave a slightly rueful smile. 'Perhaps you think we dried-up lawyers take no interest in our clients as human beings?'

Clara felt ashamed. It was obvious that Mr Ramsden really meant to be kind.

'I'm sorry,' she said. 'I always seem to be rude when people mention writing. Guilt, I suppose.'

Mr Ramsden looked quite humanly surprised.

'Guilt? How very remarkable. In connection with such a very innocent, one might say benevolent occupation. I must say I have often been tempted myself to take up the pen in my spare time. We dried-up lawyers see some curious aspects of human nature, you know. We even have to be something of psychologists in our humble way.'

'I'm sure you do,' Clara agreed.

'Guilt,' mused Mr Ramsden, laying down his quill. 'You know . . . guilt is quite one of the rarest things we come across. It is surprising how many people are genuinely convinced of their innocence, even when the facts are most decidedly against them. Unshakably convinced, you might say.'

'Yes?' said Clara, feeling none too unshakably convinced of her own.

Mr Ramsden twitched his shoulders and reassumed his professional smile.

'Which makes it all the more pleasant,' he said with unction, 'when one is convinced oneself, as one undoubtedly is in *this* particular case.'

He stood up.

'I don't think I need bother you with anything further today. We shall have to have some more interviews later on. The next proceeding will be for me to arrange an appointment for you with the court doctors so that I can obtain their evidence.'

'Doctors?' said Clara, aghast.

'I am afraid so. I wish I could have spared you, but the law is adamant. There has to be an examination by two independent doctors appointed by the court.'

Mr Ramsden looked tactfully out of the window.

'I see. Yes,' said Clara faintly.

He turned and gave her a sharp glance.

'You have nothing to fear . . . Even if there were anything, you understand me, previous to your marriage, which you could

296

not quite bring yourself to disclose to me . . . It might make our case more difficult to establish, that is all . . .'

'No. Nothing.'

'Excellent. You will forgive me. In my profession we have to be prepared for every eventuality.'

'Yes. Is there any other awful thing I have to do?'

'No, no,' he smiled reassuringly. 'Just one other small formality. One of these days, we shall have to get Mr Hughes-Follet up here so that you can identify him in my presence.'

She had risen herself but her knees began to tremble so much that she had to sit down again.

'See Archie, here?'

'Yes. But only *see*. You won't have to speak to him. In fact you will not be able to. You see that glass door leading to the inner office?'

'Yes.'

'He will be behind that. All you have to do is to tell me that the person there is indeed your husband.'

She made a great effort and stood up again.

'Behind that glass door? I'm to look at Archie through a glass door.'

'You are looking very pale. Would you like me to get you a glass of water?'

'No . . . no . . . I'm perfectly all right.' Her voice was out of control, high-pitched and shaky.

'Is there anyone with you? Or calling for you?'

She shook her head.

'Shall I get my clerk to ring for a taxi?' He sounded genuinely concerned.

'No . . . no, thank you.' Her one desire was to get away as quickly as possible without any more fuss.

'But you look positively ill. I am afraid this has been a terrible ordeal for you. You were so self-possessed . . . I did not realize . . . Try and put the doctors out of your mind.'

He took her hand and gave it a reassuring pressure, as if he were a doctor himself.

'Yes. I'll try.'

It was not the thought of the doctors that she found so hard to

297

put out of her mind, as, blessedly alone at last, she walked shakily down the stone stairs. It was the idea of seeing Archie there behind that glass door, glaring at him speechlessly like a fish in an aquarium, 'identifying' him like an object in a shop window to Mr Ramsden. Her imagination went off on one of its crazy tangents. She saw herself beating both fists on that glass door, breaking its dusty panels, crying to Archie:

'Darling . . . it's all a mistake . . . let's stop it.'

But as the chill wind struck her face outside, blowing the early-falling plane leaves round her ankles, she knew that they could not stop it now. They were no longer Archie and Clara. The squeaking of Mr Ramsden's quill had inexorably transformed them into plaintiff and respondent in an undefended suit of nullity.

Chapter Two

Clara was rather shocked at the ease with which she had slid back into the household at Valetta Road. Once they had returned from Paget's Fold and she had put away her things in her old bedroom, it was almost as if she had never left home. It was strange to be living in her parents' house with nothing to take her away from it and no work that had to be done. Before, there had been school, a wartime office job and lastly the Garrick Academy to occupy her. Now she had not even the distraction of writing free-lance advertisements. There was no immediate incentive to look for work. Father Sissons had induced Archie's uncle, Lord Fairholm, to pay Archie's debts so as to give him a clear start. He had moved into cheap furnished rooms with another man in the *My Girl Billie* company and, now that the play had opened, he insisted on sending Clara a little money for herself so that she should not be entirely dependent on her father. She was too listless to have any ambition either to earn more or to use her fitful, unreliable talent for something better than sales copy or slick magazine stories. The necessity of appearing punctually at meals, doing errands for her mother, washing her hair, and mending her clothes carried her through each uneventful day and prevented her from falling into the drifting apathy of her last weeks with Archie in Tithe Place.

She was neither happy nor unhappy, merely indifferent. If she was now unusually compliant about going up to gossip with her grandmother in the stuffy bedroom which she had always done her utmost to avoid, if she was willing to spend hours with Isabel reviewing her mother's wardrobe or discussing the merits of various shades of powder, it was from no desire to give pleasure. Any occupation, however trivial, helped to fill up the day. Better still, it prevented her from having to think or to make any decision. She seemed, indeed, to have become incapable of thought. Her father, delighted to have her home again now that he had accepted the situation, sometimes tried to lure her into a discussion. In the old days she had enjoyed talking to him about subjects in which Isabel took not the faintest interest. Now her mind dissolved at the mere threat of having to form any opinion. She could barely manage to take in what he was saying, let alone make an intelligible reply. Sometimes a phrase would lodge in her brain and go on repeating itself like a record when the needle sticks, distracting her from hearing what followed. Sometimes a word such as 'Consequences' 'Unemployment' of 'Inflation' would slowly write itself on the air as if traced in smoke and her eyes would follow each stroke, intent only on the shaping of each letter. Occasionally she caught her father staring at her with a half-angry, half-anxious expression. Then her mother would say: 'Don't bother Clara with your old politics and things. Can't you see she's worn out with all she's been through?'

Clara was not grateful for her mother's solicitude. She realized that she was supposed to have gone through a great ordeal in the few months of her marriage. Now it was over, she could no longer recapture the misery and despair. Sometimes, when she opened the black notebook in which she had recorded her feelings at the time, she could hardly believe that she ever felt anything so violently. One thing she was quite sure of: she would never feel violently again. Then she had been passionately anxious about so many things . . . about herself, about Archie, about what possible use could ever be made of the rest of a life which had been nothing but a series of false starts. She had had moods of exaltations as well as despair: a poem, a picture, the sight of a face in the street could suddenly rouse her to an excitement which made her long to communicate it to someone else. Since her return to Valetta Road she had experienced neither. She could no longer read anything but newspapers and magazines. The poets and novelists she had once loved now seemed to be writing of a totally artificial world of emotion and experience; a world she had no desire to enter.

There were, of course, moments when she was disquieted by her lack of desire for anything at all. Since she had always been restless and impatient, always longing to hurry on the future, this mood of mild indifference seemed unnatural. She avoided her old friends, not from sensitiveness, but simply because she could not be bothered to make any move. When she thought of Archie, it was with none of the old pity and affection, but with a faint envy. It was probably better to be able to feel violently as Archie did, to want something passionately even if you lost it as soon as you had found it. In any case, if Archie had lost her, he was doing what he had always longed to do. He was making a success of it. Tiny as his part was, several notices had mentioned him by name and praised him.

Nearly six weeks passed during which there was nothing Clara was forced to do but go up to Gray's Inn for an occasional interview with Mr Ramsden. Once or twice these momentarily disturbed her indifference but she learnt to master a fit of trembling or a sudden threat of tears. But the day when he said:

'Mrs Hughes-Follett, your husband is in the office for purposes of identification,' she suddenly turned faint. At the first she would not so much as open her eyes when Mr Ramsden led her to the glass-topped door and whispered: 'You need only take one glance.'

She forced them open and there was Archie, mute and staring like herself, on the other side of the glass. He looked different. His untidy red hair was sleeked down: he was wearing an overcoat she did not recognize. Her automatic control returned.

She looked at Archie as if he were a photograph and said: 'Yes, that is my husband.' Then Mr Ramsden led her back to his own office and kept her in idle chat for a few moments. She heard her own voice saying words with the right intonation but had no idea what they were. The clerk called her a taxi. When she got into it she found she was icy cold and that her right temple was throbbing in a sickening, painful rhythm. The hammer strokes fell faster and harder till, when she paid off the driver at Valetta Road, black zigzags were dancing in front of her right eye and she thought she was going to vomit. All the next day she lay in bed in a darkened room. Unaccustomed to physical pain, she was surprised that the body could feel so violently when the other sensibilities were numb.

She had another of these headaches after being examined by the two court doctors. During the examination she managed to detach herself so completely from what was going on that her body seemed to have no connection with her. She even felt an insane desire to laugh at the doctors' elaborate precautions, as if it were their modesty and not hers which had to be safeguarded. But afterwards she found that she was shaking all over and, by the time she got home, her right temple was throbbing like a dynamo. She lay for hours aware only of the terrible, insistent beat to which the words 'Virgo Intacta' fitted themselves as if to the pounding rhythm of train wheels.

Some days after this, Mr Ramsden announced triumphantly that there was a hope that her case might be squeezed into the current session and heard before Christmas. Clara felt no elation, merely a relief that, for the time being, there would be no more interviews with the solicitors and she would have to take no action of any kind. Mr Ramsden had suggested that she might like to begin preliminary enquiries with the ecclesiastical authorities. But since proceedings could not be officially begun until she had obtained the civil decree, she thankfully put it off.

When she had been at Valetta Road for over two months, she noticed that her parents were becoming a trifle restive. Her father began to hint that, now she was looking so much better, it might be a good idea for her to find work of some kind. Clara was immediately on the defensive. 'What kind of work?' she asked. 'I don't imagine you want me to go back to the stage, do you? Anyhow, I shouldn't have the remotest hope of getting a part in London. And I can't go on tour because of the case.'

'Good heavens, no, my dear. Anything but that! What about your advertisements and so on?'

'I've lost the knack. Besides you always disapproved of that too.'

He could not deny it and suggested hesitantly that, as her French was good, she might be able to coach some of his younger pupils. This suggestion alarmed her so much that, for the first time, she burst into tears. She could not tell him why the idea of giving a boy a few French lessons caused such panic. The real reason was that it revived the idea of being a schoolmistress which her father had cherished for her all his life. Home, instead of a refuge, suddenly appeared to Clara as a trap. She would never escape again. At twenty-two she was going to be condemned for life to what she had spent years trying to avoid . . . a career of teaching. Not even in a school but as her father's junior assistant. She saw herself twenty years hence, a dry spinster with pince-nez. 'Mr Batchelor's daughter. Such a help to him. A pity she never took her degree of course.' 'Wasn't she on the stage once? I even believe she got married!' 'My *dear* . . . people will say anything. You've only to look at Miss Batchelor to know neither of those absurd rumours could possibly be true.'

Her father, though disturbed by this sudden burst of crying, was inclined to press his point, though gently. Luckily her mother came to her rescue with a suggestion that silenced him.

'Claude, how *can* you be so tactless? Just when she was beginning to get over things . . . to bring up the subject of teaching boys. Charles Cressett . . . you *can't* have forgotten Archie's connection with all that tragedy?'

It was easy after that to escape to her bedroom and bathe her stinging eyes. As she did so, she was aware of a sensation she had never expected to feel again. She felt she must get out of the house, do something, above all, see someone who did not belong to her family. Feverishly she did up her face, changed her dress and ran softly down the stairs, hoping to be out of the house before the meal was finished. She was too late: her mother was already coming upstairs for her ritual afternoon rest.

'Going out, darling? What a good idea! It's so bad for you staying indoors so much.'

On an impulse, Clara drew her mother into her bedroom and shut the door.

'Mother . . . would it matter if I were out to dinner tonight?'

'Of course not, darling. Have you got an invitation? I'm so glad if you have. You haven't seen any of your old friends since you came home.'

'No. Nothing definite. I just feel I want to get away from Valetta Road. Do you understand?'

Isabel kissed her.

'Of course, darling. You don't know how often I wish *I* could. The minute dinner's over, Daddy disappears into the study and there's nothing for me to do but read or strum the piano or go to bed.' She added hastily: 'I mean there *was*, until you came home. You can't think how lovely it is having you back again.'

'I'm pretty rotten company I'm afraid,' said Clara, pulling down her eye-veil to avoid another kiss. She was grateful to her mother for her intervention at lunch but she was in no mood for demonstrations.

'What a charming hat,' said Isabel. 'I'd forgotten it.'

She stepped back and looked critically at Clara.

'Why, you suddenly look more like your old self. Your face always had so much life in it. All these weeks it's looked like a house with the blinds down. And now . . .'

This time there was no avoiding the kiss.

'Go and enjoy yourself, pet. I'll make some excuse to Daddy.'

Once she was out in the street, Clara's flatness returned. Where, after all, could she go? Whom could she see? Honour demanded that, once out of the house, she must stay out till considerably after dinner time. She ran through a list of the old friends she had shockingly neglected since her marriage but none of them appealed to her. She could not face curiosity, excited sympathy, tactfully veiled triumph. It was a sunny late October day with a wind sharp enough to make her eyes, still sore from crying, water behind the eye-veil. She pulled the fur collar of her coat almost up to her nose and began to walk fast and aimlessly. After a while, finding she was automatically walking south, she deliberately took the streets that led to Chelsea.

Chelsea seemed so remote from her present life that she could almost fancy it did not exist except in her imagination. When she found herself once more in the King's Road, though recognizing every shop and tree, she still could not believe that, only a few months earlier, it had been her daily thoroughfare. Not till she stood on the corner by the Catholic church, staring across at the 'Sugar House' did she recover any sense of connection. The orange curtains were drawn and the windows shut. She crossed the road and walked down the side street, peering guiltily through the flap of the letterbox into the shed which their landlords had called a 'studio'. She could make out a faint glitter of metal in one corner. Archie must have left some of the sleepers when he dismantled the model railway. Someone – was it Archie himself? – had piled them up anyhow against the wall. She was suddenly seized with the mad idea that it was not her life here that had been an unreal dream but her present life in West Kensington. She had an insane desire to get into the house, barricade herself in and never return to Valetta Road again. Suddenly she remembered that she still had the key to the house in her handbag. Recklessly, she retraced her steps and was just going to turn the corner to approach the front of the house when she heard the street door open. She flattened herself against the wall, her heart beating violently. A woman came out. Clara could only see her from the back but she recognized the brassy hair of Mrs Woods. The owner. Mrs Woods hesitated for a moment, then, mercifully, took the other direction.

Clara had always disliked their landlady. The idea that Mrs Woods might have found her, not merely spying through the letter-box of the shed but actually breaking into the house, made the sweat start out on her forehead. She turned and walked, as fast as her shaking knees would let her, through the back streets that led to the embankment. Leaning on the parapet to recover her breath, she took the key of the Sugar House out of her bag and threw it in the river.

The action cleared her head. For the first time she realized, however dimly, that her standing there, staring at the dancing coins of light on the dark water, was part of a continuous stream of life. Since her marriage she had had an increasing sense of unreality, as if her existence had been broken off like the reel of a film. Nothing that had happened to her seemed to have had a connection with any past or to be leading to any future. Now she perceived, though she could not yet feel it, that her life could not, in the nature of things, remain in this state of tranced immobility. However sluggishly, it would go on like the river and the mere going on must produce some changes for better or worse. Whether she liked it or not, she could not go back to the Sugar House. A startling idea occurred to her. She could not yet imagine summoning up the will to do so but, like a revelation, she saw that it might be possible for her one day to leave her parents' house again.

Excited by the mere possibility, she went into the 'Blue Cockatoo' and sat there drinking coffee and smoking for nearly an hour. Her thoughts took no practical turn: she merely let herself drift on a tide of vague, slightly guilty pleasure. On the wall was a poster of the London Group's autumn exhibition. One of the painters exhibiting was Marcus Gundry. That strange episode in his studio the night that she and Archie had parted was now the most unreal of all. It was not that she did not remember it: it was simply isolated in her own consciousness like a vivid dream. Staring at his printed name, a simple, yet astonishing fact presented itself. Marcus Gundry was a real person. In order to have his name printed on that poster, he had bought materials, stretched canvases, painted pictures, sent them to a Committee. She became aware of an even more astonishing fact – a discovery so startling that she caught her breath with excitement. What had happened to her that evening had happened also to him. He too had lived through those hours, evidently with very different feelings, but they had been part of his experience as of hers. For her experience had been disturbing, even shocking, yet, as she sat alone in the arty little restaurant, aware of the sulky glances of the waitress who was a Chelsea 'character' and obviously regarded her as an intruder, it suddenly acquired a new importance. Marcus Gundry had had no preconceived ideas about her: he had simply accepted her as another human being. And she had felt another human being in a more special sense. It was true she had behaved in the most extraordinary way; relaxed and happy one moment, hysterical with terror the next. But, throughout that evening, for one of the few times in her life she had been completely natural. She had said exactly what came into her mind; she had asked questions she had never dared to ask before; she had made an utter fool of herself and she had not minded. All that seemed important now was the extraordinary sense of being alive after months of deadness that she had had that evening. An impulse came over her, as strong as her impulse to let herself into the Sugar House. She stubbed out her half-smoked cigarette and stood up, hardly able to control her impatience at the slowness of the sullen waitress. Out in the street again, she realized that her sudden longing to see Gundry was as crazy as the other. But to want anything again was so intoxicating that she could no more control the want than she had been able, all these months, to force her will into any channel. As she hurried along, so eager to be there that, if a taxi had passed, she would have hailed it, what was left of her reason kept saying 'This is absurd. You know it's absurd. It won't even work. You know perfectly well that Gundry is only interested in you as a possible mistress. You haven't the slightest intention of becoming his mistress. It won't even be like the last time. You will be in a perfectly ridiculous situation. He'll be furious . . . He'll be bored.' She was scolding herself so vehemently that her lips moved as she almost ran along. Not looking where she was going, she muttered quite audibly 'Stop it, you idiot!' At that moment someone blocked her way. A hand fell on her arm.

'Stop *what*?' enquired a mild, amused voice.

She looked up, dazed, and found herself staring into a face she knew.

'Clive Heron!' she gasped. 'Of all people!' she added with perfect sincerity: 'You can't *think* how glad I am to see you.'

'Don't tell me you were thinking of me at that very moment because I certainly shan't believe you,' he said, turning and falling into step beside her.

'And you would be right. You couldn't have been farther from my thoughts,' Clara said, with the gaiety which the appearance of Clive Heron always induced. His appearances had always been rare and unpredictable. In the interval, Clara was apt to forget all about him yet, whenever she ran into him again, she was always aware of this sudden lightheartedness.

'I am always right,' said Clive Heron. He clutched the hat which always looked far too large and heavy above the small, delicately featured face which seemed too frail to support the weight of his pince-nez. '*Must* we walk in the teeth of this appalling gale? I was deliberately keeping my back to it.'

'We could turn round and walk up Oakley Street. Unless you're going anywhere special?'

'No. I'm merely taking my Saturday afternoon constitutional. The direction is *entirely* determined by avoiding these icy blasts. What about you?'

'I'm not going anywhere special either. At least, not now. I've changed my mind.'

'Stopped it, in fact?'

'Yes. Thanks to you.'

They turned into Oakley Street and Clara tried to lengthen her step to keep up with Heron's strides.

'You can't do it,' he observed. 'Better tittup along in your usual ridiculous fashion.'

Obediently she returned to her usual short step.

'May one enquire stop *what*?' he asked, after a moment. 'From the way you were dashing along, muttering to yourself, you seemed to be fairly far gone. Suicide?'

'Not quite as final. I was trying to stop myself from going to see the very last person I *ought* to see.'

'Hmm. Do you *want* to be restrained?'

'Yes.'

'What do you expect me to do? Escort you back to your own doorstep?'

'No. I've said I'm not going to be home till after dinner and nothing will induce me to go back to West Kensington for hours and hours and hours.'

'West Kensington? I thought you were living in Tithe Place.'

'I was. But I'm not now.'

'Dear, dear, how very confusing. I wish people wouldn't gad about so. I had just got it into my consciousness that you were living round the corner from me. In another month or two, I might even have brought myself to the point of ringing you up. Now I've got to absorb an entirely new set of referenda. Really, my dear girl, it's intolerable. What *have* you been up to?'

'Too complicated to tell you in the street.'

'Well, at least you have some grains of sense left. Oh God, now we've got to turn into this infernal wind again. What do you want to *do*?' he asked in an exasperated voice.

'I haven't the least idea.'

'For heaven's sake . . . don't expect *me* to make any decision. You know I'm *perfectly* incapable. *Suggest* something.'

She said bravely:

'I'll accompany you to *your* doorstep. If it's still the same one.'

'Of *course* it's the same one. The mere contemplation of moving would drive me into a frenzy. Come *along*. I warn you, I shan't open my lips till we're out of this howling gale.'

Only when they were outside the house in Paultons Square where Heron had rooms, did he relax his expression of tortured endurance. He carefully removed his pince-nez, wiped his watering eyes and actually smiled at Clara. Looking up at him, she realized it was the first time she had seen him without his glasses. His eyes were childishly blue and the area of protected skin round them so white that it made the rest of his pale face seem almost tanned. Without his pince-nez, which had worn a permanent groove either side of his nose, an entirely different Clive was revealed. The small features which had always seemed as impersonal as if Clive had simply selected them for their unobtrusive elegance like a shirt or tie, suddenly composed into a real face. This face seemed to belong to someone whom Clara did not know at all . . . a vulnerable creature with an odd beauty, neither masculine nor feminine. He had removed his hat along with the pince-nez and a sudden gust of wind caught his red-gold hair and tossed it up in a crest above the high white forehead, giving him a momentary resemblance to a Blake angel.

He gave a little shriek:

'My God . . . my *hair*! For mercy's sake, come *inside*.'

Chapter Three

'Very peculiar. *Most* extraordinary.' Clive Heron leant back in his chair, carefully adjusted one long leg over the other and fitted a fresh cigarette into his holder with slow precision.

They had spent all the afternoon in his rooms and had just finished the dinner sent up by his landlady. It was not till they had settled down to their meal that Clara had been invited to 'explain her situation'. During the afternoon, Clive had devoted a long time playing gramophone records. Next he had demanded 'the *precise* implication' of certain theological terms in a book he was reading and had noted Clara's replies in his small, exquisite writing on the blank page at the end. Finally, they had discussed from every possible angle, but without reaching a conclusion, the desirability of Clive's adopting a kitten.

Clara, who was far more intuitive about cats than about human beings, had long ago decided to treat Clive Heron as if he were a cat. It had worked surprisingly well. Now, by patiently allowing him to go through the rituals which surrounded all his actions, whether the placing a chair at the exact distance from the gramophone to ensure the best sound effect or the careful uncorking of a bottle of sherry, she proved that she was aware of the enormous concession of being allowed to enter his rooms. Hitherto they had always met in public places; occasionally, by pre-arrangement, for a dinner, theatre or concert; more often, by chance, in the street. Even in the street, he did not always acknowledge her. Sometimes he would walk past her, affecting an absent-minded stare which he knew perfectly well did not deceive her. Sometimes, when she saw him approaching and rashly waved to him, he would go so far as to bolt up a turning which he had obviously never intended to take. Only once had she induced him to enter her own home, since he disliked going into his friends' houses almost as much as inviting them into his. With infinite prevarications, he had 'provisionally' accepted an invitation to her twenty-first birthday party at Valetta Road. She had been quite prepared for him not to turn up. He had, however, been, not only the first to arrive and the last to go, but the success of the evening. Clara was used to her friends being enthusiastic about her father who was always at his best as a host. Clive, with his usual unexpectedness, had taken a violent fancy to Isabel. Since then he had rarely run into Clara without enquiring after 'your *marvellous* mother' or 'that *incredible* woman whom you haven't the wits to appreciate'.

The fact that he had invited her in was remarkable. His insisting on her staying to dinner was more remarkable still. He was obviously pleased with himself and with her that the rash experiment was, so far, turning out well. Nevertheless, Clara knew that she must leave all control to him. She had been fretting to talk about her 'situation', but she could see him holding her off with deliberate mischievousness. Now, with frequent interruptions from him at points where she wanted to get quickly on with her narrative and blank silences when she paused, expecting comment or even sympathy, she had at last been allowed to tell him as much as he was interested to hear.

'It sounds more peculiar than ever when I say it in this room,' she said.

'Why?'

'Because it's such an eminently reasonable, civilized room.' She glanced round at the cream-panelled walls, the orderly rows of books, the two table-lamps whose shades had just been adjusted to their present angle after much deliberation on Clive's part and groans of 'Why *can't* people leave things *alone*?' The few pieces of furniture, obviously carefully chosen for elegance or comfort, were maintained at the highest level of polish and repair. 'It suits you extraordinarily well. Did you acquire all these things bit by bit or in one grand sweep?'

'I didn't acquire them at all. They're furnished rooms.

Nothing belongs to me but the gramophone and the books. I loathe possessions.'

'I didn't know you were so austere.'

'I'm not in the least austere. I should like to have the best of everything. It's simply that I don't like owning things. Once you own things you're a slave to them. You have, in fact, to *do* something about them. Look at all these objects. Very agreeable. I can enjoy them but I'm not responsible for them. If, heaven forbid, I had to move somewhere else, I could leave them without the slightest pang. Whereas, if I possessed them, I should have to take all sorts of appalling *action* . . . get them stored or removed or whatever people *do* with objects. The mere idea paralyses me. You look ruminative. Are you attached to possessions?'

'I don't know, because I haven't had many. I'm afraid I could get attached to them all right. I can imagine thoroughly enjoying having a beautiful house of my own and quantities of good clothes and all that sort of thing. No, what I was ruminating about was something else. Something that's just struck me as odd.'

'*What?*'

'That you've got something in common with Archie, though no two people could be more wildly unlike in other ways. He hated possessions, too.'

'Hmm. Yet, if you'd stuck it for a year or two, apparently you could have had everything in that way you wanted. I'm rather surprised you chucked it so soon. After all, from the money point of view, you were on to a remarkably good thing.'

'I thought you didn't approve of riches.'

'Inaccurate, as usual. In the first place I don't approve or disapprove of anything in that sense. In the second, though I happen to dislike possessions, I don't in the least dislike money. On the contrary: "Put money in thy purse." The more the merrier. Not *keep* it there, of course. Get rid of it as quickly and agreeably as possible. Otherwise it becomes a possession.'

'That's obviously how Archie felt. Only he got rid of what wasn't there.'

'Well, it would have been there if you'd held on a little longer.

Haven't you been slightly impetuous? He sounds an amiable enough chap. I know plenty of women who'd be rather relieved to be let off the usual concomitants of marriage.'

'I was relieved,' Clara admitted. 'But it wasn't as simple as all that.'

'No doubt, no doubt,' he said equably. 'I can see the situation bristles with formidable possibilities. Now, tell me what *really* interests me. What line does your Church take about it all?'

She told him what she knew of the complex process of annulling a Catholic marriage. He nodded approvingly.

'Perfectly logical. Just as I supposed. Marriage, as such indissoluble. Query, what constitutes a marriage? When in fact is a marriage not a marriage? Onus on you to prove certain conditions have not been fulfilled and proofs independent of civil law required. Am I correct?'

Clara nodded.

'Good. I always suspected it was a fallacy that they'd trump up a case for you provided you could pour enough cash into the Vatican coffers. But I like to get things straight from the horse's mouth.'

'I *hope* I've got it right,' Clara said anxiously. 'Anyway there's certainly no hanky-panky. Rome grinds slow and grinds exceedingly small. I'll probably be reduced to powder by the time it gets through.'

'You oughtn't to complain if you are. After all, for you it's the mills of God, isn't it? Don't you *expect* to be dust and ashes in this vale of tears? I appreciate the Catholic Church *far* more than you do.'

'Not quite enough to become a Catholic though,' said Clara maliciously.

He waved his cigarette, threw back his head and emitted the half-amused, half-exasperated 'Ah' with which he savoured any characteristic 'nonsense' of Clara's.

'My *dear* girl! What a barbarian you are! I appreciate the Catholic Church . . . probably considerably more than most Catholics . . . precisely because I'm *not* involved in it. In any case, I don't believe it's possible for anyone to *become* a Catholic. If one's born into that tradition, one should accept it precisely as one accepts one's nationality. I don't approve of conversions . . . or de-conversions for that matter. One should remain in one's situation.'

'Then you should disapprove of me. It's true I was only seven when it happened but I *am* a convert.'

'Rubbish. You had no control over that any more than if you'd been baptized as a baby. Besides you were properly brought up in the whole thing . . . it comes natural to you. I count *you* as a real Catholic. The person I disapprove of . . . in so far as I disapprove of *anyone* . . . is your father. A man *soaked* in the Greeks too. A *deplorable* lapse.'

'I think it was rather magnificent,' said Clara hotly. 'He must have gone through awful struggles. Look at what he gave up. He became one at thirty-five . . . just when at any moment he might have become a headmaster. Well, that finished *that*. He'll be an overworked, underpaid assistant master for the rest of his life now. I doubt very much if I'd have had the guts to give up so much if *I'd* been in his situation. Anyway, as regards the Greeks, he said it was Plato and Aristotle that first put him on the way to it.'

'Which shows he totally misunderstood both of them. As I've always suspected.'

'Weren't they looking for truth? And if Daddy became convinced that Catholicism *was* true, wasn't he absolutely right to accept it, even if it involved giving up things? Of course *you'd* say it wasn't true so he just made a ghastly mistake.'

'There you go again,' he groaned. 'Have I ever said it *wasn't* true?'

'You can't mean *you* think it's true.'

'Of *course*, it's true. But *poetically* true, not literally true. That's the trouble with your father. He's too literal.'

'Then I am too.'

'Can't you *really* see the difference between literal truth and poetic truth? Come, come, I know you're not an idiot.'

'I think I'm rapidly becoming one – Still you can try and explain.'

'It's *perfectly* simple. There are different realms of truth. Take a Cézanne picture . . . even any typical good old apples and

313

crumpled nappies. You know perfectly well you are beholding a portion of eternal truth when you gaze at it. Poetic truth in fact. Now take the actual objects he painted . . . the physical apples and crumplers . . . verifiable, existing objects. Literal truths, in fact.'

'Yes, I see *that* difference. And in a sense the Cézanne is *more* true . . . because it is *poetic* truth . . . just as Raskolnikov's murder or Othello's is truer than a literal account of a murder in the *Daily Mail*.'

'I should prefer to say it belonged to a different realm of truth . . . to the realm of essence rather than to the realm of existence. But you've got the rough idea.'

Clara frowned . . .

'It's funny . . . I seem to understand dimly when people use analogies from art. I haven't the most rudimentary sense of philosophy and never will have. But surely religion's something beyond *all* categories . . . art, philosophy . . . everything?'

'Why? Why shouldn't it be simply another realm to be explored, another activity of the human spirit?'

'Because . . . oh, because it involves *everything* in a person. I can't argue with you. I get all muddled. Once you're convinced there is a God and that your whole life here and hereafter depends on your relation to that God . . . that truth surely transcends all others . . . Or aren't you convinced there *is* a God?'

'No. In my opinion . . . and in that of vast numbers of people infinitely more competent than I am . . . God is an unnecessary hypothesis. No . . . no . . . don't try and come it over me with those official proofs. Any logician could dispose of them in five minutes. They're simply respectable rationalizations after the event . . . cooked up by people who already *were* convinced.'

Clara's head seemed to be filled with a whirling fog.

'If only I had a *mind*,' she sighed.

'You do very well without one,' he said with his sudden delightful smile. 'Don't think I object to people believing in God. If that's your natural approach to things, you should accept it and enjoy it. It's entirely a matter of temperament.'

314

'I suppose you'll say that weak-minded people need some sort of prop and religion gives it them and strong-minded people can do without it,' Clara said rather angrily.

'Now, now . . . I'm not such a fool as to suggest anything of the kind. There are thousands of strong-minded theists and thousands of weak-minded atheists. Nor do I suppose, as people so often do, that there is anything particularly consoling about believing in God. On the contrary, I can quite see it can put one in the most agonizing predicament. "It is a fearful thing to fall into the hands of the living God." Yes, indeed.'

'You don't talk like the stock atheist.'

'Of course I don't. I'm not a stock anything. I'm unique. In fact, I often have a sinister suspicion that I *am* God.'

Clara laughed.

'It's no laughing matter, I assure you. It might be the most appalling thing to be God. Because no one could save Him from *His* agonizing predicament.' He added gaily: '*No one* has any idea what I suffer. I'm mad, you see.'

She perceived obscurely that he did suffer and said slowly:

'Am I mad too? Honestly, there've been times lately when I've wondered whether I wasn't going out of my mind . . . if I hadn't actually *gone*, in fact.'

'Very probably,' he said cheerfully. 'Definitely mad in spots. Which is why I've always had such a fancy for you. But you're quite different from me. With your amazing literalness, your passion for translating everything into immediate, violent action, I shouldn't be surprised if one day you went right over the edge and landed yourself in a strait-jacket.'

'Thank you.'

'Don't mistake me. I'm not saying you *will*. Merely that it's an interesting possibility. Because, of course, you'd recover and feel marvellous. My situation is far more deplorable, because I'm permanently in the strait-jacket. I shall never technically "go out of my mind" and I shall never be cured.'

'Cured of what?'

'My particular neurosis. My invincible horror of taking action of any kind or making any decision. Which wouldn't matter in the least if it weren't coupled with the most appalling anxiety and guilt about *not* taking action. Your Archie is impotent in one way and I'm impotent in another.'

Clara said sympathetically:

'I know about that sort of impotence. For months . . . all the time I was with Archie . . . it was like a sort of creeping paralysis. It's been the same ever since I went back to live with my family. When I look back, I can't imagine how I ever *wanted* to do anything, let alone attempted to do it. Not only things like going on the stage or writing advertisements, but even writing a letter or reading a book.'

'Don't *mention* writing letters,' he said with a sympathetic shudder. 'Or ringing people up . . . I *know*.'

'At one point it got so bad . . . that was in the Archie days . . . that I couldn't be bothered to get dressed properly or even comb my hair. I just slouched and mooched about all day in a kind of stupor.'

Clive's pince-nez glittered at her.

'Dear me! Most interesting. Evidently you're quite One of Us. Not so far gone as me, of course. Otherwise you wouldn't dare relax for one moment. With me, if once the hair weren't accurately combed, the shoes properly laced, every object exactly placed, the same bus caught every morning, *The Times* always carried under the *left* arm, the entire structure would collapse. The deluge, in fact.'

Clara murmured:

> 'But I beneath another sea
> And whelmed in deeper gulfs than he.'

'*Precisely*,' he said. 'You've got it.'

They were silent for some minutes, smoking companionably. Clara was careful to drop her ashes neatly in the tray which Clive had already emptied several times.

He said at last, with that sudden radiant smile which revealed his unusually white and even teeth:

'Astonishing, how much I like you. I did, the first time I set eyes on you, you know. *When* women are all right I actually prefer them to men, though no one would believe it.'

He had moved his head slightly so that his eyes were clearly visible behind his glasses. There was a questioning expression in them which did not match the cheerfully confident assertion. For some reason Clara felt suddenly out of her depth and could think of nothing to say. After a pause, he asked:

'By the way, have you quite got over our old friend, Stephen Tye?'

She nodded. 'I'm rather shocked at myself for having got over it so completely. And so quickly. Months before I married Archie. Yet I really and truly thought I was in love. I was completely obsessed by him for well over a year. Now I can't even remember what it felt like. I must be disgustingly shallow.'

'Not necessarily. When the fever goes, thank heaven it *goes*. But I'm surprised you can't remember the symptoms. Thank goodness, I'm sane at the moment and have been relatively free since my last Object left me. But there's not a quiver of the Object's eyelashes, not a tremor of my own knees, not one shade of the tortures of suspense and jealousy I can't recall in the minutest detail.'

Clara said stupidly:

'You mean you've been in love?'

He said impatiently:

'Of *course* I've been in love. What do you take me for? Over and over again. I've doted upon and been doted upon. Once or twice it's even been simultaneous. I assure you there's nothing I don't know about all *that*.'

This was such a surprise . . . and, for some reason, not altogether an agreeable one . . . that Clara could only say feebly:

'Of course, I don't know you very well, do I?'

'Rubbish. You know me considerably better than most people. I just happen not to have mentioned all that side of my life. I only mention it now to assure you that it does exist. Or rather, shall we say, did exist. I've certainly been immune since this last set-to . . . Possibly I'm cured forever. *What* a relief!'

'I suppose I must be, then. Yet I don't feel anything as definite as relief. Perhaps you don't appreciate being cured if you've forgotten what it felt like to be ill. You make me almost wish . . .'

'Wish *what*?'

'That I *could* fall in love again . . .'

'You will, Oscar, you will.'

She shook her head.

'No. Honestly, I don't think I could. I can't imagine doing anything positive ever again.'

'You seemed positive enough about *not* doing something when you cannoned into me this afternoon. What *was* all that about?'

'There, you see. I'd already forgotten about it. Yet, at that moment, I felt absolutely *compelled* to go and see a particular person. And I knew it was an insane thing to do.'

'Why more insane than coming here with me?'

'Too complicated to go into. Anyway, it's done me worlds more good talking to you. Even if he'd *let* me talk.'

'*Do* be more explicit. If *who* had let you talk?'

'Oh . . . a painter called Marcus Gundry . . . If you knew him, you'd realize it was crazy of me.'

Clive raised his faint eyebrows and tucked in his small chin as he did when he was, or affected to be, startled. This time, she thought he really must be startled for the cigarette dropped from his holder.

'*That* old Turk! Well, well, well!'

'So you know him?'

'Oh . . . vaguely.' He bent down anxiously to recover his cigarette. 'Intact, thank goodness,' he said with relief. 'They call him the Ram of Derbyshire. *Rather* a good painter, though. I bought a picture of his once but I've never been able to decide *exactly* where it ought to hang. So it's still reposing in a cupboard . . . I haven't even got so far as removing its integuments.' He frowned and fitted the cigarette delicately into the ivory holder. 'Gundry! Of all the unsuitable confidants for a young woman in your situation! Are you in the habit of going to see him?'

'I've been precisely once.'

'Ah, I think I see your point. You'd be lucky if you survived twice. I imagine you're very much his type.'

'He was extraordinarily kind. He let me off. But he made it very clear he didn't want me there again just to have a nice, cosy chat. Yet *that* was the part *I* found so exciting — It was the only time I've felt human for months and months. Except today.' She paused and frowned. 'Yet even this isn't *quite* the same . . .'

'Obviously,' said Clive. 'No risk. Hence no excitement. One of your flaws is that you have a craving for dramatic situations in ordinary life.'

'Have I? What a genius you have for deflating me.'

'I prefer to call it disintoxicating.'

'All right. I'm sure it's very salutary. I even like it. But when I talked to Gundry . . .' She broke off. 'No, I can't explain the difference. If I tried, it might sound rude.'

'Come *on*, you absurd creature. Don't you know I adore hearing anything about myself . . . however unpleasant? I feel I've really pulled it off when someone talks as if I actually *existed*.'

'Don't *you* feel you exist? I don't either. I believe this afternoon . . . in the Blue Cockatoo of all places . . . I suddenly realized, for the first time, that . . .'

'We are talking about Me . . .' said Clive firmly. 'Kindly stick to the point. *What* is the difference between a cosy chat with Marcus Gundry and a cosy chat with me?'

'Well . . . you're obviously a much more remarkable *person*. And I couldn't enjoy being with anyone more. I always have enjoyed it. Whatever we talk about, whatever we do. It's like a sort of enchantment. You appear and disappear like some creature from another world . . .'

'I disappear,' he murmured. '*Quite.*'

'Yes. It wouldn't be crazy to rush off frantically to look for you. It would simply be unthinkable. You wouldn't be *there*. I believe you really could become invisible when you don't want to be seen. But, given certain conditions, you suddenly materialize like a rainbow. And you produce exactly the same sort of pleasure. Whatever mood I'm in, I suddenly feel absurdly gay and irresponsible.'

'Very flattering. You said just now I deflated you.'

'That comes later. You make me realize I'm a complete nitwit. I even feel I ought to do something about it. But I don't, because when you vanish, you vanish completely. I don't even think "How nice – or how improving – it would be to see Clive Heron." I don't think about you at all.'

'Then surely we've achieved the ideal human relationship? We enjoy each other's society without impinging on each other's consciousness.'

She laughed.

'Ideal, perhaps. But not exactly human. You see, I can't think of you as an ordinary human being.'

'There you are! *You* can't . . . and I can't. Sometimes I can put it across on the Objects. Especially if they're perfectly simple, straightforward creatures as they frequently are. The more "ordinary", the more madly attractive I find them. But I *long* to be an ordinary human being. I should *adore* to be a great hearty extrovert with a moustache and a pipe, playing golf every weekend and bellowing with laughter at stock-exchange stories.'

'You *wouldn't*?'

'I'm perfectly serious. However, like most ideals, it's unattainable. So I merely *contemplate* it, which is the proper way to treat ideals. My only quarrel with Catholics is that *occasionally* they make the fatal mistake of attempting to realize theirs in the realm of existence instead of leaving them where they belong, in the realm of essence. However, we'll let that pass since it obviously disturbs you. Gundry, of course, *is* an extrovert. Most painters are, lucky dogs. Is that why you prefer his conversation?'

'I didn't say I preferred it. All I'm trying to say is that it has a different effect on me.'

'Explain yourself.'

'I'm trying to. You are *extraordinarily* like the Caterpillar in Alice . . . Well . . . when I talked to Gundry . . . and I have only talked to him once properly . . . I positively felt as if one day, heaven knows how, I might conceivably be able to *do* something. Whereas with you, though everything seems marvellously exciting or amusing . . . you make me giddy talking about things I don't understand . . . or we listen to music and you make me *listen*, not just vaguely hear a pleasant background buzz while I wonder whether or not to wash my hair tomorrow . . .'

'Put it off,' he interposed. 'One should *always* put things off . . .'

'*But*,' Clara continued firmly, 'I go away with the feeling that all one's got to do is to look on . . . enjoy, criticize . . . but not participate. Is that nonsense?'

'Not at all. But why this lust for action and participation and so on? The spectacle's *there* to be contemplated. Why not be a civilized spectator? I assure you there are none too many of them. They have enormous value. Gundry paints a picture. I have acquired the wits to see that it is quite a good picture and I buy it. The result is Gundry can live for a few weeks and paint another picture. *You* seem to think it would be better if I spent the money on canvases and paints and produced some inefficient daub of my own.'

'Of course not. But haven't you ever wanted to produce anything?'

'Not unless I was assured beforehand it was going to be absolute perfection. Why clutter up the world with a lot more mediocrity?'

'Stephen said some of the poems you wrote at Oxford were extraordinarily good.'

'Nonsense. They were exactly like the poems *everyone* writes at Oxford. I had the sense to know when to stop. For God's sake don't rouse my guilt about writing. There's a conspiracy among the Panjamdrums to force me to write. If they knew the agonies I go through at the mere though of putting pen to paper, even to write a letter. The mere idea of *pens* and *paper* causes such appalling anxiety that I never keep either in the house. If I have to write, I go to my club.'

'Don't you have to write at the Home Office.'

'By a merciful dispensation, no. Once my secretary was ill and I thought I should have to *resign*. My job is mainly criticizing what other people write. At which, of course, I am *admirable*.'

'Yes, I'm sure. If I ever wrote anything, I should be terrified of your seeing it.'

'What nonsense! I used to adore those advertisements of yours. *Gems*, my dear! They would have been works of art if only they hadn't incited to action instead of contemplation. *Most* insidious. I once *actually* bought a bottle of hair lotion because I couldn't resist your blandishments. I'm sure you could make a fortune if only you'd put your mind to it. What are you looking so glum about?'

'Because I suppose that's all I'm fit for. And I'm too stupid to do even that now.'

'Well, what the hell do you want me to do? I suppose eventually you'll have to do something owing to the brute necessity of earning a living. Now that you've flung away the prospect of living in idle luxury. Can't you eventually get vast alimony out of this chap?'

'I wouldn't take it if I could.'

'There you go,' he said affectionately. '*Quite* mad. Still, oddly enough, I see your point. D'you want to go back to the stage?'

She shook her head.

'No. I'll never make anything but a fifth-rate actress.'

'I'm inclined to agree. Old Stephen's going on all right, isn't he? I saw his Antony. Not as good as his Richard but bloody good in some ways. He's a real actor. Not interested in anything *but* acting. I must say I should adore to have been an actor. The trouble is, I'm too intelligent. So, incidentally, are you. I admit you seldom give any obvious signs of it. But I'd give all my poor old wits to have been Irving.'

'I used to think Stephen was very intelligent. I let him bully me like anything.'

'Only because you were bemused. You know as well as I do that Stephen wasn't intelligent about anything but acting. Very proper, too. He had a few stock remarks which, being a good actor, he delivered with the right intonation.'

It was so true that Clara had to laugh.

'Yes. Even when I was most bemused, I used to think he said things as if he were trying out a new way of putting across a line. Even those charming, spontaneous gestures . . . you couldn't help feeling they'd come in handy later on when he'd worked them up to look even *more* spontaneous. Do you think all good actors are insincere? Because I believe Archie's going to be quite a good actor though he's the sincerest person I know. Anyhow, he's got awfully good notices in this one tiny part. His first on the *real* stage.'

'Fluke, probably. Though I admit he wasn't at all bad.'

Clara gasped.

'You mean you've *seen* him? Why ever didn't you tell me?'

'Why should I? I can't diagnose his case history as a husband. But his case as an actor rather interests me.'

'I didn't know you ever went to musical comedies.'

'Of course I do. Especially when Sherry Blane's in them. *There's* acting for you. Pure comic genius. I wish to God I'd seen Dan Leno. Blane's obviously got something of the same thing.'

'What about Archie?'

'Oh *well* . . . all right in that particular *thing*. It was brilliant of Sherry Blane to pick him. Your great gangling gawk of a husband couldn't be a better foil to his incredible smallness and neatness. He even brought it off extremely well . . . as amateurs often do. But he hadn't the faintest idea *why* he brought it off. That's why I said "fluke", I very much doubt if he's got the real right thing. What he *has* got, of course, is an amazingly beautiful voice. My dear, I haven't heard anything like it for years. Even in that staggering rubbish he sang, it positively melted the fibres of the heart. Why on *earth* doesn't he get it properly trained and become a concert singer?'

'It *is* a heavenly voice.' Clara had almost forgotten its extraordinary beauty. Recalling it, she felt such a pang that she did not answer Clive's question. He went on talking but she was no longer listening. Suddenly she heard him ask angrily '*Why?*'

'Oh, sorry,' she said hastily . . . 'Because Archie only cares about the theatre. Also because he absolutely loathes what's called good music.'

'You're wool-gathering,' he said. 'Or didn't you want to hear what I said?'

'Weren't you asking about Archie? I suddenly began to think about him.'

'Now, no . . . none of these hankerings and regrets. Archie is *foutu*. I was making some enquiries about *you*.'

'Me?'

'*Yes . . .*' he shouted. 'I was asking why the hell you didn't do something about writing. You could, you know.'

'Advertisements?'

'*Not* advertisements. That piece of yours in the *Saturday Westminster*. Not half bad.'

'Fancy your having read it.'

'I read everything.'

'You never mentioned it at the time.'

'No. I *almost* brought myself to the point of writing to you. But the *effort* of coming to grips with pen and paper plus the appalling necessity of having to buy *The Stage* to find which provincial town you were appearing in at that moment . . . Well, I'm mentioning it now.'

'You mean you *liked* it?' said Clara, puffed up with irrational joy.

'Certainly.' He added in his mock-Bloomsbury voice: '*Very* remarkable. *Quite por-ten-tous.*'

'Obviously a fluke like Archie's.' She tried to sound careless.

'Not obviously. But conceivably,' he maddeningly agreed. He stood up, carefully picked up their two ashtrays and emptied them. Clara did not dare to renew the subject. A card on the mantelpiece caught his eye. 'Oh, Lord, I suppose I shall have to do something about *that*.'

'About what?'

'Nell Crayshaw.'

'I know that name . . . I've seen it in *Vogue* or somewhere . . . I remember now . . . photographs.'

'That's right. She's a remarkably good photographer. The *only* person who's ever managed to capture my elusive phiz. I wish she'd stick to taking photographs and not invite me to parties.'

'Do you hate parties?'

'Not invariably. But how can I possibly know beforehand whether I can face a party on a particular day?'

Clara said rather wistfully:

'I can't remember when I last went to a party.'

'Does that mean you want to go to this one? It would be perfectly all right with Nell. The more, the merrier.'

'The point is, do *you* want to go?'

'I never *want* to do anything. I might consider the possibility if you came and backed me up.'

'I'm rather tempted. It's such ages since I've done anything like that. Yet . . . I don't know. I feel terrified at the prospect of meeting new people. I've got so used to just mouldering away with my family . . . doing nothing, seeing no one.'

His eyes glinted mischievously behind his pince-nez.

'Well, it's probably time you were forced into the social whirl. You do look slightly mildewed now I come to think of it. So I presume I shall have to sacrifice myself.'

'Oh, no,' she insisted. 'I'm not going to add to your torments. Let's forget about Nell Crayshaw and her party.'

'*Actually* of course, I enjoy suffering. Anyhow we needn't commit ourselves yet, need we? If I rang you up . . . perhaps better if *you* rang me up – on the morning of this jamboree . . . we might go into the matter. We'll leave it like that, shall we?'

'Very well.'

'Wonderful. We've positively made a decision. Really you have the most *salubrious* effect on me.'

'You mean I've persuaded you to do what you meant to do all along.'

'Exactly. But by ordering me to do it, you've removed the appalling load of guilt. It's an immense relief to be forced to do something.'

'I should have thought you loathed being made to do things.'

'Ah, that's just where you're wrong. That's why I was so exquisitely happy in the army. Happiest days of my life.'

'It's difficult to imagine you in the army.'

'Of course I went through *agonies* of indecision before joining up. Not the usual ones because, oddly enough, I'm not alarmed by cataclysms in the outside world. They're *far* easier to cope with than the stresses and strains in the poor old psyche. As for death . . . what *could* be more desirable? No, it was the *small* things . . . the idea of having to sleep in a tent with other people and the *horrifying* possibility of having my hair cut by an army barber. But once I'd crossed the Rubicon, it was a miraculous relief. I was a dazzling success. Yes, my dear, actually mentioned in despatches! I had no sense of self-preservation at all. It was after two years at the front that I was afraid I was *just* beginning to crack. The noise, you know. That infernal din began to get on my nerves. And just at that *precise* moment . . . I should almost *certainly* have run away if I'd had to endure one second longer . . . my daimon arranged for me to receive a beautiful, knock-out wound and I was invalided out.'

'I didn't know you'd been wounded. Is that why you look so ethereal?'

'I've always looked ethereal. Actually I'm exceedingly robust. It was distinctly unpleasant at the time but now it doesn't cause me even a modicum of discomfort. I've lost one kidney and if I happened to lose the other that would finish me. The net result is that I receive the maximum disability pension. Very agreeable.'

'I still can't picture you in uniform. Did you have a moustache?'

'Certainly not. I even got away with that since Nature, for once, was on my side. I've got a photo of myself somewhere.'

He rummaged carefully in a drawer and produced it. Clara examined it with interest.

'Did Nell Crayshaw take this?'

'No. I didn't know her in those days. Just some hack. My mother blackmailed me into having it done.'

Clive's face had been a little plumper but it still looked extraordinarily small and frail above the stiff lapels of the tunic. The fine hair (it had been thicker then), though severely brushed, still showed a childish tendency to curl: the eyes looked out through the pince-nez with an unusually earnest expression.

'Fascinating,' she said. 'Did you really look so saintly?'

'I presume so. After all, I was only twenty-one. Seven years less contagion of the world's slow stain.'

'I'm only twenty-two now,' Clara sighed. 'I feel thirty at least. And look it.'

'You exaggerate. I admit you don't look as you did when I first met you. A little dimmed . . . and, by your own absurd standards . . . a little over-inflated. Don't think *I* object . . . I think women ought to look like Renoirs or even Rubenses.'

'So did Gundry,' said Clara crossly.

'Of course. All painters like women to be fat. There, there, don't look so enraged. You're not all *that* fat. But I agree, the bloom should be recovered. And no doubt will.'

'What does it matter whether it's recovered or not?' said Clara with sudden gloom. 'Truly, Clive, I *do* feel my life's over.'

'All right, it's over then. It's your own fault for getting into such ridiculous situations.'

'I expect so,' she said meekly.

'The fact is my dear, you're probably a poor old neurotic like myself. You're in the dust and ashes state . . . Pestilent congregation of vapours and all that . . . *I* know.'

'I believe you do.'

'Of course, I do. I very seldom emerge from the pestilent congregation. Yet, a little while ago, you observed I was like a rainbow. Let's have a good cry, shall we?'

'And smile bravely through our tears? I've lost the habit.'

'So have I unfortunately. *Sunt lacrimae rerum* . . . yes, *yess*. One registers the fact but the tears don't well up. Fortunately, perhaps. If they did, one wouldn't be able to turn them off.

> 'He weeps by the side of the ocean
> He weeps on the top of the hill
> He purchases pancakes and lotion
> And chocolate shrimps from the mill.

What could be more exquisite?'

'Yes, indeed. And you *did* purchase lotion.'

'*Yess*,' he said solemnly. 'I purchased lotion.'

Clara was suddenly aware of the time.

'It's frightfully late. I must go.'

'Nonsense, it's Sunday tomorrow.'

'That's just why. Daddy likes me to go to early Mass with him and thunders on my door at seven.'

'Of course, if you insist on your superstitious practices . . . all right. But before you go, I *must* show you something.'

He took another photograph from the drawer and handed it to her. 'This is one of Nell's. She didn't want to part with it but I insisted.'

Clara was studying the photograph of a tall young man in uniform, wearing the tartan trews of the KOSB.

'Is he a friend of yours?'

'Never set eyes on him. He's one of Nell's innumerable younger brothers.'

'He's extraordinarily good-looking,' Clara admitted, staring at the young officer's face. The eyes, under thick straight black brows, were unusually beautiful, evidently light in colour – grey, she guessed. The camera had caught what was obviously a typical expression, a one-sided smile and a confident, slightly mischievous look. As she studied it, the young man's face seemed so extraordinarily alive, unlike the usual strained composure or uneasy grin of a photograph, that he seemed to be smiling at her with a peculiar intimacy.

'Did you ever see such a perfection of the type?' Clive urged. 'I mean, Brushwood Boy, and all that. My God . . . if *only* I could have looked like that.'

She remembered the stiff little photo of Clive in uniform; the pince-nez, the small pale face with that remote, unworldly look. Nothing would have been more unlike all the subalterns in her father's study. With a sudden pang, she asked:

'Was *he* killed in the war?'

'Gracious, no. Though I admit he looks the kind that invariably did get killed. Luckily, he was just too young. He's in the regulars. Coping with the Irish troubles at the moment, I believe . . . I see he's got you, too.'

'Well, it's a marvellous photo of a marvellous young man.'

'Quite dispassionate?'

'Oh yes . . . That is, I mean, one can't help being moved by anything . . . well, so perfect of its type, as you say. One can't quite believe he's real. Yet the odd thing is, I feel as if I'd seen him before.'

'In your dreams, probably. He's obviously an Archetype. Probably a crashing bore in real life.'

'Yes, probably.'

'I suppose there's a remote chance he might be at this ghastly party. However, if we knew he were going to be present, we'd be wiser not to go. Then we could preserve our illusions. Don't you agree?'

Clara said, not quite truthfully:

'I'm completely neutral.'

He studied her face:

'Man delights not me; no, nor woman neither.'

She gave him back the photograph, half with relief, half with reluctance. The young man's picture had begun to give her an uneasy feeling. She could not be sure whether it was pleasurable or frightening. Then she smiled at Clive Heron . . .

'Not in general. But *you* delight me.'

He smiled back rather sadly.

'*Quite.* But you see, my dear, I'm not a *man.*'

Chapter Four

It was nearly midnight when Clara got home. She let herself in with a feeling of guilt, and was relieved to find that her father had gone to bed. In vain she told herself that she was grown-up and free to come and go. The fact remained that she had not told her father that she meant to go out.

She was cowardly enough to hope that she might sleep through his knocking on her door to tell her it was time to get up for Mass. They had a pact that, if she did not answer his first knock, he assumed she must be asleep and did not persist. So far, she had never cheated. But tonight, the prospect of the long walk to church alone with him alarmed her and she was tempted to avoid it. It was some time before she got to sleep and her dreams were uneasy. Perhaps because she and Clive Heron had been talking about Stephen Tye, she dreamt about him for the first time for many months. In the dream, she recaptured some of her old feelings about him. At first, aware that she was dreaming, she was surprised at having even the illusion of love. She seemed to hear Clive Heron whispering: 'There you see, my dear. *That* was what it felt like. Merely a question of disinterring it.' Soon she lost consciousness of dreaming. She was sitting in the study and Stephen, in one of his rare, gentle moods, was reading her poems from *A Shropshire Lad*. She was frightened that her father might come in and find them together. Then Stephen vanished and she was all alone on an empty stage reciting 'Summertime on Bredon'. The auditorium was so dark that she could not see if there were anyone in it. Nevertheless, she recited each verse very carefully, pitching her voice as if declaiming to a large audience and trying to get the right intonation for each line. It seemed to her she was reciting very well. Not only was her voice completely under control but it had a range and variety she had never suspected. She listened to it with interest, enjoying this unusual sense of power and freedom. By the time she came to the last stanzas, she was convinced she was reciting to a vast, if invisible audience. The reason for their utter silence was that they were spellbound by the beauty of her speaking. She was launching splendidly on the last of all . . .

'The bells they sound on Bredon
And still the steeples hum
Come all to church, good people . . .'

. . . when there was a noise like a clap of thunder from the auditorium. Was it a burst of applause? Or a furious stamping of feet to drown her? She broke off, disconcerted, frantically trying to remember the next lines. Then the auditorium melted away like a mist: she found herself no longer standing, but lying down. She was in her own bed and her father was knocking urgently on the door. Still half-asleep, she called out automatically:

'I hear you. I will come.'

As soon as they were in the street, she glanced anxiously at him to read his mood. His face was neither smiling nor stern. Anxious to know how she stood, she decided to be brave and introduce the subject herself.

'Mother did explain I'd be out to dinner last night?'

'Yes. She said she thought it would do you good to get out of the house. I hope you had a pleasant evening, wherever you went.'

'Yes, lovely,' she said volubly. 'Who do you think I ran into? Clive Heron . . . do you remember him? That man in the Home Office who came to my twenty-first birthday party. You and Mother both liked him.'

'Heron?' he frowned. 'Oh yes. Tall thin man with reddish hair and pince-nez. Very good company. Intelligent, I imagine.'

'Yes, awfully. I met him by chance and we dined together.'

'I trust he gave you a good dinner. I remember he was very knowledgeable about wine. Did he take you to Soho or somewhere more impressive?'

Clara sensed danger, but not wanting to lie, said, far too lightly:

'Actually we had dinner in his rooms. His landlady is a marvellous cook. He kept saying . . .'

Her father stopped dead on the pavement.

'You dined *alone* in a man's rooms? . . .'

Clara was so terrified by his voice that she lost her head.

'Oh no,' she gabbled. 'There were two other people there. Awfully nice . . . I'd never met them before though he's often talked about them and wanted me to meet them . . .' She searched wildly for a convincing name. 'Crayshaw . . . Nell Crayshaw . . . she's a quite famous photographer. Years older than me . . . older than Clive Heron . . . And a brother of hers in the army . . . on leave from Ireland . . .' She paused, desperately trying to think of a Christian name for the brother . . . instinctively rejecting 'Stephen' the first that came into her mind.

'I see,' said her father less fiercely. He was appeased enough to begin walking again.

Relieved, she walked on too. There was silence during which she had time to decide on 'Richard' for Nell Crayshaw's brother.

She said with a nervous giggle:

'Sorry to have frightened you, Daddy. I do realize I've got to be discreet. Mr Ramsden's always impressing on me I have to be awfully careful about appearances. Not to be alone with a man and so on.'

She was horrified at her voice. Nothing could have sounded falser and more frivolous. Even if he did not at once guess that she was lying, she was talking in the way that most exasperated him.

He said angrily:

'Really, my dear! Quite apart from your ... er ... situation, I should hardly have thought it was necessary for Ramsden to warn you. A young married woman ... for *you* are still married, you know ... You sound almost as if you were in the habit of being alone with men other than your husband.'

'Well, I'm not,' she said sullenly. But she pulled up her coat collar and averted her face: she could feel that she was blushing.

They walked almost the length of a street in uneasy silence. Clara was miserably inventing material to back up her lie. She decided she would talk about the army. Her father always responded eagerly to any talk of the war. She would tell him that Clive Heron had been mentioned in despatches. What could she think of to make the unknown Crayshaws sound convincing? The regular officer's point of view compared to the temporary officer's? Very tricky. Nell would be safer. Clive had been *so* kind ... thinking that a professional photographer who worked for the papers might be able to suggest ideas to Clara for an article. There was nearly half a mile still to be spun out before they reached the church.

Suddenly, her father spoke. From the altered tone of his voice, she realized with relief that she could stop cudgelling her imagination.

'My dear, you must forgive me. When I'm worried, I often speak more sharply than I mean to. And when one spends so much of one's life ticking boys off ... And, well, I can't help worrying about you. Your mother says I forget you are grown-up now, and that conventions have changed since the war – but I couldn't bear you to do anything people might misunderstand. I care so immensely about your reputation.'

'It's very sweet of you.'

He took her arm in sign of reconciliation.

'I'm glad you had an amusing evening. I realize what a dull time you've been having lately. Would you care to ask your friends to dinner one night? I could find something tolerable for them to drink.'

'That's awfully kind of you,' she said quickly. 'Clive's still talking about that Château Yquem. Actually Nell Crayshaw has asked Clive to bring me to a party of hers next week.'

She felt his arm stiffen in hers.

'Not one of these Chelsea parties I hope – Of course, I daresay the newspapers exaggerate . . .'

'Darling Daddy, I've no idea. Because I've never been to what's called a Chelsea party. Archie and I never met anyone who gave them. Nell Crayshaw lives in Chelsea . . . so does Clive for that matter, but I assure you she's *eminently* respectable.'

His arm relaxed. He said penitently:

'Why do I always leap to the worst conclusions about you on no evidence? I ought to be ashamed of myself.'

During Mass, her mind was nibbled all the time by distractions as it had been, Sunday after Sunday, for the past few months. This morning, tired from a late night and with scraps of her talk with Clive Heron buzzing through her head, she hardly even tried to concentrate. Up to the time of her marriage, however her thoughts might stray, the Mass had always been a living reality to her. She had never had to keep reminding herself 'This is the most important thing that happens in the entire world.' Lack of conscious fervour did not worry her unduly. She had been trained not to attach much significance to devotional feelings. The essential thing was to assent to this reality with her mind and will. Now, as she tried to affirm it, she half-wondered whether she truly believed it any more. Suppose, as Clive Heron said, God were an unnecessary hypothesis? That idea was too monstrous. To entertain it would be a sin against faith. She drove it away, saying inwardly, 'Lord, I believe. Help Thou mine unbelief.' She glanced at her father's absorbed profile, so like some Roman Emperor's. 'He is a Roman,' she thought. 'He likes everything clear-cut and definite. Once he has made up his mind, he'll stick to it, no matter what it costs him. Inconceivable that *he* should ever have any doubts about faith. Why, why can't I be like him?'

He was so utterly unaware of her that she could safely keep up her sidelong scrutiny. There he knelt, following each prayer, faintly moving his lips as he did so, in the Latin missal he had since the day he was received. It was getting battered now. She counted up . . . nearly fifteen years he had had it. There were dark marks at the bottom of the pages of the Canon where his thumbs pressed, always in the same place. She moved imperceptibly closer to him as if his intentness and conviction could communicate themselves to her uncertain, straying mind. The warning bell ran for the Elevation. Instinctively, she shifted away again to leave room for the movement he invariably made. As usual, he bent forward, placed the open missal on the seat of the pew in front, slid his elbows along the rail and bowed his head into his hands. As usual, he spread his fingers so that, looking down through them, he could read the actual words of Consecration. Looking down sideways into his missal, she too read *Hoc est Corpus Meum*. For a second, she seemed to hear Clive Heron's '*Poetical* truth . . . my dear . . . not literal truth.' She shut her eyes and was aware of the extraordinary hush that falls on the most fidgeting, coughing crowd during the interval between the two Consecrations. The bell shrilled again. On the second stroke, like nearly all the rest she raised her head and stared at the uplifted Chalice. 'No . . . *every* kind of truth,' she thought. 'Forgive me, Lord.'

But no sooner had the third bell rung and she saw the heads come up raggedly and heard the first tentative sighs and rustles of relief after tension, than her mind began to flutter again. She was oddly touched by the way her father always kept his head down instead of raising it at the second bell of each elevation as nearly everyone else did. It was one of the 'Catholic ways', those family gestures she had acquired at her convent school which were second nature to her now and which he, as a convert in middle life, had never picked up. He had a pathetic admiration for her ease among such superficial things; the accent, as it were, with which she spoke the Catholic language as if it were her mother tongue. How superficial it was, she thought, compared with his solid, unwavering piety. There was no sacrifice, she was sure, that he would not make either for his faith or to carry out what that faith enjoined. How shallow was her own religion, alternating between fervour and a cold observance that amounted almost to indifference. Was it merely part of her general numbness that religion could arouse neither her paralysed mind nor her paralysed heart? She could come to life for a moment, as she had done with Gundry and Clive Heron. But, once alone again, the stimulus faded and she was left with the same blank inertia. Was it her own fault? A terrifying text slipped into her mind. 'The lukewarm He shall spew out of His mouth.'

She saw her father turn back the pages of his missal, as he always did at a particular moment, to the prayer of St Thomas Aquinas, which he used as a preparation for Communion. The *Domine, non sum dignus* was approaching; she realized she had not made the slightest attempt to prepare herself, either by trying seriously to take part in the Mass or by any other method. Dared she go up to Communion at all? Could this deadness of hers, she thought in sudden panic, be deadness of the soul? Was she in a state of mortal sin? Her lie, on the way to church, had been cowardly, but no more than venial. She searched her mind for some definite lapse since her last Confession which conformed to the canons of 'grave matter, full knowledge, full consent' and could find none. There was nothing concrete; only the diffused general state of weariness and apathy; this sense that something in her had died and already exhaled a faint odour of corruption. She glanced across at the thumb-marked page her father was reading. She followed a sentence or two, translating the Latin of the familiar prayer into the English version she knew better: 'as sick to my physician, as blind to the light of eternal brightness, as poor and needy to the Lord of heaven and earth.' Who was sicker and blinder than herself? Who needed the Physician more, even if she did not deserve to be cured? She put all the sincerity she could into the '*Domine, non sum dignus*' and went up to the rail with the others.

Afterwards, she felt no warmth of devotion, no sense of the presence of Christ of which, when she was a child, she had occasionally been vividly aware. Neither did she feel guilt or terror, as if she might have made a sacrilegious Communion. But for some minutes her restless distracted flittings of the imagination were stilled. Her mind was enclosed in a silent, but not menacing darkness. When she tried to formulate some remembered prayers of thanksgiving, it was almost as if an invisible hand were gently laid on her mouth, forbidding her to attempt to speak. Then the ban seemed to be lifted. She made incoherent petitions . . . 'Please show me where I have gone wrong . . . Please let me come alive again . . .' She went on to vague, childish petitions for others . . . for Archie, for her parents, for friends long neglected . . . then, oddly and suddenly, for Marcus Gundry and Clive Heron.

For the first time for many weeks, it was her father who waited for her. As they walked home together, she was more than usually conscious of the change in his mood that followed his weekly Communion. On the way back he was always relaxed and gay, ready to make small jokes, especially against himself.

'I hope I'm not walking too fast for you, my dear. The fact is I am shockingly hungry for my breakfast. I'm afraid I should never make a fasting friar.'

She quickened her pace to keep up with that quick marching step of his.

'Good for me to take a little exercise. Mother keeps worrying about my having got so much fatter.'

'Ah, well, it's nothing serious at your age. Though heaven forbid you should ever acquire *my* figure.' Claude Batchelor, though far from lean, was not really a fat man. It was his full face, broad shoulders and rather short legs that gave him the stocky look about which he was secretly sensitive. 'That friend of yours . . . Heron . . . you were talking about just now. I can't tell you how much I envy *his*. Tall, without being too tall, and so amazingly slim and elegant.'

Clara laughed.

'Yet only last night Clive was saying he'd give anything to be much more solid. He loathes looking so ethereal.'

'What perversity. I suppose *you'd* like to be one of these female lamp-posts that are unfortunately becoming so fashionable.'

'Of course I would. I should also like to have smooth black hair, a dead-white face and enormous, mysterious green eyes.'

'Thank heavens you can't have your wish. Why, your golden

hair has always been one of your greatest charms, my dear.' He smiled at her. 'Look as you looked only a few months ago and you needn't envy any young woman. And, thank goodness, you're beginning to.'

'Clive said I was looking dusty and . . . oh yes . . . mildewed.'

'Infernal cheek. Well . . . perhaps the old sparkle hasn't quite come back yet. But you've lost that terrible air of strain. At least these quiet weeks have done your nerves good.'

'Oh yes. I'm a perfect cabbage nowadays.'

'I'm glad you're beginning to want to see people again. It's bad for you to lose all interest in the outside world.'

'I don't awfully want to see people, you know. Yesterday it just happened.' She added in a burst of confidence, 'When I went out – it sounds horrid when you're all so sweet to me – it wasn't with the idea of seeing anyone. I just felt I wanted to be out of the house and on my own for a bit.'

'So your mother told me. I admit I was a little distressed at first. But she said it was perfectly natural. And then she suddenly turned the tables on me.'

'How?'

'She insisted that *I* ought to get out on my own sometimes. She said I was getting into a groove, doing the same things day after day. School, pupils, writing my text books . . . one night of bridge a week, usually with the same couple. If we go out to dinner or have some people here as we do occasionally, it's all arranged beforehand. No element of the unexpected.'

'She's quite right. Well, had she any suggestions?'

'A very definite one. Of course, at first I said it was preposterous. Then I suddenly realized it was something I'd secretly longed for for years.'

'It sounds most exciting.'

'When I tell you, I'm afraid you'll find it more ridiculous than exciting . . . Simply that one evening a week I should go out on my own. No one, not even your mother should know where I was going. No one was to ask where or how I'd spent those hours. On that evening, no one . . . family, friends, parent, pupil . . . would know where to get hold of me . . . even in a crisis.'

'It's not ridiculous. But it's certainly revolutionary,' Clara said slowly. It was so revolutionary that she could hardly take it in. The idea of her father making such a violent change in his habits was faintly shocking.

'Probably it will never be more than a wild idea. There are dozens of reasons against it . . . Still, as a notion to toy with . . .'

She saw that he wanted her encouragement. Surely, if anyone deserved a few unaccounted-for hours of escape, it was her father. Why then did she feel vaguely annoyed? Did she resent the mere possibility of change in someone she thought unchangeable? Or did she think he had no right to put himself, even for a few hours, deliberately out of her reach?

'My first reaction, of course, was that I simply couldn't afford to,' he went on. 'To give up a whole evening of pupils . . . especially at the moment . . .'

The wistfulness in his voice reproached her. She took his arm and said eagerly:

'You *must* do it, Daddy. You can't go on wearing yourself out at the grindstone. Perhaps you'll have marvellous adventures. Remember the days when you used to long for the knock on the door and the appearance of the mysterious agents of the Foreign Power?'

He laughed.

'No, my dear. I don't crave for fantastic adventures any more. Absurd, though, how long those schoolboy fancies *did* last. I still embark on them in my dreams. But they . . . and my annual Oppenheim . . . indulge the old cravings enough. You forget I've turned fifty.'

'Well, that's not awfully old for a man.'

'Old enough for the batteries to begin to run down. I admit I feel a trifle tired sometimes these days.'

With a sudden stab of fear she asked:

'You're not *ill*, Daddy?'

'Good heavens, no. This temptation to a night off is pure laziness.'

'What nonsense. The more I think of it, the more I'm sure you ought to do it. As to giving up an evening of pupils . . . you take some of them for nothing. Be firm from now on. No deadheads. No reductions for hard cases.'

He shook his head.

'I couldn't do that. There are parents who just can't afford the fees. And their boys are often the brightest. I'd never forgive myself if some boy with a real gift for Classics couldn't go to the University because I wouldn't give him a few hours' coaching for a scholarship. How could I have ever hoped to go to Cambridge without one?'

'*You* didn't have any private coaching.'

'Well, I was lucky. And I doubt if competition was so fierce in my day. But that's one thing neither you nor your mother will argue me out of. My dreams of being a great classical scholar were over long ago. But if there were the remotest chance of my helping a boy with it in him . . . I'd rather take a dozen geese for nothing than miss a possible swan.'

'Don't you *ever* think of yourself? I thought for once you were going to.'

'I assure you I'm thinking quite impenitently about myself. There is *a* possible solution. Your mother is heroically prepared to agree.'

'What is it?'

'Well, for some time, a young Indian law-student – his uncle's a Rajah and an old pupil of mine – has been wanting to come as a PG . . .'

'But that's one thing you swore you'd *never* do,' said Clara, aghast.

'I know, my dear. However things are a little difficult for me at the moment. One way and another, it has been an expensive year.'

Clara said guiltily:

'That's my fault. You were so terribly generous, giving me that wedding. And now, having me back on your hands . . .'

He squeezed her arm.

'Forget all that, my dear. No, no, I've always been a bad manager of money . . . I do fairly well on paper but there are always unexpected demands . . .'

'You help too many people . . .' she muttered uneasily. In her apathetic self-absorption she had not thought, till now, that she was one of them. It had never occurred to her to offer him any of the small sums Archie sent her towards her keep. 'Daddy, I ought to be contributing something . . .'

'I wouldn't hear of it,' he said. 'If my only child can't live under my roof . . . This PG idea . . . it would only be for a time. I know how your mother hates the notion. But she says she'll agree on two conditions.'

'Namely?'

'That I don't take on any more extra work. And that I *do* take this weekly evening off. I haven't asked *you* whether you have any objection to Ullah's coming.'

'Of course not.' She was, in fact, dismayed by the idea. But something had begun to dismay her far more.

'Daddy,' she said. 'Tell me the truth. You *are* quite all right, aren't you? You're still looking terribly tired though you've had your holiday.'

'Nothing whatever to worry about,' he smiled. 'Very well, your mother did insist on my seeing a doctor. Just as I expected. Nothing organically wrong. Slight fatigue or nervous exhaustion or whatever they call it. Anno Domini, in fact.'

'But you're not *old*,' she said wretchedly.

'Well, perhaps I've been a little hard on the old machinery. Still I'd infinitely prefer to wear out than rust out.'

She clutched his arm.

'Don't even *talk* of either. Oh do please take care of yourself. When can you take your first evening off?'

'Well . . . we'll think it over. So I have your *Nihil Obstat* . . . Indian student and all?'

'Of course, Daddy.'

'Then perhaps we'll add the *Imprimatur*. Let's hope nothing happens to make any of us regret it.'

Chapter Five

That Sunday afternoon Clara retired to her bedroom and took out a shiny black notebook she had not opened since she left Tithe Place. She had begun it originally, in the first weeks of her marriage, as a sop to her conscience. It had been intended as a kind of sketchbook in which she put down anything that struck her while the impression was still fresh. She had hoped to sharpen her eye and ear so that, though incapable of producing even the smallest piece of finished work, she could tell herself she was 'Practising'. Unfortunately, the notebook had soon degenerated into mere maunderings of self-analysis and self-pity.

Talking to Clive Heron had roused her just sufficiently to think of using the notebook for its original purpose. However, her faint impulse carried no further than turning over to a fresh page and writing the date very neatly at the top. She decided to begin by reading all her former entries. By the time she had read them through twice, she was so disgusted with the spectacle she presented that her one desire was to destroy the notebook.

Honesty, however, forbade this. It would be good for her vanity to preserve this repulsive record. For one thing it would puncture the recurring illusion that she might some day become a real writer. For another it would remind her of the depths to which she could sink when her emotions were out of control. Some of the entries were almost illegible. When deciphered, they were so incoherent that they might have been written by a lunatic. One whole page, which she had no recollection of writing, was even written the wrong way round so that she had to hold it up to a looking-glass to read it. During those last weeks with Archie, had she really been, as some people had hinted, on the verge of a mental breakdown?

She felt almost grateful for her present indolence and apathy. Presumably they were signs of sanity. Evidently it was an advantage not to suffer, to have no ambitions or desires, if these things produced such shaming outbursts. At least she could now behave like a civilized person. She was astonished, as well as disgusted, to find how violent her feelings had been. Could she really have felt such passions of absurd misery, bitterness, frustration and even more absurd hope? The creature . . . she could hardly bear even to think of it as 'Clara' . . . who had written some of those pages had had a short memory too. Over and over again, some state of mind was described in almost identical words as if it were being experienced for the first time. On her second reading she could discern a rhythm in these recurring entries. It was like watching someone hurling themselves repeatedly against a wall until they fell back, exhausted and battered. The creature kept rising up again, full of absurd hope and good resolutions, only to go through the hurling and battering all over again, sometimes in a passage written at one stretch.

She shut the notebook and thrust it well out of sight at the back of a drawer. As she did so, she had a curious pang, as if she were burying something. The creature, heaving and wallowing in its morass of misery, had at least been alive. But, if that was what it meant to be alive, nullity was better. Her mind, tired by even that much attempt at consecutive thought, slipped out of gear and spun round on the word 'nullity'. A decree of nullity would be merely the outward confirmation of the inward fact. It was she herself who was null and void. Nullity had charms. It was sober and decent. There would be no more struggles, no more of those ludicrous or tragic catastrophes which result from trying to do things. Above all, there would be no more violent feelings, either of pleasure or pain. Null and void. Null and void. She sat staring at the roses on her bedroom wall-paper, saying the words over and over again till she was half-hypnotized. The mirror on her dressing-table was in her line of vision. Her eyes shifted unconsciously from wall-paper to the square of glass. Her own face stared back at her, rigid and vacant, wearing a peculiar little smile.

For the next few days she walked, as it were, on tiptoe. She concentrated intently on each small thing she did, whether brushing her hair or changing her mother's library book. How simple life was, after all. One did the next thing and then the next. No need to think or fuss, above all to feel. It was restful, even pleasant, like doing row after row of plain knitting. Her father took the first of his secret evenings off. She felt a kind of amused pity that, at his age, he should be afflicted with this craving for change. She wondered whether she ought to tell him how much more satisfactory it was to be passive and detached. No, Clive was the only person who might conceivably understand. She was almost tempted to ring him up and tell him: 'My dear, I've discovered the *only* way to make existence tolerable.' But her new code of behaviour forbade initiating any action. True to it, she was neither surprised nor curious when one morning the maid knocked on the door and said that a Mr Heron wanted to speak to her on the telephone.

She went downstairs without haste. She felt superior because her own inaction had driven Clive to the astonishing length of ringing her up. It was another proof of her detachment that she had genuinely forgotten all about Nell Crayshaw's party. She was completely indifferent now as to whether she went or not, but the new code demanded passive acceptance of anything that offered.

Clive, for once, was surprisingly definite. He was in the mood to go to a party and he wanted her company. He sounded, indeed, almost enthusiastic. She said languidly:

'All right. If you're really keen on going . . . Yes, yes. I've said I'll come. Paultons Square is on the way? Very well. I'll pick you up. Ring up if you change your mind.'

She went through the motions of dressing for the party with the same slow care she had taken to using for everything. It was the first time she had dressed for a party with neither excitement nor apprehension. Always before, she had been keyed up, anxious how she would look and what impression she would make. Until Stephen's time there had been the secret hope of meeting some new and interesting man. When she had gone to parties with Stephen there had been the secret fear of his meeting some more attractive woman. Probably because she had dressed without the usual nervous fuss, she noted ironically that she looked prettier than she had done for months. Her hair had recovered some of its old lustre. It was in a biddable mood and had fallen easily into soft, loose waves. Her skin had lost its parched look and the black velvet dress, which disguised the weight she had unaccountably put on since her marriage, showed up the whiteness of her arms and shoulders. The dress recalled the first black velvet she had ever possessed. She had been fifteen then and still at her convent school. Her father had disapproved of it as too old and sophisticated but her mother had backed her up. She remembered how excited she had been when she had first tried it on, how grown-up it had made her feel, almost as if it transformed her into a different person. But, almost at once, she had taken an equally violent dislike to it. It was not because of grief over her grandfather that she could hardly bear to wear it again after his funeral. It was because of the terrible things her father had said when Blaze Hoadley had kissed her in the orchard at Paget's Fold. The kiss had been her first and could hardly have been more innocent but he had turned on her with such savage bitterness that she had been too paralysed to attempt any defence. She could no longer remember his words, but she could still recall her own humiliation and the feeling, which had lasted for days, that she must, in some way, be corrupt.

She stared critically at her reflection, wondering how much her face had changed in seven years. Then she gave a small, cynical smile.

'What a fool you were then. And what a fool you've made of yourself ever since,' she thought. 'Well, let's hope you've learnt a little sense at last.'

To test this, she deliberately tried to summon up the face of the young officer in the photograph. Clive had said it was just possible he might be at the party. She was surprised to find how clearly his features came up in her mind. Normally she had a confused memory of faces, even those she knew well. But she could see this stranger's as vividly as if she were looking again at his photograph. She could even see details she had not consciously noticed; one eyebrow was a trifle ragged; the nose swerved a little from the straight; the smile revealed a gap between the front teeth. The slight flaws emphasized, rather than marred, the young man's striking good looks. Clara mentally examined his image, admiring it in a detached way, as she might have admired the picture of some splendid animal. Certainly she had never encountered a man as attractive as this. Yet, even in the days when she had been capable of feelings, she was not sure that he would have aroused them. His attraction was so obvious that it seemed to put him out of reach. She would have taken it for granted that she could not interest him. Now, she was delighted to find, she was not even curious enough to want to see him in the flesh. She was genuinely indifferent as to whether he went to the party or whether she went herself. Had Clive rung her up at that moment to say he could not, after all, face it, she would have taken off her party dress and gone to bed with perfect equanimity.

PART THREE

Chapter One

They arrived rather late at the party. Clive had insisted on Clara's coming up to his rooms for a fortifying drink. By the time they had found a taxi and directed it to Nell Crayshaw's studio, which was one of a group of four tucked away in a cul-de-sac by the river, the room was smoky and crowded. Except for a few candles on a shelf above the piano, it was in darkness and everyone was listening intently to the young man who was playing. Scarcely a head turned as they lowered themselves cautiously on to cushions on the floor.

'Op. 78. *What* luck!' whispered Clive. Clara nodded vaguely. She guessed it was a Beethoven sonata but could not recognize it. However, she did recognize the pianist whose face was only visible in the dimness. Avery Cass had been the most brilliant of the music students who regularly attended the Cohens' Sunday parties. The sight of him reminded her of her neglect of Patsy. She hoped Cass would not recognize her. Though she was sure he could not see her, she fidgeted on her cushion, trying to draw back still farther into the darkness. Clive hissed at her below his breath. After this rebuke, she sat rigidly still . Her eyes were growing used to the dimness; she could make out pale blots of faces. Then a theme recurred, so exquisite that she could not help attending. As it vanished in a complex labyrinth of harmonies through which her ear was not good enough to follow it, she became aware of a new distraction. She felt that someone was trying to attract her attention. None of the indistinguishable faces on the far side of the piano seemed to be turned towards her. Yet she was convinced that the person was not sitting anywhere near. She did her best to ignore this plucking at her attention but it continued with a gentle, teasing persistence. Then she tried another technique. She spoke silently to the unseen intruder: 'Stop it. I don't *want* to be disturbed.' It was almost as if she heard the reply. 'I know you don't. All right. See if you *can* stop me.' It developed into a kind of game. She forgot all about the music in concentrating against the intruder. It was like wrestling with a friendly antagonist. Sometimes she thought she had won and the other had given up. But, as soon as her mind was left blank again, she realized she had been enjoying this odd game and missed the invisible attack. The next moment, the amused inner voice (she knew by now that it was a man's) would come clearer than ever 'You may as well give in. My will's stronger than yours.'

When the sonata was finished, there was a moment's silence, followed by clapping and subdued, appreciative mutterings. Clive turned to Clara with a happy sigh. 'There's glory for you! I don't wonder it was the old boy's own favourite. And, my God, that chap can play it.' Clara, aware that she had heard barely a note of the last movement, guiltily murmured 'Marvellous.'

'If we had *any* sense,' Clive whispered, 'we'd go now.'

By her new code, Clara should have agreed at once. But the thought of going had suddenly become unendurable. She said:

'I think he's going to play again.'

Cass had stood up but Nell Crayshaw had darted over to the piano and forced him down on to the stool again. People began to call out suggestions for what he should play next. But Cass smiled, shook his head and plunged into a dance tune. Soon people were on their feet, pushing back what little furniture there was and beginning to dance. Couple by couple joined in until Clive and Clara were among the few still sitting huddled on the floor against the wall. He said irritably:

'Oh, hell. You don't want to dance, do you? Nothing will induce *me* to.'

'I'm quite happy to watch,' said Clara. 'Anyway, even if I could *see* anyone, I'm sure I wouldn't know a soul, but you and Avery Cass.'

'Avery Cass?'

'The man who's playing the piano.'

'You *know* that phenomenal creature?'

'I used to slightly. He was a friend of some people I used to know awfully well. I don't suppose he'd remember me. Frankly I rather hope he won't.'

'Why? Is he a frightful bore?'

'Far from it. It's only that he might put these people on my track. Not that I didn't like them. I just don't want to be involved again.'

'*Quite*,' said Clive approvingly. 'One should never be involved. Still less re-involved.'

'Still, if you desperately want to meet him . . .'

'I've heard him. That's all that's really necessary.' He hummed a phrase from the sonata with perfect accuracy. 'I'll have a word with him on my own, if I feel like it. At the moment, the only thing I want *desperately* is a drink. How about you?'

'All right, yes,' said Clara. She did not in the least want a drink.

'I *think* I can make out the bar through the inspissated gloom. I'll battle my way through the shuffling horde and get us both one.'

'Sure you feel strong enough?'

'I shall definitely collapse if I *don't* have a drink. Thank goodness, dear Nellie never spares the booze.'

He unfolded his long legs with agility and began to thread his way through the dancers. Clara noticed how precisely he timed each step, as if he were dancing himself, so that he slid slowly and deftly through the shifting crowd, neither jostling nor being jostled. No head turned, no couple stepped aside as he passed. He was like a ghost; moving invisible and intangible in his own dimension. It would be impossible to imagine Clive deliberately impinging on her mind as the unknown man had done.

Though she was concentrating on Clive, she was perfectly aware that the other was approaching her. It was no surprise to feel a hand beneath each elbow, firmly pulling her up to her feet from behind. Turning round, she recognized him at once though he was not wearing uniform and it was too dim to see his face properly.

She said, without thinking:

'So it was *you*.'

'Did you mind? I couldn't resist trying it on. You put up an awfully good show to keep me out.'

Someone turned on a subdued lamp. Though the room was still very dim, she could make out the small gap between his front teeth as he smiled down at her. Then he stopped smiling.

'What made you say 'It was *you*' like that? You can't have seen me before. I'd know.'

'I've seen your photograph.'

'Good Lord, where? Not in a shop-window, I hope. Or some beastly advertisement? Nell's capable of anything.'

'You needn't worry. A friend of mine begged it from your sister.'

'She's no right to give my photo to girls I don't know.'

'It wasn't a girl, it was a man.'

'Why the hell should a man want my photo?'

'He's interested in types. He thought you were the perfect subaltern.'

'I doubt if my C.O. would agree. Who *is* this man, anyway?'

'The man I came with. Clive Heron.'

'The one sitting beside you? Pale, red hair, pince-nez, mole under the left eye?'

'How could you see all that in the dark?'

'I've got cat's eyes. How else do you think I saw *you*?'

'Mental cat's eyes too, apparently. Do you often do this . . . telepathy or whatever it is?'

'Only with my own family up to now. But we know each other so well it hardly counts. I just tried it with you for fun. I was pretty astonished when it worked.'

'Not as astonished as I was,' said Clara. 'Such a thing's never happened to me before. However well I knew people.'

'All the better. Let's dance.' He put his arm round her. Before taking her hand, he said in a changed voice:

'Tell me something.'

'Yes?'

'That chap you came with. You're not seriously tied up with him? I don't approve of butting in.'

'You're not butting in.'

'Good.' Yet still he hesitated. Something seemed to have

overcast his gay confidence. Then he smiled again. 'After all, I'm only asking for a dance.'

Clara did not answer. Standing there in the circle of his arm which enclosed her firmly but without pressure, she was aware of the strangest sensation. It was as if the whole of her past self had suddenly dropped away and she were a perfectly simple, perfectly free creature. She put her left hand on his shoulder. He glanced down at it and said:

'You're wearing a wedding ring. I didn't see it before. What does that mean?'

'I can't explain now.'

He frowned and asked in a muffled voice:

'Is it all right?'

'All right? What do you mean?'

'Blest if I know what I *do* mean. Even if I did . . . I'm no earthly good at talking. I'm getting out of my depth. When you put your hand on my shoulder, I had a very queer feeling.'

'I had too,' she said softly. 'I suddenly felt absurdly happy.'

'So did I. But at the same time . . . You know that prickling they call "someone walking over your grave"?'

Conscious of nothing but this delicious irresponsible sense of confidence, Clara smiled.

'You're being morbid. I tell you it's all *right*.'

As he took her other hand, she noticed that he too was wearing a ring: a ring that did not look quite right on a man's finger. It was a gold band mounted with a small white enamel shield bearing a red cross. They danced in complete silence. An extraordinary feeling of lightness possessed her; a lightness she had known hitherto only in those pleasant dreams where she floated down flights of stairs, hardly touching the ground. She felt as if she were simultaneously asleep and awake. Far from being unaware of what was going on round her, her senses were more alert than usual. Even in the dimness of the smoky, crowded room, she noticed details of faces and dresses with a peculiar sharpness. Scraps of conversation came to her clearly through the general soft babel; she found she could follow several threads of disjointed talk at the same time, just as she could distinguish the separate layers of scent, tobacco smoke, hot wax, alcohol and human flesh which made up the smell of the room. She was almost more conscious of all these small, vivid new experiences than of the man she was dancing with. Yet she knew that they came to her only through him. If she lost contact with him, this miraculous enhancement of life would vanish. Though she was so acutely aware of what was going on around her, the two of them seemed to be moving invisibly in another dimension, just as she had fancied Clive Heron doing when he had woven his way through the dancers.

From her new world, she watched Clive weave his way back again, a drink held carefully in each hand. At first he was no more than any other strand in this web of heightened perceptions. She observed with impersonal interest the unusual length of his thumbs, clasped at full stretch round the two large tumblers. But when she saw his pince-nez peer round till they found her, a pin-point of light from a candle coming and going in each lens as they followed her movements, she missed a step in the dance. For a moment, like a sleeping top just beginning to falter, the tranced tension slackened. Cautiously, as if realizing the risk she was taking, she freed her right hand and waved to Clive over Crayshaw's shoulder. But though the pince-nez were steadily fixed on her, Clive made not the faintest acknowledgement. She felt Crayshaw's arm tighten a shade against her spine, drawing her back into the perfect rhythm of his steps. The faltering top recovered its balance and spun into its trance again. But now she was aware only of her partner.

The music stopped. They found themselves standing at the edge of the floor. For a moment, they stood motionless, still embraced. They looked at each other, blinking and vaguely smiling, as if awakened from sleep.

Crayshaw recovered himself first. He took her arm and hustled her through the crowd into a corner that was momentarily empty.

'What's happened to us? Have we both gone mad? Or is it only me?'

'Me, too,' she said.

'I simply don't understand.'

'Neither do I.'

She looked into his eyes. As she had supposed, they were grey. The thick black eyebrows were drawn together, giving his face with its aquiline, slightly crooked nose a fierce expression. She smiled.

'How angry you look.'

His eyebrows relaxed but he did not smile back.

'It's no joke,' he said. 'I started it as one and it's turned into something else – It's beyond me.'

'Beyond me too.'

Suddenly he laughed.

'Well, we can't just stand here glaring at each other and saying "I don't understand". Let's get out of this beastly atmosphere. Perhaps some fresh air will bring us to our senses.'

'I can't just go off like that . . . There's Clive . . . the man I came with . . .'

'You needn't worry about him . . . He's gone off himself.'

She said with a faint qualm, 'He can't have. He was there just now while we were dancing.'

'Do you realize we were dancing for well over half an hour?'

'Oh – that's not possible.'

'I'd have said the same. I've usually a pretty good sense of time. But I happened to look at my watch before and after.'

'You're *sure* he's gone?'

'Absolutely sure. I saw him with his coat on, saying goodbye to Nell. Go and get *your* coat. Is it a decently warm one? I've got some rugs but it's an open two-seater.'

'Warm enough.' As she moved away, her extraordinary lightheartedness returned. She turned back towards him, laughing.

'I can't say goodbye to your sister because I don't know which she is. It was too dark to see her face when we came in.'

'Don't worry. You'll meet Nell soon enough. Thank God, I've got a month's leave and this is only my first day.'

He added, smiling:

'Anyway, I couldn't introduce you now if I wanted to. I don't even know your name. Hurry and get that coat.'

'All right, Richard,' she said, without thinking.

'Good Lord . . . So you *do* know mine.'

'I didn't know I did, I guessed right, then?'

'You really didn't know?'

'No. But I remember now. Something too silly to explain. My father was cross with me about something. I told him a lie. I said I'd met your sister . . . and you . . . somewhere. I had to give you a Christian name. The one that came into my head was Richard.'

'Odd,' he said. 'Coming events? All the same . . . damn, I can't guess yours . . .'

'Clara.'

'All the same, Clara.' He paused. 'You'll think me the most ghastly prig. Girls fib, I know. But don't to me. I won't to you, either. I feel it's rather important. Do you feel that too?'

She said soberly:

'Yes. I do.'

Chapter Two

As they walked arm in arm across the courtyard round which the four studios were built, Richard halted.

'Listen. Can you hear the river?'

The air was chilly on Clara's face after the hot, crowded room. She listened and, through the noise of the piano and the laughter inside, she could hear a rhythmical sluck, sluck, that sounded only a few feet away. She shivered and moved nearer to him.

'How close it sounds,' she said.

'Much too close. I tell Nell she's crazy to live so near. If ever there were a flood, she'd stand a good chance of being drowned. There's a passage that runs down a slope between those two studios opposite. Nothing but a few iron posts at the end of it. At high tide the water comes up well beyond them. You could walk slap into it. It's always slippery, down at the end. If you went down there in the dark , even at low tide, you could easily lose your footing and fall in.'

'You sound as if you were warning me.'

'I am warning you. You strike me as being a trifle absent-minded. You're never to walk down that passage without me.'

'Very well You talk as if we . . .'

He cut in: 'I think we'll be about this place a good deal during the next few weeks. Nell has two of these studios. She and her man . . . I'll explain all that later . . . live in the one where the party's going on. She's turned the other – the one she uses for work – over to me for my leave. We could go there now. But I don't want us to be indoors any more for the moment.'

'I don't either.' It seemed natural that he should make all the decisions.

'Shall we go down that passage to the river before we set off in the car? It's rather eery down there. Like the end of the world. You'll be perfectly safe with me.'

'Yes.'

They moved slowly along the passage which ran, dark as a tunnel, between the two unlit buildings. At every yard, the rhythmic slucking sounded louder and the dank breath of the river came stronger. One of the things of which Clara had an irrational terror was the sound of water lapping over stone in the dark. She was terrified, too, of walking even by daylight, on any slippery surface. But, though the path was slimy under her thin high-heeled shoes, holding Richard's arm she trod as surely as on a carpet. She knew with absolute certainty that, as long as she was with him, nothing could ever frighten her again.

They passed through the posts. The tide was out. They stood together on what seemed a lonely shore. She could hear the river but it was invisible in a pearly mist. Above, the sky was half-veiled, half clear, with silvered clouds round the moon. A tug hooted in the distance. They stood for some moments inhabiting this world of water and sky and luminous vapours before they kissed. It was a deep, unhurried kiss more like the recognition of old lovers, long parted, than the fierceness of sudden passion. They kissed only once, then stood for a while enfolded, saying nothing, not even each other's names. Her head was buried in the hollow of his shoulder and his cheek pressed so close against her own that she could feel the movement of bone and muscle as he muttered:

'Let's go back.'

They walked in silence up through the dark passage into the courtyard again. The piano and the laughter sounded brutally loud to Clara after the quiet. But the noise of Richard starting up his car did not disturb her. Like the hoot of the tug down there by the river, it belonged to their private world. He said, above the coughing of the engine:

'If you'll be cold, I'll put the hood up.'

'I shan't be cold.'

'Good.'

They drove for some miles and she watched him as he talked in short bursts, his eyes intent on the road. He handled the car easily, with the minimum of effort. She remembered that Archie had driven a car with the same careless skill. It was the first time she had thought of Archie since that evening with Clive Heron. At that moment, Richard asked:

'Will you tell me now? About your husband and everything?'

The story did not take her long to tell. At first she spoke reluctantly, not because she found it difficult but because she did not want to be reminded that she had once had another life. He listened without comment till she had finished. Then he said in a low voice.

'Lord, that man must have been through hell. He sounds a good chap, too.'

She said eagerly:

'Oh, I'm glad you see that. People don't always. My mother, for example. She never understood him.'

'I don't believe any woman could understand what he must have felt like. Not even you. I could imagine killing myself if my body wouldn't do exactly what I wanted it to do. It would be as good as being dead already.'

'You're tremendously good at physical things, aren't you?'

'Games and all that? Pretty fair, yes. I'm not sports mad, if that's what you mean. No, it's more that it's the thing that makes me feel alive . . . exercising it, making it do something it couldn't do yesterday. Hardly matters what . . . handling a boat, picking out one bird's song among a dozen others, judging the wind when I'm shooting . . . it makes me . . . this sounds awfully pompous . . . but I can't think of another word . . . *exult.*'

'According to you, I'm half-dead already. I'm hopeless at using my body.'

'You shouldn't be. Not from the way you dance.'

'Oh, dancing . . . Even that I do shockingly badly most of the time. I've no control over it. Sometimes it comes right with one particular person . . . just for an evening. The next time, even with them, it's just as likely to go wrong.'

'It will always be all right with *me*,' he said confidently. 'I could teach you all sorts of other things. I *know* I could. All that's the matter with you is that you're a trifle absent-minded, as I said before. You've got to be absolutely inside yourself . . . really *there* in your bones and muscles and all the rest. Then you just leave it to *them*. They know by instinct what to do, if you'll let them.'

'How simple you make it sound. But, now I'm with you, everything seems simple.'

'I always thought everything *was* simple. This last hour or so, I'm not so sure.'

They drove on for a time in silence. Then Richard began to talk about himself. He told her a little about his life with the regiment in Ireland and a good deal about his family and his home in Wiltshire.

'I suppose we're absurdly clannish. We children are three-quarter Scots. Maybe that accounts for it. Anyway, we care awfully what happens to each other. When something goes wrong with one, it affects us all. Even Nell feels it, though she's least typical Crayshaw of the eight of us. She hates having to upset our father and mother over all this business. Not that they've ever said a word or ever will. It hurts them all the same.'

'What is it that hurts them?'

'It's a long story. But I want you to know. Well, she got married . . . years ago now . . . to a terribly nice chap. Naturally he joined up and went off to the front.'

'Was he killed?'

'Better if he had been. No, he got a bad head wound. Now, he's in an asylum and permanently insane. He may live for years but he'll never get better.'

'Oh, how dreadful for Nell. I can't think of anything worse if one loved someone.'

'Neither can I. Nell's tough but there was a time when she nearly went to pieces herself. Up to a couple of years ago, she used to go and see him, though he didn't recognize her. Then things got worse still. He recognized her but he hated the sight of her.'

'Mad people are supposed to do that, aren't they? Turn against the people they're fondest of? Oh, it must be almost worse to go mad than to go blind.'

'Pretty little to choose between them, I should say. I'd rather be dead than either. They had to stop her going to see him in the end. It brought on violent attacks . . . They had to put him in a padded cell. I say, you've gone awfully white. I oughtn't to have told you.'

'If just hearing about it . . . oh, how did Nell endure it? And how can *he* feel?'

'John? God knows, poor devil. I suppose you don't actually suffer when your mind's gone. Nell's got her work. She's frightfully keen on this photography and damn good at it. And, for the last year, there's been this man Gerald Moreton.'

'I remember now. You said "Nell and her man" . . .'

'That's the one. It's a shame they can't get married. Nell's well on in her thirties. She'd like to have children. But she doesn't think it would be fair to them. And you can't get a divorce for insanity. Even if it's a hopeless case.'

'It's tragic. Does she love this man as much as . . .'

'She'll never forget John, as he was. It's just as if he were dead. And she couldn't feel the same about anyone else. But she's very fond of Gerald and she'll stick to him. And he's crazy about her. He can't bear to remember she ever had a husband. That's why she's gone back to her old name.'

'Poor thing . . . You can't blame them for living together . . . After all, it's not as if they were Catholics . . .'

'I'd forgotten, for the moment, *you* were a Catholic.' He added, as if to himself, 'Funny you should be, too.'

'Why? Is Gerald Moreton one?'

'Quite the reverse. Long before he met Nell, he was going to be a C. of E. parson. Then he decided he didn't believe in it all and that the only honest thing to do was to chuck it. Now he's just an agnostic or whatever you call it. So's Nell.'

'And you?'

'Oh, C. of E. like my parents and all the rest of us. I've never thought much about religion. Just taken it for granted it was a good thing. But I'm rather impressed by Roman Catholics. They're so awfully in earnest about it. They let it interfere with their ordinary lives.'

'Do you know many Catholics then?'

He did not answer at once. She glanced up at his profile and saw he was frowning. After a moment, he said:

'Oh well. After a couple of years in Dublin, one's bound to have met a good few.'

Again they fell silent. They had driven fast but Clara had no idea in which direction. At last he turned the car up a deserted side street and stopped under a tree. She supposed they must be in some suburb on the outskirts of London. But to her the tree above them and the privet hedge on which the headlights glimmered looked like the margin of an enchanted forest. He dropped his hands from the steering wheel and she turned towards him, waiting breathlessly for him to take her in his arms. He looked at her with an odd, strained smile that was almost a grimace and said:

'Not till I've told you something.'

He pulled the leather glove from his left hand and she once more noticed the curious little ring with the red cross on the white shield. Clara felt suddenly cold. She asked:

'Something to do with that ring?'

He nodded.

'A girl in Ireland gave it to me. I didn't exactly want her to. But I took it. What's more, I promised to wear it.'

Clara glanced at the privet hedge and saw it for what it was: a privet hedge in a suburban garden.

'You're engaged to her?'

'No. But things looked rather like going that way. I like her very much. And she . . .' He broke off and looked straight ahead again.

'She wants to marry you?' Clara just managed to keep her voice steady.

'It sounds rather awful put that way. As if I were the hell of a conceited chap. Perhaps I am.'

She said, trying to sound careless:

'It's quite natural women should fall in love with you. You should be used to it by now.'

'Don't be sarcastic. Still, I asked for it, I suppose. Of course there's a certain amount of fluttering round any garrison. But very few hearts get seriously damaged. There's always a chap with an extra pip or a more glamorous mess-kit to come along and mend them. But this girl's different.'

'What do you feel about her?'

He hesitated.

'At this moment, I don't know. Almost as if I couldn't remember. Yet it was all clear enough when I walked into Nell's party.'

'How did you feel then?'

'Awfully fond of her. Not absolutely ready to settle down straight away. But when the time came, I thought I'd make as good a go of it with Kathleen as with anyone.'

'How prudent you sound.'

'We Crayshaws . . . the boys anyway . . . are canny when it comes to marriage. Though we tend to marry young and like it. Once we're roped, we make reasonably good husbands and fathers. I've got two nephews and a niece already. We usually seem to run a bit wild and then let some nice girl pick us and get on with the job. And our own jobs tend to take most of our energy and keep us steady.'

'Did you always mean to go into the army?'

He considered for a moment.

'I couldn't be anything else but some kind of soldier. Not in the modern world. I'd like to have lived when one didn't have to have a profession and just rode off and fended for oneself. But I'm getting pretty fed up hanging around in Ireland doing nothing. It's not in my idea of soldiering getting my N.C.O.s to make up to servant girls to find out if there are any arms hidden about the place. I'm jolly tempted to try and get transferred to the Flying Corps.'

Clara said, involuntarily:

'Don't.'

He stared at her:

'Why did you say that so frightfully definitely?'

'I don't know myself. It just slipped out.'

'No fibs,' he said sternly. 'You saw something, didn't you?'

She could not answer. Out of nowhere it had suddenly flashed into her mind, with perfect clarity, that some day, perhaps soon, perhaps years hence, Richard would be killed in a flying accident.

'Rather not say?' he asked, more gently.

She nodded. After a moment, she said:

'I seem to be a little crazy tonight. That game of yours . . . I'm out of my depth. I don't know what's real and what isn't.'

'Think I'm not out of my depth, too?' He gripped her by both shoulders and turned her so that she had to look straight into his eyes. 'You and I . . . This is real . . . It's got to be, hasn't it? . . . Don't ask me why. It's just a fact.'

She said softly:

'How wild your eyes look.'

'You can't see yours.'

'Richard . . . what's happened to us? Are we bewitched?'

'Would you live on a desert island with me?'

'Yes.'

'Or in one of the beastly little villas in this road?'

'Yes.'

They were both laughing but their eyes were fiercely intent. Then Richard frowned and said soberly:

'There's no risk I wouldn't take. Just for a second I was worried about *you*.'

'Why?'

'I don't know. I tell you I'm absolutely in the dark. I only know it's all or nothing for us.'

'Yes.'

'Would you risk it?'

'Yes.'

His face remained clouded.

'We might have to wait years.'

'Because of what I told you?'

'About this case and so on? That . . . and maybe something else.'

'What do you mean?'

'Don't ask me. Just a hunch. Something to do with you. I've no idea *what*. Let's call it nonsense and forget it.'

She said happily:

'Yes, forget it.'

His face relaxed.

'Good. I'm asking you to trust me. Because all I know is it's got to happen. And I can't see further ahead than the next few weeks. But I'll give you a sign.'

He took his hands from her shoulders and stripped the little red and white ring from his finger.

'Oh, no,' she cried in sudden terror. 'Too soon.'

'Too late,' he said almost harshly. His aim and throw had been so swift that the ring had already dropped in the middle of the privet hedge.

Something in her seemed to wail, 'Remember where it fell.' Whether she said it aloud or not, he ignored it. He heaved his shoulders and gave a sharp, hissing sigh before he drew her into his arms and she forgot everything but that they had found each other.

Chapter Three

During the next three weeks, it seemed to Clara that everyone and everything about her was in a conspiracy to make her happy. This happiness was of a different order from anything she had known or even imagined. It was almost like the acquisition of some magical power that transformed, not merely herself but every person she met, everything she saw and heard and touched.

She spent the greater part of her time with Richard. Often they parted without planning when or where their next meeting should be. She had become so expert at 'the game' that he had only to will her and she went instinctively to the right place at the right time. The strange sense of heightened perception she had felt when she danced with him had now become her permanent state even when they were apart. While she was with him it made everything they did or said or saw together register at the time with astonishing sharpness. Afterwards the details were apt to vanish in a vague golden haze.

She realized that, until now, she had never even begun to know what it meant to be alive. Not only everything she did with Richard but the most trivial words and objects seemed to be charged with extraordinary significance as if she were living in a fairy-tale where everything had its own language and conveyed a secret meaning. At first she had moments of doubt that the spell might break and she would find herself back in the old dull world. But soon each day not only confirmed but increased her sense that everything had become flawlessly, effortlessly right. No activity, physical or mental, any longer presented any difficulty. The flesh she had put on during those months with Archie disappeared so quickly that every morning she arose with a lighter body. Soon her clothes hung loose on her but she did not trouble to take them in. She knew that, whenever she wanted to, she could discard all her present ones and become possessed of delightful new ones, perfect to the last detail, as effortlessly as a snake sloughing its skin. Her mind worked with astonishing speed and clarity. She was full of plans and projects to be worked out when Richard had returned to his regiment. She did not tell him that soon she would be making a great deal of money. For one thing, she wanted it to be a surprise: for another, she did not yet know exactly how she was going to make her fortune. That would be revealed to her when the time came. She was also convinced that, in due course, she would write a very wonderful book. She had only to convey this dazzling new intensity of vision to make it unlike any book written before.

The new clarity of perception affected her relations with

other people. She was able to understand and adapt herself to strangers, even at a first meeting. Richard introduced her to one of his married brothers and she felt at once that she had known Angus and Cecily all her life. It was delightful how they had accepted her as if she and Richard were already married. Cecily had taken it for granted that she would like to come and help bath the baby and, though she had never handled a baby before, her new physical expertness had made it quite easy. Richard had come in when she was drying the little creature and their eyes had met above its damp, ruffled head. As they smiled at each other, she was surprised to find how natural and inevitable it seemed that she should bear his children. Something which had once been clouded with fears and anxieties now appeared as a new delight. In that quick exchange of looks she mentally accepted all the pain that it had once terrified her to imagine. She thought, 'It would be for him. Our children must be completely alive as he is. I'll refuse an anaesthetic. Nothing must take the edge off it. He'll lend me his strength.'

She was equally at home with Nell and her lover, Gerald Moreton. This was all the more gratifying since Richard had warned her that Nell did not always 'take to' people. And, indeed, there was a bluntness, at times a roughness about Nell that the old Clara would have found intimidating. But the new Clara easily pierced this slightly forbidding shell and recognized Nell's honesty and generosity. Nor was she affronted, as she would once have been, by Gerald Moreton's rather provocative teasing. Though he dared not do so in front of Richard, he could not be alone with her even for a few minutes without gibing at Catholics. He liked to insist that her nullity suit was a 'put-up job' and typical of the way 'you R.C.s can slither out of anything if you know the ropes'. Normally she would have been hurt and insulted. But she took it in good part and teased him back because she perceived that, beneath his rather aggressive 'cheeriness', he was an unhappy man, obscurely disturbed by his own loss of faith and bitterly resenting the fact that Nell could not get free from her insane husband. But it was not only with those whom she already thought of as her new 'family' that the charm worked. People in shops, bus conductors, waiters, all seemed to feel it too. They smiled at her in a special way as if they knew her secret and were grateful to her for being so happy.

Though she knew that Richard was the cause of this wonderful new access of life, her happiness was not dependent on being with him. It was like a sparkling fountain inside herself that overflowed into every detail of her daily life, even into brushing her hair or talking to her grandmother. She brimmed over with affection for everyone; she would have liked to stop strangers in the street and tell them she loved them. She found herself planning wild schemes of benevolence, not only for her father and the aunts at Paget's Fold but for people she had almost forgotten. It was difficult sometimes not to burst out singing or laughing from sheer ecstatic joy. Sometimes it seemed to her that she could savour the ecstasy even more fully when she was alone than when she was with Richard. Not long after their first meeting she discovered something so obvious that she wondered she had not discovered it before. Sleep was a sheer waste of time if one were really alive. Night after night she would lie awake, neither restless nor impatient for the next day; content simply to feel this high pulse of life throbbing through her. She would get up and dress, as refreshed and clear-eyed as if she had had nine hours' deep sleep. She also began to discover that it was hardly necessary to eat. Her appetite had almost vanished yet everyone was saying how amazingly well she looked. She wondered if she ought to tell someone about these remarkable discoveries. Supposing she had hit on the secret of life? Perhaps she ought to test it out a little longer so as to prove her theory scientifically. In any case, with the infinite prospect of time before her, she could afford to wait.

This patience was one of the things that surprised her most, for all her life she had been violently impatient. It bore no resemblance to that dull, artificial detachment she had achieved for a week or two before she met Richard. She could laugh at that now along with all the other illusions and follies and miseries of the past. Her present patience was something entirely different; it grew naturally out of her certainty that nothing could ever go wrong again. It was Richard who became impatient sometimes and wondered how long it would be before the case was settled and she was free. She felt so much married to him already that sometimes she forgot there still had to be a barrier between them. Sometimes, in his arms, her whole being seemed to dissolve into one magnetic current flowing towards him. It was he who would remind her, gently as a rule, but now and then sternly, not to try him too hard.

One thing, though reassuring, did strike her as remarkable. This was the extraordinary change in her father. In the first few days, when Richard had said he wanted to meet her parents, she had been hesitant about bringing him to the house. However casually she and Richard might behave, she knew very well there was no hiding the intensity of the bond between them. Her father would be shocked and apprehensive: she dreaded the inquisition which would follow when they were alone. Yet, when the two did meet, her father seemed to accept Richard almost as naturally and inevitably as she had herself. It was as if the magic had worked on him too. She had never known him so affectionate and so genial. She caught him looking at her sometimes with such radiant kindliness that she was impelled to go over to him and kiss him. It was as if he had forgotten all about her situation and saw her as she could not help feeling herself to be, an unmarried girl who had found her true love. Occasionally he said something which showed he had not forgotten but he said it with a gentle compassion quite unlike his old anxious severity.

On one of the few evenings she had spent entirely at home, the after-dinner pupil rang up to say that he would be half an hour late. Her father suggested that Clare and her mother should take their coffee with him in the study. He sat down in his usual place at the desk while her mother took the big green armchair and Clara a small one by the mantelpiece with its load of photographs. As she drank her coffee, she found her attention strangely drawn to these young men, most of them mere names to her, who had been soldiers like Richard. Though she knew so many of them were dead, they all seemed suddenly like living people. They seemed to be looking at her and smiling at her as if they were glad to know she was going to marry a soldier. Some of them had an urgent, almost pleading look as if there were something important they wanted to tell her.

Her father said with his new, happy look:

'It must be years since we were able to do this. It has almost the charm of forbidden fruit.'

Her mother laughed.

'You're acquiring a taste for forbidden fruit, Claude. It must be the effect of your mysterious Monday evenings.'

'I assure you they're very innocuous evenings, my dear. But I admit that the mere fact of their being secret does give me an absurd pleasure.'

'They're doing you all the good in the world. He looks a different person these days, doesn't he, Clara?'

Clara tore herself away from the compelling faces on the mantelpiece and said gaily:

'Of course he does. Darling Daddy!'

Isabel smiled at her.

'As to *you*, Clara . . . You can't think what a relief it is to see you happy again. It's as if you'd been under some kind of curse and the bad spell had suddenly been removed. She's never looked so gay and pretty in her whole life, has she, Claude? Why, she's more than pretty, she's almost lovely . . .'

'She's certainly never looked better,' her father said. He added, with the faintest touch of anxiety, 'It's almost bewildering . . . this extraordinary change.'

'Nonsense, Claude,' said Isabel. 'She's been through the most appalling experience and thought the whole of her life was ruined. Now, thank heavens, she's met the right man and everything is going to be different.'

'Don't leap too far ahead, my dear. Remember there is a very long way for Clara to go before she can make any definite plans. Clara, believe me, there's nothing I want more than to see you happy. And, personally, I've seldom seen a young man I liked more than Richard Crayshaw. When I see you together, I'm apt to forget how things are. Perhaps I ought to be more of a heavy father. Somehow it's hard to deny what obviously gives you so much happiness . . . What do you think, Isabel?'

'I can't see what possible harm there can be in their seeing each other,' her mother said. 'After all, it's only for another week or two. Then Richard has to go back to his regiment. They obviously fell in love at first sight. It's like an exquisite fairy-tale. Clara, darling, you're saying nothing. Does it hurt you to hear us talking so prosaically about you and Richard?'

Clara smiled.

'Oh no. I don't mind at all. I'm glad you see without my having to explain.'

'Of course,' said her mother, 'you can't exactly get engaged just yet, can you . . .?'

'Really . . . Isabel . . .' her father began in mild rebuke.

'We don't need to be engaged,' Clara broke in. 'There's nothing complicated about it. We just know.'

'You mean that if, and when it becomes possible, you hope to marry?'

'It's not a question of hoping – only of waiting.'

'Dear child . . . there are so many bridges to cross. And it's all so sudden . . . Can either of you be sure so soon that . . .?'

'Don't worry her,' Isabel interrupted. 'Can't you just let her be happy?'

Clara said suddenly:

'Isn't it strange, Daddy, that, after all, I should be going to marry a soldier?'

'Why strange, darling?' Isabel asked. 'And why, after all?'

Clara went on in an eager rush, talking directly to her father.

'You remember when I was little, how I loved everything to do with the army. How I hated dolls and always played with soldiers. I wanted to be a colonel of Hussars when I grew up. That Hussar cap I'm wearing in that awful photo of me at seven on the mantelpiece. I used to sleep with it on my pillow. It all comes back now when I talk to Richard. He's surprised to find how much I know about all the regiments and their battles and so on. I've told him about all those army games I used to invent for Charles Cressett.' She was aware of a sudden interchange of glances between her parents. 'Oh, don't be frightened. I often talk about Charles to him. You see nothing upsets me when I talk about it to Richard. He's very fond of children. We might even call our first son Charles. But it was about soldiers you wanted to know, wasn't it? This is the strange thing. During the war you know, I couldn't get *into* it. I mean, I somehow couldn't feel any connection with it. Perhaps because I was just too young to have anyone I very specially cared for out at the front. Oh, I used to write to people's brothers and all that and sometimes an officer on leave would take me out to tea. But I didn't keep imagining all the time what was happening to them. Not as you did, Daddy. Even when they were killed . . . ones I knew . . . I didn't really feel it. I've often felt guilty about that.'

She saw that both her parents' eyes were intent on her face and felt a sense of triumph to see how absorbed they were by her words even if they did not quite understand them. Often there were things she was only on the verge of understanding; she could not expect them to know more than she did. When she herself understood more, there were so many things she would be able to tell them. Aware that she had fallen silent and that they were waiting thirstily for her next words, she went on:

'Well, I don't any more. And, quite suddenly tonight, while I've been sitting here with you, I know why.' She swept up her arm and pointed to the photographs. 'You see, they've forgiven me. They've told me so. They're so very happy that I'm going to marry a soldier.'

The door-bell rang. Her father, looking a little pale, as was natural enough after the wonderful news she had just given him, said:

'Forgive me, my dears . . . my pupil. Clara, dare I suggest you have an early night for once? You've had some rather late ones.'

She saw that, even if there had been time, this would not have been the right moment to tell him that sleep was quite unnecessary. Instead she ran over to him and kissed him, saying . . .

'I'll go to bed this minute if that's what you'd like.'

Her mother smiled a little uncertainly.

'What a biddable child you are these days. But perhaps bed *would* be a good idea. Your eyes are so bright and your cheeks are so flushed. And you hardly touched your dinner.'

She passed her hand over Clara's hair.

'Why, it's all electric like a cat's fur. Darling, you mustn't get over-excited . . . you'll burn yourself out.'

Clara laughed softly.

'I can't burn out,' she said.

Only one thing had very faintly disturbed the radiant delight of those three weeks. This was the intrusion of the young Indian student into Valetta Road. He had arrived within a few days of her meeting Richard and she could not get used to his permanent presence in the house. It was not an intrusive presence for she rarely saw him except at mealtimes. Yet she was always being reminded of him, if only by the almost noiseless footsteps passing her door or the sight of the wrought silver vessels which he kept in the bathroom for his religious ablutions. She did not actively dislike Wajid Ullah but the glowing affection she now felt for everyone with whom she came in contact refused to extend itself to him. His face, with its dark eyes and splendid teeth would have been handsome had it not been heavily pitted with the smallpox which had also slightly coarsened his delicate features. She could not say what it was about Ullah that gave her a faint feeling of uneasiness; whether it was his scarred face, his exaggerated courtesy that seemed to have a touch of mockery or a way he had of staring at her with those dark eyes whose whites were tinged with yellow and then suddenly averting his head. She often saw him staring at her mother in the same way and occasionally covertly glancing from one to the other as if comparing them. When he did this, a curious little smile sometimes twitched his mauvish lips. Wajid Ullah slept on the top floor in the room next to her parents. Her own bedroom was on the first floor. Sometimes she fancied that those singularly quiet footsteps paused for a minute or two as he passed her door on his way upstairs. Once he annoyed her by asking her, with his polite but insatiable curiosity about all English customs:

'Excuse, but you are young married lady and yet you live under your father's roof?'

'Yes.'

'In my country that would be thought very strange. For how many months then is it custom for a bride to remain under her father's roof before husband fetches her away? With us it is only in case of very young child-bride. My sister at home is such

369

child-bride. The young man of such fine appearance who visits this house is, of course, your husband?'

She was on the verge of saying 'Yes' when she caught that look in his dark eyes she had seen before, a look of courteous insolence, almost of veiled desire. Suddenly she was seized with such a passion of rage that she could have struck him. He said meekly, with a deprecating smile on his mauve lips:

'Excuse . . . No offence meant . . . I ask only from interest in customs of country. Pray do not trouble to answer. I never wish to displease you.'

Chapter Four

Richard's leave was drawing to its end. Clara made no attempt to dissuade him from spending the last week of it with his parents in Wiltshire. He was to go down to Peacocks on the Saturday and she was to join him there on the following one for his final weekend before he returned to Ireland.

On one of his last few days in London, he said:

'I suppose there's no hope of your being able to come over to Dublin? It may be a hell of a time before we can see each other again.'

She shook her head, smiling.

'I can wait.'

'We're supposed to be posted back to England soon. But, in the army, you can never be sure of anything.'

Clara said:

'I don't even feel apart from you.'

'Nor do I. All the same, I wish we could get married straight away without any fuss and I could take you back with me. I'm beginning to feel I want us safely tied up. Oh, I know it's impossible. I'm not complaining really . . .'

'What are you frightened of? Don't you know everything *must* come right for us? *Aren't* we tied up? I couldn't feel more married to you than I do.'

'I didn't say I was frightened. It's just that ever since we met, it's been like living in some extraordinary other world. I want to see you safe and solid in *my* world. See?'

'But our world's the same. How could these extraordinary things happen between us otherwise? How could we possibly play our game? I've never been able to do that with anyone else. Have you?'

'Not in the least like this. Only somehow, I'm beginning to feel more and more out of my depth. In every other way, I'm the most ordinary of ordinary chaps. I love you most terribly . . . absolutely beyond anything I thought possible . . .'

'Ah, so do I you . . . so do I you,' she said softly.

He caught both her hands and clutched them with the palms against his cheekbones.

'I belong to you,' he said.

She looked into his face, more familiar to her these days then her own. She never looked in a mirror now except for the most cursory glance. But she knew every modulation of his, not only its structure which no expression could distort, but every slight flaw of skin or feature which made it Richard's face and not the almost ludicrous perfection of a type. Her look travelled up from the firm, mobile mouth with the small moustache which did not hide the groove of the upper lip to the grey eyes with their thick black brows and lashes. On the upper lids the straight lashes grew so close together that they looked like a crow's quill. Then she saw that the eyes themselves, usually bright as an animal's, were slightly clouded. She said quickly:

'You're worried about something. What is it?'

He shook his head between her cupping hands.

'Nothing definite. Let's take the car and go off into the country, shall we? We've hung around London rather a lot the last few days.'

'Yes, let's.'

She tried gently to withdraw her hands but he kept them clutched against his face.

'How awfully hot your hands are. In the old days they were always cold till I'd warmed them. You're not feverish or anything, are you?'

She laughed.

'Of course not. I've never felt better in my life.'

'All very well to laugh, my girl. But I've noticed that lately you hardly do more than pretend to eat. And you're getting thinner every day.'

'So much the better.'

'Hmm. I'm not sure I approve. Anyway I'm jolly glad you're coming down to Peacocks for the last weekend. Even you won't be able to resist my mother's cooking. In any case, if you're going to be one of the Crayshaw family, she won't let you off, any more than the rest of us.'

Clara said happily:

'One of the Crayshaw family. I love to hear you say that.'

He kissed the palms of her two hands and laid them gently back in her lap.

'I think you'll like my mother. People do.'

'Will she like me?'

'Of course. She would, in any case. And I'll be spending a lot of next week talking about you.'

'I wonder what you'll say.'

'So do I. Sometimes I wonder if it wouldn't be better just to spring you on her without preparing the ground. Of course the moment she sees me, she'll know without my telling her that something's happened to *me*. She won't ask me any questions. The minute she sees *you*, she'll understand.'

'You *are* worried about something,' Clara insisted.

'All right. Just a bit, yes.'

'Something to do with the . . . with Kathleen?'

He nodded.

'She's met her. She's very fond of her. Oh, she knew perfectly well there was nothing definite. But I could see she rather liked the prospect . . .'

'And she mightn't like this prospect so much?'

'She'll like it far better. Once she's seen you and seen me. She'll realize we're so absolutely . . . well, that it's just inevitable. I meant to write and tell her. But I'm hopeless at putting things into words on paper. Only I had a letter from her this morning, asking me to give her love to Kathleen when I wrote. Of course she'd posted it before I phoned her last night to say you were coming down for my last weekend. But it brought it home to me that I've been rather a swine. I *ought* to have written to Kay. But how can you say these things in a letter?'

'Has she written to you?'

'Every week. She always does. I've just skimmed through them. I can't remember a thing that was in them.'

'If you didn't answer . . . won't she guess?'

He shook his head.

'I hardly ever do answer. I've told you I'm no hand at writing letters. No, I'll just have to tell her straight when I see her. She'll understand. But I hate hurting people. I wish I'd got it over.'

'You're very fond of her, aren't you?'

'Yes,' he said frankly. 'I always will be. Once I like people, I go on liking them. But you and me . . . it's something entirely different. I could easily imagine being much more attracted by some other girl than Kathleen. But us . . . that's something I couldn't have imagined if I tried.'

'Do you think *I* could have?'

'More easily than I could, maybe. There's something about you I can't quite follow. I don't know what it is. But every now and then I feel it. Especially lately.'

'Can't you try and tell me?'

He frowned.

'I can *try*. Give me your hand,' he took it and said again, 'Burning hot. It's as if you were on fire inside. I look at you sometimes and it's as if you were melting away. Sometimes when we're together . . . even when I have you in my arms . . . it's almost as if you suddenly weren't there. Usually, it's only for a split second . . . and then you're back again and everything's real.'

'It *is* real . . . it's all real,' she said passionately. 'Perhaps neither of us knew what was real before.'

'I never knew anything like this. But at first we both seemed to be in the dark . . . sort of bewildered . . . Now it's as if you'd got cat's eyes in the dark . . . and I hadn't. Sometimes I almost feel as if you weren't a girl at all . . .'

'What am I then?'

'The Lord knows.' He looked down at her hand. 'I picked up a paper in Nellie's studio the other day. There was a poem in it. I don't often read poetry. But something about this made me think of you. Some of it actually stuck in my head.'

'Tell me.'

He muttered, still staring at her hands.

'Alone in wet Berehaven, ere Whitsuntide came in
I met a faery woman and she was white of skin
She laid her white hand on me, my own was coarse and brown
And in my veins I felt the tide of life go up and down.'

He broke off. 'Can't remember any more.'

'I believe you can,' she urged.

'Only vaguely. It was all very sad and *we're* not sad. It's one of the things I love most about you, the way you enjoy everything so tremendously. This faery female left *her* man waiting hopelessly forever in the rain.'

Clara laughed.

'You can trust me not to do that. Anyway it's you that's leaving me.'

He straightened his shoulders and laughed too.

'Thank goodness, we *can* laugh. I remember the last line . . . rhyming with "rain" of course . . . "I'm weary with the waiting but she never comes again".'

'Dear, dearer, dearest Richard,' she said happily and kissed him. 'Where shall we go in the country?'

Looking up into his eyes, she saw that they were bright again.

'That's what we need,' he said. 'Get out and blow all these morbid notions away. It's not like me to be morbid. Let's go somewhere *you* know well. I keep taking you to places and to see people I like. You don't know how I'm longing to take you to Peacocks. When I'm back in Ireland, I want to be able to think of you in places and among people I know. So as to banish the Banshee woman for good and all. I've seen you in your own home . . . good. I've seen your father and a nicer man there couldn't be. But isn't there somewhere in the country, somewhere you've known all your life . . . that's your equivalent of Peacocks?'

She said excitedly:

'There's Paget's Fold. Oh, Richard, I can't imagine anything more wonderful than seeing you at Paget's Fold. Why did I never think of it before?'

Just as they were setting out, Clara said on a sudden impulse:

'Do you mind if we stop at Westminster Cathedral? I'd like to go in for a moment.'

'I'll come in with you,' Richard said.

He followed her up the aisle and went into the bench behind her. Clara knelt for some minutes with her face buried in her hands. She was conscious of nothing but an immense overflowing of gratitude for all this new joy. Then her thoughts became more coherent. She asked God to bless Richard and herself. For the first time in weeks, the wild tension of happiness slackened to something sober. Almost sad. She found herself praying: 'Keep us safe, whatever happens. Give me grace to accept whatever Your will is for both of us.'

As they came out on to the steps of the porch, Richard looked at her with an expression that was strange to her: a gravity that made his face seem for a moment older, almost careworn.

'I'm glad you did that,' he said. 'I liked seeing you in there. You looked so much at home. It means a lot to you, doesn't it?'

The sobriety still lingered in her mind, as if a cloud had passed over its brilliant, heightened illumination.

'Yes,' she answered quietly. 'But not as much as it should mean. Nothing like as much.'

He said with the same unusual gravity:

'It might to me one day. I can't tell. Meanwhile, you don't have to worry, Clara. I know what it means, marrying a Catholic. I'm prepared to accept all the conditions.'

She said gently:

'Kathleen's a Catholic too?'

He nodded, then said hesitantly:

'I don't quite know what to do in there. I found myself sort of mentioning her as well as you. You don't mind?'

'Mind?' Clara said with a sudden pang of self-reproach. 'Oh,

Richard . . . how could I mind? It's what I should have done myself. But I forgot that anyone in the world matters but *us*. Is being happy making me frightfully selfish?'

He caught her arm.

'Of course not. Perhaps just a trifle absent-minded, now and then. Come along, let's get going.'

On the drive down to Paget's Fold, her dazzling joy not only returned but soared up to a new peak of exultation. It was a brilliant November day. Leaves and bare stems, stubble and dying grass, glowed with soft fires of crimson, amber and rosy brown. To Clara it seemed it was she and Richard who kindled all these fires as they raced through the countryside like a torch, scattering sparks of light to left and right, leaving a trail of glory. It was difficult to sing aloud as they sped along, her hair streaming in the wind. She wanted to cry out, 'We are life. We are joy. We set the world on fire as we pass.' But she had to keep her wild exhilaration secret. Richard, his face growing happier as each mile took them deeper into the country, was in a mood to talk. He was constantly drawing her attention to a bird or a late flower, speculating what fish might be in a stream or game in a covert. Moreover he wanted Clara to tell him everything about Paget's Fold and her two great-aunts. At one point, he slackened speed and asked:

'I say, do you think we ought to descend on them like this, unannounced? Oughtn't we to stop somewhere and telephone them?'

Clara pealed with laughter.

'A *telephone* at Paget's Fold, You can't think how funny that is. Wait till you've seen it. You might as well expect the aunts to have an aeroplane.'

Richard laughed, but not uproariously.

'Of course, after what you've told me. But those old darlings . . . mightn't they be a bit flustered? They might think they ought to produce one of those marvellous meals for us and be upset because we hadn't given them any warning.'

Clara was momentarily sobered.

'You're quite right, Richard. I never thought of anything but wanting to show *you* the place. I've never in my life burst in on them without warning. But I'm sure they'll be delighted to see us.'

Richard said firmly:

'We'll stop in Horsham and have lunch. Then at least they won't have to worry about feeding us.'

'I'm not hungry,' Clara assured him.

'Well, I am,' he smiled. 'Hungry as a hunter. What's more, I'm jolly well going to see *you* eat a decent meal for once.'

She swallowed some food obediently and they set off again. Soon they began to pass landmarks she recognized, the church three miles from Paget's Fold where she and her parents heard Mass on Sundays, the steep hill with the monument to the cyclist who had been killed at its foot, the ruined windmill at Owlbridge, the last village before Bellhurst. Now, as every tree and pond and gate became familiar, Clara's mood changed. Her happy exultance remained but it took on something of the quality of a dream. She could not believe that she was really here, with Richard, in these old beloved surroundings. It was almost more than she could bear. She half wished she could wake up before the dream took them to the house itself. But the next moment they were on the road that divided the two great sweeps of the green and she saw Paget's Fold. It looked so different that she only stopped Richard just in time. Looking out for the great walnut, she had seen not a green but a golden tree; the sumach by the gate was flaming crimson; a dozen details she could not immediately take in made it appear strange, almost disconcerting. At first, all this seemed to confirm that she was dreaming; then she realized that she had never before seen Paget's Fold in November.

As they stepped out of the car, Richard stood for a moment, stretching his limbs and drawing in deep breaths.

'What terrific air. You can smell the sea in it. It can't be far away, the sea.'

'Only a few miles.'

'When we've seen your aunts, shall we drive on to the sea? Do you know somewhere where it's not all built up and beastly?'

'I don't know,' she said vaguely. 'Beyond Rottingdean, there might be.'

'I'll find somewhere,' he said. 'Look, there's someone coming out of the house.'

It was Aunt Sophy, making her way down the brick path to the gate and peering uncertainly at the car and their two figures. The house might look different but Aunt Sophy was the same as ever. She wore her old black gardening-skirt, green with age, and the purple crochet shawl she pulled over her blouse on chilly days.

'Aunt Sophy, isn't it?' Richard whispered. 'She's just as you described her.'

Clara ran up to the gate and flung her arms round Aunt Sophy over the iron rail. The old woman stared at her, half-smiling, half-bewildered.

'Clara . . . is it really you? Well . . . this *is* a surprise . . . Oh dear . . . what will you think of us? But we never got your letter . . .'

'There wasn't a letter. We came as a surprise.'

'And that must be Archie with you . . . Oh, dear . . . I'm sure it's a great pleasure to see you both . . . But it's *such* a surprise . . . I can't quite take it in, dear. I'd better go and tell Leah.'

Clara felt as if the dream were turning into a nightmare. She had almost forgotten Archie's existence. Now, for a moment, she remembered all the past and realized that the aunts had still been told nothing. She clutched Aunt Sophy's tiny sloping shoulders through the purple shawl and whispered, 'Darling Aunt Sophy, I can't explain now. This isn't Archie. It's Richard . . . Richard Crayshaw. I so much wanted him to see you both. And Paget's Fold.'

Aunt Sophy said with a kind of helpless obstinacy:

'I'm sorry, dear. I don't quite understand. We're not used to meeting strangers. And the house isn't looking as we would wish. Let me go and tell your aunt. She'll want to change her dress.'

'No, please. I want Richard to see you just as you are. Come and be introduced.'

Richard had remained tactfully in the background, pretending to do things to his car. Aunt Sophy advanced with such shy reluctance in the grip of Clara's arm that she almost had to be dragged along. But when she looked up into Richard's face, her puzzled, anxious expression relaxed into a faint smile. She said gallantly:

'I'm sure you're very welcome. Clara should have warned us she was bringing a friend to see us. Then we could have made a little preparation.'

'It was my fault,' Richard said. 'It was such a marvellous day and I had my car. I was dying for some country air. I practically forced your niece to let me drive her down here. Will you forgive us?'

'Yes . . . yes, of course,' said Aunt Sophy with more confidence. 'I'm sure anyone would be tempted by the country on such a beautiful day. Clara dear, I can see the drive has done you good. You look very much better than when I saw you last. Except that you seem to have got very thin.' The anxious look returned. 'Oh dear, you must be very hungry after all that motoring. I wonder what I can find . . .'

'*Please*,' said Richard. 'We've just eaten an enormous lunch in Horsham . . .'

'That's just as well.' To Clara's relief, Aunt Sophy actually smiled at him. 'You see . . . being two old ladies living on our own . . . we don't always bother much about food.'

'You're as bad as my mother,' Richard smiled back at her. 'When my father and the rest of us are away, she lives on tea and buns and hardboiled eggs.'

'Are you one of a large family?'

'There are eight of us. Six boys. Two girls.'

'Indeed. That's very large for nowadays. More like the families there used to be when I was young.'

Clara watched Aunt Sophy with astonishment. As a rule she was too shy to talk to anyone until she had met them a great many times. Now she was talking quite naturally to Richard and almost ignoring her own presence. But suddenly the worried look appeared again.

'I mustn't stand here chattering like this. My elder sister doesn't even know you're here. Your Aunt Leah is up in her room, Clara. If you don't mind, I'll just go up and have a word with her. Perhaps you'd care to show your friend the garden, dear. Though I'm afraid it's looking far from its best.'

379

Richard said:

'My mother would envy you those zinnias. She's a pretty good gardener but she's failed with zinnias year after year.'

'They're very troublesome,' Aunt Sophy agreed. 'I can't tell you how many failures I've had with them myself. And you know, this year, I'd got so tired of pampering them I practically said, "Come up if you want to and don't if you don't. I wash my hands of you, you nasty spoilt little things." And look at them. They've been flowering away since September.' She pointed to the bright clumps of crimson and orange, ochre and magenta.

'He knows about flowers,' said Clara fondly. 'I didn't even know those were zinnias till this moment.'

'Your mother would,' said Aunt Sophy. 'It's a wonder to me how well Isabel knows all the flowers. And yet your father, who's country-bred, can't tell an aster from a Michaelmas daisy . . .' She glanced hopefully at Richard. 'Do you know our nephew – Mr Claude Batchelor? Perhaps you're one of his old pupils?'

'Not an old pupil. But Mr and Mrs Batchelor have been frightfully good to me.'

'That doesn't surprise me. We think the world of them. Have you known them long?'

'Only since I came on leave. I've been in Ireland for the last two years and I'm going back very soon.'

'Ah well, it's natural you should want to see as much of England as you can. Now you must excuse me.'

Though Aunt Sophy's face looked slightly puzzled, it was considerably happier as she trotted off into the house.

Looking back afterwards, though she remembered innumerable details of that day, Clara had no clear recollection of the time she and Richard spent inside the house. She did however remember standing in the orchard with Richard. Alone with him again, her faint uneasiness had vanished. She was back in her enchanted world where there was nothing surprising in his being there with her, his head outlined against the lichened branches of an apple tree where a few bright globes still hung. He said: 'If I sent your Aunt Sophy a young tree to replace this old Elliston that's dying off, would she think it cheek? We've got some nice little Ellistons coming on in the plantation at Peacocks. Or perhaps she'd rather have a larch. A larch would look fine in that space at the end. I like the idea of something from Peacocks being planted here.'

'Oh, so do I,' she said eagerly. 'And I know she'd love it. But please let it be a larch. That's a tree I do know. I've always longed to have one here.'

'Right. A larch it shall be. For *you*. That's a solemn promise.'

Suddenly the air was filled with the whirr of wings. He swept his arm up:

'Look. Skylarks. A whole flock of them!'

She stared up into the clear, faint blue. The birds were tumbling and flying in a wild, mazy pattern. Then for a moment, Clara saw them hang absolutely still against the sky. She saw, too, that the dark specks of their bodies were arranged in a curious way: some singly, some in clusters of two and three. She cried out . . .

'Richard . . . it's a message . . . They're writing music in the sky . . . Music for us . . . Oh, if only I could make it out!'

But the next moment, the birds had resumed their mazy dance and the pattern had dissolved before she had had time to decipher it. Almost immediately, Aunt Sophy had come out to summon them.

She supposed they must have spent quite a time talking to the aunts inside the house for, when they drove away, it was beginning to get dark. She had an odd impression that the aunts had been much more at ease with Richard than with herself. This puzzled her because, even with Aunt Leah, she had been gayer and livelier than ever before in her life. She had even made her laugh a great deal. Yet, if that was so, why had she a persistent image of Aunt Leah's pale face looking more pinched than usual, not with disapproval, of course, since that was impossible, but with something almost like fear? No, she was sure they had all been very gay. She herself most certainly had. Except during the very last moments before she and Richard left when she had suddenly stopped talking and laughing. Forgetting even Richard's existence, she had had a flash of intense awareness of all the poverty, all the bravely born frustration of the two old women's lives. Soon she would be able to make up to them for all the hardships. But first there was something she must do herself. She thought how often she must have hurt them, how selfishly she had taken all their kindness for granted. Aunt Sophy was standing at the bamboo table, looking out of the window. Clara jumped up from her chair and flung herself on her knees at Aunt Sophy's feet.

'Darling Aunt Sophy,' she cried. 'Forgive me. Forgive me for everything.'

Aunt Sophy's face looked down at her in bewilderment, two pink stains blotting her plump, finely-wrinkled cheeks.

'Forgive you, Clara? Now, dear, what's this nonsense? Get up at once or you'll spoil your nice skirt.'

But Clara would not get up. Somebody lifted her gently from behind. She heard Aunt Leah say:

'There, there, Sophy. It was just one of Clara's little jokes.'

As she and Richard stepped into the car and turned to wave goodbye to the two small figures standing very close together by the gate, the sun was going down behind the house and a mist was rising from the green. She felt a momentary sadness and said to him:

'I wonder when we shall be there together again.'

'I wonder, too,' he said, almost with a sigh. Then he turned to her and asked briskly: 'Still want to go on to the sea? Looks as if there might be fog coming up later. I'm game to risk it if you are. Or would you rather we went straight back to London?'

'Oh, let's go on to the sea.'

'Right. The sea it is.'

He started the car with an unwonted jerk. The next moment the tall screen of elms by the pond had hidden Paget's Fold completely from their sight.

They drove on towards the wall of the downs. The fast-waning light turned the western hills to pale yellow-green velvet. To the right Chanctonbury's wood lay like a dark wreath on a vast mounded grave. Neither of them spoke for some time. Clara was feeling a little drowsy with the strong air and the even speed of the car. At last Richard said:

'What dears those two are. I loved their house. It fits them as perfectly as a bird's nest fits a bird.' He paused, then said hesitantly: 'I say, darling . . .'

'Yes?' She glanced at him and saw that he was frowning. 'What's the matter, Richard?'

'Oh, nothing really,' he answered, his profile intent on the road. 'Just that . . . well, you did overwhelm them a bit, didn't you?'

'Overwhelm them? How? I don't understand.'

'Oh well, if you don't understand, it's no good my trying to explain.' He changed gear rather abruptly.

She said in panic:

'Richard, you're not angry with me? Have I done something awful?'

He put one hand on her knee.

'No . . . no . . . of course not. You just had me puzzled a bit at one time, that's all.'

She pressed her fingers to her temples.

'I don't remember this afternoon very well. But I thought we were all so happy.'

'Well . . . yes,' he said slowly. 'Somehow, I didn't feel *they* were.'

'But I so wanted them to be,' she wailed.

He said comfortingly:

'Of course. I expect it was just that. I do the same sort of thing sometimes when I feel a situation's a bit sticky.'

'What sort of thing?'

'Oh . . . you know . . . play up a bit . . . overdo the cheerfulness. It's just that I've never seen you like that. You're usually so marvellously natural with people . . . Sorry, I can't explain. Let's forget it.'

Clara said nothing. A mist seemed to be rising in her head like the mist that hung over the ditches. Her eyes suddenly smarted and turned wet. She stared ahead at the blurred, dancing road. Then she felt the car slow down and heard Richard say . . .

'Clara, why, you're crying.'

The next moment the car had stopped and she was held close in his arms . . .

'My love, my love,' he whispered. 'Don't do that. I can't bear it.'

She lay a minute or two against his shoulder in an ecstasy of relief. Her eyes were closed. She could feel his lips moving gently round their sockets, kissing away the tears that oozed under the lids. Then she recovered herself, sat upright again and managed to smile.

'Sorry, Richard. I can't think why I did that.'

'*I* can,' he said ruefully. 'You know, just for a second, I came as near being angry with you as I hope I'm ever likely to be. Whereas any fool could see this afternoon was a frightful strain on you. And it was all my fault. I shouldn't have been such a blundering ass.'

'You . . . how?'

'Well . . . practically forcing you to take me down there. Hang it all, you'd told me what they were like. They were shocked to death, poor lambs, seeing you turn up with a totally strange chap when they obviously think of you as still married to Archie. I doubt if they even know you've started these proceedings.'

'It's quite likely Daddy hasn't told them,' she said, trying to keep her head clear. 'He wouldn't in the summer. He probably wants to wait till it's all over.'

'Exactly. And I made you barge in on them unexpectedly. Which is something you say you've never done in your life. I could hardly have created a more beastly artificial situation if I'd sat down and worked it out, could I? And I expect *you* to be as natural as a kid staying with them for the summer holidays. Richard Crayshaw, you're an ass.'

She asked hesitantly:

'Was I *so* unnatural?'

He kissed her quickly.

'Just a bit wrought up. Forgive and forget?'

'Of course.'

He started up the car again.

'On to the sea, then. Absolutely nothing's going to spoil our last two days, is it?'

'Nothing,' she said happily. But she gave a little shiver.

'Cold, my sweet? There's a rug in the dicky.'

'No . . . Just your saying "last two days".'

'Silly girl. You know perfectly well I only meant till I go down to Peacocks.'

'Yes. But I suddenly realized next week is almost here. It's going to be awfully strange without you.'

'Even for a week? Who said only this morning she could wait for months? So you *are* going to miss me after all?'

'It's just that as if next week were something I simply couldn't imagine.'

'Then you must start busily imagining the weekend.'

She moved a little closer to him.

'Tell me again about Peacocks,' she said.

She drew him on to talk about the place he loved. As he did so, all the uneasiness vanished from his face. She loved to hear him talk of Peacocks but, as the dusk gathered, her strange drowsy feeling increased. Without losing consciousness, there were stretches when she was aware only of the sound of his voice but not of what he was saying. But there were no more moments of terror or unhappiness. She lay back in her seat in a gentle bliss, content that she should drive on and on with him forever.

She supposed they must have stopped somewhere on the coast and left the car for the next thing she remembered clearly was walking on the shore in the darkness with Richard and hearing the noise of the sea.

She heard him say:

'We can get up on to that ledge of rock. It's a bit slippery. Hold my hand tight.'

Then they were standing together on a narrow shelf with their backs against rock. It was so dark that the sea was only visible as crawling, broken arcs of white. It roared in their ears and flung up bursts of unseen spray in their faces. When he turned and took her in his arms so that she no longer felt the solid rock behind her, it was as if the two of them were alone in the middle of a wild dark ocean that surged and thundered round them on all sides. They clung desperately together like two drowning creatures: his invisible face was wet against hers and she could taste the salt on his lips. His voice sounded strangely, so close in her ear that it was like a voice in her own head:

'I wish we need never go back. Shall we stay and be washed away?'

She did not know if she answered aloud. Her whole self, straining so close to him that they seemed a single being was concentrated into one desperate appeal: 'Never let me go.'

The next thing she remembered was hearing his voice saying urgently:

'Wake up, darling. Sorry, but you'll have to help me.'

She opened her eyes, bewildered. They were in the car and standing still. All round them was a dense fog. Had she been asleep? She had no recollection of having got into the car. She blinked her smarting eyes and asked:

'Richard . . . where are we?'

'Dashed if I know,' he said. 'I've never seen a worse fog than this. I'd have let you sleep on otherwise. I think we're on the right road but I can't see a yard ahead. If I give you a torch, think you could walk in front and guide me? It mayn't be so bad further on.'

Suddenly her head cleared. She felt confident and efficient. She said gaily:

'Right. Just give me the torch.'

She walked slowly ahead for a mile or more. The fog was so thick that Richard's head was only a blurred shape behind the windscreen. The car followed her, nosing along like a blind animal. She began to feel a sense of elation, feeling him dependent on her guidance. At last the fog grew less dense and he called her back into the car.

'Good girl,' he said approvingly. 'Lots of girls wouldn't have done that without making the hell of a fuss. I like feeling one can depend on you in a crisis.'

She said happily:

'When you're there, nothing *seems* like a crisis. I could do *much* more difficult things.'

He tucked the rug round her, looking down at her. His eyes were reddened and his face grimed with fog: drops of moisture beaded his eyelashes and moustache. She felt a rush of warm, comradely affection for the tired, almost battered face he presented.

He said:

'You must go on feeling like that when I'm not there. Otherwise I'll worry about you.'

'What is there to worry about?'

'Oh . . . nothing, really. Just that I want you to be awfully sensible and look after yourself next week. I feel I've been making you overdo things a bit. You're looking tired.'

'It's the fog,' she said. 'You're looking tired yourself.'

'I am a bit at the moment. It's a strain having to creep along, not seeing where you're going. But there's no need for you to keep awake. Get on with that sleep I interrupted.'

She must have dozed off again for the next thing she remembered was Richard shaking her and saying:

'Come on, darling. We've arrived.'

She opened her eyes and said stupidly:

'Why, we're in Valetta Road.'

'Yes, thank heaven,' he said. 'There were times when I wondered if we'd make it. Luckily it got much better after Horsham. Even so, we've been over three hours on the road.'

She stretched her stiff limbs and got out of the car.

'Come in for a moment. I'll get you a drink. Daddy has some whisky in the dining-room.'

'Darling, it's frightfully late. Better not, don't you think?'

'Just for a moment,' she pleaded.

They tiptoed into the dining-room and Clara switched on the light. He said:

'Don't bother about a drink. I'll just say goodnight and go. It's high time you were tucked up in bed.

She was standing by the mantelpiece, half intending to do something to the dead fire, when she caught sight of her face reflected in the big mahogany-framed mirror above it.

'Richard . . . how frightful I look!'

She stared in dismay at her pale, grimy face with its reddened eyes and the tangled wisps of hair round it. It reminded her of something: she could not remember what.

'We're neither of us looking our best at the moment,' Richard laughed. 'Hardly surprising, after what we've been through.'

His face appeared over her shoulder in the mirror. It looked strange to her: almost sinister. It was not merely the tiredness and the smudges of dirt from the fog that seemed to distort it. He grinned, revealing the little gap between his front teeth. She said with sudden anger . . .

'Don't laugh at me.'

'I'm not laughing at *you*, idiot,' he said. 'Just at my own filthy mug. I look like a coal-heaver.'

'Richard . . . do you think those two people in the glass really are us?' she asked anxiously. 'When I was little I used to think it was another *person* I saw there. She frightened me sometimes. I thought she wanted to pull me through into her world. Looking-glass Land, you know. Where everything's the wrong way round.'

He pulled her almost roughly back from the glass and turned her so that she faced him.

'Stop it, darling. In a moment you'll be having morbid fancies . . . I'm going to kiss you goodnight and leave you. Just let's fix up where to meet tomorrow.'

'You can send me a message, can't you?'

He frowned.

'I'd rather not. I think maybe we've been overdoing the game a bit. It's probably a bit of a strain for you. Even for me, maybe. Let's just be two perfectly normal people tomorrow, shall we, for our last night before I go down to Peacocks?'

'Oh, very well,' she said with a touch of sullenness. 'What do you want us to do?'

'I've got to do some shopping before I go back to Ireland. Better not come along. It would be rather a bore for you. Could you bear to come and have supper with Nell and Gerald? I half-promised we would, my last night. We can get off on our own after.'

She controlled a wild, helpless feeling that had suddenly invaded her mind and said meekly:

'Very well. What time shall I go to the studio?'

'About seven?'

She nodded.

He put his arms round her. Suddenly the helpless feeling flared up all over her body into a blind, panic-stricken rage. She struck out at him so fiercely that he stepped back, staring at her with his mouth open.

'Clara . . . what on earth . . .?'

His face looked so comical, gaping at her, half-affronted, half-frightened, that her rage vanished and she began to laugh.

'You absurd Richard! You really thought I meant it. It was just a joke.'

His face relaxed but it looked guarded and uneasy.

'I really took you in,' she said, still laughing, but more quietly. 'You really did think I was angry.'

She put her arms round his neck and kissed him. He yielded, but with a certain stiffness.

'You took me in all right,' he said. 'But don't do that again without warning.'

She released him and stood silent, her head bowed. In that moment she took in what life could be without him. What insane impulse had driven her to try and shatter their perfect world? She could not plead with him. If she had killed his love, nothing could revive it. She waited, almost longing for him to go, to leave her alone in her misery.

Then she felt his arms close round her, gently but securely. His face was against her hair, but he did not kiss her. He said:

'You can't get rid of me so easily. It's just that, these days, I can't follow all your moods.'

They drew apart and looked sadly and searchingly into each other's eyes. She knew from his how haggard were her own.

'Oh, Richard. Neither can I . . . Neither can I . . .'

Chapter Five

The following morning when Claude went up as usual to say goodbye to Isabel before setting off to St Mark's, his face was overcast. Propped up against her pillows, she smiled up at him over her breakfast-tray and asked:

'Is something the matter? You look very gloomy.'

'I'm rather worried,' he said, sitting down at the other end of the bed. 'Have you seen Clara this morning?'

'No. She hardly ever comes up till after you've gone to school. Why? Haven't *you* seen her then?'

'Oh yes, I've seen her,' he said heavily.

'What's wrong then? For a moment, I thought you were going to say she didn't come in last night.'

'Oh, she came in. Though goodness knows at what unearthly hour.'

'She was out with Richard, of course. Well, she's often come in late. Isn't it rather absurd to start being a heavy father now, dearest? After all, he's going away tomorrow.'

Claude sighed.

'I suppose I ought to have been a heavy father before. But seeing the child so happy, I hadn't the heart to say anything.'

'Why this sudden attack of conscience?' She smiled up at him but, seeing no change in his troubled expression, said more seriously:

'Claude, I'm sure there's nothing to worry about. I'm perfectly certain you can trust that boy.'

'As far as one can trust any young man in love, yes. I like young Crayshaw as much as you do. But Clara seems to have forgotten that her position is a very delicate one. To do him justice, I think he is far more aware of it than she is. He had the grace to ring me up just now and apologize for bringing her back so late. They were motoring and got caught in a fog.'

'Then what *are* you fussing about?'

'My dear, do you know what Clara calmly announced to me at breakfast, as if it were the most natural thing in the world?'

'That she was engaged to Richard? She'd only be saying what's obvious to us all. Don't look so angry . . . I know there's all this wretched legal business to be got through first . . .'

'Actually, that was not what she said. Even Clara must realize that they cannot possibly consider themselves engaged even if they hope, all being well, to be married some day. But I could hardly believe my ears when she told me where the two of them went yesterday.'

'Well, where for goodness' sake?' Isabel asked impatiently.

'Of all places – to Paget's Fold.'

Isabel laughed.

'They could hardly have gone anywhere more innocent.'

'But Isabel . . . imagine what the aunts must have thought. They only know that she's married. And she suddenly bursts in on them with a young man who's not her husband.'

'Well, I daresay they were rather surprised. But I'm sure they were charmed with Richard.'

'Richard's charm is hardly the point. They have no idea that Clara hopes to have her first marriage annulled.'

'You don't mean you still haven't told them?'

'There seemed no point in disturbing them till it was all over and settled. And that, alas, may not be for a very long time.'

'I always said you should have told them when we were down there in the summer.'

'Perhaps, I should. Clara's forced my hand. I shall have to tell them now.'

'Dearest, I can't see anything very serious in all this.'

'Can't you? I know you think I'm hopelessly hidebound and conventional. I wish to heaven it hadn't happened.'

'I hope you haven't been scolding Clara. I think it's very touching she should want Richard to see the place she loves so much. She never took Archie there. It's a proof that she's really and truly in love this time.'

His face relaxed a little.

'Poor child. She's most certainly in love.'

'Why "poor child"? It's the most wonderful thing that's ever happened to her. She's a different person in every way these last few weeks. It's like seeing a rosebud you almost thought might never open suddenly burst into a rose.' She leant forward and seized his hand. 'Claude . . . You haven't tried to spoil it for them?'

'You needn't worry, my dear. I could hardly say anything in front of my mother and Ullah. I am sure Clara had not the least idea what I was thinking. The only hint I could give her was to try and change the subject. But she kept returning to it. My mother looked a little disturbed but wisely said nothing.'

'That's one thing to be grateful for. I must say your mother has shown remarkable restraint about Clara and Richard. Though she's obviously devoured with curiosity.'

'She has a perfect right to be interested,' said Clause rather sharply. 'But I wish Clara would be a little more discreet in front of Ullah. He looked at her in a way I didn't altogether like just now. Obviously I can't take him into my confidence about our family affairs. But he knows that Clara is a married woman. I'm afraid he may be getting an altogether wrong impression of her.'

'How terribly you worry about what people think. What *does* it matter? Oh, how I hate all these prying eyes and petty, unimaginative minds! Clara and Richard . . . it's all so exquisite and fresh . . . like Romeo and Juliet . . . You've felt the spell of it yourself. You've reminded me of the Claude I knew . . . let's forget how many years ago. That young man who thought nothing of walking six miles in the rain on the off-chance of seeing a foolish young girl called Isabel Maule. Now suddenly you go and turn into that severe schoolmaster who *dared* to say happiness wasn't important.'

He sighed, glanced at his watch and sprang to his feet.

'I can't make you see my point. And the severe schoolmaster must be off to his school. Otherwise he'll be late.'

When he had kissed her, she detained his hand on her shoulder for a moment and looked up into his face.

'Claude . . . I believe something else is worrying you?'

He said, after a moment:

'Perhaps, my dear. I don't know. If so, it's something too

vague to give it a name . . . When you said just now Romeo and Juliet . . .' He broke off.

'Our Romeo and Juliet are going to have a happy ending,' Isabel assured him, laying her lace-draped cheek against his hand. She was wearing the little ribboned cap she had worn that morning in the study when Claude came back from Tithe Place. 'Oh, Claude, they *must*. It would be too cruel if anything went wrong.'

'I sincerely hope it won't,' he said soberly.

'You're not suggesting anything *has*?' Her voice was anxious now. 'You said Richard telephoned this morning. Did he speak to *her*?'

'No. She wasn't down. In any case, he didn't ask to. But he asked me how she was.'

'As if he were worried, do you mean?'

'It struck me he sounded rather uneasy. He said more than once he should have brought her straight back from Paget's Fold. Apparently they drove on to the coast afterwards. He said he should have realized she was overtired already.'

'Is *that* all? That just shows what a nice, considerate young man he is. For one awful moment, I thought you were going to suggest there might have been some hint of a quarrel. I daresay she *is* a little tired. Though she's been looking so radiant, one would never guess it.'

'She was decidedly pale this morning.'

'Not depressed?'

'Not in the least.'

'Well, she's a whole week to rest in before she goes down to meet his people.'

'She doesn't seem to be thinking of resting. She talked of spending the day working.'

'Richard's last day in London . . . *Working*?'

'She's not meeting him till tonight at his sister's place. But she had a letter from those advertising people she used to work for. They want some stuff from her and are prepared to pay her twenty-five pounds if she can do it quickly.'

'Poor pet . . . if she's tired . . . But it's a tempting offer. Twenty-five pounds is a big fee, isn't it?'

'I should certainly have thought so. It represents nearly fifty hours of pupils to me. But Clara's only comment was . . . "I'll do it for twenty-five *this* time. Next time they'll have to pay two hundred and fifty."'

'Well, that was obviously a joke. Why look so disapproving?'

'Because I got a distinct impression she didn't mean it as a joke. She said it with extraordinary conviction. And there was a very odd look in her eyes.'

'Claude,' said Isabel firmly. 'It strikes me that you're the person who's overtired. You seem determined to find something to upset you this morning. If poor Clara can't go and have tea with her old great-aunts or make a little joke about money, it's high time you took one of your famous nights off.'

His face relaxed at last.

'You really think I'm being morbid and fanciful?'

'Of course you are. Stop worrying and start looking forward to Monday night. It's Friday today so the worst of the week's over.'

'Absurd how I do look forward to those Mondays. Goodbye, my dear. If I don't go this moment, I *shall* be late. Then I shall get the sack and no more Monday nights.'

She kissed him.

'There. That's the first smile I've seen this morning. Goodbye, you male Cassandra.'

But when he had gone, the gaiety left her own face. She sat, with her hands clasped round her knees under the bedclothes, staring into space trying to remember something. She wanted to recall some lines of Juliet's but the ones she was searching for did not come. Try as she would to find them, thinking back to an amateur performance in her youth when she had played Juliet to some dim, nameless Romeo, the words she wanted would not return. Instead, with such insistence that she began to whisper them under her breath, there came ones that she had forgotten:

'It is too rash, too unadvised, too sudden
Too like the lightning which doth cease to be
Ere one can say: It lightens.'

Chapter Six

Clara was glad to have an interval to herself before meeting Richard that night. Yesterday things had slipped out of focus and she wanted to recover the bright sharp image before seeing him again. At all costs they must part tonight in perfect harmony and serenity. There was a film of drowsiness over her mind. She felt she wanted to tiptoe through the day, holding herself carefully, until the turbulence of last night had subsided, leaving her calm and radiant once more. She decided to put off doing the advertisement campaign till Richard had left London. A glance at the agent's letter had shown her that it would present no difficulties. Without conscious effort, headline and slogans came into her head as she moved about her room, performing small tasks with deliberate slowness. She was not displeased at having some work, however trivial, in prospect. There had been moments yesterday when the crystal sphere of security in which she was enclosed had nearly cracked and she had been giddily aware of a whirling darkness outside. This small sign from the everyday world was a reassuring token that it, too, recognized her as destined to succeed in everything she undertook. It was significant that they had offered her double her usual fee. That was only the beginning. Soon money would begin to flow to her in larger and larger quantities, not only for her own and Richard's needs, but for all those others whom it would be her delight to help. Tomorrow or the next day she would sit down to this, the first of an endless series of commissions which would come unasked and be fulfilled with expert ease.

Today, for the first time since she had met Richard, she felt the need to think, even to analyse. In the middle of lazily tidying a cupboard, she broke off and went to the drawer where she kept the black notebook. Sitting down, she opened it and decided to make an entry. As she sat frowning and biting her pen, trying to find what she wanted to say, she remembered the last time she had looked at that notebook, intending to write in it. Since the night of Nell's party, she had not given Clive Heron a thought. Now she felt a touch of guilt. If it had not been for Clive, she would never have met Richard. The least she could do was to let him know the amazing thing he had done for her. Perhaps next week, when she was on her own, she would ring him up. Since she had seen him last, she had had experiences beyond anything Clive could imagine. She might be able to convey some hint of them to him. At least she could show him the miraculous effects in her own person. If only such a miracle could happen to him! Then her mind reverted to Richard and the dim ghost of Clive Heron vanished. After a little thought, she slowly wrote a few sentences in the notebook. She wrote slowly, not only because the words did not come easily, but because she could not control a faint, persistent tremor in her hand.

'I began to feel there must be a space between us, however one we are. We are like two spinning planets magnetized in harmony. But it is essential each should keep to his own orbit and not be drawn into the other's. If one should waver ever so slightly . . . What am I frightened of? Some fearful psychic collision? How foolish that sounds. But I nearly lost *my* balance last time. Something overwhelmed me. For a second I wanted to destroy everything. I struck out at him blindly. Was it that this happiness is almost too much to bear? This is morbid. We cannot . . . we must not be destroyed. It is just that I must be a little careful, for both our sakes.'

She arrived at Nell's studio a little before the arranged time. Remembering her wild, dishevelled reflection in the glass last night, she had dressed, for the first time for weeks, with conscious care. For the first time, too, she had looked long enough at her face to notice the changes in it. Like her body, it had grown thinner so that the shape of the bones was just discernible under the fair skin, so unusually pale tonight that for a moment she thought of using rouge. She decided against it. This pallor, along with the narrowed contours which made her eyes seem much larger gave her face a look of her mother's. She had always been convinced that she had inherited none of

Isabel's beauty; her features were mainly softened versions of her father's and her notable fairness the replica of his. But, tonight, in spite of the difference in colouring, the woman who looked back at her from the glass was unmistakably Isabel's daughter.

When she reached the studio, Nell was busy in the kitchen and her lover, Gerald Moreton, was sitting in front of the fire, reading. He closed his book and gave her a teasing smile.

'Hullo, Clara. All alone? Where's the faithful Richard?'

'I'm early, I expect. He said he'd be here at seven.'

'Running before the clock, eh? Looks almost unnatural, seeing you by yourself. However, I suppose you've been in each other's pockets all day as usual. Especially with the prospect of an entire week's separation.'

Nellie came in with a tray of plates and cutlery.

'Stop teasing the child, Gerald,' she said in her slightly harsh but pleasant voice. 'You know perfectly well Richard was helping me in the dark-room this afternoon. And that he's round saying goodbye to Angus and Cecily now. Clara's got more sense than to want to be with him every second.'

Clara looked up at her gratefully. She had a great affection for this handsome, slightly masculine woman. Nell was nearly as tall as Richard, with the same flat back, square shoulders and long legs. Her hips were so slim that her corduroy trousers, stained with chemicals, looked natural and workmanlike on her. Her hair, black as his, was cut in a straight fringe above the same marked brows but her eyes were green, not grey and her features blunter.

'Shall I lay the table for you, Nell?'

'All right . . . if you're feeling energetic.' When Nell smiled, sharp creases appeared about her mouth and eyes and one saw that the firm flesh was beginning to lose its elasticity. 'Richard seemed a bit apprehensive in case you might be tired. Apparently you two young idiots got lost in a fog and got home at some unearthly hour.'

'He might have thought of a more original excuse,' said Gerald Moreton, grinning. 'Clara, I hope you and Richard haven't been up to anything Holy Mother Church doesn't approve of. She's rather pale, now I come to look at her. And do I see dark circles under those bright eyes?'

Clara began to lay the table. She saw that Gerald was in his most provoking mood and was determined not to rise.

'Leave the girl alone,' said Nell. She screwed up her eyes at Clara. 'I rather like you pale – gives one a chance to see your face, not just that schoolgirl complexion – Richard's always nagging me to do a portrait of you. You look more photogenic than I've ever seen you. Pity we can't get down to it tonight.'

'Put your mind back on your cooking,' said Gerald. 'I'm sure I can smell something burning.'

Nell hurried into the kitchen and Clara went on laying the table. Moreton watched her without offering to help. In repose, his bony head was rather fine. When he smiled, the face lost its distinction and took on the faintest tinge of vulgarity.'

'It amuses me to see you doing something so down to earth as laying a table,' he said. 'You're not really the domesticated type, are you?'

'What type am I then?'

'Lord knows. Bit of a highbrow, I should say. You've quite a good brain if it weren't cluttered up with all this Catholic nonsense. Still one doesn't expect women to be logical. All the same, I'm surprised you should have fallen so heavily for young Richard. Triumph of matter over mind, I suppose.'

'What do you mean?'

'Case of nature redressing the balance. Your first husband was a dud. And Richard's obviously the answer to any maiden's prayer . . . physically. You needn't look so shocked. I'm not trying to be offensive. There's nothing to be ashamed of in a good, healthy sexual attraction. Quite the reverse. Of course, as a Catholic, you're bound to have appalling guilt about sex.'

Clara managed to control herself and said lightly:

'There's nothing you don't know about Catholics, is there, Gerald?'

'I know they can't possibly believe all they pretend to. No rational person could in the modern world. The C. of E.'s bad enough. But even they don't seriously expect you to believe in the Immaculate Conception and all that.'

Clara laughed.

'I never supposed they did. It's only been an article of faith for Catholics since 1854.'

'Come off it. You're not seriously suggesting they didn't have to believe Jesus was born of a virgin till the nineteenth century?'

'Of course they did. But the Immaculate Conception means something entirely different from the Virgin Birth.'

'These sophistries are beyond me. All right, explain the differences then, you little casuist.'

She was beginning to explain when Nell returned from the kitchen.

'You two at it again?' she broke in. 'Can't you ever keep off theology, Gerald? I believe you ought to have been a parson after all. Stop browbeating Clara and give me a drink.'

'Clara was browbeating me,' said Gerald. 'I must say the Jesuits teach these kids their stuff.'

'Whoever was browbeating who, you've brought her colour back.'

Gerald poured her out a drink.

'Want one too, Clara?'

She shook her head.

'Come on, you don't have to abstain from all the pleasures of the flesh, even if it is Friday. Nell's insisted on having fish for supper on account of your scruples.'

Clara said gratefully:

'That was sweet of you, Nell.'

'It was Richard who reminded me. By the way, where *is* that boy?'

Clara said, without thinking:

'He'll be here very soon. He's only just managed to get a taxi.'

Nell gave her an odd look.

'You said that as if you knew for certain.'

'Well . . . I do. Actually, I'm rather surprised. Because he said he thought we'd better stop for a bit.'

'What's this?' said Gerald. 'The famous Crayshaw telepathy? Of course there's a perfectly rational explanation of it. Anyway, half the time it's lucky guesses or one takes the Crayshaws' word for it. I won't be convinced till some of you have tried it in properly controlled conditions. But Clara isn't a Crayshaw.'

'Well, she's going to be,' said Nell. She raised her glass. 'Here's to the two of you.' When she had drained it, she asked Clara: 'Know who I ran into yesterday?'

'Someone I know?'

'Clive Heron. I thought he was looking slightly glum. Something warned me it would be more tactful not to mention I'd been seeing a good deal of you lately. I felt he was rather deliberately keeping off the subject of you.'

'More likely he wasn't even thinking of me. We often don't see each other for months and months.'

'I've never known old Clive bring a girl to a party before,' said Nell. 'And you did leave him pretty thoroughly in the lurch.'

'It was he who went off without even saying goodbye,' said Clara.

'Don't overdo the innocence, dear. I got a strong impression that night he was jealous. He arrived in tearing spirits and went off looking like death.'

'You're being the innocent one, my good Nell,' said Gerald. 'That Heron chap isn't interested in women. Even in such an attractive piece as our Clara.'

'I'm not sure you're right, Gerald,' said Nell. 'Oh, I know what everyone *thinks* above Clive. If he found the right woman . . . she'd have to be rather an unusual one, of course. I really had hopes when he turned up with Clara.'

'They could hardly have been more well and truly dashed, could they?' asked Gerald with a grin.

'Poor old Clive,' said Nell. 'Well, I'm glad, for Richard's sake they were. But I'm sure you *were* that female, Clara.'

'Which female?'

'The one he talked to me about once.' She mimicked Clive's intonation with remarkable accuracy. 'The only just conceivably *not* impossible she.'

Footsteps sounded in the courtyard.

'Here comes the chap who blighted *that* dim hope,' said Gerald. 'Still it's nice for Clara to have something to fall back on.'

Richard let himself in and stood surveying the three of them. He and Clara exchanged only the quickest glance but in that glance she knew that everything was all right. It was as if the wavering jet of a fountain had suddenly burst up straight and strong, balancing her heart like a light ball on its tip.

Gerald said:

'You're late, my boy.' He winked. 'Bus held up in the fog?'

Richard smiled.

'I stayed longer than I meant to at Angus's place – And it took me ages to find a taxi.'

Supper was a cheerful meal and they lingered over it for a considerable time. Though it was an effort for her to eat, Clara was not impatient for the meal to be over. She sat rather quietly while the other three talked and laughed, cutting her food into very small pieces to make it easier to swallow. Her security had returned so completely that she was happy merely to savour it. Her eyes rarely searched directly for Richard's. When they did, his were always quick to respond. Once again she felt her love well up and overflow to embrace not only Richard but Nell and Gerald. Looking at Moreton, she wondered how she could have found him even faintly dislikeable. She noticed how, even though he was in one of his aggressively humorous moods, his blue eyes followed Nell every time she went out to change the dishes, as if he could not bear her out of his sight. As for Nell herself, she felt a glow of admiration for this older woman who would one day be her sister. How much Nell must have suffered yet how gay and courageous she was. She loved the very lines which were beginning to mar the smoothness of her dark-skinned, rather Egyptian face. If Richard and herself were like Romeo and Juliet just as her mother said (and, for once, Clara had not reproved her being romantic), she could see those older lovers as Antony and Cleopatra.

When supper was over, they all went out into the tiny kitchen to wash up. Nell shooed her away from the sink, saying:

'Leave it to me. You've got a decent dress on.' Gerald and Richard had already seized the only two drying-up cloths so Clara stood back, looking on from the open doorway. Suddenly she felt strangely detached from them, watching them, watching their movements as if watching a ballet. She was aware of an exquisite sense of timeless happiness. Something whispered in her head: 'This is the perfect moment. Go *now*.'

Feeling completely serene, she slipped away without their noticing, tiptoed across the studio and, closing the door very gently, went out into the dark courtyard. She did not stop to think where she meant to go. She merely let her feet carry her, with slow even steps, wherever they wished. Of their own accord, they carried her down the narrow passage that led to the river. When the stones turned slippery under them, they moved on with the same, even, deliberate steps, taking her so accurately in the dark through the iron posts that her skirt barely brushed them. She gasped as the cold water came up round her ankles but did not pause in her slow, rhythmical walk. Suddenly, though she had heard no footsteps, someone grabbed her from behind and violently jerked her back.

'You little idiot,' Richard's furious voice said in her ear. 'What the hell do you think you're going?' He dragged her back till she was out of reach of the water and turned her round to him. She could not see his face in the darkness but she knew from the savage grip of his arms that he was angry. She said mildly:

'I was only walking, Richard. I just felt like walking, that's all. Don't hold me so tight. You're hurting.'

His grip relaxed a little. He said less angrily:

'I *told* you never to go down that passage at night alone. Giving me a fright like that! If I hadn't come running after you, you might have been drowned.'

'I'm sorry,' she said in the same mild voice. 'I didn't go down there deliberately. I just found myself going down it.'

'You're getting too absent-minded altogether for my comfort,' he said, marching her along again in the crook of his arm. 'Your feet must be soaking. We'd better go into the other studio and dry them.'

She walked obediently beside him. Then she asked timidly:

'Oughtn't we go back to Nell and Gerald first?'

'No. We don't want a lot of fuss and explaining – They were expecting us to go off on our own, anyway. They want to be alone, too. Gerald's in one of his difficult moods, as you saw.'

She was relieved to hear that his voice sounded almost normal again. They crossed the courtyard in silence and he let her into the other studio. When he had turned on the light and lit the gas fire, he sat her in a chair and pulled off her soaking shoes and stockings. Then, he knelt in front of her, chafing her cold, wet feet. Looking down at his bent head she could see only his hair and the dark brows drawn together in a frown. At last the frown relaxed and he looked up at her kindly.

'Better now?'

She smiled and nodded.

'Quite dry and almost warm.'

'What pretty feet you have,' he said, bending down to kiss them. He stood up and lifted her out of the chair. 'Now, my girl, you'd better lie down for a bit. I'll tuck you up warm in a rug. That must have given you a shock.'

He laid her on the camp bed that Nell had put up for him and knelt beside her with his arm under her neck. She found that she was trembling a little.

'Cold? Shall I put a blanket over you too?'

'No, I'm perfectly all right.'

All the same it was a relief to be lying down. She was not cold, but she felt numb and drowsy. She closed her eyes. After a while she heard him say:

'Darling, you will look after yourself next week while I'm away? I'm a little worried about you, you know.'

She opened her eyes at the sound of his voice.

'Why? Because I was silly last night? I can't think what came over me. It won't happen again.'

He kissed her and said gently:

'It wasn't exactly sensible wandering off down to the river like that, was it? You don't know what a fright you gave me. For one ghastly moment I thought you did it on purpose . . .'

'But I told you I didn't. I just suddenly felt like going out of doors and I found myself walking down the passage.'

He said doubtfully:

'I'm not sure that makes it any better.'

She closed her eyes again, almost wishing he would not talk.

'Clara,' he whispered. 'You *are* all right? You're so awfully pale.'

She smiled drowsily.

'Quite all right. A little sleepy.'

'You *are* happy with me? There isn't anything worrying you?'

She turned and embraced him.

'Happy? Oh, Richard, I've never been so happy in my life. Don't you know that?'

He laid his forehead against her hair and muttered:

'I used to know it. But sometimes you seem to go off where I can't follow you. You won't be absent-minded about coming down to Peacocks will you?'

'Of course not. I'm so longing to be with you there.'

He said in a tone of relief:

'Good. I'll send you a letter with the trains. There won't be much else in it. I can't say in words what I feel.'

'Neither can I. But we don't have to, do we?'

'I'll send you a token. A jay's fly-feather. They take a bit of finding. But I'll find one all right.'

'I've never given you anything. What would you like?'

'Don't give me anything yet.'

'Why not?'

'Just a superstitious hunch. But I'd like you to promise me something.

'That's easy.'

'You've got to keep it, mind.'

'What is it?'

'Just to take most frightfully good care of yourself next week. I couldn't bear it if anything happened to you when I wasn't there.'

'Why should anything happen?'

'Well, just take care that it doesn't. See?'

'I can't think why you're worrying so. I never felt better in my life.'

He considered her face. 'You look all right now. Perhaps I've been talking nonsense. All the same . . . Sure you wouldn't rather I didn't go down to Peacocks tomorrow?'

'Of course you must go.'

'Right. I will, then. I'm going by car. I could be back in three hours if you needed me for any reason.'

She smiled and shook her head.

'Darling Richard, the next time I see you will be at Peacocks.'

He kissed her gently.

'We've so little time left. Don't let's talk any more.'

He stretched himself beside her on the narrow bed and folded her in his arms. She lay beside him in utter content, past thought or desire, aware only of being in the one right place for her. Without losing consciousness, she fell into a light, delicious sleep. When at last he roused her gently saying: 'Darling, it's time I took you home,' she could hardly bear to unseal her eyes. It was as if he had roused her from the quiet ecstasy of death.

Chapter Seven

The next morning, all Clara's gay confidence returned. She was aware indeed, of a new vigour, a sense of conscious power that was even more delightful than her former sense that everything was being made easy for her. Whatever danger might have threatened her and Richard in the last day or two had been safely averted. The crystal sphere had shuddered for a moment; now it poised and spun steadily in the sunlight again. All she had to do was to refrain from touching it. The more perfectly she kept her balance, the freer she left him. He must be bound to her only by the mysterious current between them. She must simply go on from day to day, doing each thing as it came to hand, in the light of her love that transmuted even the dullest task.

She sat down immediately after breakfast to tackle the advertising campaign. It was almost a pleasure to find that it presented one or two difficulties.

By the end of the morning she had overcome them and sketched out her rough drafts.

After lunch her father said:

'I suppose you haven't by any chance an hour or two to spare this afternoon, Clara? The last thing I want to do is to interrupt your work.'

'I can easily finish tomorrow or on Monday,' she said. 'Why? Is there something you want me to do?'

'I should be immensely grateful if you could help me out. It's one of those lectures I'm giving for those Saturday night classes for my scholarship boys. I've just looked out the one on the Cyclic Epic for tonight and find it's in a terrible mess. Besides, some interesting new stuff's come out since I wrote it. I want to insert some bits about that. If you could bear to let me dictate a revised version, it would save me no end of time.'

'Of course I'll do it. Do me good to learn something about Cyclic Epics. Let's start straight away.'

They went into the study. Her father settled her at his own desk and seated himself at the one opposite. Clara did not, however, learn anything about Cyclic Epics. As soon as her father began to dictate, she became a mere writing-machine. The words conveyed no meaning to her as she transcribed line after line in her small clear writing. At intervals, he would say 'Stop me, if I'm going too fast,' but she always shook her head. Her hand moved with tireless mechanical speed, keeping up with him almost word by word. Once he asked 'Wouldn't you like a rest? Your hand must be aching, going at this rate.' But, as before, she shook her head.

When he came to the end, he said:

'Wonderful, my dear. We've done the whole thing in just over two hours. However did you keep up that prodigious speed? Can I just glance through it?'

He took the manuscript and she saw him make a few corrections. Then he put away his pen and smiled across at her.

'Really, Clara. I congratulate you. Beautifully legible and amazingly accurate. In all those pages – Greek words and all – only one tiny slip.'

'One? You made more than one correction.'

'Only because it was a word that occurred several times. Rather an amusing slip, too.'

'What was it?'

'Instead of "cyclic epic" you invariably wrote "sickly epic".'

There was a short interval before his teatime pupil was due. He made her sit in the big green armchair though she assured him she was not in the least tired.

'You're the one who's tired,' she insisted. 'It's absurd your having to work like this, even at weekends.'

He smiled at her.

'You forget that I shall have my Monday evening of wicked idleness.'

'You ought to have every evening off,' she declared. 'Never mind. When Richard and I are married, you will.'

'My dear, let's hope you and young Crayshaw will be able to get married long before I retire.'

'Well, you needn't retire unless you wanted to. I haven't worked it all out. But if I were to allow you a thousand a year?'

He stared at her for a second, then laughed.

'My dear child, for a moment I thought you were serious.'

'I am serious, Daddy. I can't do it just yet, of course. But it won't be so very long now.'

He was still looking at her in a puzzled way when the doorbell rang. She jumped up and kissed him.

'There's your pupil. I'll be off now. Only don't tell Mother yet. It's a secret between you and me.'

The next morning after she had gone, as usual, to early Mass with her father, she decided to go to High Mass with her mother as well. Armistice Day had fallen during the past week and they arrived to find that a solemn Requiem was being sung for all who had died in the war. In front of the altar was a catafalque guarded by four young men in uniform, standing with bowed heads and reversed arms.

As soon as Clara saw this, she realized it was not mere impulse that had decided her to go to Mass a second time. She had been intended to come to this soldiers' Requiem. The catafalque reminded her how easily Richard might have been one of those who had been killed. Along with her immense gratitude came sense of remorse. How lightly she had taken the deaths of all those young men. When had she thought of the ones she had personally known, however slightly, beyond an occasional, perfunctory prayer? The fact that she had been a schoolgirl when the war broke out was no excuse for her having shut it out of her mind. She had done worse: she had not merely refused to experience it, she had turned it into a game. When she was Charles Cressett's governess, she had invented for him and acted with him that toy warfare that mocked the cruel reality. It was on one of those very games that Charles had been killed. She was utterly unworthy to be a soldier's wife.

Suddenly, beyond the four bowed figures guarding the catafalque she saw a crowd of young men in torn and blood-stained uniforms. Their haggard faces were all turned reproachfully on her. She buried her own in her hands to shut them out, praying in utter abasement: 'Forgive me . . . forgive me. Give me a chance to make up for my neglect. Put me to some test. Give me some share in your suffering. All my life I have been a coward.' When, at last, she raised her head, the space in front of the altar was empty except for the catafalque and the four living men.

Gradually her mind grew calm again. She was able to follow the rest of the Mass lucidly and without distractions. But, at the end, when the priest came down from the altar to sprinkle the catafalque, she saw those other figures again. Once again their haggard faces were turned towards her but now they were smiling. An extraordinary peace descended on her. With it came a strange and indefinable sensation. It could not be called apprehension for there was no tinge of fear in it. Richard's words 'Take special care of yourself' came into her head. They seemed to have acquired a new meaning. It was as if it were not just for his sake that she must be careful. She felt there was some other reason she could not yet discern, something connected with those soldiers she had seen during the Mass. Because of Richard they had a special claim on her. Perhaps there was something they wanted her to do for them? Whatever that strange, faint intimation meant, there was no need for her to probe. At the right moment, all would be made clear.

On the Monday morning, though she had not expected one so soon, there was a short note from Richard. It contained little beyond the time of the train he would meet the following

Saturday and a reiteration, underlined, of 'Take care of yourself.' To her delight, he had enclosed the jay's feather. She could hardly bear not to pin the blue-green feather, brilliant as a jewel, to her dress. But, with the sense of making a small sacrificial act, she put it between the pages of her missal where they fell open, from yesterday, at the Mass for the Dead.

She spent the morning revising and copying out her advertising campaign. Then she sat down to write to Richard. She rejected all the passionate words and bright extravagant images that came into her head and wrote only:

'My dear love, I am glad you found the jay's feather so soon. I will never lose it. I am keeping my promise. There was a reason for your making me promise that. I do not know the whole reason yet but I shall. Perhaps quite soon. Nothing in the world would stop me from catching the 10.15 on Saturday. Only a few more days and I shall see you at Peacocks. I love you. Clara.'

In the afternoon, when she came back from posting her letters, she saw that it was beginning to get foggy. It reminded her of the day she and Richard had driven through the fog. She was surprised to find how long ago that seemed. As she walked down Valetta Road, the fog seemed to thicken suddenly, almost with every step she took. Even when she was indoors again, though it was no longer in her eyes and nostrils, a cloud of it seemed to have settled inside her head. She felt extraordinarily sleepy. She went up to the drawing-room and tried to dispel the drowsiness and the mist in her head by strumming on the piano. Then she remembered that Wajid Ullah was probably working in the room overhead and stopped of her own accord. The idea of his creeping down and putting his pockmarked face round the door with a silky request to play more quietly was extraordinarily repellent. As she closed the piano-lid, a conviction formed in her lazy mind. For the next few hours she must speak only if it were absolutely necessary. At all costs she must allow no one to touch her. How fortunate that her grandmother was in bed with a cold and her mother out at a bridge party. Her father, too, would be going straight from the school to whatever secret place he would spend this particular Monday evening. She was secure of not being disturbed.

She lay down on the sofa, closed her eyes and let the drowsiness overwhelm her. She did not, however, go to sleep. Instead, she lay in a kind of passive stupor. She was perfectly conscious but incapable of the slightest movement. Nor was she aware of any passage of time or of any separate thoughts. Her whole mind and body seemed to be arrested in a cataleptic state in which the only thing she knew was that she was being mysteriously prepared for something and that it was imperative to make no attempt to disturb this strange experience.

She heard the door open and was aware, through her sealed eyelids, that the light had been turned on. The voice of Molly, the housemaid, said:

'Ah, there you are, Miss Clara. I've been looking all over the house for you. Lying there in the dark! You must have been sound asleep and not heard the gong.'

Without opening her eyes, Clara forced herself to answer.

'I don't want any dinner, thank you, Molly.'

'Now, come along, Miss Clara. Your Mother and Mr Ullah have been waiting ten minutes and more. You're not ill, are you? Open your eyes, do.'

Clara tried to obey but her lids seemed glued to her eyeballs. Molly said anxiously:

'I've never known you to sleep in the afternoon. And not wanting any dinner. I'm sure you're not well. I'll go and tell the mistress to come up.'

'No, Molly, I'm perfectly all right,' said Clara. She had managed to make her eyes come unstuck. 'Tell Mother I'll be down in a moment.'

'Very good, Miss Clara.'

Molly gave her a doubtful glance and hurried away. It was an effort for Clara to get up from the sofa. She realized that she would have to go through this ordeal of sitting at the dinner-table with her mother and Wajid Ullah. It would be all right, provided she ate not a morsel and uttered not a word.

Her mother was sitting at the window end of the table with Ullah on her right. Clara took her place at the end opposite Isabel, with her back to the mahogany sideboard. When her mother spoke to her, she merely smiled without answering. Her mother began a desultory conversation with Ullah. With detached dislike, Clara watched the young Indian's pitted face and oily black eyes as he talked to her mother with that exaggerated courtesy that was so near insolence. Every now and then his white teeth flashed as he gave a giggle. Once Isabel addressed him as 'Wajid'. Clara was on the point of protesting when she remembered that she must not speak. To avoid being drawn into the conversation, she stared fixedly at her untouched plate. It was becoming more imperative for her not to speak. She could feel herself being slowly charged with a mysterious magnetic force. She must not speak but she could listen. Her mother and Ullah appeared to be talking the merest trivialities, about a play, about her father having overworked lately, about the fog which was so thick that it was seeping into the room through the heavy drawn curtains. Suddenly, she realized that all the words they used were a code language. What they were really doing was making an assignation. She must warn her father of the terrible danger that threatened him. But how, tonight, could she find him? Ullah wanted to be her mother's lover so as to give her smallpox. She was on the point of speaking when the magnetic currents began to run up and down her limbs with such force that she was aware of nothing else. She thought: '*Now* it is really beginning.' She mastered a moment of panic by telling herself 'Keep quiet. Let yourself go with it. No danger as long as you don't interrupt it. Something is possessing you, like a medium. Just let it *happen*.' The currents became so intense that her whole body began to vibrate. These vibrations became so strong that they communicated themselves to the chair she was sitting on. It began to rock to and fro, with a gentle, insistent rhythm. She heard her mother's voice from a great distance:

'Clara, darling. Whatever are you doing?'

The chair's gentle rhythm changed to a rapid, violent one. Suddenly it gave a convulsive heave and flung itself backwards under her so that she fell with it, striking her head against the sideboard. She heard her mother give a little shriek. The next moment someone had pulled her to her feet. She opened her eyes and found herself in Wajid Ullah's arms. She struggled and clawed at his face, screaming: 'Don't touch me! Don't touch me!' She fought, but he was surprisingly strong. He pinned her arms against her sides so that she could not move. Beyond him was her mother, making incoherent, wailing sounds. She heard Ullah say in a quiet, authoritative voice.

'Do not distress . . . do not distress . . . My sister have such attacks. . . . Go at once and telephone doctor. I can hold her . . . I accustomed.'

Clara stopped struggling. She shut her eyes and her mind went blank. She supposed she must have fainted for when she opened her eyes again she was sitting in an armchair by the fire. She looked round cautiously. She was still in the dining-room; the half-eaten meal was still on the table. There was no sign of her mother or Ullah. Yet she was sure she was not alone. The room was very foggy. There was a dull ache in the back of her head. Peering round painfully, she saw that a man was sitting only a few feet away from her in the armchair on the other side of the fire. A large, reddish, blue-eyed face was watching her intently. It took her a minute or so to realize that it was a face she knew, though she could not attach a name to it. She said:

'Hullo . . . how did *you* get here?'

'Well, so you've noticed me at last. You haven't forgotten me, have you, Clara?'

'I know your *face*,' she said uncertainly.

'So I should hope. Considering we're very old friends indeed – come along now, what's my name?'

It came to her.

'Doctor Mayfield.'

He grinned.

'Splendid. Doctor Mayfield. Whom you've known since you were so high, haven't you?'

She said suspiciously:

'What are you doing here? Nobody's ill, are they?'

'Who said anyone was ill? Can't an old friend drop in for a chat? Well, how's the world treating you these days, Clara?'

Clara said, with sudden fury:

'It's a plot. Mother and that man. They want to get rid of me.

That's why they've sent you in here to talk to me. To keep me quiet. But I won't be bribed.'

'Steady on, now' said Doctor Mayfield, with an irritating smile. 'You've given yourself a nasty bump on the head. Confuses one a bit. Did the same thing myself once, playing football for Guy's. Know what I did? Went round and round the Inner Circle twenty times without stopping. That was a silly thing to do, wasn't it?'

'Very,' said Clara coldly. 'Why are you treating me like an idiot? You can't deceive *me*.'

'Who's trying to deceive you? And who's treating you like an idiot? We all know you're a very brainy young lady. Much too brainy to fall off a chair in the middle of dinner and bang your head against a sideboard without a very good reason. Now suppose you tell me exactly what happened.' He leant forward and laid his hand on her knee.

Clara sprang to her feet and screamed:

'Don't touch me! Don't touch me! You'll be struck dead if you do.'

The doctor stood up and caught her by the shoulder.

'I'll risk that. Now, Clara, take it easy . . . Suppose we sit down again, shall we?'

His big, insolently smiling face loomed over her as he tried to force her back into the chair. He was a tall, heavily-built man. Clara sprang at him and slapped his face with such force that he staggered backwards and the imprint of her hand made white blotches on his red cheek.

'You little devil,' he said, rubbing his cheek. 'All right, young lady. We'll have to try something else.'

He went quickly out of the room. The moment the door had closed behind him, Clara became calm and lucid. She realized she must act quickly. Her senses became preternaturally acute. She could hear Doctor Mayfield talking to her mother in the study next door. She heard him say 'I'll just go back to my place and get an injection for her. Is there a key on the outside of the dining-room door? Good. Don't go in to her. She's rather excitable. My advice is, as soon as I've gone, lock her in. I'll be back in a quarter of an hour.'

She waited to hear no more. In a flash, she was out of the room, had closed the door silently behind her and was running noiselessly up the stairs. From her bedroom she could hear their voices, her mother's high and tearful, the doctor's low and booming, though she could no longer distinguish the words. Her mind was taking lightning decisions but she felt astonishingly calm. Not only did she feel in the pocket of the fur coat she slipped on to make sure that her purse was in it, she took a minute or two to write a hurried note to her father. At all costs, he must not be worried. He must understand that she had good reason for her flight. She even told him where she was going. She slid the note in an envelope, wrote his name on it and added *Private and Confidential*. Then she stood, listening. It was all right. The voices were still going on in the study. She tiptoed down the stairs, left the note on the oak chest in the hall, and closed the front door behind her with hardly a sound.

Out in the street, the fog was so dense that she could hardly see a step ahead. She made her way carefully along the street, guiding herself by the railings. As she turned the corner, a taxi loomed out of the fog and she hailed it. She gave him the address of Nell's studio. The man said:

'That's somewhere Chelsea way by the river isn't it? It'll be worse than ever down there. I doubt if I can make it.'

Clara said confidently:

'Please try, I don't mind how slowly you go. I can guide you. I know the way very well.'

'More than I do. And in this pea-souper . . . All right, if you're game to risk it, I am. But I don't guarantee to get you there. Jump in.'

Once in the taxi, Clara felt perfectly safe. She knew that she would be able to direct him, however thick the fog. Her only concern was that, as they would have to creep along, she might not have enough money on her to pay him. She opened her purse and saw that there were two half-crowns in it. Normally it would have been twice as much as she needed. But would it be tonight? She prayed that the money would hold out and felt a reassurance that it would. When at last they reached the gateway to the courtyard, she jumped out and proferred him her two half-crowns.

'I can't see what it says on the meter. But it was terribly important for me to get here. This is all the money I have.'

The man grinned at her.

'That's all right by me, Missie. Suppose *he's* waiting for you, eh?'

She smiled and said goodnight. In a moment the taxi had been swallowed up in the fog. She took a long time to cross the courtyard. Her mind was not so clear as it had been in the taxi. But at last she found the right studio and knocked urgently on the door.

Chapter Eight

Because of the fog, Claude Batchelor came straight home after his solitary dinner in Soho instead of going on to the Café Royal as he had intended. The moment he opened the door, Isabel appeared from the study and flung herself on him, sobbing.

'Oh, dearest, thank God, you've come.'

'Isabel, whatever's the matter?'

She could only gasp, with her face buried in his shoulder:

'Clara . . . She's run away . . . She's ill . . . We've searched the neighbourhood . . .'

He took her into the study and comforted her till she was calm enough to speak. When she had finished her story, his face was as pale as hers.

'The first thing to do is to find her,' he said. 'In this fog, anything might have happened to her. Have you telephoned the police?'

She nodded.

He sat down at his desk, clutching his head in his hands.

'If only I'd been here. If only I hadn't gone out in this insane way, not letting you know where to get hold of me – It's a judgement on me.'

'Darling Claude, don't start blaming yourself — Thank heaven you're here now. Wait, there's something I forgot. She left a note for you . . .'

'Why didn't you open it? It might give us a clue.'

'Oh, Claude. I was so distracted. I didn't know what to do. Mayfield and I rushed out after her. I didn't see the note till I got back, and she's put "Private and Confidential" on it.' She began to cry again.

'Hush, Isabel . . . hush.'

'It's in the hall. I'll get it.'

She went out and fetched it. He put his arm round her, saying gently:

'We'll both read it, my dear.'

He tore open the note. Together they read the scrawled, but legible lines:

'Darling Daddy,

I had to leave the house. So must you when you get this. The house is full of evil. It is not only the small-pox. Don't be worried to find me gone. I have gone to Nell Crayshaw. 3 Rivershore Studios. Chelsea Embankment. Your loving Clara.'

'Thank God for that at least,' Claude said. 'If she was enough in her right mind to say where she was going . . .'

'But . . . dearest . . . that wild talk about the house being full of evil . . .'

He said, straining after hope:

'You say she hit her head . . . Doesn't concussion sometimes cause hallucinations? I must ring up Crayshaw's sister at once. When did Clara leave?'

'Nearly two hours ago.'

'It's our one hope that she somehow managed to get there. You don't know the number?'

She shook her head. He began to search through the directory. His hand was shaking so much that it took him a long time to find the place.

He picked up the telephone and asked for the number. After a while, he said:

'It's ringing but no one's answering. Shall I hold on? Or try the police again?'

'Oh hold on,' she implored. 'They may not have heard it . . .'

There was a long pause. At last, just as he had shaken his head and was about to replace the receiver, his face changed:

'Someone's answering,' he said.

Isabel strained her ears in vain to catch what was being said the other end. Claude's almost monosyllabic questions and replies came at long intervals, and gave her little comfort except the knowledge that Clara was there. At last he heard Claude say:

'I'll get over to you as soon as possible, fog or no fog. Would you mind just giving me the directions again? Thank you. And thank you more than I can say for looking after her.'

He hung up the receiver and immediately picked it up again and asked for Doctor Mayfield's number. As he waited for a reply, he gave her a hurried glance and said:

'I'll tell you everything when I've spoken to Mayfield . . . Hullo? Is that you, Mayfield? . . . Yes, thank God we've found her . . . No . . . not reassuring, I fear . . . This friend of hers says she can't make her understand anything . . . I don't like to ask you to come out on such a filthy night . . . you will? . . . That's extraordinarily good of you . . . Right . . . I'll wait for you to pick me up . . .'

He came and sat on the arm of the big green chair and drew Isabel's head on to his shoulder. He said, trying to keep his voice as steady as when he had spoken to the doctor:

'My dear . . . we must try not to lose our heads. It may not be as bad as it sounds. Till Mayfield's seen her, we can only guess . . . These things always seem terrifying to the layman . . .'

Isabel took his hand.

'Tell me everything Nell Crayshaw said.'

'My dear . . . I don't want to upset you. Wouldn't you rather wait till Mayfield's seen her?'

'I want to know everything she told you,' she said quietly.

'Well, if you insist. It seems Clara arrived there well over an hour ago. They . . . Miss Crayshaw kept saying "we" and referring to someone called Gerald . . . were just sitting down rather late to their supper. They were very surprised to see Clara. Especially on such a foggy night.'

'How did she find her way?'

'Apparently she picked up a taxi.'

Isabel said hopefully: 'Her mind must have been clear enough, then. How did she seem when she arrived?'

'Quite normal, even cheerful. She talked quite sensibly about being afraid of not having enough money on her for the fare – She gave no explanation why she had come to their place. Apparently her manner was a little excited. Nell said she had noticed that she had seemed a trifle over-excited lately and thought nothing of it.' He broke off and said wretchedly. 'I've noticed it myself. Odd, little things she said. Why only this very Saturday . . .'

'Oh, Claude . . .' Isabel broke in. 'We both thought that it was just that she was so happy about Richard.' Her grip on his hand tightened. 'If anything were to go wrong . . . It would be too cruel . . . too tragic . . .'

'My dear . . . I'm so afraid of distressing you. I'd rather not tell you any more.'

'No . . . please, go on. I *must* know. I won't interrupt again. Every detail you can remember.'

'Well, apparently Nell Crayshaw and this man Gerald, whoever he is, asked her to have some supper with them. Clara refused. She went and sat by the fire while they ate. She sat there without saying a word though she had been very talkative when she arrived. They asked her, even if she didn't want anything to eat, wouldn't she sit at the table with them? She said no and muttered something to the effect that it would be dangerous for her to move. They thought her manner strange but decided the best thing was to leave her alone and go on with their meal. Suddenly she asked for some bread and salt. Then she said . . . Nell Crayshaw was positive about this . . . "Bread and salt is good against evil spirits." Gerald then asked her if she thought they were evil spirits but she smiled and shook her head. She became rather insistent about the bread and salt so they gave her some. She ate a little and then sat for a long time saying nothing. They noticed she was looking very pale and seemed dazed. At last they suggested would she be better at home in bed? This man Gerald offered to go out, find a taxi and bring her back here. Nell said that, at that, she leapt to her feet and began to scream hysterically. When they tried to calm her, she fought like a wild-cat. It was as much as the two of them could do to hold her. Then, quite suddenly, she collapsed into a chair and began to cry. Nell tried to comfort her, but Clara did not seem to know who she was. She said her mood had changed completely. She was quite gentle, like a child. She even talked like a child. Nell said this frightened her more than the hysteria. She thought the best thing to do was to put Clara to bed in the other studio – apparently she rents two of them – and ring us up. However, as soon as she got her into the other one and undressed her, Clara became very obstinate and tried to run away. There was no bolt on the door and Nell dared not go back to the other studio where the telephone is in case she slipped out and wandered off in the fog. At last she persuaded her to go to bed. To her relief, Clara fell asleep.

'She dared not leave her alone, even to go across the courtyard to the other studio. She opened the window and called out to Gerald. He heard her and came over, saying he would sit by Clara while Nell telephoned us. But he had hardly arrived before Clara woke up and became so hysterical that it took the two of them to deal with her. She began to sing and rave as if she were delirious. She kept running over to the door and trying to get out. It was all the two of them could do to stop her. Nell said her strength was quite incredible. But at moments, she would become perfectly quiet and normal. She even recognized them and said "Tell Richard not to worry." But the next moment, the delirium and the violence would return. That was what was going on when I rang her up.'

Isabel had begun to cry softly.

'The poor, poor child . . . Oh, why doesn't Mayfield come?'

'He'll be here any minute,' he said soothingly. 'Try not to cry.'

She dried her eyes.

'I'm sorry, dearest. It was just the shock. I'll go up and get a coat. I'm coming with you.'

'Are you sure you can bear it?'

She was already on her feet.

'Of course I can . . . My own child!'

The door bell rang. Claude started up.

'Thank heaven, there's Mayfield. Very well, get your coat while I tell him what I've just told you.'

When Isabel returned to the study some minutes later, the doctor said to her:

'I think it would be better if you didn't come with us, Mrs Batchelor. It'll only upset you . . . and it might upset Clara. She seemed to have got some wild notion about you when I saw her before. Hysterical girls often do about their mothers – My idea is to let your husband see her alone first. The fact that she left that note for him suggests that, whatever strange fancies she may have, she's not suspicious of him.'

'But why . . . *why* should she have these strange fancies?' Isabel implored him. 'You've known her since she was a child . . . Clara's never been hysterical in her life . . . if anything she was too controlled . . .'

'Controls have a way of breaking down, you know. After all you told me earlier on about how she's been ever since that abnormal marriage of hers . . . first the apathy and depression . . . then this sudden emotional stimulus . . . Perhaps this rather violent reaction isn't altogether surprising.'

Claude said hopefully:

'You really think it may be only that . . . just a temporary nervous reaction?'

'My dear man, I can't give any opinion till I've seen her again. But a little burst of hysteria can look very alarming to the layman. Not to mention the effects of even mild concussion. Let's hope that this is nothing that sedatives and a few days' rest won't put right. If you're ready, Batchelor, we'd better be on our way. Thank heaven, this filthy fog seems to be clearing a little.'

Claude said: 'Right. My overcoat's in the hall.'

Isabel murmured: 'You're still wearing it, dearest.'

He gave a painful smile.

'Of course . . . how idiotic of me.'

She kissed him and begged:

'Let me come with you. I won't ask to see Clara.'

Doctor Mayfield said with professional heartiness:

'Now, now, Mrs Batchelor. If you don't go straight up to bed, I shall have two patients in this family on my hands.'

'I'll wait down here,' she said quietly. 'Will one of you telephone me when there's any news?'

When they had gone, she knelt for a long time beside the green armchair, with her face buried in her hands. Her prayer calmed her a little. She found that she was shivering with cold, in spite of the thick coat she had put on and the gas fire which had been burning there ever since Dr Mayfield's first visit. She went upstairs and fetched an eiderdown from her bedroom, and, wrapping it round her, huddled down in the great chair and closed her eyes. She must have fallen asleep for the whirr of the telephone bell startled her only as an irrelevant noise. Then she realized what it meant and leapt up, stumbling over the folds of the eiderdown, to grab the receiver. The voice was Claude's.

'Dearest . . . how is she?' she implored.

'Mayfield can't say anything definite yet.' She could tell from the way he spoke that he was not alone. 'He's with her now – Going to give her an injection.'

'You've seen her? How did she seem? Did she know you?'

'I only saw her for a minute of two. She recognized me. She even said "Why are you here, Daddy?" ' There was a faint tremor in his voice.

'Surely that was a good sign?' Isabel said eagerly.

'Let's hope so. But I only stayed with her a moment. I'm afraid the sight of me upset her.'

'Claude . . . does she seem very ill? To you, I mean? I know you don't want to say much with Richard's sister there – Just say yes or no . . .'

After a pause before he answered:

'Frankly, my dear, yes, But remember my impressions mean nothing. We must wait and see what Mayfield says . . .'

'Hasn't he *any* idea what it may be?'

'He says it's too early to tell – Try not to worry too much. The drug will put her to sleep. There might be a considerable improvement when she wakes up.'

'Obviously she can't be moved tonight. Can we bring her back here tomorrow?'

There was another pause. Then Claude's voice said guardedly:

'He thinks probably better not. In fact, just to be on the safe side, he suggests putting her into a nursing-home for a few days. At all costs, she must have complete rest and quiet.'

'But she could have that here. I'd look after her night and day.'

'I know you would, my dear. But we must go by what Mayfield says. Forgive me if I ring off now. I can hear him coming across the courtyard.'

'Oh, wait,' she implored. 'Let *me* speak to him . . . I know you're keeping something back . . . He'll tell me if you won't . . .'

But it was too late. As she was speaking, she heard the click of the receiver and the line went dead.

Chapter Nine

When she found herself lying in Richard's camp bed, she started up in a panic. Didn't they know that was the one place of all places where she must not be? She ran to the door, stumbling over the nightdress that was too long for her. (Why was she wearing a nightdress? Whose nightdress?) Two evil spirits, one male, one female, clutched her, trying to stop her from escaping. She fought with all her might but they dragged her back and forced her into the bed again. Over and over again, she started up and ran to the door. But each time the two evil spirits dragged her back in spite of her struggles until at last she was exhausted and lay quiet, with her eyes closed. When she opened them, there was no one in the room but Gerald and Nell. At least she thought they were Gerald and Nell but they looked very strange. There was blood on Gerald's forehead and Nell's black fringe hung in jagged peaks. They looked so funny that she had to smile. She asked:

'Is it really you, Nell?'

'Yes, Clara dear. And this is Gerald. You remember Gerald?'

'Of course.' Then she asked anxiously: 'Where's Richard?'

'He's gone down to Peacocks. Don't you remember?'

She thought for a moment. Then she remembered and leapt out of bed again.

'Nell,' she cried. 'I have to go to Peacocks too. Oh, where are my clothes? I shall miss the train . . . I know I shall miss the train.'

Nell said:

'Hush, dear. You haven't to go to Peacocks till Saturday. There's plenty of time. Try and go to sleep.'

She let Nell put her back to bed. Perhaps it was all right now the evil spirits had gone. She asked:

'Why am I here in Richard's bed?'

'You were so tired. We thought you'd like to stay the night.'

Her eyelids came down suddenly like heavy blinds. She whispered:

'Tell Richard not to worry.'

When she was able to open her eyes again, Nell was not there. Only Gerald was sitting by her bed. He said, 'Feeling better? You've had a little doze.'

She wailed:

'Where's Nell? You shouldn't have let her go. Now she'll never come back.'

He tried to stop her but she was out of bed and at the door before he caught her. She fought with him, screaming, 'You fool . . . let me go to her . . . Don't you know what they're trying to do?' She screamed louder and louder trying to make him understand. Before she could make him realize that Nell had been tricked into going to the asylum to see her mad husband and they were going to lock her up there, the evil spirits reappeared and dragged her back to bed again. She shut her eyes and, to keep them at bay, sang with all her might, over and over again:

'O Deus ego amo te
Nec amo te ut salvas me
Nec quia non amantes te
Aeterno punis igne.'

At last she felt it was safe to stop. She opened her eyes. They had gone. There was no one in the room at all. Then she saw the door slowly move on its hinges. Someone was coming in. Was it the evil ones again? She sat up and made the sign of the cross.

It was her father who came in. He looked just as usual except that he was wearing the brown habit of a monk. She asked: 'Why are you here, Daddy?'

He smiled at her. She did not like the smile. He said 'Clara, my dearest child.' The voice did not sound like his. He came quite close up to the bed before she realized the truth. It was one of the evil spirits disguised as her father. He was going to try to kiss her. If this devil kissed her, she was lost for ever. She would never see Richard again. She whirled her arms and shrieked, 'Don't touch me . . . Don't touch me . . . I won't marry you . . . I belong to Richard.'

That drove him away. As the door shut after him, she lay back sobbing. 'Richard . . . hold on . . . don't let me go . . . I *am* true . . . I will be true.' For the first time, infinitely far away, she felt his presence. Silently, she called back, 'Don't be afraid. I can hold on, whatever they do.'

Something tremendous was going to happen. A terrible ordeal to prepare her for her marriage. She must go through it bravely, asking for no mitigation, as a soldier's bride should. She saw the door slowly open again. At any moment the ordeal would begin.

This time it was Doctor Mayfield. He was carrying some small object concealed in one hand. Was it an instrument of torture?

He came and stood over her, smiling falsely, and asked:

'Well, Clara, do you know who I am?'

'Doctor Mayfield, of course.' She was careful not to let him see how she hated his red face and false smile.

'Splendid, splendid! And you're not going to slap poor old

Doctor Mayfield's face again? Shall we shake hands and make it up?'

His free hand slyly pulled one of hers from under the sheet. But she had seen what his other hand concealed. It was a hypodermic syringe. She tore her wrist away, imploring:

'No . . . no . . . I mustn't be drugged. Richard doesn't want me to be drugged. Please, please not that.'

'Now, now,' he said hypocritically. 'Who's talking about drugs? Wouldn't you like to have a nice long sleep and dream about Richard?'

Her whole body was suddenly convulsed with such pain that her mind became confused. Why was it so essential she must not be drugged? Was it because she was in travail with Richard's child and, as a soldier's wife, she must not be spared any pang? When the doctor grabbed her arm again, the pain made it difficult to struggle with him. She fought as best she could but he was too strong for her. She felt the needle pierce her arm. In spite of her desperate effort to remain conscious, the heavy wave of the drug submerged her.

She was awakened by the distant noise of a car. Her mind was numb and drowsy but lucid. She was too exhausted to move her limbs, but she managed to raise her eyelids. Nell was sitting beside her.

'Nell,' she said. 'That car . . . I can still hear it?'

'What car, dear?'

'It's a long way away . . . Listen, can't you hear it now?'

'I'm trying to, dear – But I can't yet.'

'It's a very long way away still,' said Clara and closed her eyes.

She lay in a stupor aware of nothing but the sound of the car. It was a long time before she realized it was Richard's car. Then she saw it quite clearly, driving very fast along the dark roads with its headlamps on. She could just make out his face, pale and concentrated, behind the steering wheel. His voice sounded in her head: 'Hold on, darling. I'm coming as fast as I can.' At intervals she dozed off but in each conscious interval she saw and heard the car. Suddenly she saw some larger, heavier vehicle approaching from the other direction. She called out 'Take care'. But she was too late. The next moment she heard the crash of the collision and screamed.

She felt Nell's arm round her.

'Clara, what's the matter?'

She controlled herself and said:

'Wait . . . let me see what's happened.'

After a minute or two, she said:

'Oh, thank God. He's not hurt.'

'Who isn't hurt, dear?'

She opened her eyes and smiled at Nell's anxious face.

'Richard. It's all right. The car's smashed up but he's not hurt at all.'

'You've had a bad dream. Try and go to sleep again.'

She said quietly:

'No. It wasn't a dream. Richard started to drive back from Peacocks. That was his car I kept hearing. I saw it all happen. He ran into something. I couldn't see exactly what it was. But it's only his car that's smashed.

'Richard's quite safe, dear. So go back to sleep.'

'Yes. Now I know he's safe. He'll have to come on by train now. You won't let them do anything to me till he comes, Nell?'

'No, dear. Of course not.'

She slept. When she woke again, it was to the grey light of early morning. Her head had cleared; she felt sick and exhausted. She turned her head painfully and saw that the doctor was sitting beside her. She did not trust him but she no longer feared him.

He said:

'We're going to move you somewhere where you'll be more comfortable.'

She did not protest. She knew what they were going to do. They were going to take her away and use her for some kind of experiment. Something to do with the war. She was willing to go. But when they lifted her out of bed, she cried out desperately:

'Richard . . . Richard . . . Oh, you're too late.'

She was in a cab, with her head on a nurse's shoulder. Two men were sitting opposite her. One was a stranger. The other looked like Gerald Moreton. It was odd to be driving through the streets in broad daylight wearing only a nightdress that did not belong to her and the black imitation sealskin coat her father had given her. She was very sleepy. She kept trying to remember when she had last put that fur coat on but her mind was a blank.

They came to a tall house. Someone, Gerald perhaps, carried her up flights and flights of stairs. Now she was in a perfectly ordinary bedroom. An old nurse with a face she liked sat by the fire; a young one, very pink and white and self-conscious, stood near her. Clara wandered over to the window and looked out. A red bus went by. It was comforting to see the bus. She wanted to stand there and watch other buses going by. If she could see the numbers, she might be able to tell what road it was down there. But the young nurse took her by the elbow and led her away.

'I shouldn't look out of the window if I were you, dear,' she said in a soft, hateful voice. 'It's so ugly.' Clara did not resist. Now she was puzzled and frightened; she wanted to explain something, but her head was too muddled. Presently she was in bed, alone but for the old nurse. Then she found that she was clutching a rosary. It was her father's old black one. She knew that her parents were downstairs, praying for her. Her throat was dry; a fearful weariness weighed her down. She was in her last agony. She must pray. As if the old nurse understood, she began 'Our Father' and 'Hail Mary'. Clara answered. They recited decade after decade in a mechanical rhythm. A cold sweat came out on Clara's forehead; all her limbs felt numb and bruised. Her strength was going out of her on the holy words. She was fighting the overpowering sleepiness that she knew was death. 'Holy Mary, Mother of God,' she forced out in beat after beat of sheer will-power. She lapsed at last. She was dead, but unable to leave the flesh. She waited; light, happy, disembodied.

Now she was a baby again. It was as if she had died and been reborn. She was not in her own home but in Charles Cressett's night nursery at Maryhall. Yet she knew that she was still Clara. She lay very peacefully watching the nurse knitting under the green lamp. Her body was a baby's but her mind understood what had happened. She had been given a chance to live her life all over again. This new life would unfold perfectly day after day through a new childhood lapped in warmth and security. But just as she was savouring the bliss of this rebirth, the pleasant, firelit room and the old nurse vanished. She was standing alone in a dark crypt. Beside her, on a bier, was a glass-lidded coffin. In it, dressed as a First Communicant, lay a girl who had died at her convent-school. Instead of white flowers, Theresa wore a gilt paper crown on her head. As Clara watched the dead girl, a worm crawled out of her mouth. She screamed and woke out of the nightmare to find herself back in the firelit room. But she was no longer a baby and another nurse was sitting by the green lamp.

'You must be quiet, dear,' said the woman.

There were whispers and footsteps outside.

'I hear she is wonderful,' said a woman's voice.

'Yes,' said another, 'but all the conditions must be right, or it will be dangerous for her.'

'How?'

'You must all dress as nurses,' said the second voice, 'then she thinks she is in a hospital. She lives through it again, or rather *they* do.'

'Who . . . the sons?'

'Yes. The House of Mirrors is full of them.'

One by one, women wearing nurses' veils and aprons tiptoed in and sat beside her bed. She knew quite well that they were not nurses; they were women whose sons had been killed in the war. Each time a woman came in, Clara went through a new agony. She became the dead boy. She spoke with his voice. She felt the pain of amputated limbs, of blinded eyes. She coughed up blood from lungs torn to rags by shrapnel. Over and over again, in trenches, in field hospitals, in German camps, she died a lingering death. Between the bouts of torture, the mothers, in their nurses' veils, would kiss her hands and sob out their gratitude.

'She must never speak of the House of Mirrors,' one said to another.

And the other answered:

'She will forget when she wakes up. She is going to marry a soldier.'

At last the ordeal was over. She lay back in the bed, too

exhausted to open her eyes. Gradually she realized that, all through it, Richard had been in the room below. The horrors were over now. Any moment now he would be coming up to tell her that she had done everything that was needed. She had earned the right to marry him.

She heard the door open softly and knew that he had come in. She turned her head to look at him, but her eyelids were clamped down with leaden weights. She struggled desperately to speak to him but she could not manage even a whisper. She had gone dumb. Perhaps she had gone deaf too. She knew that he was speaking to her but she could not hear the words. He was close to her now but she could not get through to him nor he to her. At last, with a huge effort, she lifted her eyelids. He was standing close by her but she could not see him clearly. His face was a blur. The only thing she could see distinctly was the shepherd's plaid pattern of his suit. She strained her eyes to keep it in focus but, almost at once, that too began to blur. With her last remnant of consciousness she tried to force herself to keep aware of him, to implore him, in her agony of dumbness, to wait. But she could not get through to him. For one tiny flicker, her senses returned. She heard someone say:

'It's no use. She doesn't know you.'

Before she could cry out 'I do, I do,' the darkness closed down.

PART FOUR

Chapter One

Months, perhaps years, later, she woke up in a small bare cell. The walls were whitewashed and dirty, and she was lying on a mattress on the floor, without sheets, with only rough, red-striped blankets over her. She was wearing a linen gown, like an old-fashioned nightshirt, and she was bitterly cold. In front of her was the blank yellow face of a heavy door without a handle of any kind. Going over to the door, she tried frantically to push it open. It was locked. She began to call out in panic and to beat on the door till her hands were red and swollen. She had forgotten her name. She did not know whether she were very young or very old. Had she died that night in Nell's studio? She could remember Nell and Richard, yet she knew that her memory of them was not quite right. Was this place a prison? If only, only her name would come back to her.

Suddenly the door opened. A young nurse whom she had never seen before stood there. As suddenly as the door had opened, Clara remembered her own name. She cried out: 'It's come back – I'm Clara Batchelor. Ring up my father and tell him I'm here. The number is Hammersmith 2159.'

The nurse did not answer, but she began to laugh. Slowly, mockingly, inch by inch, though Clara tried with all her strength to keep it open, she closed the door.

She lost herself again; this time completely. For months she was not even a human being; she was a horse. Ridden almost to death, beaten till she fell, she lay at last on the straw in her stable and waited for death. They buried her as she lay on her side, with outstretched head and legs. A child came and sowed turquoises round the outline of her body in the ground, and she rose up again as a horse of magic with a golden mane, and galloped across the sky. Again she woke on the mattress in her cell. She looked and saw that she had human hands and feet again, but she knew that she was still a horse.

She became a human being again. One day a nurse came in, put a coarse brown serge dressing-gown over her nightshirt and took her out of her cell. They went out into a long passage with a shiny waxed floor. There were more nurses there and several other women, all dressed in the same coarse brown dressing-gowns. The nurses all looked fresh and trim but the women were haggard and unkempt. Some of them were old and repellent and all had matted, untidy hair. The nurses formed the women up in a long line, pushing them back when they tried to break out of it. Her own nurse pushed her into the line too. She did not know what was going on at the top of the line. She thought it was some form of torture for she could hear the women ahead of her screaming. At last there was only one in front of her and she could see what was happening. One nurse held the woman down on a chair while another roughly dragged a comb through her tangled hair. Then she took a needle and thread and sewed it into a tight plait. But when her own turn came, they only dragged the comb unmercifully through hers. Someone said:

'It's too short to sew up. Lovely colour isn't it? My goodness, I'd give something to have natural waves like that. What a waste on one of them.'

Then two nurses dragged her, one on each side, to an enormous room filled with baths. They dipped her into bath after bath of boiling water. Each bath was smaller than the last, with gold taps that came off in her hands when she tried to clutch them. There was something slightly wrong about everything in this strange bathroom. All the mugs were chipped. The chairs had only three legs. There were plates lying about with letters round the brim, but the letters never read the same twice running. After the hot baths, they ducked her, spluttering and choking, into an ice-cold one. A nurse took a bucket of cold water and splashed it over her, drenching her hair and half blinding her. She screamed, and nurses, dozens of them, crowded round the bath to laugh at her. 'Oh Clara, you naughty, naughty girl,' they giggled. They took her out and dried her and

431

rubbed something on her eyes and nostrils that stung like fire. She had human limbs, but she was not human; she was a horse or a stag being prepared for the hunt. On the wall was a looking-glass, dim with steam.

'Look, Clara, look who's there,' said the nurses.

She looked and saw a face in the glass, the face of a fairy horse or stag, sometimes with antlers, sometimes with a wild golden mane, but always with the same dark stony eyes and nostrils red as blood. She threw up her head and neighed and made a dash for the door. The nurses caught and dragged her along a passage. The passage was like a long room; it had a shiny wooden floor with double iron tracks in it like the tracks of a model railway. The nurses held her painfully by the armpits so that her feet only brushed the floor. The passage was like a musty old museum. There were wax flowers under cases and engravings of Queen Victoria and Balmoral. Suddenly the nurses opened a door in the wall, and there was her cell again. They threw her down on the mattress and went out, locking the door.

She went to sleep. She had a long nightmare about a girl who was lost in the dungeons under an old house on her wedding-day. Just as she was, in her white dress and wreath and veil, she fell into a trance and slept for thirty years. She woke up, thinking she had slept only a few hours, and found her way back to the house, and remembering her wedding, hurried to the chapel. There were lights and flowers and a young man standing at the altar. But as she walked up the aisle, people pushed her back, and she saw another bride going up before her. Up in her own room, she looked in the glass to see an old woman in a dirty satin dress with a dusty wreath on her head. She herself was the girl who had slept thirty years. They had shut her up here in the cell without a looking-glass so that she should not know how old she had grown.

Then she was Richard, endlessly climbing up the steps of a dark tower by the sea, knowing that she herself was imprisoned at the top. She came out of this dream suddenly to find herself being tortured in her own person. She was lying on her back with two nurses holding her down. A young man with a signet ring on his finger was bending over her, holding a funnel with a long tube attached. He forced the tube down her nose and began to pour some liquid into the funnel. There was a searing pain at the back of her nose, she choked and struggled, but they held her down ruthlessly. At last the man drew out the tube and dropped it coiling in a basin. The nurses released her and all three went out and shut the door.

This horror came at intervals for days. She grew to dread the opening of the door, which was nearly always followed by the procession of nurses and the young man with the basin and the funnel. Sometimes, instead of a signet ring, the young man wore one mounted with a white shield that had a red cross on it.

She changed into a salmon. The salmon was suffocating in a dry, stone-floored cell behind iron bars. Just beyond the bars was the life-giving waterfall. It lay wriggling and gasping, scraping its scales on the stone floor, maddened by the noise of the water it could not reach.

Perhaps she died as a salmon as she had died as a horse, for she woke in a small six-sided room whose walls were all thick bulging panels of grey rubber. The door was rubber-padded too, with a small red window, shaped like an eye, deeply embedded in it. She was lying on the floor, and through the red, a face, stained red too, was watching her and laughing.

The rubber room was a compartment in a sinking ship, near the boiler room which would burst at any minute and scald her to death. Somehow she must get out. She flung herself against the rubber walls as if she could beat her way out by sheer force. The air was getting hotter. The rubber walls were already warm to touch. In a second her lungs would burst. At last the door opened. They were coming to rescue her. But it was the torturers who entered: the young man and the two nurses with the basin and funnel.

One day she found herself sitting on a heap of straw in a small room that was dusty and friendly, like an attic. She was a child of about twelve, dressed in an old blue pinafore. Her name was Clara. She sat patiently, with crossed legs and folded arms, making a spell to bring her brother Richard safe home. He was flying back to her in a white aeroplane with a green propeller.

She could see his face quite clearly as he sat between the wings. He wore a fur cap like a cossack's pulled down to his black eyebrows, one of which was a little ragged. Enemies had put Clara in prison, but Richard would come to rescue her as he had always come before. She and Richard loved each other with a love far deeper and more subtle than any love between husband and wife. She knew at once if he were in pain or danger, even if he were a thousand miles away.

Richard came to her window and carried her away. They flew to Russia, and landed on a plain covered with snow. Then they drove for miles in a sledge until they came to a dark pine forest. They walked through the forest, hand in hand, Clara held close in Richard's great fur cape. But at last she was tired, dazed by the silence and the endless trees, all exactly alike. She wanted to lie down in the snow, to sleep.

Richard shook her: 'Never go to sleep in the snow, Clara, or you will die.'

But she was too tired to listen, and she lay down in the snow that was soft and strangely warm and fell into an exquisite dreamy torpor. And perhaps she did die in the snow as Richard had said, for the next thing she knew was that she was up in the clouds, following a beautiful Indian woman who sailed before her, and sifting snow down on the world through the holes in her blue pinafore.

She was sent back to the world. She was no longer a child. There was someone whom she must reach at all costs. He was a soldier. His name was Richard. She saw a huge, tiered wedding cake. On the top of it was a tiny figure in uniform, wearing a glengarry and tartan trews. The only way to reach him was to be turned into a mouse and gnaw patiently through tier after tier of the cake till she reached the top. She became a mouse. But when she began to gnaw, she found that the cake was made of painted tin. After working painfully for hours, she had only gnawed through an inch and her teeth were too blunt to bite any more.

She became a human being once more. She was no ordinary human being but Lord of the World. Whatever she ordered, came about. The walls of her prison turned to crystal. Beyond them was a garden full of larches and apple-trees, with peacocks strutting on the lawns. One of them had a blue jay's feather in its beak. She turned that peacock into a beautiful young man and the other into children lovelier than dreams. Then she tested her powers by ordering destruction. She changed the garden into a sea and summoned up a storm that blew great ships out of their courses as if they were paper boats. Only herself she could not command. She grew weary of making magic and longed only to sleep. But there was no one powerful enough to order her to sleep.

She raved, she prayed, but no sleep came. At last three old women appeared.

'You cannot sleep unless you die,' they said.

She assented gladly. They took her to a beach and fettered her down on some stones, just under the bows of a huge ship that was about to be launched. One of the three gave a signal. Nothing could stop it now. On it came, grinding the pebbles to dust, deafening her with noise. It passed, slowly, right over her body. She felt every bone crack; felt the intolerable weight on her shoulders; felt her skull split like a shell. But she could not sleep now. She was free from the burden of having to will.

After this she was born and re-born with incredible swiftness as a woman, as an imp, as a dog, and finally as a flower. She was some nameless, tiny bell, growing in a stream, with a stalk as fine as hair and a human voice. The water flowing through her flower throat made her sing all day a little monotonous song, 'Kulalla, kulalla, kullala, ripitalla, kullala, kulalla, kulalla, kulla.'

This happy flower life did not last long. She found herself a human being once more in a cell unlike any she remembered. She was lying on a mattress in what looked like a great wooden manger clamped to the floor. Over it was stretched a kind of stiff canvas apron, like a piece of sailcloth, fastened to the manger with studs and metal eyelets. At intervals the blank yellow door without a handle opened. Sometimes it was the two nurses and the young man with the funnel; sometimes the two nurses or even only one. When they unfastened the sailcloth and took her out of the manger as they sometimes did, she found she was wearing not a nightshirt but a curious white garment, very stiff and rough, that encased her legs and feet and came down over her hands. She was frightened of the nurses. Sometimes they were rough and called her 'naughty girl': sometimes they were friendly and said 'good girl'. But she could not discover what it was that she did that made them say 'naughty' or 'good' though she was very anxious they should not be angry. They addressed her as 'Clara'. She did not know what her name was but she was sure it was not Clara. At first she sulked but soon she saw it pleased them if she answered to it like an animal.

Between the visitation of the nurses and the torture with the funnel, she dozed and dreamt. Or she lay quietly, content to watch, hour after hour, the play of pearly colours on the piece of sailcloth. Though she did not know who she was now, she could remember places and people from another world in which she had once lived. She found she knew several poems, both in English and French and enjoyed saying them over to herself. But if a word or a line had gone, she could only fill the gap with words she made up in a language of her own.

Among the people she remembered was the man who had been her father in that other life. She thought about him quite often: she had been very fond of him. She remembered a mother too: a very beautiful woman with big dark eyes. She remembered her coming up to the nursery to say goodnight, wearing an evening dress that sparkled with gold sequins. But a terrible punishment had fallen on her mother. She had taken a lover and caught small-pox from him. Her husband came home one night and found her face pitted with the marks of it and all her beauty gone. He knew then that she had been unfaithful to him and drove her out of the house on a night of thick fog. In the fog, her mother lost her way, wandered into the river and was drowned. Once her father's face was so vivid to her that she actually fancied he was sitting there beside the manger. She clearly saw not only his face but his shoulders in a grey tweed overcoat she recognized. Everything about that head and shoulders was familiar except the scarf he was wearing. The illusion was so complete that she said aloud:

'Daddy, you've got a new scarf.'

But, as she said it, the face crumpled into a grimace which made it unrecognizable and, the next moment, it vanished.

One night there was a thunderstorm. She was terrified. The manger had become a little raft; when she put out her hand she could feel waves lapping right up to the brim. In that other life she had always been afraid of water lapping in the dark. She cried out: 'Star of the Sea, pray for us.' The Litany of Our Lady came back to her. She began to say it aloud, very slowly and distinctly, in Latin. She had just said 'Vas insigne devotionis' when the door opened and a light shone in on the waves that surrounded her. In the doorway stood a nurse she had never seen before. The nurse was very young, with a gentle face, blue eyes and black hair. She knew at once that this girl was not really a nurse. Her name was Kathleen and she was Irish. She had disguised herself as a nurse so as to get into this nightmare place. The Irish girl said softly:

'Rosa Mystica.'

'Turris Davidica,' she herself replied.

'Turris eburnea.'

'Domus aurea.'

And thus, turn by turn, they completed the litany. Then the girl disguised as a nurse smiled and closed the door. But now it was light, the storm was over and the manger was no longer a raft on the sea but clamped as usual to the floor and surrounded by dingy yellow walls.

One day she discovered that the sailcloth and the stiff enveloping garment had gone. She was lying under coarse grey blankets and wearing the nightshirt once more. The change was as delicious as if she had been wrapped in silk and covered with swansdown. Her body felt as light as if, but for the weight of the blankets, it would have floated up to the ceiling. She found that she could stand up in the manger. For the first time she saw that there was a window high up in the wall behind it.

Through this window which was barred and covered with close wire netting she could see into a garden. This discovery gave her great pleasure. In the garden women and nurses were walking; they did not look like real people but oddly thin and bright, like figures cut out of coloured paper. And she could see birds flying across the sky, not real birds, but bird-shaped kites, lined with strips of white metal, that flew on wires. Only the clouds had thickness and depth and looked as clouds had looked in the other world. The clouds spoke to her sometimes. They wrote messages in white smoke on the blue. They would take shape after shape to amuse her, shapes of swans, of feathers, of charming ladies with fluffy white muffs and toques, of soldiers in white busbies.

Soon she became more daring. She leapt from the manger on to the high window-sill and crouched there like a cat. But one day she was so absorbed in watching the doll-like figures in the garden that she did not hear the cell door open. Two nurses dragged her down from her perch. She fought with them. One slapped her and said:

'You know what happens to naughty girls. Do you want to go back to pads?'

The other said:

'The gymnastics they get up to! Almost like animals. She's been so quiet lately, too. Have to put the sheet on her.'

They stripped her, forced her struggling limbs back into the heavy canvas garment and fastened her down under the sailcloth again. Exhausted, she fell asleep.

When she woke up again, a nurse was sitting beside her, holding a plate with some porridge in it and a spoon. The nurse kept spooning up bits of it and trying to make her eat. She did not want to eat, because she knew the porridge was poisoned, but the nurse forced a little between her teeth and she had to swallow it. The nurse smiled.

'There, that's a good girl.'

Suddenly she noticed the plate the nurse was holding. It had letters printed round the rim. She could not make them all out because the nurse's hand covered part of them. But she could distinctly read the word HOSPITAL. Her mind suddenly became sharp. She asked:

'Is this place a hospital?'

'That's right, dear.'

'What kind of a hospital?'

'Ah, that'd be telling,' said the nurse slyly.

'Please, I must know. What *kind* of a hospital?'

'A hospital for girls who ask too many questions,' said the nurse, thrusting the spoon into her open mouth. Now she knew for certain the porridge was poisoned. She spat it out and her mind went blank again.

Chapter Two

One Sunday in April, Claude Batchelor returned later than usual from his weekly visit to the asylum. He let himself in so quietly that Isabel, who was waiting for him in the study as she did every Sunday afternoon, did not hear him. When he came into the room and she saw his face, she sprang up from her chair and ran to him.

'Dearest . . . Is the news bad?'

He held her close, without answering. Then he moved stiffly and haltingly over to his desk and sat down, still not saying a word. Isabel stood, with her hand on his shoulder, anxiously watching his efforts to clench the quivering muscles of his face. He could not control them. With a choking cry, he buried his head in his hands and sobbed.

In all those months he had broken down like that only once: the day he had had to sign the certificate of insanity. Isabel was too shaken by his anguish to formulate any questions, even in her own mind. It was not till the loud, racking sobs ceased as abruptly as they had begun that she asked, with lips gone so dry that she could hardly shape the words:

'She's not dead?'

He lifted his marred face.

'No, thank God. Forgive me for frightening you like that.'

'But what is it? . . . What have they said to you?'

'Just let me pull myself together.' He fished out his handkerchief and blew his nose violently. Then he put her in the big green armchair and came and sat close to her. Taking her hand, he said:

'My love, we may have to face a rather dreadful possibility. But remember, it is only a possibility.'

'Not that she will never get well?' she gripped his hand. 'Oh Claude . . . I can't believe it . . . I *won't* believe it.'

'No. They are fairly sure now that she will recover eventually.'

'Oh, thank God . . . thank God . . .'

'But, alas, it may not be for a long time.'

'How long? A year? Two years even?'

Instead of answering, he leant forward and kissed her.

'If you can bear it, I would rather tell you exactly what he said. It was the head doctor I saw today. Brooke. I had a long talk with him.'

'Yes?' she said, staring at him with sad expectancy. Much weeping had dulled her great brown eyes and permanently reddened the lids. 'She's no better than she's been all these last weeks?'

He answered slowly:

'In some ways . . . from their point of view . . . there is an improvement . . . No, wait, my dear . . . This last violent phase seems to be passing . . . I was even allowed to see her today . . .' His face began to twitch again.

'My poor darling . . . how did she look?'

He swallowed hard and went on:

'Very pale and thin. Not, thank God, unhappy. She even smiled sometimes.'

'But she still didn't know you?'

'Isabel . . . just for one flash, she did. She said, absolutely in her normal voice "Daddy, you're wearing a new scarf." His voice broke and tears came back into her eyes.

'Dearest . . . don't,' she said, clasping his hand tight. 'Surely that was a hopeful sign? . . . All these months . . . she's never recognized you.'

'I thought it hopeful, too.'

Ignoring the deadness of his voice, she went on eagerly:

'And the scarf. She was *right* about the scarf. It's the one I gave you for Christmas, and it was November that she was taken ill.

She couldn't have seen it when she was well. Oh, darling, she's getting better.'

'Hush, my dear. Try and be patient. I haven't told you all the doctor said.'

'Very well. But I don't promise to believe it. Doctors aren't infallible.'

'He would be the first to admit that. He kept stressing how little is really known about these things. There is some research going on, especially abroad, but so far they are only feeling their way – He impressed me as a remarkably honest man. I felt I could trust him to tell me the truth.'

'How can he tell you the truth when he admitted no one knows it?'

'He has immense practical experience. And some facts are known. There are forms of . . . insanity which are recognizable. They know the symptoms . . . they have a fair idea of the course things will take. At first, just because her attack was so sudden and so violent, they thought she might recover, almost as suddenly, in a matter of months. There would have been a danger of its recurring but she might have had long intervals of being perfectly normal . . .'

'To live with that horror always hanging over her? Could anything be worse than that?'

'Perhaps not. Perhaps not. At any rate, that is not what he thinks now.'

'What *does* he think?'

He answered, speaking slowly and heavily again:

'That the symptoms are changing. There may possibly be a very marked improvement. What he fears is that she may develop a milder but more chronic form of mania. He has seen it happen before, in cases like hers. When she recovered . . . he says such patients nearly always do recover eventually . . . she would almost certainly be perfectly well for the rest of her life . . .'

'She's still only twenty-two. What does he mean by the rest of her life?'

He took both her hands.

'My dearest . . . I don't know how to tell you. He can't be sure

441

. . . But he says the chances are that she may not come out till she is between forty-five and fifty.'

She wrenched her hands out of his and covered her face. He moved them gently away. For a moment her eyes glared at him with a terrible bright blankness so like Clara's that he had to look away. She said on a high note:

'How can God be so cruel? Why didn't he let her die? I'd rather . . . far rather you'd told me she was dead.'

'Hush, my love, hush.' He gathered her in his arms. Her body was rigid and trembling. Then suddenly it went limp against him, and, to his relief, she wept.

He soothed her like a child, kissing her hair and wiping her face with his handkerchief. When at last she was quietened, he said:

'Lie back in the chair for a moment while I get you some whisky.'

She lay with closed eyes, hearing him unfasten a cupboard, clink glass against glass, squirt a siphon. Her mind was numb. She could not remember why she had been weeping. She only knew she had lived through all this before, this lying back in a chair with burning eyelids, utterly spent, while a man moved about a room clinking glass, pouring out whisky. When, at last, she opened her eyes, she was half-dazed to find herself in the study. The man holding the glass to her lips was not Reynaud Callaghan but her husband, Claude.

She drank meekly. Her head cleared. She even made a wry mouth and said:

'How I hate the taste of whisky!'

'It will do you good. I've given you so little – See how much I've given myself.'

Claude swallowed his in gulps. Faded patches of the old fresh pink came up in his cheeks. Isabel felt hers flush too: a reviving warmth ran down her back. She said:

'I don't wonder people take to drink.'

Exhausted as she was, she suddenly felt inclined to talk. She became almost voluble. As if this were any other Sunday since the middle of last November, she began rehearsing over again every circumstance of Clara's breakdown; making all the old conjectures, stirring up all the old hopes as if somewhere there must be something they had overlooked, something they ought to have done, something they might still do. She said, for the hundredth time:

'If they'd left her in the nursing-home just a little longer. Instead of rushing her off to that dreadful place and making you certify her. Oh, I know Mayfield said it was the only thing to do. But how could he *know*? How could a stupid, commonplace man like that understand anyone as sensitive and imaginative as Clara? What she must have gone through in that terrible time with Archie . . . And then that exquisite, idyllic happiness . . . Wasn't it enough to unbalance her a little? . . . If they'd only waited . . . given her a moment's breathing space . . .'

'My dear,' he said, as he had said it so often before: 'What else could we do? . . . We were in Mayfield's hands . . . He thought it was the best place . . . Remember, when he and I took her there, there was no shadow of doubt in any of *their* minds . . .'

'A public asylum. Our darling child in a public asylum.'

He said wearily.

'You know how terribly against the grain it went to send her there. If he thought a private home would have been better, I'd have sold what little I have, taken on any amount of extra work to pay the fees. But his argument seemed sound . . . still does seem sound. With a private home, there's always the suspicion they might want to keep them longer than strictly necessary, just because of the fees. And, if I were to die, who could go on paying them? Nazareth has the best record of all the public ones. They've got the best doctors. Mayfield's not the only one who's assured me of that. And, since they always have people waiting for admission, they *want* to discharge patients as soon as they reasonably can. Dearest, we've been into it all so often before.'

'The fact remains she's been far, far worse since she went there. And the terrible things they do to her. This forcible feeding . . . oh, it's unbearable to think of.'

'I wish I'd never told you about that, Isabel. But you dragged it out of me.'

'It's what they did to those poor suffragettes in prison. I heard a woman who'd been forcibly fed speak once. I've never forgotten her description of it.'

'It was only done as a last resort. She was starving herself to death. They don't think she knew what was happening.'

'Don't tell me you can't feel pain, however deluded you are.'

'Well, at least he thinks that will no longer be necessary. The nurse has managed, at last, to persuade her to eat a little. They've been very patient with her.'

'Not as patient as I would be . . . But they won't let me see her. Her own mother.'

'Dearest, you know it only upsets you both.'

'How can it upset her when she doesn't even recognize me?'

'Isabel, you know what happened the last time. Obviously it isn't you she sees or thinks she sees, but some terrifying hallucination.'

'She doesn't know you yet she's not frightened when she sees you. Not since that dreadful night at Nell Crayshaw's. Why of me? In real life it was you she used to be frightened of. Never me.'

'Isabel,' he pleaded. 'Don't remind me of that. If you knew how I'd searched my conscience, wondering if I were in any way responsible. I hadn't often been too harsh with her.'

Her voice dropped its high, monotonous note of complaint . . .

'Dearest, of course it's not your fault. You mustn't let that terrible conscience of yours torment you. How could it be your fault?'

He sighed.

'I don't know. That first night, it seemed like a judgement on me.'

'A judgement for what? There's not a better, more conscientious man in the world.'

He shook his head.

'Only God knows how much evil there is in me. That was how *she* saw me that first night . . . as an evil spirit.'

'She was obsessed with the idea of evil spirits. You even thought the poor child was possessed, and wanted to call in a priest. It wasn't till you gave her your rosary . . .'

'How often I've thought of that . . . that Catholic nurse telling us how she said the rosary aloud with her before her mind went altogether. They tell me even now, in there . . . they sometimes hear her praying . . .'

'Why doesn't God hear her prayers? . . . and ours? Is there one single day we haven't prayed from the bottom of our hearts?'

He took her hand.

'My dear, we must be patient. Perhaps He will hear them. At least, He will give us strength to bear it.'

'I haven't your resignation,' she said. 'I can't believe God could be so cruel. Wasn't it enough to strike her just when she had her first real chance of happiness? But to condemn her to this living death. Not to let her get well till she's almost an old woman . . .' Her voice rose. 'I can't believe it. I won't believe it. I trust Richard more than any doctor. *He's* always been certain she'd get well.'

'Dearest, how can he know? He wants to believe it. And he wants to comfort us.'

'He has intuitions about her. Didn't he know she was ill that night? Didn't he start to drive back from Wiltshire to London? And she saw everything that was happening all those miles away . . . the accident . . . everything. That wasn't delusion. Richard told Nell that Clara was right in every detail.'

'I know . . . I know, my dear. It was as if she had second sight. But in her abnormal state . . . I believe there are other instances . . .'

'It doesn't account for Richard's knowing something was wrong with her. He was as sane as you or I. No, there is some extraordinary bond between those two. They belong to each other. They can't be torn apart for ever.'

He put his hand to his forehead and made no reply. After a while he said in a changed voice:

'Isabel. There's something I want to talk to you about. In the first shock, I could only think about Clara . . . and ourselves . . . But there are others to whom this is going to be a terrible blow.'

'Richard? He won't believe it. Any more than I do.'

'Richard, yes. And also, Archie.'

She said angrily:

'That eternal concern of yours for Archie. If anyone is to blame for her breakdown, he is.'

'What right have we to say that? God knows it's what the poor boy feels himself. Don't you know how utterly wretched he's been ever since I had to tell him? Haven't you any pity for him?'

'Oh, I'm not saying he deliberately wrecked her life – But think of the change in her after three months of that ghastly marriage. Have you forgotten that morning you went to Chelsea? You told me – here in this very room – that she struck you as nearly out of her mind . . .'

'Must we go over it all again? Does it make things any better for her – or us? I believe *she* would be sorry for Archie.'

'She was always far too generous about that wretched boy. All right . . . he loved her in his feeble, selfish way. But how can you think of him in the same breath as Richard? That's *true* love. I think he'd have gone out of his own mind if it weren't for that wonderful confidence . . .'

He said slowly:

'Yes. But I shall have to break this to him. He rang me up last night from his sister's place. He knows I was seeing the head doctor today.'

'Need you tell him all you told me?'

'I promised faithfully.'

'He won't believe it.'

'I'm not so sure.'

'Why? Claude, ever since he's been back in England, he's come to see us every time he was on leave. And every single time he's told us he was certain she'd be completely cured. He was sure it would be quite soon.'

'Yes, poor boy. He's kept it up with us. Yet I've fancied lately that, in his own mind . . . Remember there's already one tragedy of this kind in his own family.'

'Nell's husband's case is entirely different. His brain was damaged. I never have . . . I never *will* believe that Clara is insane. Certainly not permanently insane.'

'My dear . . . there's a terrible problem we all have to face. Even supposing our worst fears aren't justified . . . the cruel fact remains – Is it ever going to be right for Clara to risk marrying and having children?'

'Children . . . perhaps not. But if there were any real risk for her or for them, surely even the Church would allow . . .'

'No, my dear. That is out of the question.'

'Oh, the Church is inhuman about marriage. If it weren't entirely run by men . . . if women were only allowed some say . . .'

'My dear, there are times when we all feel that the Church demands the impossible. When we're calmer, we remember *why* she demands it.'

'I can't believe that God Himself would wish to keep those two apart. Two creatures made for each other – Aren't they to be allowed any human happiness . . .?'

'Isabel, my dear – What use are these wild speculations? You're only torturing yourself. We must . . . we *must* realize the facts. We can't let that boy wreck his life in impossible hopes . . . It's only common justice.'

'Justice,' she said bitterly. 'What justice is there in all this?'

'Oh my dear . . . that's something we can't understand.' He put his arms round her. 'We can only go on in the dark. Let me ring up Richard. He'll have been waiting in suspense all this time.'

'What are you going to say to him?'

'Just what I said to you. Go into the next room, my dear. It would be too painful for you . . .'

'And to him? To hear that on the telephone? Claude, you can't be so cruel. Ask him to come here and tell him yourself.'

He said remorsefully:

'Yes. Of course. What a coward I am . . .'

'Would you like me to be there too?'

He hesitated.

'For my sake, yes. For his sake, no . . . Men sometimes find it easier . . .'

Within an hour, Richard arrived. Claude was listening for his ring. When it came, he hurried at once to answer it. But before he reached the study door, he stopped and, on a sudden impulse, went to the mantelpiece, took down the two photographs of

Clara as an obstinate child in a Hussar cap and as a demure, uncertain girl of sixteen and shut them in a drawer of his desk.

Two hours later, when Richard had gone, he took them out again and put them back in their old place. His eyes filled as he did so but he had no strength left to weep. He went and sat for a long time at his desk staring blankly at the rows of green-backed files in the bookcase and the dusty plaster cast of Athene. At last he took out the much-mended black rosary that had never left him since he picked it up from the floor by Clara's bed the day they had taken her from the nursing home to the asylum. Pressing its cheap white metal crucifix against his forehead, he muttered over and over again in his mind:

'If it be Thy will . . . If it be Thy will.'

Then as the weary certainty came to him that he could live through another day and then another, he whispered aloud:

'If I have done wrong, punish me. But, oh my Lord, spare *her*.'

Chapter Three

Gradually she became aware of certain changes. The most remarkable was that, whenever she was fully awake, she was always the same person. This person was called Clara. She was almost sure that, in the other life, her name had also been Clara. She wished she knew what she looked like but there was no looking-glass in her cell. The stiff garment and the sailcloth had gone: she no longer dreaded the opening of the door since the torturers with the funnel never appeared now.

Sometimes nurses came in and washed her. She grew interested in the body they washed and began to recognize certain features of it. If it was not the body she had had in the old life, it seemed definitely to belong to her. It was very thin, with hipbones that stuck out like knobs and shrunken, weak-looking legs. One day, as the nurse was washing her left arm, she noticed that about an inch of skin on the inner side was marked with small red blotches like a rash. In the other life, she had had a birthmark in the same place on her left arm. Her gaze moved down to the hand the nurse was washing. The bones stood out and the nails were discoloured and broken yet she could have sworn it was the hand she had had long ago.

One of the nurses said:

'What are you looking for, dear? Your wedding ring? Don't worry. It's put away safe. It kept falling off your finger.'

'Wedding ring?' she asked. 'Am I married, then?'

'Must be, dear. You're down on the list as Mrs Something-Something. Never can remember these double-barrelled names. We always call you Clara, don't we?'

'Yes. But who *is* Clara? And what am I doing here?'

'Never mind that now, dear. Give us your other hand like a good girl.'

When they went out, they forgot to shut the door of the cell. She could hardly believe her good fortune. At first she was too delighted to have something new to look at, instead of the blank yellow surface of the door, to do more than stare contentedly. She could see a section of a passage and, in the far wall, a large window. The window gave on another wall, covered with a creeper that was just showing tiny shoots. Occasionally a nurse passed down the passage and, once, an untidy-looking woman in a brown dressing-gown. A similar brown dressing-gown hung on a peg in her cell. She was shivering with cold, even under the blankets. Very cautiously, she got out of the manger bed. The stone floor was like ice under her bare feet. As she put on the dressing-gown, she was seized with violent curiosity. She tiptoed out into the empty passage. At the far end it opened out into a kind of hall. In the hall was a fireplace in which was a beautiful leaping fire. There were women sitting round it; some in brown dressing-gowns, some in ordinary, but very ill-fitting clothes. Irresistibly drawn by the warmth and the flames, she padded silently down the passage and joined the women by the fire. They stared at her sullenly, but let her come close and hold out her hands to the blaze. But, just as her chilled body had begun to enjoy the heat, two nurses seized her under the armpits and dragged her away from the heavenly fire. They forced her back along the passage back into her cell and slammed the door on her.

There came another time when they left the cell door open. Remembering what had happened before, she resisted the tremendous temptation to go in search of the fire again. She contented herself with staring at the creeper on the wall beyond the window and was rewarded with a charming sight. Slowly, the tiny shoots lengthened and unfurled until they became green leaves. Then, suddenly, all the leaves began to dance, beating one against the other like thousands of miniature clapping hands. This made her very happy. She knew the leaves were dancing and clapping to encourage her.

A small space about her became solid and recognizable. In that space objects and people were always the same. There were two nurses who were quite distinct to her now whereas, before, there seemed to have been fifty different faces under starched caps and shapes in blue dresses and white aprons. Both were young and pretty: she liked one and feared the other. The one she liked had red hair and green eyes; the other was blue-eyed and fair. Once, when they were making up the manger bed, she heard them address each other as 'Smith' and 'Jones'. The red-haired one was Jones. She must try and remember that.

It was extraordinarily difficult to remember things. Words like 'before' and 'after' no longer had any meaning. There was only 'now'. Very occasionally there was a tiny thread of continuity, such as walking to the fire and being dragged away from it. But it always snapped off short and she would find herself in the middle of doing something without any idea how she had come to be doing it. Once she found herself standing on a rostrum in a room full of desks. At every desk a young man was sitting, with a notebook open in front of him. Beside her stood an elderly man with a beard, writing something on a blackboard. She snatched up a piece of chalk from the table in front of her and threw it at one of the young men. He laughed. Gradually all the rest of them began to laugh too and she joined in. The man at the blackboard turned round and said:

'That's enough, gentlemen. However, you have now

observed that this patient's reactions are entirely different from those of the typical melancholic you saw a few minutes ago.'

Often she found herself in a long tiled washroom with a row of basins at which other women were washing themselves. On the other side of the washroom was a row of lavatories unlike any she had ever seen. They had no doors to them and, instead of a chain, a thick brass rod hung down from the cistern. She so often found herself in this place that she came to recognize some of the other women who used it. Nearly all of them were middle-aged or old. Stripped to the waist, their shrivelled or pendulous breasts repelled her. But there was one quite young with a milk-white skin and firm round breasts. Clara always tried to take the basin next to the white-skinned girl. Sometimes they smiled at each other. Occasionally the girl gave a peculiar look and said, as if she were telling a secret:

'We're going to have lots of little sunny breezes today. And lovely sunny weather.'

She never said anything else.

One day, in the washroom, a shaft of tempered sunlight came in through a high barred window at one end. There was a tree beyond the window, so that the light was tinged with green. The girl was standing full in the shaft so that her torso looked almost translucent. It was no longer white but touched with faint rose and green reflections and dappled with moving shadows of leaves. Clara stared entranced at this beauty. It reminded her of something. She said:

'You look exactly like a Renoir.'

The girl gave her a suspicious glance. For a moment, Clara thought she was going to be angry. But immediately she gave her usual smile and said confidingly:

'We're going to have *lots* of little sunny breezes . . .'

Another thing that recurred was finding herself sitting up in the manger bed with a plate of food balanced on her knees. The food looked strangely unreal, like the painted cardboard food in dolls' teasets. The knives were blunt, too, like doll's knives. She usually ate the unreal, completely tasteless food because she wanted to see the pattern on the plates. She could see all the printed letters round the rim now. They read NAZARETH ROYAL

HOSPITAL. When the centre of the plate was visible, it showed a picture of a rather handsome building with a pillared portico and a dome. The dome was like some dome she had seen before, but much more slender. She puzzled a great deal about the words and the picture. What and where could this hospital be? And why was she in it? One day it occurred to her that Nazareth was a misprint for Lazarus. Hadn't there been something called a Lazar House? Wasn't a Lazar House a place where lepers were segregated? But how could she have caught leprosy? Her mind became muddled and she gave up the effort to think.

Two things made it very hard to think consecutively. One was that, though she could now recognize certain sections of the place she was in, there was no way of connecting them together. They were like islands with a blank, featureless stretch of sea between them. How did one get from one to the other? It was the same with people; Smith, Jones and 'Sunny Breezes' materialized and dematerialized. What happened to them in between? Even more confusing was the impossibility of establishing any sequence in time. For time behaved in the most extraordinary way. Sometimes it went at a tremendous pace, as when she saw the leaves of the creeper unfurl before her eyes like a slow motion film, or the nurses, instead of walking along the passage, sped by as fast as cars. Yet, often, it seemed to take several hours to lift a spoon from her plate to her mouth.

Nevertheless, she continued to try desperately to piece things together, to find some connection between Clare *here* and Clara *there*. She was becoming slowly convinced that this extraordinary place not only existed but existed somewhere in the world she had once inhabited.

One day she was looking beyond the open door through the window when a bright idea struck her. Why had she never realized it before? She was in Looking-glass Land. Of course everything was peculiar. Of course time behaved in this extraordinary way. She was so delighted at this discovery that she laughed out loud. At that moment Jones appeared in the open doorway. Jones said, smiling:

'You seem very cheery all of a sudden. That's a nice change. Going to tell me the joke?'

'I've discovered where I am. In the Looking-glass.'

'There's no looking-glasses in this ward, dear.'

'I mean I've gone through. I'm like Alice Through the Looking-glass.'

'Who's she when she's at home?'

'A girl in a book. Not me. I'm Clara.'

The red-haired nurse looked very pleased.

'Well, did you ever? You *are* coming on. Doctor B. will be ever so bucked. Ta-ta for now.'

She smiled and hurried away. Later she came back with a bundle of old magazines.

'It was you mentioning books. Thought you might like to look at 'em to pass the time. They're old ones, so it doesn't matter if you mess them up.'

Clara was very grateful for the magazines. She turned the pages and looked at the pictures. They reminded her of the other life. But soon they began to make her unhappy and confused. In one was a photograph of a dark, handsome young man in uniform who seemed to stare at her challengingly and ask: 'Now who am I like?' She threw that magazine on the floor and picked up one called *Punch*. She read some of the words under the pictures but they did not seem to make much sense. Suddenly she noticed something extraordinary . . . the date of the magazine. It was January 4th 1922. Another of those bright flashes came into her head. She was quite sure the year in the other life was 1921. If this place was in the same world, it should be 1921 here too. But Jones had said these were *old* magazines. Was it a misprint? Then she grasped it. Here – in Looking-glass Land – one could read things before they were written. Excitedly, she picked up the *Punch* again. Under a drawing she read:

Butler. I'm afraid I shall 'ave to give notice, my Lady. Roulette and chemaing-de-fur I 'ave countenanced, but I cannot bear to see your guests stoopin' to 'put-and-take', which I understand is all the rage of the lower classes.

Of course she could not understand the meaning of such

words as 'chemaing-de-fur' and 'put-and-take'. They belonged to the language of the future. Exhausted by her discoveries and by the effort of reading, she fell asleep.

She often stood up in the manger and looked out into the garden where the nurses and the women walked. They looked more like real people now. She came to recognize some of the women, especially one with a swarthy, cheerful face and a mass of short frizzy hair, who sometimes waved to her as she passed. One day, Jones came in and caught her waving back. Clara cowered down, terrified that this would mean some new punishment. But Jones only said:

'Keep on like this and we'll be getting *you* out in the garden one of these days.'

The cell door was open all day now and only locked at night. Clara guessed now what the big keys that hung on Smith's waistbelt were for. At night she could hear the sound of grinding locks approaching all down the passage, sometimes followed by screams and the sound of fists beating on wood. One night, Smith came in looking cross and dishevelled. Clara implored:

'Please don't lock me in. I promise not to get out. *Please* . . .' She put out her hand and touched the key.

Smith said furiously:

'None of that, my lady. I've had enough trouble with you bitches for one day.'

She rapped Clara hard on the knuckles with the great key. Clara cried out and pressed her hurt hand to her mouth.

'Oh God,' said Smith. 'Now I suppose you'll split on me.'

Clara looked at her and saw that Smith's pert, pink and white face was frightened as well as angry. She said:

'I won't. I'll tell Jones I banged it on the door. People do bang on these doors.'

Smith looked relieved.

'You've more sense than some of them,' she said, as she went out. Clara fancied she locked the door less fiercely than usual.

One day, Smith and Jones came in carrying some clothes over their arms.

'Come on, Clara, we're going to dress you.'

It felt very strange having clothes put on her. Stranger still, she seemed to recognize some of the clothes. There was a dark blue dress she was sure she had seen before. It hung on her thin body like a tent. She said:

'Where's the belt? It had a red belt.'

'Well, it hasn't got one now,' said Smith.

'But it *must* have some kind of belt. Look how loose it is.'

'Miss Particular, aren't we, all of a sudden?'

Jones said kindly:

'Don't worry, dear. No one'll notice. None of the other ladies have belts either.'

'You and Smith have belts.'

'That's enough of that. And we're *Nurse* Smith and *Nurse* Jones to you.'

Jones said:

'Oh, Smithy, stop narking at her. Put your coat on, Clara dear. Look . . . a nice new coat.'

Clara frowned.

'It's not my coat. I had a fur coat once.'

Smith began to giggle.

'Oh, stop it, Smithy. Yes, dear, I'm sure you had. But it's too warm to wear it today. It's a lovely spring afternoon.'

Clara put on the unfamiliar beige coat. Jones ran a comb through her hair.

'Lovely natural waves, you've got,' she said kindly.

'Have I?'

'Yes, dear. Lucky you're a real blonde. You can't fool us with peroxide here. There. You look quite sweet.'

'Almost human, if you didn't know,' Smith said it under her breath, but Clara heard. She asked:

'Jones . . . I mean *Nurse* Jones . . . have I got leprosy?'

'Leprosy? What an idea! Of course not.'

'Or . . . or small-pox?'

'Whatever next?'

'Promise?'

'I'll prove it.' She bent forward and gave Clara a quick kiss. 'There!'

'You make me sick sometimes, Jones,' said Smith. 'What's the good of being soft with them? Only leads to trouble.'

Her legs were so weak that they had to support her, one on each side. They took her along the corridor, through the hall-like space where the grate was empty now, and out through a glass-topped door. To her disappointment, Clara found herself, not in the pleasant garden she could see from the cell, but in an asphalt yard surrounded by high brick walls. On one of the walls was chalked in big, sprawling letters:

Baby
Blood
Murder

There was no green in the yard except a trampled patch of grass in the middle, surrounding a plane tree whose buds were barely visible. Under the tree was a broken bench. Smith and Jones led her to the bench and sat one each side. Clara no longer wanted to talk. She was watching the other women walking round the asphalt yard, all in charge of nurses. She recognized some she had seen in the washroom. 'Sunny Breezes' was there. She stood out from the others because she looked like a neat schoolgirl with her plaited hair and her trim dark blue coat. She walked with precision, as if at the head of the drill file, whereas the others loped or shambled. There were two faces she had not seen before. They were both terrifying. One belonged to an elderly woman who wore a hat and a tweed coat and skirt. It could hardly be called a face for the features were partly obliterated and the skin was red-glazed and puckered as if the flesh had been burnt away. The other face was that of a monster, half-human, half-animal. The human part was almost classically beautiful with a broad forehead under wiry black curls and great eyes that seemed to be carved out of green stone. But the mouth was hideously deformed. Two long yellow eye-teeth grew down over the lower lip, like the fangs of an old tiger. Suddenly, the creature, who was tall and strongly-built, caught sight of Clara and made a dash for her. Her nurses ran and pulled her back, but not before she had cuffed one and torn the other's cap off.

Smith said:

'That Micky playing up again. Bet she'll have to go back to pads.'

Clara cowered against Jones's shoulder. Then she noticed something that made her forget her fear. Beyond one wall, she could see a high, slender dome like the one on the plates. There was a gilt spearhead at the apex that glittered in the sun. At the same moment, she heard the sound of a motor horn beyond the walls. Something stirred in her mind. That car belonged to someone called Richard. He was looking for her, to carry her away from this dreadful place. But how could she let him know that she was so near, on the other side of the wall? She called despairingly: 'Richard . . . I'm here . . . I'm here.'

'Stop that now,' said Smith.

The asphalt yard became another fixed point in her life. She learnt to associate it with the ringing of a bell and a voice calling: 'Ladies for the garden, please.' She joined the sad procession that trailed round and round the patch with the plane tree. Smith and Jones no longer held her arms: sometimes they let her walk alone. She liked this, for she could snatch a blade of grass as she passed. She knew now that it was useless to hope anything from the motor horns. He would never be allowed to pass through the walls. But he might have found another way to communicate with her. In the lines ruled on a blade of grass there might be a message, if she could only decipher it.

She spent much of her time wearing ordinary clothes now. They did not seem to mind if she wandered up and down the passage and even looked through the open doors of other cells. What strange-looking people there were in them. There was one who fascinated her. She was an old lady who wore very elaborate white draperies and a strange headdress like the Duchess's in Alice in Wonderland. The walls of her cell were covered with water-colours of garden scenes. The old lady was often standing at a small easel, painting. She took no notice of Clara until, one day, she said rather severely:

'You should curtsy to me, you know.'

Clara curtsied obediently. It seemed quite natural to do so. This person so obviously belonged to Looking-glass Land.

'That's better,' said the old lady more agreeably. 'I see you are quite intelligent. You know a queen when you see one.'

'I wasn't sure if you were a queen or a duchess.'

'I am here incognito, of course. Just until my lawsuit is settled. My solicitors think it is safer for me. I have so many enemies who wish to defraud me of my rights. Of course I cannot mix with most of the people here. I am used to intelligent society.'

After that Clara always curtsied when she passed the old lady's cell, whether the occupant acknowledged her existence or not.

Chapter Four

One day, she woke to find herself in entirely new surroundings. She was lying, not in the manger but in a real bed . . . an ordinary iron bedstead that had not only blankets but coarse sheets. She stared about her in delight. It was almost like being in a tiny bedroom in the other world. The walls were painted blue and on them hung a small mirror. The floor was of stained boards and had a narrow strip of carpet on it. Best of all, there was a handle on the door. She got out of bed excitedly and put on her clothes which were lying neatly folded on a chair. It worried her more than ever that her dress had no belt. She thought of tying a stocking round her waist and then realized it would look even more absurd to go about wearing only one stocking than a loose-hanging dress. That was the sort of slovenly thing those dreadful women in the yard did. At all costs she must avoid looking like them. By the window (it was barred, but it looked otherwise like an ordinary window and gave out on the familiar garden) was a small low cupboard on which lay a brush and comb. The brush and comb were marked 'Hughes-Follett'. Since they obviously did not belong to her, she wondered if she dared to use them. But she had such a desire to make herself as neat as possible in honour of this wonderful room that she went to the mirror and began to brush and comb her hair. The face it reflected reminded her strongly of someone she knew, someone who might even once have been herself. The hair was thick and golden and wavy. It seemed more familiar than the face. She went on brushing it till it shone, trying to get used to this rather odd-looking face with the sharp, pointed chin and the neck that showed the collar-bones. The lips were almost as pale as the cheeks. In spite of its haggardness the face seemed strangely young, almost like a child's.

The door opened and a nurse whom Clara had never seen came in. She was fat and middle-aged, with a severe expression. Clara guiltily dropped the brush.

'So you've got yourself up and dressed, have you?' said the nurse. 'Actually brushing your hair too. Good.'

'I'm sorry I used this brush,' Clara stammered. 'You see I haven't one of my own.'

'They're yours, all right. Can't you read?'

Some instinct warned Clara to make no comment. She said humbly:

'What a lovely room. May I really stay in it?'

'As long as you behave yourself, yes. Now, do you think you can keep it tidy?'

'Oh yes,' said Clara eagerly.

'Hmm. When I come back, let me see if you know how to make a bed.'

The nurse went out. At first the task seemed impossible. The sheets and blankets tangled themselves into a shapeless mess. But she persevered with desperate concentration. Suddenly she remembered how one made a bed. She smoothed and tucked and folded slowly, but competently. Somewhere, a long time ago, she had done this every morning for critical eyes. She remembered a long row of white-curtained cubicles, and children in blue uniforms and black aprons making beds. The door clicked open with a sound so much like that of a nun's wooden 'signal' that she turned and said, without thinking:

'Are my corners all right today, Mother?'

The woman facing her wore, not a black habit but a nurse's uniform. She examined the bed.

'You've done that very nicely, Clara,' she said. 'You could give some of my nurses points. Your mother certainly taught you how to make a bed properly. But I'm not your mother, you know. I'm Sister Ware. Try and remember that.'

'Yes, Sister Ware.'

The room brought very definite changes in her life. Instead of having plates of food brought to her, she had her meals with other women at a long table in a big, bare dining-room. These women did not look so shabby and forlorn as the ones in the asphalt yard. When she tried to talk to them they answered, often very politely, but entirely at cross-purposes. The asphalt yard had vanished too, along with Smith and Jones and Micky and the woman with the burned face. She was sorry never to see Jones now. She did not like Sister Ware, though she made great efforts to please her. But there were conpensations. She did at last find herself in the real garden. It was summer there. Flowers were coming out; peonies and irises. There were daisies in the grass. No one seemed to mind if she wandered off by herself, provided she joined the line of other women when the bell rang. There were still gaps in time she could not account for but the recognizable islands had grown much larger.

One day, the door of her room opened and Sister Ware came in followed by a young man in a white jacket. Clara gave a start of terror when she saw his face. It was the young man who used to come in with the funnel and the basin.

'Now, don't be frightened, Clara,' he said. 'I see you recognize me.'

She asked miserably:

'Is that going to begin again?'

'No, no, no. Not as long as you go on being so good. Sister Ware's very pleased with you. I just thought I'd drop in for a little chat. How nice and tidy your room is. Do you keep it tidy yourself?'

Sister Ware said:

'Yes, she does. Mislays her things sometimes, but pretty fair considering. She's improved a lot in Ward C.'

'How would you like to have something to do? Some knitting, for example?'

'I don't know how to knit.'

Sister Ware looked disapproving.

'I'm told you used to be very fond of reading. Would you like some nice books?'

'Thank you very much,' said Clara meekly.

'How are you getting on with the other ladies? Made any friends?'

'I don't know what to talk to them about. They don't answer what I say.'

'Dear, dear, that's very rude of them. Well, now is there anything you feel you *would* like?'

He looked so amiable that she faltered bravely:

'I couldn't go away from here, could I?'

'What, away from your nice room and Sister Ware? Don't you like it here?'

'I don't know,' she said dully. She saw Sister Ware frowning and added hastily: 'I mean, yes. It's very nice.'

The young man said cheerfully:

'You'll see it can be nicer still if you go on being good. Lots of people would rather be here than anywhere else. We have good fun sometimes. Concerts, you know. And twice a year we have a dance. I bet you dance well. I'll book you as a partner for the next one. Doctor Bennett, my name is. Cheerio for now.'

Sister Ware prompted reproachfully:

'Say, Goodbye, Doctor.'

'Goodbye, Doctor.'

When they had gone, she sat for a long time on her bed, trying to puzzle things out. Later, Sister Ware returned with a book.

'Don't read it all at once. You can't have another till next week.'

The book was by someone called Dornford Yates. She began to read it without much enjoyment. But, as she was reading, a wonderful idea came to her. The next time Sister Ware came in, she said daringly:

'I suppose I couldn't have a pencil and some paper, could I?'

'I'll have to ask doctor about that.'

'Please . . . he did ask me if there was anything I would like.'

'Give some people an inch and they take an ell,' said Sister Ware crossly. 'You'll be asking for the moon next, I suppose.' She went out, banging the door behind her.

Clara could not help crying a little. But, for the next few days, she made tremendous efforts to be 'good'. She noticed that some of the other women helped the nurses clear away the plates at mealtimes and she imitated them. The nurses seemed pleased. She heard one say to another 'H.F.'s coming on. She'll settle down all right.'

She made more effort to talk to the other women. She was beginning to feel cut off and lonely. She noticed some of them giggled and chattered together quite happily. But, when she listened in to their conversations, they sounded almost meaningless. It was like listening to children talking. Each seemed to be talking aloud to herself and taking no notice of what the others said. Yet they seemed to have some sort of communication with each other. She began to wonder what was the difference between the women and the nurses. The nurses' chat was dull but easy to follow. And their faces looked different. There was something odd about the women's faces even though some of them were quite good-looking and had powdered cheeks and carefully arranged hair. It was something about their eyes, she decided. They had a sly, shallow look and they were always straying restlessly as if looking for something or someone. She wished she could find out what secret they all had in common and which she seemed unable to share. One afternoon, in the garden, she discovered what it was. Three of them came up to her, looking sly but friendly. One asked, with a giggle:

'Do you play croquet, dear?'

With astonishing confidence, Clara answered:

'Yes.'

'Come on . . . we'll have a lovely game.'

She went with them to a lawn she had not seen before. As soon as she saw the wide, bent hoops, she knew they were the wrong shape. The hoops at Paget's Fold were straight and narrow. Someone gave her an old mallet. She said firmly to the woman nearest her:

'You and I will be partners. Shall we take blue and black?'

'I'd rather be red.'

'All right, we'll take red and yellow.'

'No, dear. You have blue and I'll have red. I always have red. Up the rebels!'

In vain Clara tried to explain the rules of croquet. They had come back with absolute clarity. But it was hopeless. No one could understand. In the end she left them running gaily about the lawn, hitting any ball they saw and usually all playing at once.

Her first thought was: 'Alice in Wonderland again. They might as well play with hedgehogs and flamingoes.' But the next moment, it came to her. These women were mad. All those women she saw at mealtimes were mad. No wonder she could make no contact with them. She was imprisoned in a place full of mad people.

She controlled her impulse to break into panic-stricken tears. She must think with all her might. She sat down on the grass frowning with the effort. Croquet. A place called Paget's Fold. Who was it she used to play croquet with there? Her *father*! She could not remember when she had last thought about him. Perhaps he was still there in the world beyond the walls. How, how could she let him know where she was, since she did not know herself?

She stood up and began to pace up and down a path, not looking where she was going. Someone bumped into her.

'Hullo, all on your lonesome?'

It was Doctor Bennett.

'Yes. I was thinking.'

'Were you now? And what were you thinking about?'

She was going to say 'My father' but one had to be careful here. She smiled and said:

'Did Sister Ware ask you if I could have that pencil and paper?'

'So we'd like a pencil and paper? I daresay it might be managed. May one ask what you want to do with it?'

She said cautiously:

'Can people send letters from here?'

He gave her a considering look.

'Well, that depends. Who were you thinking of writing to?'

She decided to risk it.

'My father,' she said.

'Well, well. And who is your father?'

It came to her as clearly as if she were reading it off his white coat.

'Claude Batchelor, 22 Valetta Road, W.14.'

He asked gently:

'How long have you known that?'

'I've just remembered it.' With sudden despondence, she added:

'Perhaps he's dead.'

'No, Clara. He's not dead.'

'How do you know?' she asked, suspiciously.

'You must take my word for it. Come, come, we aren't enemies, you know. Would you like to write your father a note?'

She shook her head and began to cry a little.

'I haven't a stamp . . . And where could I post it?'

'Now, now we're not going to be silly and cry, are we? I'll give you some paper and a pencil and a stamped envelope. You can come with me and I'll give you them now. I'm trusting you and you must trust me. If you write a nice, tidy letter, I'll see that it's posted.'

She looked at his finger and saw he was wearing the signet ring, not the white shield with the red cross.

She said hesitantly:

'Very well. I'll trust you.'

He took her into a room with a desk in it. Out of the desk-drawer he took three sheets of paper, a pencil and a stamped envelope.

'Now mind. If you spoil that envelope, you won't get another. And if you break the pencil, no one will give you a knife to sharpen it.'

'Sister Ware . . . Suppose she thinks I've stolen them?'

'I'll fix Sister Ware. Come on, I'll take you back to your room.'

She could hardly wait to be left alone with her treasures. As soon as the door closed, she sat down, put a sheet of paper on the flat top of the cupboard and tried to write. But she had forgotten how to make letters. She took the Dornford Yates novel and began laboriously copying the print. It looked all wrong. She

464

took another sheet, started at the left and tried to write cursively. But she could not do it. Then she realized her mistake. She was trying to write the wrong way round. In Looking-glass Land one must use looking-glass writing. She began again at the right hand side and wrote backwards, reversing the letters. Her hand moved quickly and easily. She wrote a few sentences and held them up to the mirror on the wall. The writing was a little shaky but perfectly legible. Then it occurred to her that her father was on the other side of the looking-glass. It would be more sensible to write the way they did there.

She sat down again and stared at the third and last precious sheet. With a great effort she made her hand begin at the left. It was extraordinarily difficult to make the letters go that way. But she persevered, using all the concentration she could muster. Though it became a little easier after the first few words, she was tempted again and again to give up the task as hopeless. But, at last, she got to the end and read it through.

> 'Dearest Daddy,
>   I do not know where I am but I think it is Nazareth Royal Hospital. That is what it says on the plates. Please try and find me. I want so much to see you again. Please try hard. Perhaps you thought I was dead. I am alive but in a very strange place. Doctor Bennett (?) has promised to post this.
>   Your loving daughter,
>   Clara.'

She sealed the envelope, addressed it carefully, and put the letter under her pillow. That night she could hardly sleep for fear the doctor should forget his promise.

In the morning he came in while she was still in bed. But someone else came in with him; an elderly man with a beard. Clara looked at the stranger and said:

'I've seen you before, I think.'

'Have you indeed?' said the bearded man. 'And where was that?'

'On a rostrum. Writing things on a blackboard.'

The two men exchanged glances.

'Quite right,' said the one with the beard. 'My name is Doctor Brooke. We shall meet again. I've only come in to say goodbye. I'm going away on a holiday.'

'Oh, you're *lucky*,' she said, before she could stop herself.

He frowned, but he did not seem angry.

'Well, one never knows. Now I want you to be a very good girl while I'm away. You must do everything Doctor Bennett says.'

She nodded gravely. They were moving towards the door. The bearded doctor had already gone out. She looked imploringly at Doctor Bennett. He had not said a word. Had he forgotten? Suddenly, he smiled: 'Well, Clara, how about that letter?'

She snatched it from under the pillow and held it out to him. He scrutinized it carefully.

'Very nice . . . very nice indeed. I'll see that it goes.'

As he went out, she heard him say:

'Just look at this, sir . . . Pretty good, eh? When you thought she'd never . . .'

The door closed before she could hear the rest. What . . . oh what was it that they thought she would never do?

Chapter Five

Claude Batchelor walked down the brick path to meet the postman at the gate as he did every morning since he and Isabel had come down to Paget's Fold. They had been there for nearly a fortnight but, every single day, he had to fight down the memory of this time last year when Clara had been with them. He had grown used to her absence from Valetta Road. But here, where there was no work to distract him and where everything reminded him of their happiest days, the dull, accustomed ache flared up once more into anguish. Though the aunts were kinder than ever, their careful avoidance of Clara's name only made him more conscious of her absence. He longed for this travesty of a holiday to be over

466

so that he could resume those fruitless Sunday visits to the asylum.

It was months since they had let him see her. As Doctor Brooke had foretold, that Sunday in April, she was, in many ways, much better. When the new phase was 'established', when she had settled into that twilight state that might go on till she was as old as he was now, they would let him see her again. Meanwhile they feared that, precisely because she might recognize him, it might over-excite her and bring on a relapse into the violence and delusions of the first attack. Though he could not see her, those visits to Nazareth brought him a faint consolation. At least, for a little while, he was under the same roof as Clara. Somewhere, in the dreary hinterland behind that ironically splendid façade, some part of her lived on. Taking down changes of clothes for her, though it tore his heart, reminded him at least that she still inhabited the same world. The red belt they had made him take back was still hidden in a drawer of his desk. He had not told Isabel that belts and cords were forbidden, any more than that the pretty, flimsy nightdresses it comforted her to make never reached Clara. There was a little pile of them locked away, along with a hand mirror and three bottles of scent, in a cupboard to which only he had the key. For Isabel seemed almost to have convinced herself that Clara was suffering from some physical illness and he could not bear to remind her of the truth.

The morning walk to the gate to meet the postman had become a kind of substitute for the Sunday visits. There was always a chance there might be a note from Brooke or Bennett with the news of some slight change in her condition or a request to bring something for her next time he came. He had left them his holiday address, though they had assured him they were unlikely to need it as he would only be away three weeks.

On this brilliant August morning, the postman was later than usual. Isabel called from the window:

'Dearest . . . your breakfast's getting cold.'

He was on the point of turning back to go indoors when he

saw the postman coming across the green. He held out only one letter. It was the wrong shape for the Nazareth envelopes. Claude took it half-heartedly, merely noting it was something re-addressed from London in his mother's writing. When he glanced at it again, his hand shook so much that he could hardly tear it open. He took out a folded sheet. At first the writing jigged so wildly before his staring eyes that he could not read the words. When he had managed to read them, and take them in, he cried out:

'Isabel . . . Isabel . . . come here at once.'

She came running down the brick path.

'Dearest . . . what is it?'

'You'll never guess . . . Tell me I'm not dreaming . . . This letter . . .'

'It's not? . . . But it *is* . . . It's from Clara.'

'From Clara herself . . . Look, dearest . . . Perfectly clear . . . perfectly reasonable . . . Even the doctor's name . . . Yes, dear child . . . quite right . . .' He became incoherent in his joy. They clung together, half laughing, half crying.

'I must go up to London at once,' he said. 'This very moment. They *must* let me see her after this . . . They might even . . . No . . . I must be reasonable . . . Oh, Isabel, was there ever such a glorious morning?'

She kissed him.

'I always knew she'd get better.'

'We mustn't hope too much . . . But, oh, I can't *help* hoping . . .'

It was she who made him come in and eat some breakfast, reminding him that there was no train from Bellhurst for another two hours. He could hardly eat in his excitement. He called the aunts to hear the news. They put on their steel-rimmed spectacles and read the letter, looking a little dazed.

'Her writing was always so clear,' said Aunt Sophy. 'I could almost read it without my spectacles. It hasn't changed.'

Her faded blue eyes brimmed over.

Aunt Leah said tremulously:

'Now, Sophy, dear . . . This is good news, you know . . .'

But when the first exultation had died down, Claude's face clouded over.

'Shall we take a turn round the garden, Isabel? There's plenty of time before I need leave. I want your advice.'

They walked up the grass path towards the orchard.

'Why are you looking so worried, Claude? After this wonderful, wonderful sign . . . If she's well enough to write a letter . . .'

'I know . . . I know. The doctors never hinted at such an improvement as that . . .'

'Then why do you sigh like that? When she's remembered you of her own accord. When she longs to *see* you . . .'

'If they let me see her . . .'

'They wouldn't be so heartless as to stop you – Surely . . . now that her memory's obviously coming back . . .'

'That's just it, Isabel. How much does she remember?'

'She doesn't want to see *me* . . . perhaps it's only the first glimmerings . . . Even so, oh, Claude . . . if there'd been just one word.'

He put his arm round her.

'I know how you must feel, my dear. But perhaps the less she remembers the better.'

'Even her own mother? Oh, Claude, why?'

'Dearest . . . mightn't every memory make her suffer more? I was too overjoyed at first to think what this might mean to her. Suppose she asks me today to take her home? How can I bring myself to tell her it's impossible?'

'It will be possible one day. Perhaps quite soon. I *know* she's going to get well.'

'Isabel . . . we *daren't* hope . . . How can I help being obsessed with the same idea? . . . But we mustn't let ourselves . . .'

'*I've* never given up hope. I've always believed – like Richard – that she'd recover. Recover completely.'

'Richard,' he said heavily. 'That's what's troubling me most of all. Suppose she asks about *him* . . . wants to see him, even?'

'Poor darling child . . . You can only say he loves her and that, as soon as she's better . . . Why . . . it might be just the incentive she needs to get completely well . . .'

'Isabel,' he said slowly. 'Supposing I'm not justified in saying that . . . We haven't seen Richard for a long time . . .'

She stared at him.

'What do you mean? It's true he hasn't written . . . But he never did write. He always came to see us when he was on leave from Plymouth. The regiment may have gone back to Ireland . . . abroad even. I agree he ought to have let us know.'

He said, more slowly still:

'He's still at Plymouth. I heard from him about three weeks ago.'

'You never told me.'

'I didn't want to upset you.'

'Was it such a very sad letter? All the more wonderful for him when he hears *this*. I'll write as soon as you've gone . . . No, before . . . You can post the letter in London. It'll get there sooner.'

'Wait, Isabel. There's something I have to tell you about Richard. I'm afraid it will come as a great shock.'

He told his story quietly, calming her fierce, incredulous interruptions. When he had finished, she was in angry tears.

'I can't believe it,' she sobbed. 'Of him . . . Or of you. He *did* love her . . . If you hadn't dashed all his hopes. What *right* had you? . . . Why, here, in this very orchard . . . The little larch tree he brought from his home and planted for her . . . Only this very spring.'

'Dearest, I implore you . . . I *had* to tell him what I believed to be the truth. What else, in fairness, could I do?'

'He shouldn't have believed you. Even if he did . . . how *could* he go back to this girl as if Clara had never existed? . . . I wonder the creature herself hadn't more pride than to take him . . . Perhaps he never even told her . . . Of course he didn't . . . The coward . . . the liar. Oh, what a fool I've been. *You're* not to blame. He's rotten to the core.'

'Isabel, you're far too harsh. Richard's neither a coward nor a liar. He did tell her. What's more he told her, just as he told me, that he could never feel for anyone again as he felt for Clara.'

'She must be despicable too. Snatching up another girl's leavings . . .'

'Isabel . . . Isabel . . . She'd cared for him long before . . . She put his happiness before hers. Because he loved Clara, she wanted her to recover . . . Yes . . . to marry him.'

'No doubt she *said* so. Clever minx. Was he so blind as not to see through that? Oh, the weak-minded *fool*. Thank heavens, he'll suffer too. He's got the sort of wife he deserves.'

'You know nothing about her.'

'Don't tell me you've met her . . . that she's taken you in too?'

'I've never met her, Isabel . . . I've known of her existence for some time. In those first terrible months, when Richard was nearly beside himself . . . when he could think of nothing but Clara . . . he said he seemed to bring nothing but misery wherever he went . . . But, as long as there was any hope of Clara's recovery . . . Isabel . . . I know that girl's sincere . . . She's a Catholic . . . She made a pilgrimage to Lourdes to pray that Clara might be cured . . . Cured to marry the man she loved herself.'

'Very saintly, no doubt,' said Isabel with scorn. 'Pity she couldn't wait to see whether her prayers were answered. Or that *he* couldn't.'

'My dear . . . have any of us as much faith . . . or strength . . . as we'd like to have? I didn't know about it at the time . . . it was long ago, when the delusions were at their worst. If I *had* known . . . and month after month had gone by with no sign of Clara's getting better . . . would I still have expected a miracle? As for Richard . . . he wasn't a Catholic . . . He'd hoped against hope for a natural recovery. But after that dreadful Sunday night . . .'

She said, still with bitterness, but more calmly:

'I went on hoping. Mothers are more faithful than lovers. After all *she's* suffered . . .' Her eyes filled again. 'Oh what a cruel world for her to come back to . . .'

He took her in his arms.

'My dearest . . . I can hardly bear to remind you . . . But it may be a long, long time before there is any question of her coming back.'

Chapter Six

Ever since she had given Doctor Bennett the letter, Clara had realized that it was of the utmost importance to hold on to her new awareness. There was the possibility that her father might write back. It would be unendurable if a letter came during one of her blank spells. She might lose it or never even know it had come.

By forcing herself to attend vigilantly to every detail, she managed to piece together the run of a whole day without once finding herself unable to account for how she came to be in a particular place or doing a particular thing. By the time she had done this for four successive days, it had become habitual. This awareness brought perplexities of a new kind. For one thing, she had never realized how long and monotonous a day could be. Now, when she woke, she knew what the routine would be . . . tidying her room, wandering about the ward outside, turning over magazines, lining up with the other women waiting for the bell and the call of 'Ladies for the garden'. At mealtimes she listened to the bird-like, meaningless twitter, feeling more and more isolated. If, for some reason, she was condemned to live among mad women, would it not be wiser to try and enter into their world? She began to study them, not only what they said, but their glances and gestures. If she learnt their language, she could make some kind of contact to appease her loneliness. Some of them seemed ready enough to be friendly. Alone in her room she began to imitate certain gestures they repeated, their darting looks, their irrelevant scowls and giggles. Soon, she saw how much easier it would be to slip into their ways than to keep up this tremendous effort of piecing things together in logical sequence.

Trying out these looks and gestures was rather soothing; it dulled the new sharp edge of her mind, as if she were a little drunk. If there were no sign from her father, why not gently relapse to a state where no more effort was needed? She felt she could easily become so like the rest that she would not even have to make the effort of acting.

Four endless days and not a sign. If only she knew what day of the week she had given Doctor Bennett the letter. But how could one know what any day was here? She did not even know the month, except that it was high summer . . . July or possibly August. There was nothing to distinguish one day from another. Not knowing where she had started was like sewing with an unknotted thread. Suppose she assumed that the first day had been Saturday? The fourth day would have been the first when she could hope for any reply. The fifth day passed, more slowly and wearily than any of the others. Agonizing doubts began to assail her. He had received her letter but he could not find her. No one was allowed to know where Nazareth Royal Hospital was. Doctor Bennett had forgotten to post the letter. Worst of all, he had never meant to post it. The whole thing had been a cruel trick. She became more and more convinced that this was the real explanation.

It was on the afternoon of the sixth day, as she was lining up for the garden file, that she saw Doctor Bennett appear from a door in the passage. He smiled and beckoned to her but she pretended not to notice. She was not going to trust that lying smile again. He came up to her, took her arm and drew her away from the others.

'Don't look so frightened, Clara. I have a very pleasant surprise for you.'

She asked, with wild hope:

'A letter?'

'Something better than that. Come in here.'

He took her through the door from which he had appeared. Someone was standing on the far side of the room. She took one look and ran into his outstretched arms.

'Daddy . . . it's really you . . . Oh, Daddy, Daddy.'

She heard the doctor's voice say:

'I'll leave you two together. I'll be back in a quarter of an hour. Then we'll have our little talk.'

At first the two of them could only look at each other, then kiss and laugh and kiss again. It was Clara who recovered her sobriety first.

'Then you *did* get my letter?'

'Indeed I did, dearest child. I couldn't believe my eyes – It reached me at Paget's Fold this morning. I came up straight away . . .'

'Paget's Fold . . . I never thought of that . . . is it the summer holidays then? What day is it today?'

'August the fourth.'

'However did you find me so quickly?'

He said, with a touch of hesitation:

'Well, my dear . . . I knew where you were.'

'You mean you've known all along?'

'Yes . . . Let's sit down, shall we? You mustn't get overtired or upset . . . You see, you've been ill.'

'But I feel perfectly well.'

'You're much much better, thank God.'

'Oh, Daddy, there are so many things I want to ask you.'

'Very well, my dear. But take it easily. What is it you want to know?'

'This place. It's a hospital, I know. But such a peculiar one. How do I come to be in it?'

'You were too ill to remember coming. My darling, you've been very ill indeed.'

'How long?'

'A long time . . . Many, many months – If you knew how wonderful it was to see you looking better! Your mother will be so happy when I tell her.'

'Mother . . . where *is* Mother?'

'Down at the cottage. We read your letter together. You can't think how excited we were to see your very own writing. She sends you her fondest love.'

'Oh, give mine to her . . . And the aunts . . . they're still alive?'

'Yes, indeed. And Granny too. She sent your letter on. She must have recognized your writing. How she must have wondered what was in the letter.'

Clara laughed.

'Poor Granny. She must have been dying to open it and see. Curiosity's her ruling passion, isn't it?'

Her father laughed too.

'Well, she likes to be in on things. And I haven't had time to tell her yet. I came straight from the station. I couldn't wait.'

'From Victoria?'

'Yes.'

She thought for a moment.

'Is this place in London?'

'Yes. Just over the river . . . on the Surrey side.'

'Have you ever been here before?'

It was his turn to look thoughtful. He said, after a pause:

'Yes, dear. Very often.'

'Have you seen me ever?'

'Sometimes, dear. You weren't always well enough to see me.'

'Funny,' she mused. 'I thought I saw *you* once. Long, long ago. When I was down in the manger. But you had a scarf I didn't know. A black and white one.'

'I have a black and white one. It was your mother's Christmas present.'

'Christmas!' she said. 'Has there been a Christmas then? Where was I at Christmas?'

'You were here, dear.'

'How extraordinary not to remember . . . Wait . . . You said it was August . . . I must have had a birthday too.'

'Yes . . . dear child.'

'How old am I now?'

'Twenty-three.'

'Twenty-three,' she said. 'Fancy being twenty-three . . . and not knowing it. How long have I been here? Oh, Daddy it seems forever. If only I could tell you the extraordinary things that have been happening . . . If only I could sort it all out . . .'

'Don't try, dear. You mustn't tire your head.'

'Have I had brain fever or something?'

'Something of the kind, yes. Try not to think about having been ill. Think about getting better.'

'Oh, Daddy . . . aren't I better enough? Can't I come home

now? I don't think I can *bear* being here any longer. Please, please take me home with you.'

He put his arms round her . . .

'Dearest, dearest child. One day, we hope . . . but the doctor thinks you're not quite well enough yet . . . There, there, don't cry . . . If you cry, the doctor will say it's bad for you to see me . . .'

She checked her tears.

'Anything but that. I'll be good. I promise I'll be good. Only don't go away and never come back.'

The door opened and the doctor came in. He had a file of papers under his arm.

'Oh, Doctor Bennett . . . please don't take him away,' she implored.

'There, there, Clara. I'm not going to take your father away. I just want to borrow him for a few minutes. Will you be a good girl and wait outside the door.'

She stood up obediently.

'Yes. But promise you won't take him away without my seeing him again?'

'I promise. And I keep my promises, don't I?'

'Yes. So far.'

It seemed hours that she waited outside. It was torture to be separated from her father by that door. At any moment the bright, empty ward would be filled again with the nurses and the crazy women. Sister Ware might pounce on her, ask her what she was doing, and send her back to her room. She might never see him again. At last, just when she had given up hope, when she could hear the approaching twitter of the procession returning from the garden, the door opened and Doctor Bennett called her in.

The first time she had gone into that room, she had been aware of nothing but her father. Now she noticed that it contained a desk with some papers strewn on it. Her father was sitting in a chair against the wall. He looked anxious, she thought. He smiled at her when she entered, but the smile seemed strained. To her dismay, the doctor did not go out and leave them alone. Instead, he sat down at the desk and motioned

Clara to take the chair on the other side. She glanced nervously from his face to her father's.

'Don't look so worried, Clara. I only want to have a little talk to you. Would you like your father to stay or to come back when we've finished?'

'Oh, stay, *please*.'

'Very well. Mr Batchelor, would you mind moving your chair farther back where she can't see you? I want her answers to be quite spontaneous.'

Doctor Bennett clasped his hands before him on the desk and leant forward, looking searchingly into Clara's face.

'Now, Clara, I'm going to ask you one or two questions. Not difficult ones . . . but I want you to think carefully before you answer.'

'Yes?'

'To begin with, you know you've been ill, don't you?'

'Yes.'

'And that when people are ill, they often have to stay in hospital quite a long time?'

'Yes.'

'Now . . . I want you to be quite frank with me . . . you're getting rather tired of being in this particular hospital, aren't you?'

'I'm afraid I am, yes,' she said cautiously.

'Can you give me any definite reason why? For example, how do you get on with the nurses?'

'Quite well, I think. If I do what I'm told.'

'How about the other patients?'

She hesitated.

'Well . . . it's rather hard to get on with *them*. I do try. But they don't seem to understand what I say. And what *they* say doesn't always make sense.'

'I see. Now, when you talk to the nurses or to me nowadays . . . do *we* seem to talk sensibly?'

'Oh, yes . . . And when I talked to Daddy . . .'

'So you feel *you're* like me and your father and the other ladies in the ward are different in some way?'

'I'm afraid I do, yes.'

'Could you tell me what you think makes them different?'

'I know what I think. But I don't like to say it.'

'Come, come . . . you can say it to *me*.'

'I'm not sure . . . I'd rather not . . . You see, you're a doctor . . .'

'What's that got to do with it? No . . . no . . . don't look round at your father . . . I'm asking you the questions.'

'Yes. But I'm so frightened of giving the wrong answers.'

He said more gently:

'Why, Clara?'

'Because I think you're trying to find out something. Whether I'm mad or not . . .' Her lips began to tremble. 'It seems to me that those women are mad . . . But people say . . . don't they? . . . They say . . .'

'Now . . . now . . . don't cry . . .'

She heard her father make an inarticulate noise but forced herself not to look round. The doctor raised his hand . . .

'It's all right, Mr Batchelor. Well, Clara? *What* do people say?'

She rallied herself.

'That mad people think everyone is mad but themselves.'

'But you've just said your father and I and the nurses seem all right. So you don't think everyone's mad.'

'No.'

He pulled a piece of paper towards him and began to write on it. There was a good deal written on it already. At the top were two words in block capitals, that were easy to read upside down.

'Hughes-Follett,' she said. 'That's my name.'

He pulled the paper nearer him.

'Yes, Clara. But it's rude to try and read what people are writing, isn't it? It might be something private.'

'I'm sorry,' she said, and stared at her hands.

After a minute or two, he spoke again.

'Clara . . . Come along, it's all right to look at *me* . . . Now how would you like to go somewhere else? A very nice place . . . out in the country?'

She burst out . . . she could not help it:

'Oh please . . . *please* mayn't I go home?'

'Well . . . not yet, I'm afraid . . . Some day not far off . . . Maybe even in six months. If you go on as well as you've been doing lately. It all depends on you.'

'. . . Six whole more *months* . . . I couldn't bear it.'

'Now, Clara, be reasonable . . . We're delighted with the progress you've made . . . But only a week or two ago, you were still far from yourself, you know. Listen, let me tell you about this place in the country. You'll have far more freedom – You can have your own books and things – they'll even let nurse take you to a cinema sometimes.'

'There'll still be nurses . . . And . . . and those women.'

'Oh, it'll all be quite different from here. A thoroughly cheery atmosphere. They play tennis – Some of them even play a remarkably good game of bridge. You'll be able to get on with *them* all right.'

She said slowly:

'That's just what I'm afraid of.'

'Now whatever do you mean by that?'

'I was beginning to here. It's so awfully lonely . . . having to be with the same people always and not being able to talk to them. They seem to understand each other in a sort of way. I've been trying to be like them . . . deliberately . . . copying their gestures . . . the sort of way they talk . . . It was beginning to work . . . And in time . . .' she glanced at him, afraid she was talking too much. But he did not look angry. Instead he prompted her:

'Go on . . . And in time . . .?'

'I might get really like them. Just from being so bored. And *stay* like them. For ever. It's so hard keeping it up all by oneself.'

There was a silence. She could see that Doctor Bennett was exchanging glances over her head with her father. She gathered a little courage.

'Please . . . please . . . if you'd let me go home . . . With ordinary things round me . . . And Daddy and Mother . . . It would be so much easier to keep things clear in my head. Why can't Daddy take me with him?'

She turned desperately round to him: 'Don't you want me home?'

'My dear . . . of course . . . of course . . .'

'Then why don't you just take me?'

'Clara . . . I can't. Not yet. I'm not allowed to.'

'Why? I'm not a prisoner, am I?'

Doctor Bennett intervened. He said softly:

'Now, Clara, don't get excited . . . Listen . . . Do you think we're keeping you here against your will?'

Something in that soft voice made her suspect a trap. She did not answer at once. This was the test question. Everything depended on how she answered it. She searched wildly for the right answer, but she perceived that either alternative was fatal. Instead of replying, she burst into tears. Her father started forward and put his arm round her.

'There . . . my dear, dear child. Try not to cry. Can't you tell *me* if you can't tell the doctor?'

'What's the good,' she sobbed. 'If I say yes, he'll think I'm mad. And if I say no, he'll think I don't want to go home.'

Through her tears, she heard Doctor Bennett say:

'You know, Mr Batchelor, that strikes me as an extraordinarily reasonable answer. I wonder if I dare . . . What do you think?'

'That's not a fair question . . . You know only too well what I think . . . what I long for you to say. But we're both entirely in your hands.'

Clara sat up, clasping her father's arm. He was there . . . he was her ally. She blinked back her tears and managed to say: 'Dearest Daddy . . . It's just as bad for you, isn't it?'

The doctor bit his fountain pen and surveyed them thoughtfully. At last he said:

'The pair of you . . . You almost convince me . . . But, no, I don't think I dare . . . After all, I'm only second-in-command . . . Dr Brooke's on holiday . . . If anything went wrong, I might be in danger of losing my job.'

'Yes . . . I understand that,' her father said. 'One couldn't expect you to take such a risk. Perhaps, you think . . . just as an experiment . . . for a few days even . . . there would be a risk for her too?'

They seemed to have forgotten Clara's presence. She listened in a mute agony of hope.

The doctor went on frowning and biting his pen. The sun flashed on his signet ring and struck coloured rays from it.

'It would be a big responsibility for you, too.'

'I'd willingly undertake that. Her mother and I . . . We wouldn't let her out of our sight.'

'Well, she's certainly improved beyond all expectation. A return to normal surroundings *might* be a good thing. But you realize there's no question of decertifying her yet. This may be only a flash in the pan. The very utmost I'm empowered to do is to let her out for a short time on parole. But Brooke will be back in a fortnight . . . Hadn't we better wait till he's had another look at her?'

Her father sighed.

'I suppose . . . If you think that best . . .'

Clara clutched his hand. She stared imploringly at the doctor but did not say a word. At last he remembered her existence and looked at her.

'And what does Clara think?'

'Oh – As if you didn't *know* . . .'

He gave her a long look. She looked back steadily, beseechingly. Suddenly he smiled.

'I'll take a chance on it. You can take her back with you to the country for a fortnight. No excitement, mind. And in bed by ten at the latest. Bring her back here at three o'clock a fortnight from today to report. I can trust you?'

'Of course . . . of course.'

'And you, Clara? You'll be a good girl and not make a fuss about coming back to see me and Doctor Brooke?'

'I promise,' she said.

He smiled and stood up, holding out his hand.

'Good. Now be off, the pair of you.'

Clara and her father blinked at each other. Her father said:

'You mean . . . we can go now . . . this minute?'

'As soon as you've signed this paper. Clara, go and ask Sister Ware for your coat. Need any other things?'

'We've everything she wants at home.'

'Good. I'm sure you don't want to hang about more than necessary. Wait a moment, Clara . . . I'd better give you a chit for Sister.' He scribbled a few lines on a piece of paper and put them in an envelope. 'Say nothing . . . just give her this. And don't say a word to any of the others. It might upset them. They're not as lucky as you.'

'Oh, poor things,' Clara said remorsefully. 'I'm so happy . . . I'd forgotten . . .'

'Well, perhaps they'll be lucky one day. See you in a fortnight.'

She had one moment of panic, back in the ward without the protection of her father and the doctor. Sister Ware looked disapproving as she read the note. She muttered under her breath:

'Hmm. Very irregular. I wonder what Dr Brooke will say to this – *I* haven't even been consulted.'

She marched off without a word to Clara and returned with the coat.

'Here,' she said ungraciously. 'Now be off with you. I don't want any other ladies upset.'

Clara put on the coat and said meekly:

'Thank you. Goodbye, Sister Ware.'

'Oh, don't think you're leaving for ever. There's many goes out on parole. I'll say orryvoir. And you'll be lucky if it *is* orryvoir. If you don't behave, I won't have you back in Ward C.'

But not even Sister Ware could spoil the joy of finding her father waiting for her in the room with the desk. They did not stop to kiss. She could feel he was frightened as she that something would happen to stop their getting away. Holding her hand tight, he hurried her so fast down staircases and along unfamiliar passages that she could hardly keep up with him. She was amazed how easily he threaded his way through the great labyrinth of a building she could never piece together. Through a window, she caught a flying glimpse of the asphalt yard with the plane tree now in full leaf. It existed then: it was not just something she had imagined. She almost wanted to stop and investigate: to try and identify other places; the washroom, the cell with the manger-bed, even the terrible room with the convex rubber walls. She longed to know what had been real and what had been dream or nightmare.

'How do you know your way so well, Daddy? I could never find mine,' she panted excitedly. 'Have you been here very often, then?'

'Almost every week, my dear. But let's forget all that now.'

Sometimes a nurse gave them a curious glance but no one stopped them till they came out into a great circular vestibule with a parquet floor and white walls garlanded with gilt mouldings. Just as they were reaching the double doors that were flung open, showing a vista of pillars and steps, a man in uniform appeared from a glass cage, demanding:

'Passes, please.'

Her father handed him two things that looked like tickets: the uniformed man scrutinized them and gave them back to him.

'Right, sir. Don't forget these when you bring her back, on the eighteenth.'

They ran down the steps hand in hand, like children escaping from school, and did not pause for breath till they reached an iron gate at the end of an avenue. Beyond it, buses and trams were racing past. Clara was nearly deafened with the noise. Her father waved his free arm shouting frantically 'Taxi! Taxi.'

One came at last. As it turned and threaded its way through the traffic, Clara looked back. There was the façade she had seen on the plates – the pillared portico and the slender dome rising behind it.

'It's beautiful from the front,' she said. 'You'd never guess from the back. No grey stone *there* . . . beastly browny-yellow brick. But, from here, it looks like some famous building, doesn't it?'

Her father said wonderingly:

'Beautiful? I suppose it is. I'm afraid I shall loathe anything Wren built to the end of my life. Here's our taxi . . . Jump in.'

As the door slammed on them, they hugged and kissed each other like reunited lovers. He was even more wildly gay than she was.

'We're free . . . We've escaped . . . Dear child . . . you'll have to

483

restrain me . . . Otherwise they'll have to put *me* away . . . My blessed, darling girl . . .'

He broke off his babble of joy for a moment as they passed a huge church:

'Look, Clara. St George's Cathedral. How often I've gone in on a Sunday after going *there* . . . I'd almost like to go in now with you. Ah, well . . . perhaps better get you straight home. It's absurd . . . I can't help feeling they're pursuing us and we shan't be safe till we're back on our own side of the Thames.'

'It might have been the other side of the *sea*. Or in another world altogether. You actually used to come there and I never knew. How often?'

'Every Sunday except these last two.'

She laughed.

'Fancy . . . just as you used to at the convent.'

'You look hardly older than you did at school.' He stroked her hair. 'Thank God, it's golden, still.'

Chapter Seven

As the taxi approached West Kensington, her father said:

'I really must collect my wits. Your Granny doesn't even know I'm in London. Let alone who's with me.'

Clara laughed.

'I say, won't Mother be jealous! To think Granny will see me before she does . . . You'll have to break it to Granny gently, I suppose . . . Look, why not stop the taxi at the end of Valetta Road? Then you can smuggle me in quietly. You know how deaf she is. Anyway, she's probably up in her room. She usually is between tea-time and dinner-time.'

'Fancy your remembering that,' he said fondly.

'Oh, things are coming back with a rush. I can't cope with them all. The old streets . . . even the colours of front doors . . . Except that it's summer now . . .' She broke off and said 'Fog . . . There was a fog . . .' She asked anxiously:

'Daddy . . . that Indian student . . . Wajid someone . . . he'd had small-pox . . . Is *he* still there?'

'No, dear, he left long ago.'

'I'm glad . . . I'd have been rather embarrassed . . . I had some sort of row with him, didn't I?'

Her father stopped the taxi.

'We're so near, we might as well get out now.'

As they turned into Valetta Road, she said:

'Daddy, I don't want Granny to see me like this. Let me go up to my room and tidy up. And change into some clothes. I won't feel really myself till I've got out of *these*. You can break it to her while I'm changing.'

Alone in her old bedroom, her first impulse was not, after all, to tear off the clothes she had worn in the asylum. She went straight to the wardrobe glass and studied her full-length reflection. *There* she had never been able to see more than her head and shoulders. She took off the hated beige coat which had never seemed to belong to her any more than the uniform brown serge dressing-gown. The old navy dress that hung so loose on the body whose thinness she approved had had its place in her real life. She felt a sudden affection for it, as if it were a loyal friend who had followed her into exile. If she could find its belt, she might even keep it on. She began to rummage through drawers in search of the scarlet belt.

She became so fascinated in discovering things she remembered and things she had forgotten she possessed that, soon, it seemed no more astonishing to be back in that room than if she had just returned from school after a particularly long and dreary term. Presently, she gave up the search for the missing belt and sat down on the bed with its faded Indian cotton bedspread. The springs sagged so violently that she realized that there was not even a mattress underneath. Then she grasped that this was a very different homecoming. Perhaps they had never expected her to return at all. She pressed her knuckles to her temples, trying to remember when she had last slept in that bed. What had she been doing before *it* happened? Who had taken her to Nazareth? She had a confused memory of driving somewhere in a taxi, wearing a fur coat over a nightdress. She brushed it aside. It was something *before* that she wanted to recover. Something desperately important in the real world . . . a *person*. Before she could recover this vital missing piece, her father knocked on the door:

'Nearly ready, dear?'

'Give me five minutes,' she called back.

She hurriedly changed into the first dress she pulled out of the wardrobe, went to the dressing table and combed her hair. Her brushes were still there; their silver backs tarnished. There was a bowl with a little powder and a worn puff still in it. She fluffed some powder over her face. It smelt delicious after the smell of hospital soap which still clung to her hands. The scent was not only delicious – it brought her so much nearer to what she was trying to track down that she could hardly bear to leave the bedroom to go downstairs.

Dinner with her father and her grandmother fell curiously flat. She managed not to comment on the fact that her grandmother was now wearing a white wig instead of the curled chestnut one she had known from childhood. After the first tearful, excited greeting, old Mrs Batchelor seemed more bewildered than happy. She kept staring at Clara and then hastily averting her eyes. Even her father seemed to be suffering from a reaction after his wild spirits of the drive home. Her grandmother did little more than keep repeating how nice it would be for Clara to get down to Paget's Fold tomorrow and that she hoped the weather would stay so wonderfully fine. Every time the maid came in, there was an awkward silence, followed by more comments on the weather, the state of the croquet lawn or the best train for them to take in the morning. On Molly's first entrance in, Clara said:

'How nice to see you again, Molly.'

The girl turned fiery red.

'Very pleased, I'm sure, Miss Clara. Such a surprise. We didn't even know the Master . . . And Cook on her holiday too . . . I hope there's enough to go round, sir. No time to make a pudding even.'

The conversation flagged so desperately that, in the effort to keep it going, Clara had to give up searching for the missing piece. She began to ask for news of people in whom she was not particularly interested, merely to prove that she remembered their existence. At each 'How is . . .?' or 'Where is . . .' she fancied her father looked apprehensive until she mentioned the name.

When she had run through various acquaintances, she remembered someone whom she really wanted to hear about.

'Goodness, I'd almost forgotten . . .' she began, then broke off: 'No, I don't suppose you'd know . . . You'd be hardly likely to have seem *him*.'

'Seen whom?' her father asked faintly. This time he looked really frightened.

'Clive Heron. I don't suppose you even remember him. You've probably forgotten his existence. I think he's only been here once.'

Her father's face relaxed as he answered volubly:

'Heron? Most certainly, I remember. Tall, thin, red-haired man in the . . . let's see . . . Home Office, wasn't it. A most amusing man . . . Very intelligent. Extraordinarily likeable chap altogether. No, my dear . . . I haven't set eyes on him. Wait now . . . I'm sure someone told me he'd rung up to enquire after you.'

'Rung up? But Clive loathes telephoning. Actually rung up *here*? . . . I can hardly believe it.'

'Not here, I think. Some mutual friend I fancy . . .'

'I wonder who. We've hardly any mutual friends . . . Let me think . . .'

Her father said hurriedly:

'I've probably got it wrong . . . Mistaken the name. So many people enquired . . . Shall we have coffee in the study?'

To her relief, her grandmother announced that she was going straight up to bed.

'I'm getting an old lady now, dear,' she said. 'I daresay you noticed my hair had gone white but were too polite to say so. You always had such nice manners, like your Daddy. At my age, even a pleasant surprise can be quite a shock. And I'm sure you and Daddy must have a lot to talk about after all this time.'

In her gratitude, Clara gave her quite a demonstrative goodnight kiss. Her grandmother's flabby cheek made her think again, as she used to as a child, that it was like kissing a poached egg.

Once she was sitting in the big green chair in the study, with her father at his usual place at his desk, stuffing his burned-down pipe, her joy returned.

'Oh, Daddy . . . it's so wonderful to be back in this room. I can't believe a single thing in it's changed. Do you know, I remember the last time I was in it.'

'Do you, my dear?'

'Yes . . . I was sitting where you are now and you were dictating one of your lectures . . . Wait . . . it was a Saturday afternoon . . . I don't believe it was long before I was . . . all right, darling . . . ill.'

'It was only two days . . . Don't let's talk about your having been ill . . . Ah, I've just remembered something pleasant. I've got twenty-five pounds for you. A cheque came, so I cashed it for you.'

'How exciting . . . A present?'

'No . . . you earned it.'

'I earned it? . . . Wait a minute . . . I remember writing some advertising copy . . . I believe it was *after* that lecture . . . Was it?'

'Actually, it was, yes. But don't cudgel your memory.'

'Two days,' she said with interest. 'Well . . . if they've paid me, I must have been in my right mind when I wrote it. I say . . . it must have happened very suddenly.'

'Yes. Dear child . . . just to please me . . . will you stop talking about the past?'

'Very well. How wonderful to have all that money. I shall buy some new clothes tomorrow. Heaven knows I need them.'

'Won't the old ones do, just for the country? Your mother's expecting us by the first train – I've sent her a telegram – She'll be so disappointed if we're late.'

'Very well. I'll wait till we get back. Oh – I'd almost forgotten. I'm not officially free yet, am I?'

'I'd almost forgotten myself . . . to see you now . . . No one could believe . . . Please God, in a fortnight you'll be home for good.'

Clara hardly heard him. Something had caught her attention.

'Daddy, there *is* something new in the study. That photograph . . . I hardly realized it *was* Mother at first. She looks so much older . . .'

'Well . . . after what she's been through since last November . . . She'll look as young as ever, as soon as she sets eyes on you.'

Clara thought, with interest, 'November, was it? When the fog came down . . . A *fog*? . . .' She said aloud, 'Older . . . older . . . but in a way, *more* beautiful. I've seen her with that face before . . . It's a wonderful photograph. Who took it?'

He did not answer at once. Perhaps he had not heard. The next moment, she was straining eagerly for the answer herself.

'Wasn't it Nell something . . . Nell . . . Nell . . . Nell . . . *Crayshaw*?'

Something lit up in her brain. She said excitedly:

'Daddy . . . I've found it . . . the missing piece . . . Darling! You must tell me one thing about the past . . . It's most desperately important. Nell had a brother . . . Oh, was he real? Or did I once just see a photograph? . . . Richard his name was . . . Did I really know him?'

'Yes . . . my dear . . . you did . . .'

'Tell me . . . oh, was *this* something I imagined? Or was it real? Oh, Daddy . . . tell me . . .'

'My child . . . don't look so distressed. What is it you want me to tell you?'

'Richard and I? Were we going to be married one day . . .? Oh, I know it couldn't be for a long time – I *know* I'm still married to Archie. Poor Archie . . . I haven't given him a thought. He did love me . . . that was real . . . But Richard . . . did he . . . Oh, did he? Or was I having delusions? Women have them, don't they . . . about men wanting to marry them? . . . Lots of them did *there* . . .'

'Hush . . . darling . . . listen . . . It was no delusion. Richard . . .'

'Have you seen him?' she broke in. 'Does he know where I've been all this time?'

'Yes, Clara,' her father answered slowly. 'I've seen him many times. He was very, very unhappy about you.'

'Where is he now? When did you last see him?'

'Well . . . not for some time.'

'You don't think he's forgotten me?'

'No, no. Wherever he is, I am sure he hasn't forgotten you.'

'Why do you sound so miserable? Why do you look away like that? Is there something you're afraid to tell me? Daddy . . . he's not dead, is he?'

Her father looked at her again.

'No, my dear. He's not dead.'

'Oh, it's so wonderful to find that it was all true. He's alive . . . He hasn't forgotten me . . . In there, I used to think about him all the time at first . . . I used to see him even . . . and, in the asphalt yard, when I heard a motor horn I used to think it was Richard trying to find me . . . How extraordinary that during all the last part, I forgot all about *him* . . . It wasn't till after I'd got home . . . Oh, I must write at once and tell him I've come back . . . You've got his address?'

'Yes . . . But, Clara, one moment . . . wouldn't it be better to wait a little?'

'Why?'

'I hate to remind you on our very first evening . . . But, in a fortnight, we have to report to the hospital. Please God, then you'll be home for good with no conditions . . . Wouldn't you yourself rather wait till you're absolutely free?'

She said with a sigh:

'You don't know how hard it is to wait . . . Still, perhaps you're right . . . After what he saw happen to Nell . . . It might be kinder to *him* not to tell him till they let me out for good . . . Perhaps they told him I was incurable, like John. Perhaps he's given up hope . . . Do you think that was why he stopped coming to see you?'

'Dear child . . . there were times when we were all tempted to despair.'

'Then it will be all the more wonderful when I *can* tell him . . . Daddy, stop looking so sad . . . What is it? . . . Wait . . . I think I know. It's all coming back now . . . I'm still married to Archie . . . You didn't want to have to remind me of something else . . . the nullity suit . . . It was only just beginning . . . Oh, to think of all the time I've wasted in there . . . Nearly a whole year . . . The civil part might have been settled by now . . . And then there's Rome.'

She wrung her hands . . . 'Oh, Daddy, it may be years before we can get married . . .'

He sighed.

'My child, you will have to be patient . . . But you're so young . . . you've all your life ahead . . .'

'Oh, I don't know how to wait . . . After all, I'm twenty-three . . . And I've lost nine whole months of my life . . .'

'Clara . . . can't you be grateful that it wasn't much longer? Must you begin to worry about the future so soon? Can't you just rejoice in this wonderful thing that's happened today? If you knew what it means to me . . . to your mother . . .'

She went over to him and kissed him remorsefully.

'Dearest Daddy . . . I'm sorry. You must have been unhappy, too. Of course, I rejoice . . . But we know and he doesn't . . . It's just that it won't be quite perfect till he does too.'

Chapter Eight

It was bliss at first to be back at Paget's Fold. But, after the first joy of seeing her mother and the old aunts and the place she had loved so much, Clara began to grow secretly restless. As each hot, lazy day went by, her restlessness increased. She concealed her impatience, so as not to spoil everyone's delight in her return, but there were times when the hours seemed to drag as slowly as they had done in that last week in Nazareth. The two worlds were quite distinct to her now. She was not even frightened of the interview ahead. Something told her that, when they saw her again, they would know as well as she did that she no longer belonged to the world beyond the glass. There were moments when she almost wished she did. She had forgotten two tortures of the world this side: boredom and suspense. Beyond the glass, however agonizing the nightmare experiences, they had had a peculiar intensity. If some had been terrifying, others had been exquisite. When those experiences had ceased, she had been as passive as a child until the tremendous, absorbing effort of willing herself back to consciousness. Here, for all the kindness and love about her, she felt frustrated and only half alive. Her days were regulated to a routine of meals and walks and games of croquet; to conversations which always edged away from the only two things that really interested her: Richard and her memories of Nazareth.

Whenever she tried to tell them about anything that happened *there*, they looked so pained that she had to give it up. Once Isabel said:

'Darling . . . it's so bad for you even to think of these dreadful things – Can't you try to forget? Don't you ever think of what Daddy and I went through during that appalling time?'

'I'm sorry. Yes . . . I expect it was horrible for you . . . but some of it was pretty bad for me . . .'

'My poor pet . . . Still you were unconscious, mercifully, most of the time. Daddy and I had to live through each awful day . . . That Sunday . . . only last April . . . when they thought you mightn't get well for years and years . . . *I* never believed it. But poor Daddy did. He broke down and cried like a child.'

'How awful,' said Clara with a shudder. But she knew, with the cold clarity that was becoming her permanent state, that she shuddered, not with sympathy but with distaste. There was only one point left where she could feel intensely and that point was daily becoming more painfully inflamed by her enforced silence. Soon, she no longer wanted to talk about Richard. She dared not, even yet, envisage the hope of seeing him. All she wanted was to be alone, so that she could think about him and try and reconstruct everything she could remember of their three weeks together.

After a week at Paget's Fold, she could look back, almost with amusement, to her parents' obvious distress the first time she went into the orchard and saw the little larch, no bigger than a Christmas tree. Why had they been so frightened? Did they think the remembrance of her love would turn her brain again? Didn't they know that the thought of Richard was the only thing that kept her alive, still able to feel and suffer and hope? Without it, she would have sunk back into an apathy in which she hardly cared whether she were here at Paget's Fold or back in Ward C.

When she saw the tree, she had merely said:

'Did Richard send that? From Peacocks?'

They told her, yes. They told her he had planted it himself. She had answered coldly, with no pity for their anxious, tender faces. 'Thanks. I only wanted to make sure.'

She began to long more and more to return to London. Paget's Fold was beginning to be haunted with disturbing thoughts. That day she and Richard had driven down here, something had gone wrong. What was it? There were gaps in that day that, try as she might, she could not fill. She could remember more and more of what she had been through in the asylum but those last days with Richard remained a curious dazzle of brilliant light and utter darkness. Was it possible she had been going out of her mind then and that he had known it? Desperately, she tried their old game, crying in her mind.

'Richard . . . Richard . . . Wherever you are . . .'

But she did not feel his answering call. Was he deliberately avoiding her? Did he fear her . . . even hate her? In an unguarded moment, her mother had told her about his driving up from Peacocks the night she had been taken ill. Had he ever seen her in the asylum? Had she terrified or repelled him as Micky and the others had repelled her?

She became convinced that something was being kept from her. If her parents knew the truth, as she now suspected they did, they would not tell her. Who . . . oh who . . . both knew and would have the honesty to tell?

The agony of her suspense made her sullen and irritable. In the second week, her father began to look at her with increasing anxiety. He asked her one day:

'Are you sleeping all right, my dear? Not overdoing things? You wouldn't like a day in bed?'

She was going to answer crossly but the sight of his face touched her.

'I'm quite all right, Daddy dear.'

'You're not worrying about the interview next week?'

'No . . . not that . . . But there's something I awfully want to do.'

'Yes?' he said, rather apprehensively.

'If I mayn't write to Richard, can't I at least write to Nell?'

He hesitated before answering.

'Well . . . just at the moment, she's on holiday.'

'How do you know?' she pounced. 'Have you heard from her, then?'

He said hastily:

'I wrote to her . . . to say you were so much better . . . She's been so kind . . . I thought she would like to know.'

'And she answered. Did she say anything about Richard?'

'Er . . . only to say she agreed with me that it would be better not to tell him just yet.'

'Till I'm decertified, you mean?'

He sighed.

'I hoped you didn't know . . . But we had no alternative . . . Can't you think of it, as we do, as an acute nervous breakdown?'

'I'd rather call a spade a spade. After all, Richard knows the facts . . .' She added suspiciously, 'Or doesn't he . . . Is that it?'

'Oh, he knows, my dear. We couldn't conceal it from him. But there's no reason why anyone outside the immediate family need ever know. Please God, this time next week, we can all forget it ever happened.'

She was a little reassured. He included Richard in 'the immediate family'.

She kissed him, mollified.

'Poor Daddy, don't worry. *That* will be all right. Sometimes I forget it means a lot to you too.'

'It means more than anything in the whole world,' he said.

The day they had to report at Nazareth came at last. On the way up in the train, her spirits were almost as high as his on the day they had driven away in the taxi. She was thinking only that, at last, she would be able to write to Richard. Her father was obviously anxious though he did his best to conceal it. He kept saying:

'The doctors can't say you don't look well. You look splendid. At the worst, it can only be a question of weeks.'

The interview, in which Doctor Brooke took the leading part, did not last long. The moment she came into the room, the bearded doctor said:

'Well, well, so this is really the young woman I saw before?'

He asked her a few questions to which she replied confidently. She did not feel in the least afraid of either of them. It was almost impossible to connect these obviously routine enquiries with the agonized tension of that other inquisition.

At last, he turned to Dr Bennett.

'Well, your rather rash experiment seems to have been successful. I admit I was somewhat sceptical but results appear to have justified it. Let's hope they are permanent. Yes . . . I think we can quite safely give this patient her discharge.'

She heard her father's deep sigh of relief.

'I can't tell you how grateful I am, Doctor Brooke. And to you too, Doctor Bennett. I'm sure she couldn't have been in better hands. I'm thankful we were advised to send her to Nazareth.'

'Well, we fancy we have as good a record as any. Pity so many people are prejudiced against us. Partly snobbery . . . the idea of having a relative in a public institution. And partly our name . . . there's still a stigma attached to the idea of a Nazarite . . . though that old term's never used now.' He turned to Clara, who had been listening with faint resentment. 'Well, Mrs Hughes-Follett . . . so you can go out and begin a normal life again and forget you were ever here. But you'll have to take things easy for the next six months . . . Bed at ten, no overworking of that brain of yours . . . no gadding about and getting over-excited.'

Clara said sullenly:

'I thought I was supposed to be well.'

His face became stern.

'Look here, young lady. You're very lucky to be getting your discharge so soon. If it had been left to me, you'd have spent the next six months in our convalescent home. Remember, I can still change my mind.'

'Oh please no. I'm sorry. I'll do everything you say.'

'Hmm. That's better. You can say goodbye to me now and Dr Bennett will take you to the office to collect your things. Your father and I have a few little matters to settle up.'

She went out, feeling as if she had been dismissed from a headmaster's study.

Outside, Dr Bennett smiled at her.

'You didn't seem awfully grateful to the Head. In fact, you jolly nearly got on his wrong side.'

'You're the one I'm grateful to,' she said. 'If it hadn't been for you, I might still be here.'

He looked pleased.

'Well, I'm glad I took the risk. Now I suppose you hope you'll never set eyes on any of us again. No one else you'd like to say goodbye to? Sister Ware?'

'Do I have to?'

He laughed.

'No. She's a bit of a tartar, isn't she? Still, she had to be.'

'I would like to say goodbye to Nurse Jones?'

'What, the red-haired one in Ward J. Fancy your remembering her. She'll be pleased. Suppose I just give her a message? Ward J isn't an awfully pleasant place, you know. I don't want to upset you.'

'I'd like to see it again. It helps me to remember.'

'You're an odd girl. Don't you want to forget it all?'

She shook her head.

'No. My family won't let me talk about it. But I think about it. Some day, perhaps, I'll be able to piece it all together.'

'All right, then. I'll take you down there. You've got a knack of getting your own way, haven't you?'

Once again she found herself in the ward on the ground floor. It hung together now . . . the long, narrow corridor, the wide space with the fireplace, the glass-topped door giving on to the asphalt yard. The dreary procession of nurses and patients was walking round it. She recognized Micky and the woman with the burnt face and forced herself not to feel sick. Nurse Jones was on duty in the narrow passage, sitting, with her back to them, by the window that looked on to the wall with the creeper. Facing her was a row of doors, all shut but one. Through that one open door Clara saw the old lady in the white draperies and the strange headdress, busy at her easel.

'I remember her,' she whispered. 'My cell was the one next door to hers.'

The doctor whispered back:

'She's very clever. Had pictures in the Academy when she was young. She's been here fifteen years. We're all quite fond of her.' He said aloud:

'How's Your Majesty today?'

'Tolerably well, thank you. Who's this young person with you? Doesn't she know who I am?'

Clara curtsied.

'That's better, my dear. You may go now, both of you. I'm busy with my painting.'

The doctor went up to Nurse Jones and tapped her on the shoulder. She jumped up and turned round.

'Well . . . if it isn't our Clara! My goodness, what a difference!'

'She's come to say goodbye . . . She's leaving us.'

'Well, isn't that wonderful? I thought as much when I saw her with a hat on. Fancy you remembering Jones.'

'You were sweet to me,' said Clara.

Jones kissed her.

'There . . . isn't that nice? We miss you, dear. I bet you won't miss us, though. You used to sing like a lark sometimes. Quite a pleasure to hear you.'

'Sing?' asked Clara with interest. 'But I always wanted to be able to sing. I'm sure I can't now.'

Doctor Bennett said rather severely:

'Say goodbye, Clara. We've still got to go to the office.'

'Well, cheerio, Clara, dear. See you in the great big world some day, perhaps. Remember Smith?'

'Yes.'

'She won't half be furious. I had a bet with her. Five bob that you'd be out within the year. She's lost. God bless and lots of luck.'

At the office, she asked the doctor:

'Did I really sing quite well?'

'Yes. Very well indeed.'

'How extraordinary.'

'Hmm. It's remarkable what people *can* do when the brakes are off.'

At the office, the nurse in charge said:

'It'll take some time to pack her things. Will you wait or shall we post them on?'

'I don't want anything I had here,' said Clara. 'Please keep them.'

'That's against the rules. I'll post them on. You'd better take your wedding-ring though.'

She fumbled in a pigeon-hole and produced a small packet. Clara opened it and there was Archie's ring.

'Thank you,' she said slipping it in her pocket.

'Sign the receipt please.'

Suddenly Clare remembered something else.

'Nurse . . . didn't I have a fur coat? . . . a black one . . . Not real sealskin. But almost new. Perhaps I could just take *that* with me.'

'I'll look at your list,' said the nurse. She opened an index file and took out a card. After a minute she said in an embarrassed voice, glancing not at Clara, but at Doctor Bennett, 'That's correct. But I'm afraid there was a bit of a mishap.' She showed the card to the doctor. 'Wouldn't be much good to her now, I'm afraid.'

'All right, nurse. We'll forget about the coat, shall we, Clara? Your father will be getting impatient.'

As they were approaching the room where she had been interviewed, she said to Doctor Bennett:

'It doesn't matter . . . Except that Daddy gave it to me . . . But what *did* happen to my coat?'

'What an inquisitive young woman you are. Do you really want to know?'

'Yes, I do.'

'When you arrived here you were in pretty bad shape, you know. The fact is, before we could put it safely away, you tore it to shreds.'

She stopped and stared at him.

'*I* did? Tore a fur coat? . . . why, that's *leather*. I'm frightfully feeble with my hands. I can hardly tear *cardboard* . . . However could I have been capable?'

'Well, Clara . . . As I told you just now, people develop some strange capacities when the brakes are off.'

Chapter Nine

When they returned to Valetta Road where she was to stay the night, Clara said:

'Daddy, I don't want to go back to Paget's Fold. Now that your holiday's finished I'd rather stay on in London with you.'

'But my dear, the country air and peace is so much better for you. And your mother will be so disappointed not to have your company for her last two weeks.'

'I'm sorry. But I'm getting awfully restless down there.'

'All the same, I'm sure it's better for you. Doctor Brooke thought it might be a good idea for you to be altogether out of London for a time. He suggested you might get some sort of outdoor work . . . on a farm, perhaps. That would give you something to do without tiring your brain.'

'There's nothing I should loathe more, Daddy. I'm no longer a certified lunatic. Have I got to go on being treated like one? Am I never going to be allowed to decide anything for myself again?'

'Come, my dear, there's no need to get angry. You heard yourself what they said. You've got to go quietly. But no one's going to force you to do anything you don't want to do. It's very unkind of you to talk like that.'

'I'm sorry. I didn't mean to be unkind. But London's so much easier to get to – Suppose Richard manages to get leave when he's heard from me – I don't want him to waste any of it in travelling.'

'Well, my dear . . . I'm afraid you can't count on his getting leave . . . And, I confess, at the moment, I haven't his address . . . I believe his unit has been moved since I saw him.'

'Then I shall ring up Nell. She's sure to know . . . Oh, I know you said she was away. But I'll ring up on the off-chance.'

Before he could say any more, she picked up the receiver and asked for Nell's number.

'I remember it, you see,' she said triumphantly, while she waited for a reply . . . 'Ah, you see, she *is* back. Nell . . . Hullo, Nell . . . who do you think this is? It's Clara.'

Nell's voice said at the other end:

'Clara . . . what a wonderful surprise . . . I thought you were in the country.'

'Daddy and I have just come back from the hospital. Everything's all right. I've got a clean bill. I don't ever have to go back.'

'That's splendid news, dear. I'm so glad.'

'Nell . . . I want most awfully to see you.'

'Yes . . . we must meet some day. Actually, I'll be out of town for a bit. And I expect you'll be going back to the country for some time, won't you? Give me a ring when you come back. Well, goodbye for the moment, dear, and tremendous congratulations.'

'Please, Nell, don't ring off. I want to see you today . . . before you go. It's something very important.'

Nell said slowly:

'Well, Clara, I don't know . . . Actually I've got a frightful lot of things to do . . .'

'I promise I won't stay long. If I came over right away? Please, Nell . . .'

'Well, perhaps . . . Clara . . . is your father there? He must be frightfully pleased.'

'Yes. He's here in this very room. He knows why I want to see you . . .'

'All right . . . in that case, come over now.'

'Oh *thank* you . . . Nell . . . Oh, just one thing . . .'

'Yes?'

'Is Gerald there?'

'No . . . he's out at the moment.'

'Good. I'd rather like to see you alone . . . this first time. I'll be over in twenty minutes . . . less . . .'

Half an hour later she was talking to Nell in her studio. At first, she had felt strangely shy being in that room again. She suspected she might have behaved rather strangely the last time she had been there. She devoted the first minutes to proving that now, at least, she was perfectly normal. She asked Nell about her work and congratulated her on the photograph of Isabel. Gradually Nell's manner, which had been friendly but constrained, began to thaw.

'Let's make some tea, shall we? G. won't be back for ages.'

As Clara helped her in that once familiar kitchen, Nell suddenly smiled and said:

'You must ring poor old Clive Heron, and tell him the good news. He's been in quite a state about your having been ill. Rang me up at least once a month. Quite sensational for him. You know how he loathes phoning anyone.'

'Ah . . . it was *you* then. Why didn't Daddy tell me? He pretended he'd forgotten who it was. He even said he must have muddled Clive up with someone else. Nell, I'm getting sick of all these mysteries. That's why I so much wanted to see you today.'

A look of fear came into Nell's green eyes.

'What mysteries, Clara?'

Clara looked steadily at the face that was both like and unlike another face.

'First and foremost about Richard. Daddy made me promise not to write to him till I'd been . . . been decertified. Well, I could just see the point of that. Then today . . . when I was really free at last, he pretended he didn't know his address. And when I suggested asking you for it, he made every excuse to stop me.'

Nell said faintly:

'Do you want so very much to write to Richard?'

'Why . . . of course. Nell . . . you look so strange. Is there some reason why I shouldn't? . . . Do you mean he doesn't *want* to hear from me?'

Nell grabbed a cigarette and lit it.

'Clara, dear . . . he'll be very, very glad to know you're well again. That I'm sure of.'

They seemed to have changed parts. It was Clara now who

felt assured and self-possessed while Nell seemed to be growing every moment more diffident.

Clara pressed her:

'I think there's something everyone's trying to keep back from me. Whatever it is, I believe Daddy knows and I'm quite sure you do.'

Nell said miserably:

'Your father . . . I thought, perhaps, from the way you talked on the phone . . . I daresay, this last week or two, everything's slipped his mind except that things should go right today . . .' She rallied her voice to a false cheerfulness. 'And they *did* go right. It's simply too marvellous. You look splendid. A bit thin . . . but *I* think it suits you.'

"So you said that last night I was here with Richard. Before he went down to Peacocks. Remember?'

'Did I? I'm sure I did if you say so. It's amazing how your memory's come back. You always did have a frightfully good brain. I expect that's why you got well sooner than anyone hoped.'

'Nell, if I'm well, I'm well enough to be told the truth. I can't explain to Daddy that what I can't stand is not knowing. That's why I came to you. You've always been honest with me.'

Nell frowned and puffed at her cigarette.

'It's nice of you to say that . . . But sometimes it's jolly hard to be honest.'

'Why? Because you're afraid of hurting someone? Or because it's not always easy to know what the truth is?'

'Both, sometimes,' said Nell, still frowning.

'I understand that. Nell . . . look here, I don't want to talk about that place because it might hurt *you*. But I don't want to forget it, as Daddy thinks I should. You see . . . it was real, in its way. And it's desperately important for me now to know what's real and what isn't.'

Nell's face softened.

'Poor kid . . . You've certainly been through it, haven't you? It's changed you. You're more grown-up.'

'Am I? Nell, will you tell me this much? How much did I imagine about me and Richard? *Before*, I mean? Suppose, already, I was beginning to have delusions . . .? Perhaps he didn't love me as much as I thought?'

Nell answered slowly:

'You certainly didn't imagine he was in love with you. I've never seen him like that about any girl. After all, one knows one's own brother pretty well. No, there was something between you two that was almost uncanny.'

'The game, you mean? And his coming back the night I was ill and me seeing the car and the accident . . .'

'So you know about that?'

'Mother let it out by mistake. Perhaps she was exaggerating. She's apt to, you know, sometimes.'

'No, she wasn't exaggerating. I was with you at the time. When Richard got here, his story confirmed yours in every detail. Even Gerald was convinced. And you know what an old sceptic *he* is.'

'I certainly do.' The relief of being able to talk about Richard almost naturally was so great that she laughed. But, the next moment, she was serious again.

'You say he *was* in love with me . . . My going mad . . . was that so repulsive for him that . . .?' Her face contracted. 'But the larch tree . . . Nell . . . that was months *after* . . .'

'Yes . . . dear. No . . . no . . . he was just terribly unhappy . . . Clara I'll be frank with you . . . I couldn't bear to see him going through what I'd been through. You know about John. You'll think it beastly of me but I tried to persuade him to forget you. He wouldn't listen to me. He was absolutely convinced you'd get better. But when, last April, your father had to tell him they thought there wasn't a hope . . . at least not till you were round about fifty . . . Dear, do you really want me to go on?'

'Yes,' said Clara, summoning up all her strength . . . 'Wait . . . Nell . . . I don't think you have to tell me. I think I know.' She paused. Her lips had gone so dry that she had to run her tongue over them before she could whisper:

'Kathleen?'

Nell nodded. Then she came across and knelt by her chair.

'Sure you're all right dear? Shall I get you a drink?'

'No . . . I'll be all right in a minute.'

The room steadied itself. When Nell's face was in focus again, she said:

'They're married? I think I knew it . . . It's queer . . . I believe I saw her in *there* . . . There was a thunderstorm . . . We said prayers together . . .'

Nell was holding a glass to her lips. She refused at first, then drank the brandy obediently. After a moment she said:

'Thank you. I'm all right now. It was just the shock.'

'I should think so, dear. You took it magnificently.'

'It's a relief to know. I think I'll go now.'

'Not for a minute or two. Just get steadied up. I'll come back with you, shall I?'

'No, thank you, Nell. I want to be alone for a bit. Before I see Daddy again . . . There's so much he didn't tell me . . . That about being fifty . . . I can't face him just yet . . . I'll go for a walk . . .'

'Good idea. Just sit quiet for a little first.'

They sat in silence for some minutes. Then Nell said gently:

'Your religion means a lot to you, doesn't it, Clara?'

'It did once. Even in *there*, it did sometimes. And in that queer place I was in before. More like an ordinary house: you could see buses going past the window. But since I've been back . . . it's seemed awfully remote. Everything has . . . except wanting to know about Richard. Well, now I know. There's nothing more to know.'

'There's one thing . . .' said Nell. 'It might even be a sort of comfort.'

Clara smiled painfully. 'I doubt it. But you may as well tell me.'

'He's become a Catholic. Gerald and I aren't religious, as you know. We weren't awfully pleased about it. But, if it's the least little help to you . . . why, even G. would be delighted.'

'A Catholic? . . . It's hard to take in. I've got such an awful lot to take in . . . I don't even feel anything much . . . Kathleen . . . Of course she'd want him to be a Catholic . . .'

'Certainly, she wanted it. But I don't think she expected it. He was thinking about it before there was any question of their marrying. I believe it had something to do with you . . .'

'I can't take that in either,' she said. 'Some day perhaps . . . At the moment, I just feel numb.'

'Poor child, no wonder . . . you've had about enough for one day.'

'Yes . . .perhaps . . . I daresay I'll work it all out in time . . . I think I'll go now.

They both stood up. Nell kissed her and said, almost with her old roughness:

'You've got guts. Life won't let you down. One of these days, you'll get some sort of real happiness too. I have, you know. I could have sworn I never would.'

'I wonder,' said Clara. She gave a rather strained smile. 'Funny, the only time in my life I should have been really happy was when I was on the point of going out of my mind. That would amuse Clive Heron.'

'Would it? You understand him much better than I do. He told me once you were the only person who *did* understand him.'

'We're both mad in a way, I suppose. I'm very fond of him . . . But I don't think I could bear ever to see him again . . . *He* brought me here that night . . .' Her voice faltered: 'Oh . . . if Richard had only trusted me . . . If he'd only told me himself . . . given me some sign . . .' The tears came into her eyes. 'He won't even want to know I'm better . . . There's no point in writing to him now . . .'

'Clara,' Nell said urgently. 'There's something I'd forgotten . . . He left me something for you. Something I was to give you when you came back . . . however long it was . . . He said you'd understand what it meant.'

She went to a drawer and took out a small silk purse. Clara watched her in silence.

'I know just when he bought it,' Nell went on. 'It was the morning after that awful Sunday night your father told him . . . He went off early to catch his train . . . he couldn't bear to be even with me and Gerald. Afterwards he told me he went into Westminster Cathedral on the way . . . He'd been there once with you . . . There was a shop opposite that sells statues and crucifixes and so on . . . He wanted something Catholics used often . . .'

The red purse was lying in Clara's palm now. She did not open it. She knew from the feel of it that it was a rosary. She could not say anything, not even a word of thanks to Nell. She felt Nell's kiss on her cheek and, a moment later, she was standing alone in the courtyard.

She stood for a while, clenching her wet eyelids together and clutching the little red purse. Then she became conscious of the faint sluck, sluck of the river. She remembered the narrow stone passage. A quiet, urgent impulse came over her to walk down it; to walk on and on with her eyes shut until it would be impossible to return. But, even more urgently, she felt the small weight pressing against her palm like a detaining hand. She forced herself to open her eyes. For a moment, she was no longer alone in the courtyard. She whispered, knowing that he heard:

'Richard . . . I'll hold on . . . Go in peace.'

Antonia White

FROST IN MAY (1)
Frost in May
The Lost Traveller

FROST IN MAY (2)
The Sugar House
Beyond the Glass

The **Frost in May** quartet consists of a series of novels about a Catholic girl growing up in the first decades of this century. The heroine's intense relationship with her father, and the all-pervading influence of the Catholic faith are their dominant themes.

Frost in May is a portrait of a child's life in the enclosed world of a Catholic convent.

In **The Lost Traveller**, Clara experiences the vagaries of adolescence against the background of a world at war.

In **The Sugar House**, Clara, now twenty-one, strives to come to terms with a doomed love and an equally doomed marriage. Her dream of life crumbles, and in **Beyond the Glass** Clara has a strange, passionate love affair which erodes her fragile sense of identity – the glass wall shatters and she descends into madness . . .

All four novels have been filmed for BBC TV

All are available in Fontana

Simone de Beauvoir

She Came to Stay £1.50
The passionately eloquent and ironic novel she wrote as an act of revenge against the woman who so nearly destroyed her life with the philosopher Sartre. 'A writer whose tears for her characters freeze as they drop.' *Sunday Times*

Les Belles Images £1.25
Her totally absorbing story of upper-class Parisian life. 'A brilliant sortie into Jet Set France.' *Daily Mirror*. 'As compulsively readable as it it is profound, serious and disturbing.' *Queen*

The Mandarins £1.95
'A magnificent satire by the author of *The Second Sex*. *The Mandarins* gives us a brilliant survey of the post-war French intellectual . . . a dazzling panorama.' *New Statesman*. 'A superb document . . . a remarkable novel.' *Sunday Times*

The Woman Destroyed £1.50
'Immensely intelligent, basically passionless stories about the decay of passion. Simone de Beauvoir shares, with other women novelists, the ability to write about emotion in terms of direct experience . . . The middle-aged women at the centre of the three stories in *The Woman Destroyed* all suffer agonisingly the pains of growing older and of being betrayed by husbands and children.' *Sunday Times*

FONTANA PAPERBACKS

Beryl Bainbridge

TWICE WINNER OF THE WHITBREAD AWARD

'A brilliantly talented writer.' *The Times*.
'It is a joy to find writers with the skill and observation of
Miss Bainbridge.' *Daily Mirror*.
'Alarming humour . . . a powerful talent.'
Sunday Telegraph

A Quiet Life   £1·50

The Dressmaker   £1·25

The Bottle Factory Outing   £1·25

Harriet Said . . .   £1·25

Injury Time   £1·50

Young Adolf   £1·25

Another Part of the Wood   £1·25

Winter Garden   £1·50

Fontana Paperbacks

Eric Ambler

A world of espionage and counter-espionage, of sudden violence and treacherous calm; of blackmailers, murderers, gun-runners—and none too virtuous heroes. This is the world of Eric Ambler. 'Unquestionably our best thriller writer.' *Graham Greene*. 'He is incapable of writing a dull paragraph.' *Sunday Times*. 'Eric Ambler is a master of his craft.' *Sunday Telegraph*.

SEND NO MORE ROSES £1·25
THE DARK FRONTIER £1·25
JOURNEY INTO FEAR £1·25
JUDGMENT ON DELTCHEV £1·25
THE LEVANTER £1·25
THE LIGHT OF DAY £1·25
THE NIGHT-COMERS £1·25
PASSAGE OF ARMS £1·25
THE CARE OF TIME £1·25

Fontana Paperbacks

Fontana Paperbacks

Fontana is a leading paperback publisher of fiction and non-fiction, with authors ranging from Alistair MacLean, Agatha Christie and Desmond Bagley to Solzhenitsyn and Pasternak, from Gerald Durrell and Joy Adamson to the famous Modern Masters series.

In addition to a wide-ranging collection of internationally popular writers of fiction, Fontana also has an outstanding reputation for history, natural history, military history, psychology, psychiatry, politics, economics, religion and the social sciences.

All Fontana books are available at your bookshop or newsagent; or can be ordered direct. Just fill in the form and list the titles you want.

FONTANA BOOKS, Cash Sales Department, G.P.O. Box 29, Douglas, Isle of Man, British Isles. Please send purchase price, plus 8p per book. Customers outside the U.K. send purchase price, plus 10p per book. Cheque, postal or money order. No currency.

NAME (Block letters) _____

ADDRESS _____

_____

_____